The Scarring Underneath

a post-apocalyptic romance

T.S. Dickerson

Sturnella
Publishing LLC

THE SCARRING UNDERNEATH

Copyright © 2017 by T.S. Dickerson.

Published by

Sturnella Publishing LLC

www.sturnellapublishing.com

Edited by Jane Curry

Cover design by Renee Barratt

ISBN: 978-0-9982147-0-2

First Edition: February 2017

10 9 8 7 6 5 4 3 2 1

To Matt
– for listening to me talking about imaginary people. Constantly.

One

THE SUMMER HEAT LEFT a sheen of sweat across her skin but did nothing to alleviate the numbness in her limbs as she pulled the trigger. Cassidy Hood did not flinch as the shot sounded but watched the deer's body crumple to the ground with a thud. Birds squawked and scattered away from the meadow, but Cass was stiff and quiet, eyes narrowed on the buck. When she was sure he had breathed his last, she sighed, lowered her rifle to the ground, and collapsed beside it, face buried in the damp grass.

Tension flowed out of her. Now it wouldn't be so imperative to organize a hunt today. They could rest, adjust to all the changes, and prepare.

Cass rolled onto her back and sucked in a too-large breath, causing herself to cough. Her lungs still felt thick and pinched from the smoke. The scent of fields and forests, houses and animals burning lingered in her nostrils and she opened her eyes to check that they had truly outrun the fire. She swallowed and nodded to herself. Yes, the sky was clear here. It was only her memory that was poisoned with smoke.

She was lifting herself to stand when she heard her name shouted just beyond the trees. The sorrel gelding who grazed nearby lifted his head and snorted in the direction of the voice.

"Cass! Cassidy!"

"Shit," she said under her breath. Then she called, "Drew! I'm fine! I'm here!" She coughed a few more times and stared back at the horse who was now staring at her. "I shoot a deer, and you don't even stop grazing, but my *cough* disturbs you?" she asked the animal. Huckleberry swished his tail and lowered his head into the lush, green grass, kicking the hind leg which bore a white sock, his only marking.

Drew burst through the trees and looked around. He relaxed when he spotted Huck grazing calmly, and his frown disappeared when he spotted the downed buck. Finally, he saw Cass sitting in the grass at the edge of the meadow.

"Nice," he said. "You okay?"

She nodded as Drew stepped back through the tree line and shouted something. When he reappeared, he crossed the meadow, limping. His limp was the result of two toes taken by frostbite the first winter after the end of the world. It was more pronounced in the tall, wet grass. He extended a hand, and she took it, letting him haul her to her feet.

"It's hot," he said.

"It's the humidity back here in the trees. Especially with the pond right there." She gestured to the small body of water just beyond the grazing horse.

Cass pulled her wet shirt away from her body, wafting it back and forth a few times. She glanced down the neck at her small breasts and the ribs protruding beneath them. She frowned. She could see *through* her shirt; it had worn so thin.

She looked up to see Drew already unbuttoning his own.

"Sorry about the gunshot," she said. "I didn't think dinner would just wander in, or I would've warned you." She took the shirt as he offered it and buttoned it over her own.

"We were *hoping* it was dinner." He headed for the deer carcass. "I thought Rovers." Then, with a laugh, "Your brother was sure someone from the Oregon clan had gotten handsy and you'd lost your temper."

She rolled her eyes. "Do I need to go get the butcher kit?" she asked.

Drew said "no" just as a second male voice said "no" and Cass looked up to see her brother Cameron trudging through the high grass with a battered case.

"Did I see a smile on your face, Cass?" he asked.

Cass raised an eyebrow and headed for the deer. "The heat's getting to you, big brother." Cam laughed, and Cass allowed another small smile to lift her mouth. "Will you help us? It's fucking hot."

Cam nodded, and the three of them set to work, Drew and Cass gutting the deer while Cam buried what they discarded. By the time they finished, all three were sweating. Cass's gaze turned to Drew's skin, shades darker than her own even when she was tan. His muscles stretched and pulled, and she was struck once more by how well he kept his weight even when they'd gone weeks without decent food.

Conversely, Cam looked sunken, the leather of his belt frayed around the new holes. He hadn't lost a lot of muscle yet, but it was clear the three of them needed this meat. Cass patted the hide of the shoulder in appreciation.

"Let's get him cooking," Cam said. His blue eyes glowed with thanks he hadn't spoken as he gave her a nod. "Drew and I will drag him out." A frown creased his face as he said it and she felt his eyes moving over her thin body.

"I have to get water, anyway," she said, already walking toward the small pond. She knelt and dipped the first of two five-gallon buckets into the slowly trickling creek that fed the pond. The two men dragged the deer carcass back through the trees. After they'd passed from sight, she could still hear them grunting with effort and occasionally laughing.

As she switched the full bucket out for the empty, she felt a second wind rejuvenating her. She heard the slow hoofbeats as Huck ambled up to the pond and dipped his muzzle in for a drink. The horse was a little thin, his ribs protruding a bit more than she'd like, though considerably less than her own. The rapid pace they'd been forced to keep on the trip down from Montana had kept the horses from having decent grazing time, and they were all a bit worse for the wear. But, Huck was the oldest, and he still looked sound and strong. A few more days here, where there was ample grass, would prepare them.

Cass wasn't sure what would prepare her. In the nearly five years since civilization ended, Cass had fought for survival. She had killed people to defend herself, her group, and their supplies. It didn't faze her, anymore. She'd watched people she cared about die, sometimes slow and miserable and sometimes so suddenly it didn't feel real. But, she'd dreaded nothing with such strength as she dreaded this move.

The bucket overflowed, spilling water over her hand and she stood.

"Huck," she said, hefting a bucket in each hand. "Let's go."

The horse began to follow her, stopping every few feet to yank another mouthful of grass from the earth. Cass wove through the copse of trees, stopping to rest now and then. As she was crossing a short field toward camp, Huck trotted up behind her, catching up.

She smiled at the sound of his hooves swishing through the tall grass, his tail periodically brushing a fly from his rump. Free of the smothering humidity in the trees and out in the cool breeze, she felt her body reviving. Her mouth watered for the venison that would soon be cooking. Ahead of her, Drew was smiling as a dog licked dried deer blood off his fingers and for a moment, Cass thought maybe, with a little luck, she might manage to get everyone she cared for safely to their destination. Maybe this cross-country journey could work.

Just three—maybe four—more months of exhausting travel, lucky hunts, and managing to avoid Rovers. And of course, getting along with two other bands of survivors with their own rules and agendas. Right. No problem.

CASS HAD JUST PULLED a clean shirt over her head when she heard a shout, then another. She scrambled across the tent on her knees and unzipped the flap. She had barely stood upright when a teen girl ran up, blocking her path.

"They're here," Lena said, apprehension in her voice. "The California band. They're just down the valley a ways. Your brother went to meet them, and he told me to tell you to change and get ready to stand on the platform with him."

Cass cursed mentally and rolled her left shoulder in its socket. When she caught Lena watching the action, she forced away her frown and managed a half-smile.

"Thanks, Lena," she said.

The girl began to pull her unruly, red hair into a ponytail and stepped to Cass's side, keeping pace as the older woman began to walk toward the circle of burnt-out buildings where the people would gather.

"I guess they have several horses. And wagons," Lena said, lowering her voice as they moved closer to the group assembling in the ranch yard.

Cass felt her stomach lurch. When the Oregon band had arrived two days earlier, she'd been shocked to find they had more people than her group. Rumor had it, the California band was double the size of the Montana and Oregon bands combined. Until two days ago, Cass hadn't known this many people were left on this side of the country, much less all convening in one spot.

"Horses and wagons are good news. I can handle horses and wagons," Cass said to Lena without looking at her. "It's the people that concern me."

Those people were assembling around a long-rusted and overgrown semi-truck and flatbed trailer conspicuously jackknifed in the middle of the ranch yard between the buildings. Cam and the Oregonian leader, Hank, planned to do all their speaking to the group standing on the flatbed.

Gone were the days of chatting around the fire like a family. Now there were so many people one would have to be elevated to speak to them.

Cass jumped as a hand closed around her arm. She turned to see Trista, her brother's girlfriend, shooting her an apologetic look. Drew was with her, looking ill and angry at the same time.

"Sorry," Trista said. "I just thought you might be able to convince Drew that this isn't the second end of the world."

Cass smiled and gave a shrug. "I'm not sure it isn't." She kept her voice quiet.

Trista scoffed and shook her head, but Drew gave Cass a wink and moved in to throw an arm around her.

"You both agreed to this," Trista said. "And you would've been outvoted if you hadn't."

"If there'd even been time for a vote," Lena said as she scanned the crowd. Everyone seemed to have turned to the left.

Cass turned as well and caught sight of her brother riding into view beside a large man on a black horse. Cam's horse, Whiskey, was taller than the black one but this man's height easily made up the difference. His shoulder length, curly hair rested just above his muscular arms, exposed by a sleeveless shirt which completed an entirely black wardrobe. He was an intimidating sight.

"I never had a problem with going to Stronghold," Drew said near Cass's ear in a voice muffled by lips that barely moved. "I just wish we'd traveled alone."

The group of onlookers had to shift and move aside to allow the entire party to enter the ranch yard. There were murmurs and even a gasp or two as three mounted men came into view all wearing pieces of police riot gear despite the heat. Cass noted the look of pleasure on the California leader's face as his obvious attempt at intimidation had the desired effect.

Cam had already dismounted and seemed to be searching for someone, but Cass ignored him, instead turning to count the new horses. Most bore riders, but four were hitched in pairs to two wagons loaded with supplies and people. Other people walked beside the wagons, including a group of half a dozen scantily-clad women.

"That's interesting," Trista said.

Cass was about to ask what was interesting when Drew leaned in close again and said, "Your brother is looking for you."

Cam stood near the makeshift staircase of cinderblocks leading up to the flatbed. He was indeed scanning the crowd with a soft frown. She sighed.

She didn't mind the responsibility of being her brother's second in command. She'd have taken it on without his asking. It was the appellation that irked her. And the fact it often drew attention she didn't appreciate.

"Duty cal—" Cass was cut off by a gasp from Trista. Several other people in the crowd let out sounds of shock. A man with bound hands was tied to the back of the last wagon and had just been drug into view. At least she thought it was a man. The figure was quite skinny, the head covered by a feed bag

The leader of the group nodded at one of the men dressed in riot gear, and he freed the rope from the wagon and led the man toward the flatbed like a two-legged pet. Hank and Cam were already standing atop the trailer. Hank's arms were crossed over his chest, and Cam's frown had deepened. As Cass studied her brother, he met her gaze across the crowd. He gave his head a single shake, a signal to stay away for now. Cass nodded and turned her attention back to the prisoner.

The imposing Californian leader grabbed hold of one of the prisoner's arms and helped hoist him onto the flatbed. The man who had led the prisoner initially turned his back to the trailer but stayed by the stairs with the strict posture of a sentry.

The crowd had fallen silent. Tension seemed to weight the air. The lowering sun blazed beyond the trees causing Cam to squint as he looked across the crowd and then took a step toward the Californian leader with his hand extended.

"On behalf of the Montana band, I would like to welcome you. My name is Cameron Hood."

The large man shook the offered hand, then turned as Hank approached.

"My name is Hank Gleason. I represent a group of survivors from Washington, Oregon, and Idaho. We call ourselves the Coltonites for the city where most of us met," Hank said as he offered his hand in turn.

When Hank and Cam had stepped back, the larger man turned to the crowd. "I am Derrick Mason, leader of Clan Mason. We are pleased to join you."

There were a few awkward claps, but the sentiment did not catch on, and soon the crowd returned to heavy silence.

"There is a matter I'd like to take care of before we say any more," Derrick said, giving the rope a sharp tug. The bound man stumbled forward and dropped to his knees.

"On our way here, we found this man locked in the basement of a house. Rovers killed the owners, but this man was alive in his cell," Derrick cleared his throat. "He refuses to tell us why he was there, but he says he's done nothing wrong." Derrick moved to stand beside the prisoner who made no effort to get up but sunk back onto his legs with sagging shoulders.

"I don't have food and clothing to give to someone who may be a criminal. Especially when he won't confess his crimes. I would have killed him. But, some of the softer-hearted people in my clan convinced me to bring him here to see if any of you would have a use for him in your groups."

Derrick reached down and pulled the bag off the man's head, bringing on more gasping and murmuring. He had a split lip, and his mouth was caked with dried blood. His jaw was swollen, and his eye was an angry purple. The man blinked and raised his bound hands to shield his eyes from the brightness of the unfiltered sun. As he did, his bare chest was exposed through his torn shirt, sickly-thin and likewise covered with bruises in various stages of healing.

The man sat up straighter and pushed matted clumps of dirty, blonde hair away from his eyes. He squinted first at the crowd and then at the other men on the platform. When his eyes adjusted, he set his jaw and straightened his shoulders, unable to keep from wincing as he did.

When the pain passed, the struggle to control his expression began. Cass recognized resignation and fear in his eyes and the only way to mask that was with bravado. So, his look was brave to the point of arrogance. And Cass had seen it before.

Cass recognized the man with a rush of happy familiarity, like finding a favorite possession long lost. But just as the chaos of years running and fighting for survival made it impossible to name where her belongings had scattered, she couldn't remember how she knew him. A cloud of confusion settled in on her mind.

She must have made a sound because Drew grabbed her hand and gave it a squeeze. "You okay?" he asked.

Cass shook her head and pulled away, taking a few steps forward hoping to see better. The conversation had continued on the flatbed as she'd been mesmerized.

"So, what's the alternative here?" Hank was asking. "What do we do with him if neither of our groups takes him on?"

Derrick shrugged. "That's why we bagged him. He won't know how to get back here. Someone can take him back through the city and leave him."

Cass could see Cam was about to speak, but the prisoner interrupted.

"You may as well kill me then," he said.

Cass felt like someone had sucked the air from her lungs. The recognition was even stronger when she heard his voice. *What the hell? Why can't I remember?*

"We might if you don't shut up," interjected the man who waited on the ground near the stairs.

"You may as well. I'll die on my own and I'd rather it went quick," the prisoner said. Then he coughed several times and slumped forward, wincing in pain.

Hank and Cam turned to confer with one another, and Drew was at Cass's side once more.

"What's wrong?" he asked.

"Do you recognize him?"

"Derrick?"

"The prisoner." Cass's voice was sharp, impatient. She moved forward again, pushing through the crowd.

"No." Drew followed. "Should I?"

"I dunno. I think *I* do."

Cass glanced at Drew long enough to see his eyebrows shoot up. "From where?" he asked.

"I can't remember." On the platform, Cam and Hank were shaking their heads. Neither one of them would want to take on a new member at the start of a long and already perilous journey. Much less someone who might be a criminal.

"Are you gonna let him die?" Drew whispered. Cass glanced up to see Cam had stepped forward stuttering and running his hand up and down the back of his neck the way he always did when he had to give bad news.

Drew's question echoed in her ears, and she felt her body pumping with restless energy. Am *I going to let him die?* She felt her body leaning forward, ready to leap, which was answer enough for her. She pushed her way through the front row of people and stepped toward the flatbed.

"I will speak for him," she said, her voice ringing out and halting conversation on the platform.

There was some scattered muttering in the crowd behind her, but she took steady steps toward the stairs. The man on the ground raised a hand as if to stop her but Cam spoke.

"Let her pass," he said.

Cass shot the man a threatening look as she climbed onto the flatbed. She passed behind the leaders, managing not to glance at the prisoner, and stood beside her brother.

"This is Cassidy," Cam said. "My second." Cass saw her brother's gaze harden and turned to find Derrick looking her up and down with a raised eyebrow and an appreciative smile. "And my sister," Cam added.

"What use does the lovely Cassidy have for *this* man?" Derrick asked. As he turned to face her brother, Cass made note of his slightly off-center nose. The cartilage of his ears was thickened like a boxer's.

"We've experienced losses recently, and I could use an extra pair of strong arms to help care for our livestock," Cass said, surprised she'd come up with an excuse and been able to speak it with confidence.

Derrick let out a harsh laugh, reached down to grab the rope still attached to the prisoner's bound hands and jerked it up, stretching the man's arms above his head.

"These arms are a bit scrawny, don't you think?" he said, dropping them. Then he raised his brows, stepped closer to the prisoner and grabbed the man's chin. He lifted the man's face and tilted it left and right, presenting each side to Cass in turn. "His face is pretty, though. Maybe you have another need for his arms?"

There were a few snickers from the crowd, and the prisoner seemed to shudder in Derrick's grasp. But Cass was aware of little but the heat blooming in her chest and radiating out into her limbs. Her arms grew heavy, her fists clenched at her sides, and her nostrils flared. Then Cam was standing in front of her, a hand loose on her arm.

"Let it go," he said. His clenched jaw showed his order was firm, but his eyes were understanding. "First impressions, Cass." She took in a breath and nodded. "Are you sure about this? Taking him in?"

"You'd rather let him die?" Her voice carried a bite that surprised even her.

Cam looked down for a moment. "What if he's trouble?"

"I'll take responsibility for him, Cam. I know what that means."

Cam nodded once and turned back.

"My sister is taking responsibility for this man," he said.

Derrick bent and hauled the prisoner up by an arm. "See that? You've been pardoned. Don't make her regret it." He led the man over to Cass and handed her the rope with a smile. He glanced between brother and sister. "I don't know how useful he'll be to you really."

"Cass will make him useful," Cam said. "She's quite a teacher."

"Quite a hunter, too," Hank said, stepping forward as if to remind everyone he was there. "That venison you smell was her kill. Let's get this over with and eat."

Derrick nodded and stepped away. He started to speak to the crowd as Cam put an arm on Hank's shoulder and guided him around her and the prisoner, blocking them from the view of the crowd.

The tension in the air seemed to dissipate. As the men spoke of the journey to come and the promises of Stronghold, a buzz of excitement radiated from the crowd.

Cass had dropped the rope the moment Derrick had stepped away from her, but she remained stationed beside the prisoner. She turned her head as if she were listening to the leaders when really she was trying to banish the awkward feeling that had come over her; a feeling of not quite fitting in her own skin. She stole glances at the prisoner in her peripheral.

He stood stiff, gaze fixed on the boots of the speaking men. Close up he seemed less familiar. He was thinner than she'd realized and there were several more cuts on his face than she'd noticed. Cass wondered if the recognition had faded because it was harder not to focus on his injuries from this distance. Or maybe she was loony from hunger and trauma, and she'd never seen the man before.

She was startled by a loud whoop from part of the crowd. Then, the rest of the people joined in, shouting and clapping. Cam and the others were directing everyone to the tarp-shelter where dinner would be waiting. Cass watched as the separate groups began to mingle. Coltonites and Montanans stepped forward to help members of Clan Mason unhitch their wagons. Some split into smaller circles and shook hands.

For a moment Cass longed to merge with the welcoming, mingling groups below but she knew stepping down there would not change the tense set of her body or the cool, shielded look in her eyes. She had no room in her head for all those people—just enough for her band.

The prisoner beside her shifted his weight and a twinge of regret played in the back of her head. She hoped she had the energy for this new responsibility.

When she turned, he was looking at her. Taking in his face as a whole, overlooking the injuries, it again seemed familiar; the shape of his cheekbones and the sharp jawline. Most disturbing was the fact she had known his eyes would be blue.

Cass's jaw dropped open. A puff of air left her lungs and behind it were words she'd not planned to speak.

"Do you recognize me?

Two

WILLIAM WYSON HAD THOUGHT being enslaved to a crazy person and imprisoned in her basement was the worst thing that could happen to him. Being "rescued" had topped it. Now, it was all about to start again. When none of the Californians had recognized him, he'd thought he was safe. He'd thought enough years had gone by, enough people had died, and his appearance had changed enough no one would recall him again.

But, here was reality with vivid green eyes and a gun on her hip. Another woman who owned him, another debt to pay. And how would it be taken *this* time?

He sucked in a shaky breath and took his chances.

"Should I?" he said.

Her mouth snapped shut and her brow knit together in a frown.

"I don't know." She shrugged and shook her head. "I thought maybe I knew you. What's your name?"

She didn't know him. He wanted to scream with joy and collapse with relief all at once, but instead, he coughed and winced as pain exploded over his side. He swore he felt every rib like they were razors rather than bone. He jerked his hands to his side and let them hover there, unable to do much to ease the discomfort while bound.

"Shit," the woman said. Cassidy, was it? She reached for her left arm and pulled a knife rapidly from a sheath. He stepped back, eyes widening before he'd even had time to think she probably wasn't planning to hurt him.

"Easy," she said, her voice low and airy. "Give me your hands."

He found himself not only extending his wrists toward her but taking a couple of steps closer. She tipped his hands down and slid the knife blade carefully between his palms.

"Hold still." She sliced the restraints with two smooth cuts. He watched her face as the ropes fell away and she winced. "Shit." Her eyes met his and she raised an eyebrow. "Doesn't that hurt?" she asked. This close, he could watch her lips move and light shimmered on a scar on the right side of her bottom lip. She was waiting for an answer. He blinked and glanced down.

His wrists were red and blistered; coated with thin, brown chunks of dried blood like morbid tea leaves. He was used to the aching and throbbing of his hands by now. The only thing missing was a sense of relief at the removal of the ropes. There was only a continued, dull burn.

"It'll be alright," he said. He noticed she was appraising him, her eyes lingering on his injured side, almost completely exposed behind his torn, filthy shirt. No one was exactly clean anymore, but he hadn't looked this bad in years. Awful as captivity had been, at least he'd been cared for. Days walking behind a wagon had coated him in muck. She looked fairly put together in comparison. Cassidy. It *was* Cassidy, right?

"What's your name?" they said in hopeful unison.

The woman snickered, then smiled, half her lip turning up and her eyes widening like she was half-surprised at the action. William felt like electricity itself. His skin tingled with energy and pain was a memory.

"My name is Cassidy," she said, tilting her head to the side, still wearing her smile. "But, everyone calls me Cass."

Cass.

"And you?" she asked.

Bollocks. What was the name he was planning to use?

He cleared his throat and said, "Billy. My name is Billy."

Cass nodded, still smiling but shaking her head as if she wasn't sure why. "Nice to meet you."

She headed for the stairs only to stop before reaching them. Following her gaze, he realized she was staring at the bag that had covered his head, still crumpled where Derrick had tossed it. William swallowed back a lump in his throat, wondering what she was thinking. With a smooth kick, she knocked it from the platform. He watched the bag fall to the dirt beside the trailer, then met her gaze. Her smile was gone but the expression replacing it was deeper and full of solidarity.

She nodded and said, "Billy. Follow me."

And from then on, Billy he was.

BILLY WRUNG THE WASHCLOTH over the bucket of warm water and watched as Drew disappeared around a corner, headed toward the noise of the feast. The last gleam of sunlight would soon be gone, and he was grateful for the lantern Cass had left him. He began to wipe the dried blood and dirt from his face. The last hour of his life had been turmoil and the warm water dripping down his chest provided a relief he'd never expected to feel again.

He'd thought the people were going to turn him away. He'd

been sure of it. All those years he'd spent locked in a basement he had prepared for escape. He'd done what he could to keep in shape, everything he could remember from the days he'd needed to bulk up for a role while traveling; pull-ups on the window bars, lunges across the room, even running the length of the basement when he had the energy. Usually, he was well fed but times had gotten hard for his captors, and they ate before he did, of course.

All that time he kept his hope, hatching plans to get away, run off, and find people who didn't recognize him. After his captors had died, he'd spent so many hours screaming out the window, praying to be found, and believing those who found him would grant him freedom. Mental.

He knew the nature of the outside world, now. People tended toward violence and cruelty, and it was ridiculous to think he could survive alone. He couldn't start a fire or hunt. If he had ever managed to get away, he would've starved, died of exposure, or ended up in the hands of people worse than those who'd locked him up.

All of this had been clear while he knelt up on that lorry trailer, listening to Derrick's uninspiring petition for his "adoption" into a new band. So when he'd heard himself declaring he'd rather be killed quickly than be left to die alone, Billy had known it was true. And it was what he'd expected. But then—Cass.

He slid his shirt over his head, grunting in pain as he stretched his broken ribs. He bent over the bucket and scooped handfuls of the cooling, now dirty water over his head, scrubbing away the filth. The water against his scalp was a welcome relief, and he had to catch his breath and steady himself in the rush of gratitude.

"No," he said aloud as he reached for the towel. "None of that." He couldn't afford to get comfortable. He couldn't afford to let himself feel safe. He couldn't afford the fire Cass lit inside him either. Though it was good to know he could still feel attraction.

Cass seemed kind. She'd introduced him to Drew as if he were a new member already; there had been no sense he was indebted. Drew had been kind, if quiet. He'd been happy enough to run for water and soap while Cass had shown Billy the first aid supplies and the small shed where he was to spend the night. But, she'd said she needed "strong arms" to "help with livestock." Billy had no illusions about his appearance. He looked—and felt—like rubbish.

So had she lied? Did she have some other plan in mind? Had she only pretended not to remember how she recognized him? Was it possible her motives were the same as the last woman to "take him in"?

And if she'd meant it—if she intended for him to help with livestock—then his staying here depended on his being useful at something he'd never done. He'd ridden horses for roles once or twice, taken lessons to keep from falling off on camera, but those were controlled circumstances. This would be nothing like that.

As if on cue, a horse walked toward him from the nearby field. It came within a few feet of where he knelt and stopped. He had forgotten how big horses were. He'd forgotten horses existed while trapped in the dank, claustrophobic basement.

"Hello," he said to the animal. The horse snorted and ambled away. "Nice to meet you, too."

He felt a smile on his lips as he watched the animal move toward a patch of grass near a partially collapsed barn. He took in a deep breath. At least the air was fresh. The breeze carried the scent of cooking meat, reminding him of his hunger. He fought away nausea, grabbed the backpack full of clothes and his lantern and ducked into the shed to change.

CASS STEPPED OUT OF the shadow of the partially collapsed barn to greet Huckleberry. She swung an arm over his neck and pressed her face into his mane, breathing him in.

"What do you think?" she muttered into the horse's coarse hair. "Is he dangerous?" She listened to the horse's breathing and wondered why she had done this to herself. She could be eating already, going over the maps with Cam, or discussing with Lena her plans to test out the newly arrived horses and mules to ensure they could all be hobbled or tied to a high-line for nights on the journey. Instead, she was lurking in the shadows keeping watch over this potential problem.

She stepped back from Huck just enough to see the door of the small shed and waited for her charge to exit. When he did, he dumped the bucket of water and headed toward the light of the campfire and noise of the crowd without looking her direction. She waited a few seconds and followed at a distance.

The atmosphere around the fires was jovial. Everyone was talking, most with food in their mouths and excitement in their eyes. Cass slowed her pace. So many new faces made it hard to find familiar ones. She found Cam's first. Her brother was crouching, deep in conversation with a gray-haired but vibrant man who was smiling and nodding knowingly. He made to stand up, and Cam assisted him, taking his empty plate. With a hand on his shoulder, Cam led the man to a rusted picnic table where Trista sat with Drew.

Drew caught Cass's eye and waved her over. She glanced at the collapsible steel table where food was laid out. Billy had taken a plate and was moving to sit on the outskirts of the crowd on an old tractor tire. She'd be able to keep an eye on him from the picnic table, so she gave a nod to her friend and headed for the food. There were only a few plates left, but each was brimming with meat from the deer she'd shot or from miscellaneous small game they'd trapped since arrival. There were also pans of beans and canned corn, some smoked fish the Oregonians had brought, and baskets full of avocados. She took one and eyed it in disbelief.

"Clan Mason brought them," said Lena, stepping up beside Cass and selecting a plate. "They're delicious."

"I'm sure," Cass said, moving her plate away to allow Lena access to the food.

"You should come meet Katie and Conrad," Lena said. "This food is for Katie. Conrad wants her to rest."

Cass followed the girl's glance and saw a serious-looking man she recognized from the Oregon band and a heavily pregnant woman. Cass sighed at the reminder they would be stopping somewhere along the way to allow the woman to give birth. It was also likely they would need to stop more frequently and stay extra days more often to allow her rest. All of this would leave them exposed to discovery by Rovers.

Cass sensed Lena looking at her, so she controlled her expression. "Sure."

Lena led Cass to the small group and introduced her as she handed Katie the plate. Cass nodded to Katie and Conrad in turn. Then she realized why the pensive man with a heavy expression was someone she recognized.

"That's right," she said. "Conrad. You're the man I need to talk to about your group's horses and mules."

Nodding, Conrad said, "That's right. But, we didn't have as much stock as you to begin with and we lost one on the trip here."

"Chip," Katie said with a melancholy smile. "He was special."

Conrad's entire body rotated toward Katie as she spoke and his eyes lingered on her face.

"Well, I have to make a supply run, but we'll get to working with the horses after that. Maybe day after tomorrow?" Conrad tore his gaze away from Katie and gave Cass a nod and a half smile.

"Can I come with you?" Lena asked.

Before Cass could reply, her father Waylon answered, "No, Lena." The kind-faced man with steady hazel eyes settled down next to Katie with a plate of food.

"I didn't ask you, Dad," Lena said, her jaw clenching as her gaze continued to rest on Cass.

"I'm sure that Cass will take Drew along to help her," Waylon said, his tone growing firmer as Lena's temper heated.

"That's not fair. I know more about what we'd need than Drew."

Cass could feel Lena's anger transferring to herself. This was a common argument. Lena seemed to feel Cass could override her father's wishes and give her the freedom she craved. But, Cass didn't mind Waylon's restrictions for his daughter, and she had no intention of undermining them. Lena had more responsibility on her than any sixteen-year-old should and it made her reckless, ready to clutch at the risks of adulthood before she'd prepared for them. No, Cass wanted Lena safe in the camp.

"You do," Cass said, noticing Katie's bright eyes watching with rapt attention. She felt conspicuous dealing with the teen's temper in front of strangers. "Which is why I need you here. Almost all of our horses need their hooves done before we take off. Cam will need help."

Protests spun behind Lena's eyes, but her shoulders relaxed. "Fine."

"Nice to meet you both," Cass said and extricated herself. She high-tailed it over to Drew, glancing up to check that Billy was where he'd been. She met his gaze and paused mid-step, feeling liquid building in her eyes she couldn't explain. After sitting, she found herself unable to eat until she took a few deep breaths and swallowed back her confusion.

Once she dug into her food, she was voracious. She'd polished off half the plate before she realized Drew was watching her. He wore his smile like he was in on a private joke.

"What?" Her mouth was full, and the word came out muffled.

"Nothing," he said.

"Bull." She swallowed and glanced at the other end of the table where the gray-haired man was standing to leave. Trista held his hand between hers and smiled up at him with angelic gratitude and Cam smiled at Trista until he noticed Cass watching them.

He cleared his throat and said, "Doc, have you met my sister Cass?"

Cass swiped the back of her hand across her mouth and forced a smile.

"I have not," Doc said. "Pleasure."

Cass nodded, then frowned. "Doc?" she asked. "A nickname?"

"No. He's a doctor," Drew said.

"Not exactly," Doc said. "I was an EMT and my wife was a surgeon. But, I'm the closest thing we had in our area, so everyone calls me Doc."

Cass saw the way he wavered as he mentioned his wife and hurt for him for a second. The next second she steeled herself again. No new relationships. No new responsibilities.

"Well, lucky us," she said, "to have you on this trip." Doc smiled and nodded, raising a hand as he turned to leave.

Cass flinched. New responsibilities. "Hey, Doc?" The man turned back and noted Cass's hasty glance around them, then closed the distance between them to allow discretion.

"The new member of our band—the prisoner," Cass said.

"Yes?"

"His name is Billy, and he's injured. Would you mind having a look at him after dinner?" Cass searched the man's lined and hardened face, seeing nothing but concern and kindness.

"Of course," he said. "It's done."

Cass nodded, surprised at the level of gratitude she felt. So surprised in fact, she missed her chance to thank him before he left. She watched him leave, then let her glance return to Billy, still bent over his plate, before she turned back to her dinner.

Cam had again clasped hands with Trista across the table. They shared a long, secretive look and then Cam lunged impulsively forward, wrapped a hand behind Trista's blonde head, and kissed her.

Cass looked back to her plate and then half-turned to check on Billy. He wasn't alone, anymore. One of the barely-dressed women she'd noticed earlier was smiling up at him from the ground beside his tire seat.

Cass turned back to find Drew staring at her again, wearing the same stupid smile.

"What?" she asked.

"Let's talk about your new charge." Drew leaned forward, elbows on the table and head propped on his clasped hands.

"You're sure you don't recognize him?"

"You didn't figure out where you know him from?"

Cass shook her head and took another bite.

"Weird," Drew said, raising up to peer over her shoulder at Billy with a frown. "I dunno, Cass."

With her mouth full again, Cass asked, "Maybe from a school we competed against?"

"I doubt it." Drew looked around them. Cam and Trista were still making eyes at one another, and no one else was within earshot. Still, Drew leaned in and lowered his voice. "I mean, it's been years, but I feel like I would've remembered *that* face." Drew raised an eyebrow and stuck his tongue out to press it against his top lip. He sat back with a lascivious smile.

Cass frowned. Billy *was* handsome; it hadn't escaped her notice. But, she had been so preoccupied trying to figure out why he was familiar and providing accommodations for him she hadn't had time to think about it.

But, now she was thinking about it. Too big clothes and still-damp hair notwithstanding, he was attractive. Without the dirt and blood caked on, even the black eye and fat lip only served to make him look somehow—tested. Strong, even.

It took her a moment to realize Billy was looking back at her. Neither of them looked away, even when a few people passed through their sight line. Then, noticing he was distracted, the woman who sat with him wrapped a hand around his thigh. Billy's eyes widened, and he leaped up and away from the woman, who raised both palms and leaned back. He shook his head and said something before snatching the lantern up and jogging away from the crowd.

"What happened there?" Drew asked.

Cass just shook her head. "I don't know why I did this; I don't have time for this." She rubbed a hand over her eyes. "I had one goal: get everyone to Stronghold and be done with it."

"I wish you'd stop talking like there won't be a place for you there, Cass," Drew said. This was a common argument from him. "I mean, what exactly are you planning to be "done with"?"

Cass met Drew's eyes and shrugged. She stuffed the last bites of meat in her mouth, palmed the avocado, and followed the way Billy had gone.

CASS WATCHED AS BILLY entered the shed, and waited. The excitement of the merger died down as the Californians set up tents, and slowly everyone began to make their way to bed. Cass turned toward a light bobbing her direction through the dark.

"Do you think he needs to be watched?" Cam asked when he'd come to stand next to her.

"Honestly," Cass said, "no. But, I don't know why I feel that way. So I don't trust it."

Cam nodded and bumped her shoulder with his. "Go get some sleep. I'm on watch tonight. I'll keep an eye on him."

"It's not your night to be on watch."

"I volunteered. Won't be able to sleep tonight, anyway." Cam measured Cass's skeptical, searching look and shrugged, turning away. "Excitement. The merger."

Cass raised an eyebrow, but stretched and turned toward the row of tents. Just as she lifted her foot to leave she set it back down. "Is everything okay with you, big brother?" She watched his response carefully.

"Of course," he said. His smile was relaxed, but his eyes shifted away as he spoke.

She thought about pressing for more. He'd been acting strangely for weeks. But, she was tired and strained and decided to let it go. "Good night," she said.

She met Doc on her way. He raised a canvas bag with a red cross taped on the side and tilted his head in question.

Cass pointed at the shed, "He's in there. Thank you."

Doc nodded. She watched him approach the shed for a moment, then continued to her tent.

Drew was snoring as she shimmied down into her sleeping bag beside his. Her head had barely dented her pillow before she was asleep.

CASS DIDN'T HEAR THE first gunshot, but the second shattered the atmosphere of her dream world, and the third jolted her fully awake. She sat up straight, sucking in a breath and freezing, hoping she'd imagined it. Drew groaned from his sleeping bag beside her and mumbled something. She heard stirring in the neighboring tents and whispered voices.

"Was that gunfire? Drew, get up." Cass grabbed her jeans from beside her bed and jerked them on. She stumbled through the tent flap before she'd fully unzipped it, whirled back around and reached inside for her pistol which she'd tucked in the corner. As she stood up, she heard someone call her name, and an icy panic curled through her gut.

She headed in the direction the shots had come from. As she rounded the corner of the row of tents, she ran smack into another person. With matching grunts of pain and surprise she and the other fell backward away from one another.

"What's going on?" she said, her voice a strained growl. The pistol had slipped from her sleep-weakened hand, and she patted the earth at her side until she felt the cool metal. She squinted into the low light, straining to see who she'd collided with. "Who are you?"

"Cass?" The voice was male and somewhat familiar, so her tension eased minutely. "Your brother sent me. He's out by the shed."

Cass struggled to stand. She bumped into the man, accidentally kneeing him and stumbling again as she ran in the direction of the shed.

A light appeared ahead, and she picked up her pace, ignoring the bite of rocks and twigs into her bare feet. As she neared, she realized the light was a lantern, and it was illuminating two shapes on the ground; one small and dark, the other large and—sorrel.

"Oh, God," she said, picking up her pace. Her feet pounded into the grass of the field, and the realization of her fears brought her to a full and abrupt halt. It was Cam, kneeling beside a sorrel horse.

She let out a sound—half gasp, half moan—and Cam turned.

"Cassidy," he said, raising a hand to her. His mournful tone confirmed what she already knew. She stepped forward, only now registering the sharp scent of blood.

The horse's breathing was labored and loud, filling her ears until all sound became a dull roar. She rounded his head and glanced down. The whites of his eyes glowing in the lantern light were the only coloring on his face. No markings. Her heart sunk still further. Clinging to scraps of hope, Cass turned her gaze to his right hind leg, looking for Huck's white sock.

But, his leg wasn't where it was supposed to be. It was twisted at an odd angle, and blood soaked the ground below it. Patches of red marred the white sock.

Cass fell to her knees, yanking at the hair on her head as she let out a pained, guttural cry. She ran a hand across her face to clear away the tears already soaking her cheeks. Her fingernails dug into the flesh covering her cheekbone. She sucked in a few strained breaths and looked back up at her horse.

Blood seeped from claw marks running down his back and side, and a chunk of flesh stood out from his flank, held on only by skin. She suppressed the urge to scream into the sky and crawled to Huck's head. His eye rolled toward her, and she laid her head against his neck, running her hand across his cheek.

"Not you, boy, not you," she said, breaking off to sob. "Not my Huckleberry."

"I'm so sorry, Cass," Cam said, his voice hoarse. His hand brushed along her head.

"What happened?" Her voice sounded surreal and distant.

"Mountain lion," Cam said. "He got away at first, I heard him scream—" Cam broke off, and Cass could tell his teeth were gritted when he continued. "He stepped in a hole and went down, and the cat was on him again by the time I got here. I wounded it, but it got away."

"I didn't hear him scream," Cass said as a fresh wave of agony closed in on her. She sobbed into Huck's neck and felt her brother lay his head and arms across her.

"Shh…" he whispered, his breath separating the hair behind her ear. His hand tangled into Huck's mane beside her own.

They remained there for a few moments until Huck shifted beneath them and let out a quavering noise like a groan. Cam sat up quickly, and Cass moved to bend over Huck's head.

"Easy, buddy," she said. "I know. I got you." Then, turning to

Cam. "I dropped my gun." She turned to look for it and saw Drew standing a few feet away, holding the pistol out to them like a sad offering. His sympathetic eyes shone with tears.

Cass reached for the gun, but Cam stood up, blocking her hand.

"I'll do it," he said. "You comfort him." There was a hitch in Cam's voice, and his breathing was tremulous as he moved to the front of Huck's head.

Cass moved herself to be next to Cam and slightly to the side, never taking her hands off the warm flesh of the horse. She managed to steady her shaking and focus on Huck's eye, ignoring the glint of silver shining off the gun.

"Ready?" Cam asked.

"You're the best horse there ever was Huck," she said. "I'm so sorry." Taking a shuddering breath, Cass nodded.

One violent, cold report and Huck was gone.

Three

BILLY SAT ON THE cool earth, back against the shed, watching as Drew and Cam knelt by the horse's body and talked to Cass. She had fallen across the animal's neck when Cam had shot it and clung so tightly Billy was sure they'd have to pry her away with force.

People had wandered over to see what the early morning commotion had been. A ginger girl had streaked past just after dawn and crashed to the ground next to Cass. She'd said her goodbyes and Cam had led her back to an older man, who seemed to be her father. After hugging the girl and speaking to Cam in whispers, the man had left.

Now, the redhead was striding toward him, and Billy moved to stand.

"No, sit," the girl said, nose stuffed from crying. "I just want to introduce myself. I'm Lena."

"Billy," he replied.

"I already help Cass with the horses," she said, a touch of peevishness in her voice. "But, I guess we get to teach you, now."

Billy sat up a bit straighter and contemplated. What to say to someone who clearly didn't want him around? "I hope I learn fast so I can be useful."

Lena raised an eyebrow and turned to watch the action on the field again, crossing her arms. Billy had just given up on her saying anything else when she added, "I don't think we need you. I think Cass wanted to save you."

Billy's mouth dropped open, and he groped for something to say. He was spared when a commotion broke out in the field.

Cass had sat up, though she kept a protective hand on the horse's neck. She was saying something to Cam and Drew, both of whom had taken steps back. Hands stuffed into his jeans pockets, Cam looked down at the ground, shaking his head. Drew held both hands in front of himself, palms toward Cass. Her voice was loud, her anger evident in the stiffness of her shoulders and the jerking of her head. Billy couldn't make out her words.

Her voice died out, and Cam looked up and spoke. Apparently, he said the wrong thing because Cass rocked smoothly to her feet and advanced on him, fists clenched at her sides. Cam stood his ground as she leaned into his space. Drew turned away, running both hands through his dark hair.

"I told them," Lena said. "I knew she wouldn't like it."

"What?" Billy found himself on edge, desperate to know what had wrought such a change in Cass's attitude. "What's happened?" He heard a twinge of his accent when he spoke, and he chided himself. *Careful*, he thought. *Don't forget to be American.*

"They want to eat him," Lena said. Her blunt tone didn't tell much of her opinion. She looked down at Billy as if she was slightly disgusted to be talking to him about it. "You know. No wasted meat."

This information hit Billy in the gut, and he looked back to the field. He could only imagine how Cass must feel. It was clear this horse was important. *Wasn't it? Did she lose the plot like this over every animal?*

"But, isn't this horse—um—special?" He didn't look at Lena as he spoke, anticipating a nasty expression.

"Obviously," she said. "Huck has been with Cass for like—ever. He was her first horse. She got him Before. Before "The End"."

"They're going to make her *eat* her horse?" Billy watched as the row continued in the field. Shouted words occasionally reached them—some of them curses. Cass bounced and gesticulated, but Cam remained still and calm.

"Oh, she won't eat any. She never eats the horse meat when we have to put them down. But the rest of us..." Billy looked up to see Lena rubbing at her arms with a frown. She must not like it, either.

The concept of horse meat was not foreign to Billy. In Europe, people had eaten it often but not the meat from a horse they had owned and loved. His chest felt hollow as he watched Cass's anger burn out. She hung her head, covering her face with her hands.

"It's the right thing to do." Lena's voice and attitude had quieted. "She knows that. It's what we always do. It's just as easy to butcher as it is to bury and we don't always have luck hunting. We used to have cows, goats, but now..." Lena spoke as if trying to justify it to herself all over again.

Billy watched as Cam took a step forward, laid a hand on Cass's arm and spoke to her. She lifted her head, jerked her arm away and slapped her brother across the face. Cam's head whipped aside, and he kept it turned as she leaned in to say something.

A moment later, she bent to stroke the horse's neck again. Beside Billy, Lena spat on the ground and walked away.

Billy rubbed at the scabbing burns on his wrists and watched the girl leave. When he looked up, Cass was heading his direction, followed closely by Drew. Billy scrambled to his feet, his rib cage surging with fresh pain. He bumped against the shed, aggravating the fresh bruise he'd gotten from colliding with Cass that morning.

"...think you should lay low, today," Drew was saying. "Grieve."

With an exasperated sigh, Cass ground to a halt, "And what? Hide in our tent? Listen as they cut him apart?" Cass's voice cracked, and she coughed.

Our tent? Billy's brow furrowed.

"And dammit, Drew, I can't sit here and smell the smoke as they cook my horse."

A group of men was approaching. Most Billy recognized from Clan Mason, Derrick among them. He looked away, fighting to keep his body from recoiling as they stepped up to Cass and Drew.

"Cassidy." Derrick's voice slithered up Billy's spine and seemed to tighten the back of his throat. "I'm so sorry. This one was special to you, I hear." Billy couldn't help but look up. Derrick had thrown a massive arm over Cass's shoulders, and Billy's own arm muscles spasmed as he watched.

Cass had tensed, but she didn't shrug his arm away. "He was." Her voice was stiff now, bearing none of the heated quaver it had a moment ago.

"Well, at least we'll be well-fed when we head out in a few days," Derrick said, squeezing her shoulders and then removing his arm to clap his scarred hands together. Billy flinched and then cursed himself for it. "Well! I hear there's a wounded mountain lion in those woods." Derrick nodded his head toward the ridge.

"One step ahead of you," Drew said, his voice raising to rival Derrick's volume. "I was just about to get up a hunting party. We'll get the cat."

Cass's jaw dropped open, and her gaze might've shattered glass. "Aren't you coming with *me*?" she asked. "For supplies," she said to the other men as an afterthought.

"I want that cat, Cass," Drew said, not meeting her gaze.

"You headed to Provo?" Derrick asked. "Would you go tomorrow? I'd be happy to ride along. Keep you safe."

The smarmy way Derrick looked at Cass turned Billy's stomach, and he watched her body harden. Then, she looked at him. He hadn't known she'd noticed him there and his posture straightened.

"No need," she said. "I'll take Billy."

A HALF HOUR LATER, Billy stood beside a gray horse, reins looped around his hand. He shifted his weight from foot to foot. Not far away, Cass was saddling a horse with practiced speed as Cam hovered around her, talking with his hands.

Billy knew they were fighting about him. Derrick had been quick to point out Billy's supposed questionable morals. When pressed, Billy had admitted his complete lack of skill with a weapon. Drew had suggested several other people she should take while fixing Billy with a dark stare that promised violence. Hot embarrassment and cold fear had battled through him as he listened. But Cass had dismissed them all without fanfare, told Billy to get ready, and left to clean herself up and get her boots.

A few minutes later, Lena had appeared with this saddled horse and tossed him the reins. Now the girl scuffed the toe of her boot into the ground, kicking up clumps of grass, her face flaming to match her hair. She loosely held a rope attached to a mule wearing some type of frame saddle with leather and cloth bags on either side. It looked complicated, and Billy was again rinsed with a shower of dread that he'd never learn fast enough.

The mule jerked its head away from the girl's kicking foot and shifted further from her. Billy was struck by the knowledge that, though she was young and skinny, this girl was not someone he wanted as an enemy.

"What are you staring at?" Lena asked. She seemed ready to

burst into flame at his answer so he couldn't help but sigh in relief when he was spared giving one by Cass's arrival.

"Thanks, Lena," she said reaching for the mule's lead rope.

"I can still saddle up and come along," Lena said, not yet giving up the rope.

Cass cleared her throat and glanced over the mule's back. Drew's group of hunters were organizing themselves nearby, and a couple of people had gathered next to Huckleberry's prone form, shifting in discomfort and trying to hide the short ropes and gleaming blades they held.

"I need you to stay and make sure Cam keeps his promise," Cass said. "I don't want the dog gnawing on his bones; I don't want to see a single piece of hide I can recognize, or a drop of blood uncovered in that field. Okay?" Cass had spoken very quickly, but her words hadn't wavered.

Lena nodded, and it seemed some of the heat seeped from her. "I promise." But, she pulled the rope away again and jerked a thumb in Billy's direction. "You'll probably need to teach him how to get on and steer."

Cass glanced at Billy and he swallowed. Then, she looked at the group of men. Derrick and a couple of others were watching and smirking. When she looked back at him, he wanted to shrink away. She handed her reins to Lena, ducked under the horse's brown neck, and jogged over.

"Have you ever ridden a horse before?" she asked.

Billy nodded. "A long time ago."

"Well, these days, in our group, horses are the cars, cabs, and ambulances. So you've got to be able to ride even when you're dying." A memory shadowed Cass's eyes briefly before she glanced down at his hand.

"First, don't ever hold the reins like that. Or a rope, or anything. Never wrapped around your hand, unless you'd like to lose it." She took the reins and passed one under the horse's neck, flipping it around and crossing the other over it. She settled them into the horse's mane. "Smoke will stand, it's what she loves best."

Cass moved between him and the saddle, brushing against his chest. He couldn't stop himself from sucking in a breath and pulling away. His skin crawled almost as badly as it had the night before when the woman who'd called herself Marie had touched him.

"Sorry," Cass said. "Are you hurting?" She indicated his side with a glance and he nodded. She shook her head. "I'm sorry to do this, but if I go, you have to. You're my responsibility." She cleared her throat. "And you're gonna want to make a good showing, here. You have an audience." She shot a hooded glance at the hunting party.

Billy nodded and cleared his throat. "I'll be fine."

Cass slapped one hand onto the raised back of the saddle and the other onto the horn. "Hands like this, stand like I'm standing, and I'll give you a leg up." She moved back so he could take her place and when he did he was consumed by her earthy, honest scent. The heat of her behind him was distracting.

She knelt and clasped her hands together, palms up. "Left leg," she said. He flashed back to doing this once before. People had watched then, too. He bent his knee and this time her touch did not bother him. "One, two, three," she said, and he jumped, pulled—his side screaming as his muscles engaged—and swung his right leg over. Cass was strong, and he almost went too far. The thought of vaulting straight across the horse and slamming into the ground on the other side to a chorus of laughter caused a second's panic, but he caught the horn and flopped into the saddle.

Smoke's head jerked and her ears pinned, but she stood still. Cass rotated his ankle and tucked his sneakered foot into the stirrup.

"Wasn't that long ago," she said, looking up at him and offering an unexpected smile. "That was perfect. You're pale. You alright?"

He nodded and took a deep breath, risking a half-smile.

She gave him a quick lesson on how to steer or "neck rein" as she called it. She only paused for a second when her hand brushed his and he jerked away.

"If you have to fall off," she said, "do yourself a favor and wait 'til we're out of sight." She gave him a cheeky look as she turned and walked back to her horse. She mounted, accepted the mule's rope from Lena and headed off.

At first, Smoke was reluctant to move. Billy kicked her several times, his injuries burning in protest. She huffed and grunted, but her hooves seemed planted in the ground. The laughter Billy had hoped to avoid came at last.

"Lena," Cass said, turning around in her saddle, rocking slightly with each step of her horse.

Before Billy understood what was happening, Lena had approached and landed a smack on Smoke's rear. Having turned to see what the girl was doing, Billy was off balance when the horse jolted forward into a trot. He pitched back, over corrected forward, clutched the saddle horn and righted himself. The mare quickly caught up and slowed to a walk, following the horse and mule ahead without further complaint as the party passed through the camp and headed down the long dirt drive toward the highway.

They traveled in silence for a bit, Billy straining to remember everything he'd learned about riding so long ago, Cass scanning the valley for threats or maybe just landmarks. Now and then, she turned to check he was still firmly in the saddle and each time he thought she looked somehow more haggard. When they passed out of the valley, Cass led them off the road.

Abruptly, she stopped and dismounted.

"Cass?" he asked.

"Just wait here," she said without looking at him. Her shoulders were high and stiff as she gave a soft, downward tug on her horse's reins and said, "Stand."

She headed off across the field, walking first, then running full out, fists pumping. Her brown hair came free of its band and flew behind her like a flag.

Finally, she stopped and released a wretched scream into the air above her. She hugged her middle and fell to her knees, nearly disappearing in the tall grass.

Billy's chest collapsed as he watched her, each ragged breath an agony. Tears welled hot in his own eyes as his hands gripped the saddle horn until it was painful. He laid the reins across his thighs and flexed his fingers.

He knew it was a risk to feel this; to empathize with her this way. He couldn't trust her. What would happen if he mucked it up and failed to be useful? Worse, what would happen if she remembered where she recognized him? How useless would he look to her then? And relying on her, feeling her pain? That *was* trust. That was dependence. That was vulnerability he could not accept again.

CASS SHOWED BILLY HOW to tie the knot in Smoke's lead rope for the second time, pulled it loose, and watched him try again. She was starting to feel like he was too careful in his movements, avoiding any contact with her. Something about it stung. He hadn't said anything about her breakdown on the way here; hadn't tried to talk about it or comfort her. She was thankful to him for sparing her that discussion, that uncomprehending sympathy.

She'd given him an on-the-go riding lesson, and she was pleased he'd picked it up quickly. She almost doubted it had been that long since he'd ridden. But, it was possible for someone to have a naturally good seat, so she put the thought on the backburner for now.

"Is that right?" Billy asked. "Did I get it?"

Cass shook herself out of her reverie and checked the knot.

"Yep," she said. "The knot is right but do it once more for good measure and this time leave her a bit more room to move." Cass measured along the rope. "Like this much."

Billy bent to work again, and Cass forced herself to look away from him to check their surroundings. She didn't want to be here any longer than they had to be.

On the way into town, they'd passed a burn pile. Cass always avoided examining them too closely, but she'd noticed Billy gaping at the bleached white bones, recognizably human. Many were still piled together, overgrown with green weeds and grass, but some had been scattered around by scavenging animals. The horses' hooves had clicked against them as they'd passed.

Still, just because they didn't have to worry too much about stumbling upon gruesome remains in a store or a car didn't mean there couldn't be threats in the area; people living there or Rovers looking to resupply.

The ranch supply store looked overgrown and faded like all buildings did these days, but other than the shattered sliding glass door, it was in decent shape. The inside had looked worse when she'd checked it. People had raided the place before, turning over shelving and scattering merchandise in the process. They would find no ammo here but, the tack department seemed nearly untouched, and there was quite a bit of clothing left. They should be able to get what they needed.

Billy stepped back from the rope and turned to her.

"You got it," she said, and she couldn't help but smile at his proud expression. "Riding—check. Knot tying—check. Now let's see how good you are at shopping."

Billy laughed, and it was a nice sound. It made laughter tickle inside her as well. They paused once inside the store, eyes adjusting to the low light seeping through dirty skylights high above. She assigned him with outfitting himself with clothing and gathering extra for the rest of the camp.

Billy was looking around, and he let out a surprised "huh" as he spotted the old-time candy shop at the front of the store.

"What?" Cass asked.

He shook his head. "That's crazy. It still smells like popcorn." He waved a hand at the debris on the floor—leaves, garbage, and the rocks that had evidently broken the doors—then widened his gesture to include the store at large, its downed shelves and ransacked cash registers. "After all this."

Cass sniffed and let out a laugh. It did smell like popcorn. She didn't think she'd have noticed if he hadn't brought it up. She studied his sharp jawline, his hair brushing against it as he spoke. It reminded her of a song from Before. A melody began in her memory.

"Popcorn was my favorite food," Billy offered, turning back to her. "What was yours?"

"It doesn't really matter anymore, does it?" Her tone was contemplative, making the question seem almost rhetorical. Their eyes met for a moment too long, and they both shifted away.

Cass cleared her throat and struggled to remember what she'd been about to say a bit ago. "I don't think we'll have much luck getting you a tent here. The outdoor department is bare." She shook her head. "Some knives or fishing gear would have been nice. But, the tack we need is here, so..."

He was looking at her again, and she chafed under his gaze. She couldn't afford any more distractions. She sucked in a breath and said, "Okay. To work."

She took a step forward at the same instant he did, and they almost collided. They both chuckled and stepped back to allow the other through. Cass gave a terse nod and sped forward, tucking her shoulders and not looking back.

When she'd passed behind a tall, metal shelf that somehow had not been knocked down like a domino along with the rest, she paused and released her breath in a huff. Drew's comments had gotten into her head. Here alone with Billy, she couldn't stop noticing the weightless feeling she had when she was near him.

This quiet wonder he seemed to have for everything, including her, was making her crave sensations she'd been avoiding for quite some time. Not only the physical pleasure Drew had alluded to, but curiosity, connection, and yes, even the innocence that made Billy seem so naïve. She let out an audible growl and rushed into the tack department.

But, as soon as she spotted the halters, still neatly sorted into rows arranged by color, her focus turned to the bright purple ones—the color Huck had always worn. She remembered standing in a tack store just like this with her uncle as she fussed over which color to buy with the first money she'd earned in her life.

"You know the horse don't care what color you put on 'im, right?" he'd said, teasing.

"I care," Cass had said. She'd hung the blue back on its hanger and turned, clutching the purple.

"Purple?" her uncle had said, mockingly pained.

"Like huckleberries," she'd said.

Years later, when Huck had needed a new halter, her uncle had returned from the store one day and tossed another the same color across her lap as she lounged on the living room couch. They'd laughed about it and refused to explain the joke to Cam when he'd asked.

"Dammit," Cass said. These were memories she didn't need right now. The distraction of an attractive face was better than memories of the dead. But, it was hard to feel one without letting the other in. She winced as salt stung the scratch she'd given her cheek that morning and wiped tears from her already swollen eyelids.

She was quick in gathering what she needed and some extra

supplies she thought they might want along the way. She piled her haul at the end of an aisle and listened for Billy. Shuffling and footfalls seemed to indicate he was still working.

She wandered into the stockroom at the back of the store and put her hands on her hips, craning her neck to see into the darker room. She could make out a large garage door where they had received shipments. She crossed to it, making a face as rats squealed and scattered away from her feet. She looked for a way to open it manually, but in the end, settled for propping open the walk-in door beside it.

She scanned the boxes and wrapped pallets stacked above. Mostly dog kibble and horse feed. There were a few boxes stacked together in the furthest, darkest corner. Her hand brushed the pistol in its holster, but she felt confident she was alone, so she walked into the dreary corner. She couldn't read the markings on the cardboard at first, so she climbed up a ready-made dog house and then onto a rabbit hutch that creaked under her weight.

The first box read "power tools" and she scoffed. No need for those anymore with no electricity. But the second box read "overstock: camping" with a list of items in smaller print below. The third read "clothing: Winter".

"Score," she said. It took her a few minutes to find a good place to climb up onto the shelf. Once there, she had to shimmy between two pallets of chicken feed and dog treat boxes which wouldn't have been possible if the rats hadn't made the bags flexible by eating away at the contents. She shuddered and worked her way down beside the boxes she wanted.

Neither was damaged, despite the rat infestation. They seemed to be sleeping primarily in the various piles of dog bedding and horse blankets. At least that was where the majority of the squeaking was coming from. Cass decided it would be easier to push the boxes off to look through them.

Wedging herself against the cool metal of the wall, she pushed and let out a screech as the first box tumbled over and she almost fell with it. The box crashed into the rabbit hutch below. Wood cracked, and the legs of the hutch scraped across the cement with a sharp grating sound.

The second box was heavier, and she leaned into it. It tipped free just as Billy darted around the corner.

"Watch out!" she yelled, the second word cut off by the smack of the box against the cement. She peered over the edge of the shelf to find Billy staring up at her with wide eyes. "Sorry," she said. "What's up?"

Billy put a hand on his side. "You scared me. I thought I heard you scream and then there was a crash..."

"God, I didn't even think to warn you," Cass said. He looked genuinely concerned, breathing heavily from running across the store and tense as if he'd expected to find her dead. "That's the second time I've scared someone like that lately." She perched on the edge of the shelf, facing the back wall and swung herself down, gripping the orange metal frame. She dropped to the ground with a clatter of boot heels and turned to Billy.

He had changed out of the too-large sweatpants he'd been wearing and now wore jeans that fit, a pair of work boots, and a long-sleeved black button up over the white t-shirt they'd given him last night. He looked less like a refugee, now, and even more familiar to her.

"I'm done with the clothes except," Billy held out a hand, "do we need any baby things?" He was showing her a set of booties with little tractors embroidered on them. Cass's first thought was, as always, to dismiss such cutesy, domestic items, but something about the way he held them, one hand cradled underneath...

"I noticed that there's a woman—a pregnant woman. Cass?"

Something clicked in Cass's mind, and she knew why her

brother had been acting strangely. She knew why he'd switched his vote before the fire, suddenly wanting to travel to Stronghold. She flashed back to the night before, to Cam's excitement about Doc and kissing Trista across the table.

Cass's breath came out in a huff. "She's pregnant."

BILLY HAD JUST WATCHED Cass swing down from a shelf higher than his head without a moment's preparation, and *now* she was pale? How could she not have known the woman with the massive abdomen she'd spoken to the night before was pregnant?

"Well, yes," he said. Cass took a couple of steps back and rolled her left arm in a circle. She began to pace back and forth in front of him. He couldn't understand why she was so miffed. "Didn't you know?"

Cass shot him an exasperated look. "I'm not blind," she said, then seeming to think of something, "and I'm second in command. I do tend to hear about things like a birth we'll have to stop for."

Billy started to apologize but instead asked, "What's wrong, then?"

Cass stopped her pacing and dropped her head into her hands. After a moment, she raised her face. Her color had returned. "Yes," she said, her tone resigned and sour. "We need the baby clothes." She glanced down at the booties still in his hand.

He stared at her, trying to decide whether to question her further.

"Okay. Onward," she said. She clapped her hands and bird wings flapped against the skylight overhead. A chunk had broken out of the panel, letting brighter light stream down. Cass dragged one of the boxes under the beam of light and Billy hurried to push the other one over. She sliced open the tape on both. Replacing the knife in the sheath on her arm she said, "Let's start with this one."

She became lost in thought as she worked. He held back a moment, marveling. The booties had put her off balance but not slowed her. This woman was driven. First, a tragedy and now a serious stress and she was sorting through the boxes, flinging unwanted items aside at record speed. Only a slight wrinkle in her forehead gave away her disturbance.

Billy pushed up his sleeves and dug into the boxes, helping her toss aside what they didn't need and sort what they wanted into the sturdier of the two. At one point, she reached into the same box he did, and their bare arms brushed. He sucked in a sharp breath and almost pulled away, but stopped himself. He glanced at her, and she looked away immediately, but he had already seen the wounded look in her eyes.

Regret twisted in his chest. First the woman, Marie, who'd been coming on to him. Now, Cass. Neither situation was anything like what had happened in that basement. Neither woman was anything like *her*. Especially Cass. She'd saved him. She was teaching him.

He shook his head. No. She recognized him; owned him. He couldn't afford to forget.

Maybe it was for the best if he offended her. Wasn't she involved with Drew, anyway? Didn't they share a tent? He just needed to get by until the group got to Stronghold, avoiding conflict or recognition until then. If only he could also avoid the feeling of sick disappointment that grew from his determination to do so.

When they'd assembled the things they were taking, Cass stood and brushed off her jeans. "Let's just set this box outside that door." She gestured to the propped-open door where much of their light was coming from. "We'll come around and grab it. Save carrying it back through the store."

By the time Billy turned back, Cass had already hefted the large box and was maneuvering around shelves with it. "Uh—I can help," Billy stuttered, chasing after her. It was clear the box was heavy. Cass seemed bent under the weight, but she moved quickly.

"Just get the door," she said as she neared it. Billy darted through ahead of her, pulling the door fully open behind him and kicking the rock she'd used to prop it out of her way. Cass scraped the back of her hand on the door frame and sucked in a breath as she waddled past.

He turned and gaped as the door shut behind him. Beyond Cass was an open field. A mobile phone tower was fenced far on one end but, otherwise, it was nothing but long grass from the store to a wooded area beneath an overpass. A huge expanse overrun with elk.

Billy heard a noise slip from his mouth as he walked numbly forward. He planted his feet on the cracked asphalt at the parking lot's edge and stared. There must have been over a hundred of them, many of which had turned their heads to watch him.

"Blimey," he said, under his breath. This was one of the reasons he had bothered staying alive all those years he'd been locked in a basement. Because things like this still existed in the world, even if so much of his old life had been destroyed. There may not be art anymore but nature was stronger than ever. He'd seen it in packs of feral dogs barking through the neighborhood where he'd been kept— in the sight of deer clopping down streets unhindered by traffic. He'd known these things existed but had so often given in to despair long enough to think he'd never see them.

When he felt Cass move up to stand beside him, he turned. She wasn't looking at the elk, but at him. Her expression was inquisitive, and a half smile played around her lips.

Breathless, he asked, "Aren't they beautiful? So many!"

Cass chuckled, and her smile grew. She shook her head at him and then turned, hands on her hips, assessing the elk. "Yes," she said after a moment's contemplation. "They are beautiful." The two of them watched the herd pick up the pace of their escape into the woods. Cass cleared her throat and said, hesitantly at first, "That's actually not that large a herd, though. There are bigger in Montana and Wyoming. At least, there were. A virus wiped out a lot of elk last summer around where we lived."

"That's too bad," he said.

Cass shrugged, "Just nature. It was inconvenient, though."

Billy turned back just as the last of the elk passed almost single file into the trees.

"I still feel like I know you from somewhere," she said. "Where are you from originally?"

Billy's heart began to pound. Was the moment he dreaded already here? Could he tell her? Part of him wanted to, but the dominant part was putting on the brakes. Anytime people had learned who he was it had ended badly. He'd been traded away, kept as a bargaining chip until it was obvious there was no one left to bargain with, and ultimately, he'd wound up locked up for years and used...

Cass was waiting for an answer. He had to decide.

"California," he lied easily.

"Really?" Cass pressed. "Did you ever live anywhere else? Travel?"

"Well," he turned, making his eyes blank, "my family visited the Grand Canyon once."

Cass raised an eyebrow, but a loud meowing stole her attention. A small, gray cat was approaching. It trotted right up to Cass and began to rub against her boots.

"It likes you." Billy bent and wiggled his fingers, and the cat came to him. He plopped onto his bum, letting the animal put its front paws on his leg.

As Billy dug his fingers into the cat's oily fur, scratching, he looked up at Cass. Her mood had changed, and she was tense, spinning a slow circle as she scanned the area around them. When she'd completed her circuit, she pushed air out between her teeth.

The cat ran off.

"Time to go," she said.

"Something wrong?"

"That cat's not feral," she said. "Someone cares for it."

Billy's jaw dropped. He hadn't even thought about that. Nothing was simple; he had to remember. He couldn't help but wonder how long he might've lasted on his own if Cass hadn't spoken for him.

A surge of unwanted gratitude was interrupted by his running into Cass's back. Following, he hadn't noticed she'd stopped. He was preparing to say so as he backpedaled fiercely, but Cass spoke instead.

"Did you shut the door all the way?" she asked.

"Bloody hell," he said under his breath. Immediately, he regretted it. Americans didn't say that.

Cass turned to him and laughed. She'd thought he was being funny? He smiled and shrugged apologetically.

"Sorry," he said. "It's been a while since I've had to—well—have common sense."

Cass led the way around the store. After they'd loaded their haul onto the mule, she tied the lead to her horse and directed him to take the animals around to wait for her by the last box.

A few minutes later, the door he'd accidentally shut burst open at Cass's kick, and she passed through, carrying an oddly-shaped duffel bag that clanked like tin. He helped her stuff the items into the pack as best he could. His smashed up ribs made him almost useless.

As Cass tied off the box, jiggling it to make it secure, her shirt lifted away from her abdomen. Billy's gaze was drawn to her hips, belt fastened tight across them as her clothing was large on her skinny frame. Her ribs were well-defined, similar to his own starved appearance and he felt a wave of kinship with her. However, the outline of muscles beneath her skin proved her luckier. At least what flesh she had was strong.

There was a trace of brown near her belly button he first

thought might be a birthmark. When he realized it was blood – the dead horse's blood – he longed to reach out and scrub it away. He told himself the longing to touch her came from a desire to protect her from the ugly reminder she'd get when she saw the blood, not from curiosity about the softness of her skin. Though it didn't matter—both desires were insane.

"Cass," he said. "I'm wondering something."

She finished balancing the duffel bag among everything else. "What?"

"Who's pregnant?"

Cass looked at him for a second, then two, her eyes narrowing. It took concentration for Billy to keep from looking away.

"Let's get moving," she said. "We'll talk on the way."

CASS COULDN'T BELIEVE SHE'D told Billy about Trista. She'd needed to talk to someone, and for whatever reason, she felt drawn to this man. Still, she wasn't yet sure if she could trust him not to stab her in the back—literally. She shouldn't be spilling her guts.

They had turned into a stand of trees for the third time and were waiting. She'd varied their path back to the ranch and had more than once turned abruptly into shadows, watching and listening for any sign someone had seen them in the town and followed. Her worry had faded each time. Whoever had cared for that cat either hadn't noticed them or had no interest in a fight.

Billy was taking her order not to say a word seriously. She almost wished he would screw up so she'd have a legitimate reason to be angry at him rather than herself. But, he seemed to be a quick learner and eager to be useful. She wasn't sure if that helped her trust her instinct to save him or just confused her.

He was flicking flies off Smoke's neck, and he looked down, pulling his sleeve away from his torn wrist. He flexed his long, thin fingers and recognition struck Cass again. Chords of a song played in her mind.

He met her gaze, and a question came into his eyes.

"I think we're okay," she said. "We can travel straight now." She nudged Cowboy forward and passed from the trees into the light. It was already near sunset; they'd been away all day. By now, all remnant of her favorite companion would be gone except what was cooking on grills and spits over the fire. Her stomach rolled.

Smoke caught up to Cowboy. "I'm sorry it took so long. We won't be back before dark."

"That's okay," Billy said. A few minutes went by in silence before he spoke again. "So, do you not like Trista or do you not like babies?"

Cass's jaw fell open, and she shut it with a frown, turning to look at Billy's cautious expression. The features of his face were lit up by the sinking sunlight.

"Why would you think either of those things?" she asked, knowing full well why he'd think them.

"Your expression when you figured it out. Plus, you said Cam's been hiding it from you, so..."

Cass thought about not answering. She thought about kicking Cowboy into a fast trot and letting Billy think about staying on his horse instead of musing over her feelings. Finally, she decided she might as well tell him. The important part was already out in the open. Besides, share and share alike, right? Maybe if she told him about herself, she could get him to open up, too.

"Trista is the right person for my brother. And I don't dislike her. We're very different, and we didn't get along at first, but we do now." Cass sighed, her stomach beginning to groan with hunger. "And babies? Well, look around. This isn't exactly the safest time to be having children."

"You think it's irresponsible," Billy said. "You're worried about keeping the baby safe."

"And healthy." Cass was chilled as she thought back several months. "No doctors, no medicines. We lost a lot of people last winter. To something that was probably just the flu."

"I'm sorry." His voice was sincere though his expression was hard to decipher.

"Mostly I'm irritated because Trista was sick for weeks. I see now that it was morning sickness, but Cam was still just—beaten down with worry."

"So you were worried, too," Billy said. Cass nodded. "But, now you know she's okay. And we're going to Stronghold. They have doctors, don't they? The baby should be safe there. We all should be."

"That's the idea," Cass said.

"You don't believe it? You don't believe in what the recruiters said?"

Cass turned to him again, surprised. "You know about the recruiters?"

"Well, I heard things." Billy shrugged. "No one really talked to me on the way here, but I overheard plenty."

Cass cleared her throat. "I never had a chance to make up my mind about the recruiters. They came to us twice. Once on their way to the West Coast, and months later, on their way back. We had decided not to go to Stronghold by then. But, shortly after they left us, we were forced to evacuate." At Billy's questioning look Cass explained. "A forest fire. Destroyed everything we couldn't carry or ride out."

Billy gave a solemn nod, his eyes sympathetic. The quiet moment left Cass desperate to change the subject.

"If you knew about the recruiters, you must've known where they were going," she said. "Why were you so afraid to be left behind? You could have found a map or followed us. Gotten there on your own." Cass's voice sounded doubtful even to her.

"Fear, I guess," he said. He took in a deep breath and let it out in a gush. "I don't know how to survive. I don't know how to start a fire or find food." He broke off, staring at the ground at Smoke's hooves. "I sat in that basement planning to escape—trying to be ready. And once I got out I realized I was better suited to being locked up."

His tone was darkened by memories of torturous years. Anger welled up inside Cass, followed by sympathy.

"No one is suited for that." Her tone was sharp, almost a reprimand, but she didn't soften her expression when he turned to her in surprise. She held his gaze, remembering how helpless she'd once felt. How she'd felt like a household appliance; just a dishwasher or a stove begging to live.

She broke the intense stare and cleared her throat, now striving for a more conversational tone. "I'll teach you the rest," she said. "How to fend for yourself. Everyone in our group knows basic survival and self-defense. You're part of the group, now."

She glanced back to find tears welling in his eyes. He turned away. "Thank you," he said, his voice unwavering.

Cass pulled Cowboy to a stop near the road they had followed down from the ranch. "Whether Stronghold is what it claims—we'll know soon enough. But, will it last?"

Billy crossed an arm over his saddle horn and leaned forward on it, gingerly touching his injured ribs with the other hand. "I see your point, I guess."

Cass gestured to the road where it went uphill and turned. "Think you can find your way back from here?"

"What?" Billy sat up straight, brow furrowed. "You're not coming?"

"I don't want to be there right now," she said. She couldn't meet his eyes, though—couldn't tell him how much it would hurt to sit and watch the bellies of so many grow so full with her beloved friend. She drew out of her dark thoughts to find Billy watching her.

"I'm staying with you," he said.

Cass shook her head. The company sounded appealing, but she would have chosen Drew or Lena, not a relative stranger. "You need to eat."

He nodded and tugged on the stiff shoulder strap of a backpack he'd picked up at the store. "I've got a couple of avocados I never got around to eating last night," he said. "They're a bit bruised from being in my pockets, but I'll share."

Cass shook her head but didn't say anything. She chomped on the inside of her lip, assessing her options. He raised an eyebrow, a persistent smile finding a place on his lips.

"Let me stay," he said.

Cass sighed. "Fine. I have some water. And smoked jerky—it's pretty hard but..." She turned Cowboy and moved to the tree line nestled against the hill.

After dismounting and tying the horses, Cass helped Billy gather kindling in the quickly dying light. She started teaching him to build a fire, and they divvied up their food and ate.

"I picked up more fire starters like mine at the store," she said around a bite of jerky. "I'll make sure you get one. And that tent is for you. We'll set it up when we get back to camp."

Billy stared for a moment before giving a deep, strangely reverent nod. "Thank you."

Cass looked away and found herself babbling on, unable to handle his gratitude. "I think we'll set your tent up right next to mine an' Drew's. That way you can find me in the mornings. I'll be keeping you busy helping out. There's lots to do before we leave."

"You mean, of course, that you want me where you can keep an eye on me," he said. "I'm not going anywhere, Cass. And I'm not a killer."

Cass nodded. "I don't believe you are. Still—you're my responsibility."

"Are you sure I won't be—uh—intruding?"

Cass felt her face twist up in puzzlement. "Intruding?"

Billy cleared his throat. "On you and Drew." She could see his face flushing pink in the firelight.

Cass let out a laugh, then laughed harder at Billy's surprise at her laughter. "Firstly, you've seen the tents. We don't have many secrets, sleeping that close together. Second, it's not like that between Drew and me." Suddenly, Cass was the one blushing. She hadn't felt *shy* in years.

Maybe it was because she and Drew hadn't had a chance to discuss things. In the past, among strangers, they had played along— letting people assume what came naturally. It had often made them both feel more comfortable. She felt odd about spilling it so easily. It was half a betrayal of her best friend and half the removal of a shield. She could just as easily have said it wasn't an intrusion and left it at that.

But, Cass knew the real reason she felt exposed was the way Billy was responding to the news. His expressions and posture were less guarded, now; more intense.

"Oh, I'm sorry," Billy said. "I just assumed."

Cass changed the subject.

Usually, when people got together, they talked of The End and the ways they had survived after. No one knew exactly what had happened, but it could be interesting to speculate. Some people seemed incessantly driven to decipher it, hoping new people meant new information. And what people *believed* had ended the world revealed a lot about them.

Conversely, talk about Before was taboo. Before meant talking about the people lost.

So Cass was surprised when Billy didn't want to talk about what had caused The End. She had tired of the discussion herself. But, Billy didn't want to talk about himself much, either, which was vexing. He wanted her to tell him about herself and Cam. Were they twins? A common misconception due partly to their similar coloring. They were born sixteen months apart. How did they know so much about horses? Who taught *her* to build a fire? And so on.

So Cass found herself talking about her uncle, an outfitter and horse trader, who had taught them all he knew. She talked about Cam at the rodeo, about the first time she shot an elk, and even about Huckleberry. The conversation wandered to funny stories of being thrown from horses, and they were laughing raucously together when the wind switched, and the smell of cooking meat wafted thickly down from the ranch.

They both grew quiet, an awkwardness between them like people who'd been caught playing cards at a wake.

"You know what the sick thing is?" Cass said when she couldn't ignore the issue any longer.

"What?"

"I'm starving." Cass laughed and then the sound was strangled and cut off as she sucked in a breath. Her face morphed into a mask of disgust. "It smells good to me, and that makes me sick."

A tear squeezed from her eye and dripped from her downturned face, then another.

"It was my fault," she said. "He wasn't hobbled. He always stayed near camp. I think he wandered back to the pond because I took him there yesterday. And that's where I shot the deer. The blood—it must have drawn the mountain lion."

Billy shook his head. "None of that sounds like your fault."

In the following silence, Billy's stomach growled as if to be heard a mile away and his eyes widened in horror. But Cass let out a burst of airy laughter, snorted, and laughed harder.

Billy joined in tentatively at first and then more freely.

"I guess it smells good to you, too, huh?" she said, wiping away tears.

"I'm so sorry," Billy managed to gasp out between peals of

laughter.

When the two of them composed themselves, they stared across their little fire at one another. There was a change in the tone of their companionship. The air grew hotter and heavier, their eyes darker. Cass jerked her gaze away and rubbed a hand along the knee of her jeans, picking at a threadbare spot.

"Maraschino cherries," she said, then coughed.

She glanced up to see Billy's eyes narrowed in confusion, his head tilted.

"My favorite food," she said. "One time, we hadn't had much to eat in a while. We were hungry like this. Not starving, not sick hungry. We weren't desperate yet, but times weren't great. There were only six of us then. We stayed the night in this house. Someone had already raided the kitchen, but they'd left the wet bar in the basement untouched. We drank whiskey, and Lena and I slurped Maraschino cherries by candlelight."

Billy wore a soft smile, and he nodded when she looked up at him again.

"Delicious," he said. His stare heated, his eyelids lowering as he studied her in the flickering flame light.

"I haven't thought about that in a long time," she said.

"Why?"

She frowned and shook her head without answering. She sprawled back on the grass, watching the stars and wondering if remembering was really so bad.

"We'd better get back to camp. People will worry," she said. They kicked dirt over the fire, mounted, and left, grateful for the light of a nearly-full moon.

Four

LENA WATCHED AS CASS reached up and tied a horse's lead on the high-line she had strung between a sturdy pole at the corner of the half-fallen barn and a tree. The pretty appaloosa sniffed the rope, glanced at the next horse down the line and shifted her feet, settling in. Lena smiled. Their day had been going better than expected. Cass rolled her left shoulder, fingers pressed into the ligaments and a frown on her face.

Seeing Lena looking, Cass raised her brow. "Not bad, huh?" she said. "Just that bay mare—what's her name?"

"Eclair," Lena said.

Cass headed into the sparse shade the building provided. "She came around. And everyone else has done fine."

Lena nodded. "I wouldn't have bet it'd be this easy." She decided to get the apology out of the way before she forgot.

"I'm sorry about my attitude, yesterday," she said, leaning against the scorched wall only to stand up again immediately as a sharp splinter poked into her back, exposed in her tank top. "Ow."

"You okay? Here, let me see." Cass turned Lena away with a hand on her shoulder and peered at her back. "And don't worry about yesterday. You were fine."

Relief washed over Lena and the tension she'd been carrying released. She hated feeling awkwardness or separation between herself and Cass. They hardly ever fought and Lena walked around sick all day when they did, feeling like nothing quite fit together.

Cass pulled a couple of slivers of wood from Lena's back and gave her shoulder a sharp pat.

"I never asked you how it went," Lena said. "Did you find everything we needed?"

"Yep," Cass said. "Horse-wise, anyway. We didn't go anywhere else 'cause I wanted to get out of there." Cass crouched down, and Lena followed suit.

"Really? I thought you'd made a couple stops. You were gone so long." Lena watched Cass carefully in the seconds it took before she answered. The older woman's cheeks took on a pink tinge, and she cleared her throat.

"I was worried we might have been spotted, actually," Cass said. "There was an obviously domestic cat hanging around." The faraway look vanished from Cass's face as she turned and made eye contact with Lena. "I varied our route on the way back to keep a look out."

"Oh," was all Lena could muster. Disappointment dragged on her even as she fought it. There was no reason to worry about Cass. Cass didn't fall for guys. Cass might be the sister Lena wanted, but she wasn't at all like the sister Lena had. In all the years she'd known and worked with Cass, she'd never seen her behave as foolishly as Darcy did on a regular basis, falling for any handsome face no matter the age or whether he was passing through with another group.

Lena spotted her sister, now, heading into the meadow with a woman from another band. Both of them carried buckets for water. They laughed, Darcy running a hand through her long, well-maintained brown hair. Beside her, Cass was retying her blue bandana in her own brown hair. No primping, just practicality.

Cass hadn't gone soft even when she had been having sex with Trace. When Cam had found out his best friend and his sister were screwing in secret, he'd flipped his lid. Trace had broken it off, and Cass hadn't even seemed to care. Cass wasn't stupid, and she wasn't going to fall in love. She'd had reasons for saving Billy. But, it wasn't love.

Lena's thoughts wavered as she saw the daydreaming blankness grip Cass again.

"How long are we going to leave them?" she asked.

Cass blinked a few times and shrugged. "Let's go get some water and we'll come back in a few."

Lena stood and followed Cass around the barn, happy for more time with a kindred spirit. Darcy had been on her nerves more than ever since the other bands arrived.

"Did you see the girls from Derrick's band?" she asked. "They're wearing nail polish."

Cass raised her eyebrows. "Wow."

"No kidding," Lena said. "Darcy said they have to find nail polish remover and alcohol and stuff to mix it with 'cause it's dried up."

"I used to paint my nails for holidays," Cass said, looking down at her hand. "You know, red, white, and blue, orange and black." Lena almost choked. It was strange enough that Cass had mentioned Before, but she couldn't picture her friend fussing over her appearance. "It's amazing they've had time for things like that."

Lena wrinkled her nose, unsatisfied with the conversation. "They shave their legs, too, so now Darcy's after my dad to get her a razor and—" Lena realized Cass had stopped and was no longer listening. The last person Lena wanted to see was approaching with his arms full of metal and plastic water bottles in various sizes.

"Mind reader," Cass called, hurrying forward to take some of the bottles from Billy. Lena's eyes narrowed. They seemed inordinately happy to see each other for people so careful not to touch. Billy offered Lena a bottle and she took it, hoping her expression would keep him from hanging around.

"Thought you might need a break," he said. He watched Cass tip up her bottle and drink from it, then seemed to realize Lena was watching him and turned away. "Conrad and I finished oiling that new tack, but he has a question for you."

Cass fell into step beside Billy and called over her shoulder, "Coming Lena?"

Lena decided she may as well go. Where Conrad was, Katie seemed to be, and she was excited to chat with her again.

Sure enough, as they walked under the tarp set up for shade, she spotted Katie sitting on a blanket working something between her fingers. She hastily stowed whatever it was under a pillow when the group appeared.

"There's the water, Katie," Conrad said, his statement filled with relief as if he'd been holding his breath until it arrived. Billy delivered a bottle to Katie while Cass wandered to Conrad's side.

"That is a beautiful knife," Cass said. Lena began to move closer to see what was special about the tool. She found her path blocked by Billy who had set the remaining water bottles down and stepped close to Cass's side.

Lena went to sit beside Katie, who smiled and nodded but seemed distracted by the conversation. Lena noticed with a smile that Katie had set her untouched water bottle next to a still half-full glass at her side. Conrad's concern for the pregnant woman reminded Lena of her mother and father. Lena felt for a moment as if someone had hammered a nail into her sternum as her mother's face filled her memory.

"Tell them what your brother said when he gave it to you," Katie called over to the others. Her voice nudged Lena out of her gloom. The woman turned and put a hand on Lena's knee. "Workin' hard out there?" she asked. "I guess the heat doesn't bother tough women like you two." Lena shrugged and played with the tattered corner of Katie's blanket.

"It belonged to his brother, you know," Katie said. "Sam. He served in Iraq and before he left, he gave that knife to Conrad. He told him that in this case, the antler end wasn't the sharp end." Katie chuckled. "When Sam got back, and Conrad tried to return it, Sam said, 'No. You'd better hold on to that. You've figured *that* one out, and I'd hate to have you buy a new one and not know how to use it.'" Katie chuckled. "He tells it better." Her face turned downward as she went on. "My boyfriend had Sam's initials carved into the end of the handle when Sam passed. Kind of a memorial gift to Conrad."

Katie's half-closed eyelids and downturned mouth reminded Lena that the boyfriend she spoke of was gone. Lena was no good at comforting people, and she floundered through her brain for something to say that didn't sound stupid. But, Katie turned to her and gave her a confident, gentle smile, and she felt she didn't need to say anything, after all.

Lena looked up as Derrick swooped into the tent with long, imposing strides. He walked right up to Cass. Billy shied away like a beaten horse. Lena felt a swell of sick delight that was quickly tamped down as Derrick slung his huge arm across Cass's shoulders. Cass stiffened, and Lena's temper flared. They talked quietly for a moment before Cass nodded and turned to leave with Derrick. She shrugged out from under his arm as they moved and glanced back at Billy.

"Come with," she said. "Let me show you the high-line."

Billy nodded, raised his hand to Conrad in farewell and followed behind Derrick and Cass as they left. Lena's jaw tensed, and her mouth was suddenly dry. Cass had left without her. She took a swig of her water and looked over to see Katie watching with sympathetic eyes.

PREPARATIONS FOR LEAVING WERE set back when rain drenched the camp early one morning. Billy woke to the sound of the drops striking his tent and scrambled to dress and climb outside. The camp was quiet. The cloud cover must have delayed everyone's waking, or they were staying dry in their tents for a bit longer. But, Billy turned his face up to the sky, opening his mouth to it. The droplets rolled down from his top lip onto his tongue.

He wandered toward the shed he'd slept in his first night here, wondering how the rain sounded on its metal roof. He hadn't been able to hear the rain from his basement prison unless the wind blew it at an angle, so it struck his barred window.

He remembered one night after his captors had been killed. He'd already broken out the window glass, hoping to call out to someone passing by and his throat was hoarse from shouting and thirst. A cold breeze had blown in, carrying a damp chill he hadn't felt in years. He'd thrust his hands out and felt the cool water running over his fingers and wrists. He'd enjoyed it so much he'd nearly forgotten to catch any. That rain and the drinking water it provided had probably saved his life.

Someone cleared their throat and brought him back to the present. Cass stood a few feet away with a bucket in each hand and an amused half smile. He swiped water away from his eyes and slicked back his wet hair. He had been leaning against the shed staring up at the sky, and he was soaked.

"Morning," she said. She'd been out here longer than he had from the look of her. Her jeans and boots were darkened by water and her hair was plastered to her scalp and the sides of her face. Rain slid off her jacket, and Billy noticed it had a hood she wasn't using.

"Good morning," he said. He watched her set the buckets under streams of water running off the small building. He felt horribly selfish. He hadn't even thought to do that, despite the fact he'd just been remembering the rainstorm that had saved his life.

"I heard the rain," Cass said, adjusting the bucket. "Thought I should catch some. All these people and horses. We'll dry up that little spring."

For a moment, the two of them studied each other. The dome of clouds brightened as the sun rose. A strand of hair stuck to Cass's face, just below the scar on her lip and Billy was thinking how much he wanted to brush it away—wondering if he could still do such a thing—wondering if he'd ever be able to touch anyone again. Cass looked away, shifting her weight back and forth.

"Did the rain wake you?" she asked.

He nodded. "It's amazing." He held his hands out to his sides and watched the water collect in his palms. She was silent for a bit, and he felt her watching him. He looked up.

"Didn't rain much in California?" she asked.

"I haven't seen much weather for the last few years."

"Sorry."

He shook his head. "What about you? Out here collecting water with your hood down while everyone else sleeps through it. You like rain?"

She tilted her head to the side as if considering. "I suppose so," she said. "We were in a drought." Billy remembered what she'd said the other night about a forest fire.

"Right. I'm sorry."

Cass shrugged and moved to walk away, tipping her shoulder to invite him. He followed. The wet grass squelched beneath their feet until they ducked into the dilapidated barn. Further back, the roof was caved in, and water poured through. But, near the door, they were sheltered.

As they brushed water from their clothes, she said, "The smell—the burning? The rain makes me forget." Billy felt his head bobbing in a stupid nod. He tried to think of something meaningful to say. He used to be good with people—especially women. He used to be smooth and bold.

"How long did it take to get here?" he asked.

She wasn't listening, and Billy followed her gaze. Out in the field by the shed, the place where Huckleberry had died and been slaughtered was darkening again and red puddles were forming. They'd covered the area with rock and dirt from the long driveway. Dirt that must've been brought in from elsewhere, as it was a red clay. It made the puddles of water look like blood.

Cass looked sick. She stared down at her feet.

"Cass," he said louder, "was it a long trip? Down to here?" She looked up and blinked.

"Almost two weeks," she said. She cleared her throat and looked at him a little desperately. Her eyes shone with tears.

"Do you want to go?" he asked.

She shook her head, eyes still locked on his face. So he kept asking her light questions until the rain seemed to dilute Cass's tension. After a while, she stared out at the field and the red puddles intentionally, answering his questions with half-interest. The rainstorm slackened and stopped, and still they chatted.

Their solitude was broken when Lena and Drew joined them. They headed out to check on the horses and dry out any wet supplies. He and Cass had just tightened a tarp back over a wagon. After climbing down, he turned to offer her his hand, intending to help her off the back. But, as he raised the arm, hot pain burst across his injured rib cage, and he folded in two, clutching his side.

"Bloody fucking Ch—" he snapped his teeth closed and focused on his breathing. When the pain faded to a bearable level, he raised himself up again to find Cass crouched on the wagon, eye level with him. She searched his face.

"Do you need Doc?" she asked.

"No, no. I just forgot."

He had not yet straightened to his full height when a voice he loathed spoke from behind him.

"Not giving you any trouble is he?"

As Billy turned, he put distance between himself and Derrick. Derrick stood with his arm outstretched, offering to help Cass out of the wagon in the same manner Billy had attempted. Cass looked at Derrick's hand but didn't yet take it.

Going on as if having his arm hanging there was a normal position Derrick said, "Adam and I heard that you've got some experience with martial arts. I was an MMA fighter back before The End, you know. We thought we could get a group together—do some sparring? While the weather's cool."

Behind Derrick, Adam stood with Drew and Lena, all waiting for Cass's answer. Billy waited with them.

CASS DIDN'T WANT TO admit the way she'd truly felt about the rain when it had woken her that morning. She'd had a nightmare about Huck, and when she woke to the sound of a downpour, her first response had been to curse it. It meant a delay in leaving and worse, a morning without much to do. Since Huck's death, she'd only kept her mind quiet by working her body.

Well, technically, nothing's stopping me, she'd thought. So she'd risen and thought of things to do in the rain.

Seeing Billy standing out in it—enjoying it—had set her wondering. When was the last time weather had been more than an obstacle to work around? She'd watched him offer his bruised face up to the rain, felt the droplets tapping her skin and realized it did, in fact, feel good. It smelled good. It washed away more than dirt and sweat.

She'd enjoyed it, and the sight and sound of Billy in it. She'd felt connected to him. Too connected. Not to mention what he'd done for her—distracting her from memories of Huck seeping up through her control as the blood had appeared to seep up from the dirt.

She'd felt her own side pulse when he'd doubled over in pain beside the wagon. And her gut had contracted in embarrassment when Derrick arrived and shamed him by offering his hand. Such responses would make it hard for her to think clearly.

So she tried to sever that connection, once and for all, as she nodded at Derrick.

"I'd go for a workout," she said. "Up for it, Lena? Drew?" Lena's enthusiasm was clear in the bobbing of her damp ponytail as she nodded. Drew shrugged, one eyebrow raised.

Derrick's hand was still in her face, and she took it, pretending not to notice the way Billy frowned and turned his eyes away as she did. She felt a moment of guilt. He *had* offered her his hand. Even after the flinching and dodging he'd been doing to avoid physical contact with anyone. What did that mean?

She had no time to mull it over. Derrick pulled her under his arm as soon as her feet touched the ground. His lips were near her ear when he spoke, but his voice was loud enough that Adam, who had come up on her other side, could hear his words.

"You look good wet," he said. "Doesn't she?" As Derrick spoke this question to Adam, he looked away from Cass, and she took the opportunity to slip backward, out from under Derrick's arm. As she did, she reached up and grasped his wrist firmly in her hand. She cranked it around his back, his body sinking as she pulled the bent arm upwards.

He went down to a knee, grunting, but smiling. Cass knew it hurt, but he was strong; every bit as powerful as he looked. Her move hadn't surprised him.

"I wasn't ready," he said over his shoulder.

"You should always be ready," Lena said, watching. Cass nodded. She released Derrick's arm and stepped away.

"I need to change." Cass indicated her wet clothes.

"Need some help?" Adam asked.

Cass hoped her expression stayed neutral as a shudder of disgust rolled up her spine. "Fifteen minutes? In the clearing with the spring?" Derrick and Lena nodded.

As she jogged up toward the tents, Cass glanced back over her shoulder. Billy was leaning against the wagon a few yards from where Derrick was getting to his feet. Though she didn't look long enough to take in his expression, she could feel his gaze on her, long after she'd passed out of sight.

WATCHING CASS SPAR WAS an enlightening new torture for Billy. She'd arrived already stretching, jacket gone, and wearing tighter fitting clothing. She was thinner than he'd realized, and of all thoughts he might've had, he found himself wishing the hunters had found and killed the injured mountain lion so she'd have more to eat.

It didn't keep her from being attractive. That came less from the flesh on her bones than the way she carried herself. It wasn't a strut; on the contrary, she seemed not to desire attention. Her motions and her walk were simply—self-sufficient. Not that you would know it from the way Derrick leered at her when she arrived. He bent to whisper something in her ear, and Billy tore a clump of grass from the ground beside him.

Less than a dozen people had come to fight, though, like him, a few others had taken up spots on the ground to watch. Three men from California were there, and the rest were from Montana. No Oregonians had shown except Hank, who sat beside Drew, observing. To Billy's relief, it was decided they would warm up with people from their own groups until everyone got comfortable.

Cass was facing Lena, now, though they weren't just sparring. Cass was shouting instructions to the younger girl while besting her again and again.

At one point, Cass's focus drifted to a fight nearby, and she called out, "Too close! He's bigger than you so don't give him that chance! Use your legs." While Cass's attention was split, Lena got the better of her, landing a kick across Cass's jaw that forced her to retreat and steady herself.

Billy's eyes widened and he half-rose but Cass came back smiling and high-fived Lena. He settled back to watch as Cass began to move among the combatants, arms across her chest as she called out directions. "Vary your tempo! Keep your hand up!"

Billy was startled when a blond woman sank onto the grass beside him.

"I'm Trista," she said, offering her hand. Billy shook it.

"Billy," he said. "You're Cam's girlfriend."

Trista smiled and nodded. Then, she turned back to the sparring which was lucky as Billy had inadvertently glanced down at her stomach as if he'd be able to see that she was pregnant. He didn't think Cass had confessed what she'd realized.

"She's something, isn't she?" Trista asked.

He followed her gaze to where Cass had just taken a stance against her brother, who must've joined the game when Trista arrived.

"Cass?" he asked, though he knew who she meant.

"Mmm-hmm," Trista said. "She taught all of them, you know."

He glanced at Trista, raising his brows in surprise. "All?"

She nodded. "Even Cam. She started learning self-defense in high school. I think she was still practicing with her instructor when The End came. She made a point of teaching everyone in our group." She glanced back at Billy. "Survival skills, too. Didn't want anyone to be helpless."

Billy watched as Trista laid a hand across her abdomen. "Why aren't you out there?" he asked. Trista didn't miss a beat.

"Pride." She laughed. "I'd rather not embarrass myself in front of all these people."

Billy nodded and felt instantly sorry he'd tried to trip her up. She was a nice person. Cass had said so herself—even through her anger. It was the couple's right to keep quiet about the baby if they chose.

He turned back to watch. His voice sounded distant as he spoke, never taking his eyes off Cass. "Do you think that's why she spoke for me? Because she thought I was helpless?" Cass threw Cam to the ground and pumped her fist in the air, laughing.

"I don't think she thinks you're helpless," Trista said. "But I'm not sure why she spoke for you."

Billy nodded and sucked in a breath. Adam was approaching Cass, now.

CASS TOOK ADAM DOWN quickly and regretted it right away. She couldn't help herself. His and Derrick's earlier comments had disgusted her. Unable to impose any other punishment on people from another band, she'd taken her revenge in the form of embarrassment. She'd broken his hold, forced him to the ground, and laughed so only he could hear.

The look he fixed her with was more threatening than she'd expected. But, it was better than the look of excitement on Derrick's face as he came to stand in Adam's place. Cass was tiring. She admitted it to herself as she was slow to block a punch and took a partial hit. Hell, she'd started out tired.

Derrick was stronger than her and fast for someone as large as he was. He was a pro; that much was clear. He kept his defenses tight, and he was never sloppy. He conserved his energy. As she dodged a kick, she found herself slow to guard her face and she saw a gleam in his eyes. He'd noticed. Thank God he didn't actually want to hurt her. The thought gave her a chill.

It had been a while since she'd faced someone she knew she couldn't beat. She'd played teacher for so long; it was odd not having the upper hand. No one was shouting encouragements or reminders to her, and she missed having an instructor. Many of the others had stopped their matches to turn and watch, and she wondered how it looked from out there. Did Derrick look like a house cat playing with a fly? Or did she look like David, holding her own against Goliath?

This fight had gone on too long, and she decided to end it. Derrick seemed fresh so she knew she'd either have to let him take her down or concede. Neither was in her nature. She almost smiled when she made her decision. She took a clumsy swing with her right, which he easily blocked. Then, intentionally leaving her guard down, she waited for him to swing at the opening. When he did, she ducked down and spun, bringing her clenched fist whirling toward his crotch. She stopped it just before it struck and he jerked back and covered himself a split second later.

"Breaking the rules, are we?" he said. His eyes were wide, but a small smile crossed his lips.

"There wouldn't be rules if it were for real." She took his offered hand and let him pull her upright. A few soft claps sounded around the clearing. "I was done. We both know it."

Derrick shook his head. "I think you've got more stamina than you know."

Cass blinked and stepped away as Derrick called, "Who's next?"

Lena was approaching, but Cass held up a hand. "I'm done," she said and dragged her heavy limbs over to the side, flopping into the grass beside Conrad. Breathing heavily, she sunk onto her back.

"Good show out there," Conrad said. "Except the dirty move."

Cass raised her head to see him smile. "He had me and he knew it. I just didn't want to concede." Conrad chuckled, and she found herself relieved she hadn't offended him. She pushed the feeling away. She couldn't start caring what he thought of her. She couldn't start caring what anyone thought. Her gaze drifted over to Billy, where he sat in conversation with Trista.

A minute passed, and Conrad cleared his throat. "Recovered enough to talk?" he asked. Cass nodded.

"Hank said you'd be the one to ask about extra pillows. Said your supplies are better than ours or Camp Mason's."

Cass shook her head, already knowing they didn't have any. She and Drew had given their extra to Billy. "Sorry," she said. "We'll probably pass some houses or stores as we leave, though. We've had some luck salvaging supplies from cars on the roads, too. Don't you have one?"

"Oh, I do," he said. "It's for Katie. She doesn't sleep well. Can't get comfortable 'cause of the baby."

Cass sat up, nodding. The pair sat in silence and Cass got sucked into the last memory she had here. Huckleberry had grazed this very spot on his last day on Earth. She slammed the door on the thought, saying the first thing that came to mind.

"The horse Katie mentioned. Chip? Was he hers?"

"Nah, he was her boyfriend's. Frank's. She liked him, though. Only horse she ever trusted, even after she got pregnant."

Conrad continued to talk about Katie; how far along she was, when she'd stopped being sick, her heartburn, even what times of day the baby was most active. Cass was overwhelmed that he seemed so comfortable talking to her when she'd hardly heard him say a word to anyone else.

He paused for a moment and Cass thought the onslaught might be over. Then, he said, "The baby's father was my best friend." Cass froze. He gave this information to her like so many fragile eggs held out in offering. It seemed so important he said what he was thinking, she was scared to breathe.

"I was there when he died, and I made him a promise to care for her and the baby," he said. He turned to Cass now and smiled. "I'd have done anything for him. But, Katie… she makes it easy to watch after her—she's—she's something. Even dead, Frank is a lucky man." Conrad's jaw fell open. "God, that was awful. I shouldn'ta said that."

Cass shook her head, reading the longing and love on his face. "No, you're right. I get it."

Cass watched as Conrad's head whipped to the side. He was looking at something over her shoulder. She turned to see that Katie herself had just stepped through the trees into the clearing. Again, Conrad's whole body rotated toward the woman, like she was the sun and he was a flower contorting himself to take her in.

Katie must have waved because he smiled and his face was washed over with joy for a moment. The joy faded to a soft frown. Attracted by movement, Cass glanced down to see his thumb rubbing against the hilt of his knife as if to erase the initials etched there.

Cass wished she was skilled with words. She found herself wanting to give him advice, wanting to tell him something trite like "life is short" or "seize the day." She wanted to ask what the point of survival was if you never let yourself live. But, the words sounded hypocritical even in her head.

She let the silence hang over them as she turned her gaze back across the clearing to where Trista now sat alone.

DREW KNEW HE'D FIND Cass with the horses, and it was no great shock to see Billy with her. It *was* a surprise to see Hank appear and call Cass aside. Drew ducked into the shed and tried to appear busy sorting through the first aid kit as the pair of them stepped closer.

"I have a favor to ask of you and your brother," Hank said.

Drew's stomach gave a disapproving turn, but he decided it was hardly eavesdropping. There was little Cass didn't share with him.

"What kind of favor?" Cass asked.

"Look." Hank cleared his throat. "I was named the leader of the Coltonites because of my survival skills and because I'd served in the military." Drew heard another clearing of the throat and some shifting of feet. "The truth is, my time in Iraq left me—broken. It's only by the grace of God and the work of Conrad and Frank, too, before he died, that my band is alive today."

The silence was awkward even to Drew, who was separate from the conversation. He winced, wishing Cass would say *something* to encourage the man.

"What I'm asking is if you could look after my people, too. Sort of, take them under your wing until we get to Stronghold..."

Again, silence. Drew risked a glance at the two of them. He could see Cass's face now; her forehead creased with a deep frown. Finally, she spoke.

"I have more on my plate than I can handle. I won't make promises," she said. Hank's face fell, but he nodded. Cass looked back over to where she'd left Billy grooming one of the horses. She sighed. "But, I *will* make an effort."

Hank was more than satisfied with her concession, and he patted her on the back with vigor as he offered his thanks. Drew was overcome by the various feelings pummeling him. He worried for his friend and at the same time felt overjoyed she was embracing the things that gave her purpose.

He watched her rejoin the newest recruit, showing him where he was going wrong in convincing the horse to lift its hoof. Drew wondered at the change in her and whether it would last.

*   *   *

DERRICK LEANED AGAINST A wagon watching as Cass Hood bent and lifted a horse's hoof for her brother to inspect. The prisoner held the horse's lead and listened, his boyish face filled with rapt interest.

Derrick nodded as one of his men passed by him. When that man wandered by the group looking at the horse, he openly eyed Cass's rear and Billy bristled. This wasn't the plan. The prisoner wasn't supposed to be falling into everyone's good graces; especially Cass's. She was standing now, one arm resting along the horse's withers as she and her brother discussed. She stepped back to include Billy in their talk. Cam nodded at the other man's response, hooking his thumb into the belt loop of his jeans and looking like a Cowboy Ken doll.

Derrick had intended Cass's interest to fall on himself. He should be the one there getting looks of respect from the leaders of the Montana band. He should be getting to know her, banging her, getting into her brother's good graces and rising in the eyes of the rest of their group. But, despite his several attempts to engage her over the last few days, she had no interest in him and brushed him off at every turn.

Not that he had any *real* interest in Cass himself. She was attractive enough. In some ways, she even reminded him of Abby, the long-dead love of his life. The two women couldn't have looked more different, one thin and muscled with dark hair, the other curvy, soft and blonde. But they were both strong and loyal to a fault. Cass's voice was also similar to Abby's, deep for a woman and forceful. He felt the familiar tension in his chest as he remembered Abby and what had happened.

His shook his head. No, his interest in Cass had been aligned with his ultimate goal—gaining the Montanans as allies and making himself an obvious choice for leadership once they reached their destination. He'd formed this thought the moment she'd stepped up onto the trailer and confidently claimed the prisoner.

But Cass was like stone to most the outsiders; blank and cold.

The group split and Cass walked beside Billy, leading the horse back out to graze. She talked, demonstrating something with her hands. She wasn't stone to the prisoner. He found her lack of interest in himself much less troubling than her growing bond with Billy. He'd brought the boy along for a purpose, and though he might not be needed, he'd be useless if he became a leader's friend or lover.

The wagon shifted under his weight as Drew wiggled its wheel, checking that it was secure. The man crawled out from under the wagon looking every bit the high school football star he'd been, though he moved like he'd taken a few rough hits. Derrick wondered what had caused the man's limp.

As Drew bent to retrieve his tools, he was attacked by a licking dog.

"Get off 'im, mutt," Derrick said, nudging the dog away from the other man's face with his leg. "Finished already?"

"It was no trouble," Drew said, clapping Derrick on the shoulder. "It's good to go." Drew wiped sweat from his neck with a hand towel and turned to leave. The red dog began trotting back and forth in an arc behind the man, occasionally looking up and wagging his tail. Derrick fell in step beside Drew.

"Cass is sure lucky to have such a handy guy," he said, eager to see the other man's response.

Drew cleared his throat and took his time flipping the towel up onto his shoulder. "I've had to repair those wagons so much that I pretty much built them by hand. But, I think everyone is grateful we have them, now. How'd you come by yours?" He turned and fixed Derrick with a similar scrutinizing stare. "They're in great shape for you not to have anyone who can repair them."

Derrick flashed a smile like Drew was a buddy in on a secret. "Spoils of war. And we have someone who can do repairs; he's just not as good as you."

"Ah." Drew seemed content to let the conversation die, but Derrick stayed with him, walking toward the dinner tent, where people had begun to gather already.

The group was supposed to leave the next day, so dinner would be before sunset to allow everyone time to sleep well. But, there was a possibility they'd be staying one more day, now. It depended on what Cass and Cam decided regarding a couple of the horses.

When Drew took a seat on a rusty picnic table, Derrick sat across from him and decided to push a bit more.

"So, tell me about Cass," he said. "I can't seem to get a feel for her."

Drew shifted in his seat, scanning the growing crowd. "It takes her a while to warm up to people. Sometimes she doesn't."

"Warm up?"

"Right."

"But, you two seem close," Derrick said, leaning forward a bit, forcing Drew to make eye contact. "I bet you could tell me how to warm her up."

Anger flared in Drew's eyes, but the arrival of Rylynn and Marie quieted his response. Marie wrapped herself around Derrick and Rylynn slid close to Drew on the opposite bench.

"Hey, guys," Marie said. "Last night here. Are you ready?"

Derrick kept his focus on Drew, who ignored Rylynn and scanned the crowd again. He spotted something and stood.

"Looks like Cam has an announcement," Drew said. "See ya." Derrick's blood began a slow boil. He brushed Marie's arms away from his body and stood. Cam wouldn't be making the announcement alone; that was for damn sure. Not to *his* people. Not after ruining his chance to gauge Cass and Drew's relationship. He spotted Cam and crossed through the crowd toward him, funneling his anger into long strides that caused the crowd to part before him.

Cam smiled and nodded as Derrick came to stand beside him. Hank was nowhere to be found. Still, two leaders standing together, especially with Derrick's conspicuous size, were enough to quiet the crowd.

Cam turned to him and asked, "Do you want to tell them?" At Derrick's questioning look, he added, "We're good to leave tomorrow."

Derrick lifted his hand. "We leave tomorrow as planned."

A whoop rose up from the group, and a couple of fists punched into the air. People began to chatter again, but a man in the front stepped forward to Cam.

"The horse is sound?" he asked.

Cam nodded. "He's sound. I'll be working on correcting the damage to his hoof as we go and we'll pack him light, but he moves fine. Cass agreed. We're good to go."

Cass herself appeared from behind Derrick's shoulder. To his great annoyance, Billy was close on her tail, carrying an oddly-stuffed duffel bag.

"And in celebration," the woman said, pointing to Billy and the bag he held. "Billy would like to share his favorite food with us all, tonight." She nodded at a confused Billy and he unzipped the bag. He let out a quiet laugh and peeled the bag away from a large tin of popcorn.

People laughed, and a few gave little cheers as word of the rare treat passed through the group.

"Nice," Cam said. "Is it still good?"

"I checked at the store," Cass said, smiling. Derrick wasn't sure he'd ever seen her smile. "The container is airtight. I have a plan for how to pop it."

She gestured for Billy to follow her toward the cooking fires and a couple of people nodded or thanked Billy as he passed. Drew patted him on the back and joined them as the crowd closed behind them, cutting Derrick and the other leaders off as they filtered into lines at the table.

Cam turned to speak to him, but Derrick's mind was elsewhere, frustrated with the reek of spoiling plans. He couldn't have her making the prisoner look good. This would never work.

DREW WOKE COLD AND would have shrugged down into his sleeping bag and gone back to sleep if Cass hadn't been talking at him already.

He interrupted her with a groan and said, "You know I'm not going to remember any of this, right?"

"I know," Cass said. "I'm just getting it straight in my head and waking you up in the process."

"Well, stop."

Cass let out a little huff of laughter and Drew opened one eye to watch her. She had already rolled up her sleeping bag and was stuffing her things into her pack with the swiftness of practice. She shoved the items through the open tent flap. *No wonder I'm cold.*

Once Cass had put on her belt, secured her pistol in its holster, and tightened the knife sheath over the scar on her left arm, she glanced at him. He quickly shut his eye but couldn't keep from smiling.

"Get up," she said, smacking his leg through his sleeping bag. "Or I'll pinch your bad toes."

"Bitch."

Cass chuckled and crawled away. Drew waited for a moment, listening to others grumbling as they awakened in nearby tents. Someone out there was clapping while someone else laughed. The light filtering through the tent was a soft blue. The sun wasn't up yet, but the birds were. The rustling of nylon and clacking of tent poles as people tore down told him he couldn't avoid it anymore.

Drew quickly dressed, packed, and broke down the tent. Strangely, Billy's was already gone. He had thought he'd need to help him pack it; often a tricky process the first time. As he gathered his belongings, the dog bounded up, brightening his morning with a few quick yaps and a wagging tail. Drew bounced around, playing with the dog as he walked.

By the time he made it down to the shed and the old burnt-out barn, his group's wagons were already hitched. Cowboy, the brown horse Cass would be riding and Smoke, the gray she'd assigned to Billy were tacked and tied together to an old crossbar on the barn. Billy was tacking up Whiskey for Cam. When Billy spotted Drew, he jogged over.

"Cass just told me that you usually ride Smoke," he said. The man's face was healing well, but the crease of concern caused the bruises to stand out. "I hope I'm not causing a problem for anyone." Billy paused and looked around. When he spotted Cass chatting intently with Lena, he lowered his voice and said, "I know your group is down a horse, now."

Drew shook his head. "Cass knows I'd rather drive the wagon, anyway. I'm not as in love with saddle sores as she and Cam are. We'll trade off along the way. For now, you need the practice."

Billy nodded, and Drew went to pack up some of the cold breakfast of dried meat and nuts. Cass's new charge seemed genuine and had certainly gotten into her better graces. Drew felt less doubt about him than some of the others from Derrick's band—including Derrick himself.

The group was surprisingly efficient at getting ready. It was less than an hour before people began to mount. He stifled his laughter at the several Oregonians who were riding bikes—so short in comparison to those on horseback. A bell rang and Drew moved aside as another bike zipped past to join the others. There was a miniature vanity license plate on this one with a fairly graphic silhouette of a man biking naked. "Keep Portland Weird" the plate begged. Now Drew did laugh.

His smile was still wide when Cass slid her arm through his.

"Ready for this?" she asked.

"Oddly, yes. The sooner we leave, the sooner we get there."

"You okay with the supply wagon?"

"More than okay. Let jailbreak boy have the fleabag," he shot Cass a smile as she shook her head. There was a ready grin on her face. Surprised, Drew pulled away to look at her. She seemed to buzz with adrenaline, which was to be expected on a big day, but her shoulders were relaxed, and she looked well-rested. She had color again. He hadn't seen her look like this since before Stronghold's recruiters showed up in their field last summer.

It had been one disaster after another since then. A hard winter had decimated their livestock. A lot of life was lost to illness. The return trip of the recruiters was followed by pressure from some to join Stronghold. Then, of course, the fire that had forced their hand. Cass's tendency to take everything onto her shoulders had made him fear he'd never see that little spark of hope in her again.

"What are you looking at?" she asked, hands on her hips.

Drew shook his head. "My best friend in the world."

She looked touched for a moment; then she crossed her arms, and her expression turned snarky. "What a distinction. Best friend in the *whole world*. Out of all the—what? Maybe four, five hundred people that are left?"

He shook his head and started to spit a clever comeback only to find her looking away from him, through the crowd. He followed her gaze to Billy, who was mounted already, holding one of Cowboy's reins for her. He'd dropped the other and was giving Cass a sheepish, comical look. She tried to look annoyed as she turned back, but Drew knew her well. She was hiding a smile.

He raised an eyebrow at her, his mouth pinching together in a way that suggested he was holding his tongue.

She cleared her throat and ignored the bait. "Billy and I will be bringing up the rear. I talked it out with Cam. So, that's where I'll be if you need me."

"I bet," Drew said.

She looked at her boots and shook her head. "Bye, best friend."

He laughed as she jogged away, then moved to climb up onto the waiting wagon. He stifled a groan as he saw a few of the women from Derrick's band waiting to ride with him. He knew the names of two; Rylynn who had hit on him more than once, and Marie. She'd slept in a different tent each night since they arrived and was working her way through men from all three bands already. Rumor had it Derrick encouraged this behavior.

Drew forced a nod and cursed himself. He'd meant to talk to Cass about this. The trip would be easier if they were a "couple." He settled on his seat, pulling on a pair of leather gloves and glanced at Cass and Billy. Both were mounted now, Cass pulling the reins through her fingers, explaining something. Somehow, for the first time in years, he had a feeling Cass wouldn't want to use that arrangement. She'd shield him from anything in the world, he knew. But how could he ask her to do that? What if she wanted to be open—available—to someone? What if *he* wanted to?

Drew gathered up the reins as Derrick's voice rose above the eager hum of the crowd. The three leaders had ridden up a rise just ahead. It was time for the big speech—the christening of the journey. Drew's thoughts took precedent over the words, leaving him out of the loop when the crowd laughed or hollered. But a line spoken by Hank captured his attention.

"—and so my hope is that we will come to view those differences as assets. And we will enrich Stronghold with all we have to offer."

Drew didn't join in the cheering but gave a decisive nod. He flicked the reins and maneuvered into an open space in the caravan.

Five

CASS SAW THE EXCITEMENT of the first days of travel quickly subdued. Though glad to be underway, people were physically underprepared for the rigors of riding into rough terrain in the higher elevations. They followed the highways and interstates where they could; sometimes railroad tracks. But they avoided major cities in hopes of avoiding territorial residents or Rovers. So, they spent much of their time in wilder areas, less populated Before and entirely deserted now.

One morning a fight broke out between Adam and one of the other men of Clan Mason. The man complained of the heat and refused to strap on his riot gear. The group of three men that served as the primary guards for the Californians had been wearing it each day on the road.

When the man stuck to his refusal, Adam grew angry, and just when it seemed the two would come to blows, Derrick swooped in.

"We do not fight each other," he said, looming over Adam until the man apologized and backed down.

Derrick then wrapped an arm around the other man's shoulder and spoke to him quietly. As Derrick relieved all three of their riot gear and tucked it away in a wagon, Drew joined Cass and Cam where they were replacing a worn latigo on Whiskey's saddle. He ducked his head behind the horse.

"How benevolent of him," Drew said. Cass raised an eyebrow at his sarcasm but cracked a smile.

"I don't get why they wore it in the first place," Cass said. "There's no one to intimidate."

"What do you expect from someone who names his group 'Clan Mason'?" Cam asked. Cass let out a snort and went to mount her horse.

Early that afternoon, they came to a picturesque spot that had been set up for picnics and camping. Several picnic tables were still in good condition and a few faded trailhead signs boasted of a waterfall half a mile away. The group stopped, and Cam directed his horse back to Cass.

"What do you think?" he asked.

Cass made a face and glanced around. "Less than half a day's travel." She watched as Cam's face fell and a soft frown creased his forehead.

"Good spot, though," he said. "Like it was made for us. Clean water."

Cass glanced at the surrounding areas, looking for decent spots to set up watch. There were a couple of RVs parked off to the side, the near one lopsided due to a flat tire. They'd make good watchtowers, and there just might be pillows left in them for Katie and Trista, though Cass was angry at herself for thinking of non-essential things at a time like this.

She took in the excited murmurs of the group. Finally, she

glanced at Billy. Smoke had dropped her head to graze, and he gazed up at the treetops, then turned hungry eyes to the trailhead sign. Cass cracked a half-smile.

"Okay." She nodded at Cam. "We'll camp here."

In under an hour, people were heading for the trailhead in droves. Cass watched Lena and Billy covertly as the three of them finished brushing down the horses. Her helpers were only half present, their glances continually darting to the trail where almost the entire camp had disappeared.

Lena returned from hobbling a horse and turned to Cass. "Okay. Done, right?"

Cass shook her head. "The saddles are chaos."

Lena groaned and cursed under her breath. "They're fine."

"And if it rains? Or we have to leave in a hurry in the night?"

"You are such a hard-ass sometimes." Lena glanced at Billy as he passed, leading the horse he'd finished brushing. She clamped her hands onto her hips. "Have Billy do the saddles."

Cass's face grew hot, and she took a breath. "Lena."

"He's healed enough," Lena said. "Why are you favoring him?"

Cass raised her voice for the first time in quite a while. "Lena. Set the saddles up properly and cover them with a tarp. Now." Cass took in a shaky breath as Lena shot her a glare and went to the haphazard grouping of saddles.

She wasn't mad at Lena. She was mad because she'd been appointed to the first watch. Normally, this wouldn't bother her, but she found herself almost as desperate to see the waterfall as everyone else.

She moved around the horse she was grooming, picking the hooves on the opposite side. Her eyes met Billy's as he walked over to help Lena. Cass bent and ran a hand down the horse's leg, expelling a breath.

By the time Cass released the last horse, Lena and Billy were done.

"Can I go now, boss?" Lena said. There was still a bit of defiance in her tone, but her expression was teasing.

"Thanks, Lena. Enjoy the waterfall."

Lena took off at a jog, but Billy stood in place, rubbing his grubby hands against his jeans.

"What are you waiting for?" she asked. "Go join them. See the natural wonder."

"I could keep you company," he said. "They haven't been giving me watches, which I understand—they don't trust me. But, it hardly seems fair that you should miss out. You won't be off duty until dark, will you? You'll miss the view."

Cass shook her head, shoving her hands into her pockets. "Someone has to stand watch. Always. It may as well be me. I wouldn't get as much out of it as everyone else."

"Maybe you need it more, then."

Cass searched Billy's eyes, her lungs unable to pull in decent breaths which gave her the feeling of swaying on her feet. She swallowed and smiled.

"You need it," she said. "That much I know. So go. I'll see you at dinner."

After a moment's hesitation, Billy conceded. He raised a hand in farewell and left. Cass watched him go as long as she dared and then went to retrieve her rifle and find a good vantage point. She tried to enjoy the light playing on the trees and bird song, but it was lonely in camp with just herself and one other watchman. She could sometimes catch laughter or the fuzzy roar of the falling water in the distance.

Sunset came too slowly, and she found herself wanting things she'd forgotten the appeal of long ago.

*   *   *

BILLY MEANT TO HEAD back right away to keep Cass company, but he'd been so enjoying exploring around the waterfall and chatting with Waylon and Trista that he'd forgotten. By the time he re-entered the main camp, the smell of roasting meat already filled the air. A couple of small groups had gone hunting and fishing. Dinner tonight would be fresh.

He found Cass handing off her rifle to a man from Oregon. She smiled when she spotted him, and he felt the same rush he had at the waterfall. Then, he felt awkward, like he couldn't stand or walk right. He felt like a child who fancied a girl for the first time.

The set themselves up on the ground with Drew, Cam, and Trista, near a loaded picnic table. The elderly couple from Oregon, David and Rain, were on the end nearest them, and they all chatted together.

"Hank's convinced it was the government," Rain said through a mouthful of rabbit.

"Ours?" Trista asked.

Rain and David nodded. "He doesn't think it was intentional, mind you," David added. "He thinks it was testing gone wrong." The man shrugged and screwed up the wrinkles around his mouth. "I think he saw something when he was in the army."

Rain smoothly picked up David's thought. "Something that made him doubt the government's concern for its people."

There was a quiet moment as more than one person glanced over toward a laughing Hank at a nearby table. It was Cam who broke the silence.

"I just don't see how a government weapons test could do all the things that happened all at once all over the country."

"The world," Billy said. Everyone glanced at him, seeming surprised he'd spoken as he was usually quiet at dinner. Cass nodded at him, eyes wide and expectant. He cleared his throat. "I mean I agree. What weapon would be powerful enough to have an instant global effect like that?"

"We can't be sure it was global," David said.

Rain scoffed. "He's convinced our enemies got together to destroy the U.S."

"It's as plausible as any other theory," David said. There was no hint of irritation in his voice or the way he looked at Rain. Just the comfort of knowing she would disagree as she always did.

"Why wouldn't they come to claim their victory, then?" Trista asked. "Why wouldn't they be here taking the land?"

"Maybe they're on the East Coast," David said.

The conversation continued, but Billy zoned out. It had been a long time since he'd contemplated the possibility that his family might be alive and well in London. He'd had so many nightmarish visions of them as corpses rotting in some building or buried in a mass grave. The thought of them still living and aging was a shock. But, he couldn't fully enjoy the idea. They'd have been worried about him. They'd have wanted to come for him.

"—don't think it was a virus." Cass's voice brought Billy back to the discussion. "I mean, viruses take time. They don't simultaneously drop 99% of the population at once."

"And they don't choose to affect certain areas and not others," Cam added, nodding as he wiped his mouth.

"Right," Cass said. "And they're contagious. Cam and I—" she paused and sniffed, setting down the rabbit's leg she'd been eating. "Cam and I helped burn the bodies from our hometown," she glanced at Drew, "and some of the neighboring towns. No one who handled the bodies died."

"So do you subscribe to the alien invasion school of thought?" Rain asked. There was some chuckling from the group. Billy let a smile creep over his lips, too.

Cass shook her head, unconcerned with the teasing. "No. I guess I don't really care what happened. I just don't want it to happen again."

The mood was somber for a moment, and Cass's cheeks took on a fetching flush as Billy studied her out of the corner of his eye. She started laughing and he turned. There had been some leftover popcorn from the start of their journey. They'd brought it along in the large tin. Rain had a small plateful that she and David had been sharing. Now, she was tossing pieces of it to the red dog everyone had come to think of as Drew's.

The dog lifted himself up on his hind legs and caught a piece. Then, to everyone's amusement, Rain tossed a piece in David's direction. The old man caught the popcorn in his teeth and crunched it loudly, showing off for the crowd. She alternated tossing the pieces between human and canine.

As the dog missed the second piece in a row and scrabbled to find it in the grass, Drew said, "The old man is a better catch than the young dog."

The group laughed and David added, "Reflexes of a ninja, I always say."

"Geriatric ninja," Rain teased.

As the group laughed, Billy glanced at Cass. Her smile was fading as she stared at the trailhead. The wording on the sign was growing harder to read as the night darkened. Still, he wasn't surprised when she stood and piled her plate with the others. He watched as she checked the pistol at her side and the knife on her arm, then walked onto the trail with purpose.

When she disappeared, he turned back to the group. Cam met his eyes and held them for a second as if trying to read his intentions. People started to separate and wander toward the tents. When Trista yawned, Cam took her arm and escorted her away. Soon, only Billy and Drew remained.

Drew set to picking burrs out of the dog's fur and mumbling to it. "Dumb as a brick," he said, smiling. "Maybe that's what we should call you."

Billy stood and meandered toward the trailhead. Pausing beside the sign, he glanced behind him, then down the dark trail into the trees. It felt as if someone still had ropes around his wrists; such was the pull to follow her. He glanced down to check that those wrists, though still red and scarred in places, were free.

He was free. And so was she. He moved into the woods, walking slowly until his eyes adjusted and he could find the trail more confidently. He fought with feelings of inadequacy the whole way there. What was he doing? He was a prisoner she'd rescued, and she probably thought he was a criminal. Except when he seemed familiar to her which she hadn't mentioned in a while. But, he still saw the recognition in her eyes from time to time.

If she was to figure it out or he was to come clean as he should, she'd be completely put off by him. Some useless actor paid to have good hair once upon a time. No need for such people, now. The world needed people with skills. If he were lucky, she'd continue teaching him. But, the spark between them would be gone.

He came to the waterfall and spotted her boots first. She had taken them off and rolled up the bottoms of her jeans. She was wading into the pool at the base of the falls where water collected before separating off into two streams. Moonlight poured down from the sky and reflected in the water, lighting up Cass's figure.

Her arms were out before her, hands open to catch the spray as she made her way across the slippery rocks. She turned a bit toward him, picking a more promising path through the water and he saw that her lips were moving. He held his breath, straining to hear over the sound of the rushing water. The falls were small, but still loud.

He heard a note here and there, a part of a word. He began to string them together and his innards sunk to his feet. Horror and elation warred inside him, making his heartbeat echo through his head. It was *his* song she was singing. A song he had written and recorded.

He risked one last look at her, just as her hand reached the flow of water. Then, he turned and left.

BILLY'S STOMACH GRUMBLED AND his shoulders sagged as they came to a stop for lunch the next day. His mood was as downtrodden as his body. After hearing Cass singing his song the night before, he'd been a mess; trying to build up a wall between her and himself and simultaneously waiting for the other shoe to drop— for the moment when she realized who he was and called him out.

In his exhaustion, he wasn't paying attention to his feet as he climbed down from Smoke's back. His right boot landed in something slick and went out from under him. His lower body almost slid underneath Smoke's belly. It was only by taking a firm grip of the saddle that he remained upright. He couldn't stop himself from crying out in surprise, attracting the attention of everyone in the area.

He heard Derrick's booming laugh floating out like toxic fog over the sounds of the others. He ignored them as he righted himself and glanced down to see what had made him slip. *Of course*, he thought. His boot was covered in green tinted manure.

"Bollocks," he said under his breath. With a sigh, he loosened Smoke's cinch, careful to step around the feces. He led the horse away from the sounds of fading laughter.

No one had begun eating yet, as the group leaders were bent over a map, discussing making camp nearby and setting traps near the small lake to catch whatever food might wander past. Billy walked toward the water and began to scrub manure from his boot in a patch of tall grass. He picked up a stick, scraped out the treads, and reeled back his arm to toss the stick into the lake. Someone grabbed his wrist and squeezed, digging fingers into the healing rope burns. Dropping the stick, he jerked his arm away and turned to find Adam smiling at him.

"Maybe not in the same lake where we're getting our water," he said. "Eh, basement boy?"

Billy's jaw clenched as he held back a thousand retorts about them needing to boil the water anyway and Adam minding his own business. His eyes flicked up to Cass, where she'd been talking to Cam and Trista. Though she didn't return his gaze directly, she turned her body to allow herself a sight line over her brother's shoulder.

"Sorry," Billy mumbled, turning his eyes back to Adam, who stood far too close. Billy refused to step away from him. Adam's smile had widened into a grin that allowed Billy to smell his foul breath.

"Trying to be the good boy for her, huh?" Adam asked.

Cass called out his name and Billy glanced over to see her walking away with Trista. Her head was turned, and her arm was out, gesturing him to follow.

"Come with us a minute, will you?" she called across the distance.

"Coming!" He moved to step around Adam, but the other man again grabbed his arm. Billy's skin crawled, and his face contorted into a grimace before he could prevent the reaction.

"You think you're safe with her, don't you?" Adam said, his voice just above a whisper. "Because she spoke for you? Well, don't. You know what it really means that she took responsibility for you? It means that if you start causing problems—if you don't toe the line—*she'll* be the one to kill you."

Finally catching his breath, Billy pulled his arm free once more and started walking away.

"She'll be happy to do it, too," Adam called after him. "From what I hear."

Billy caught up to Cass and Trista. Cass's eyes searched his for a moment, but it was Trista who smiled and greeted him.

"I thought you'd like to join us," Trista said. Billy's shoulders grew heavier. It had been Trista's rescue, then. Cass hadn't wanted him to join. "I needed to stretch my legs." Trista groaned and ran a hand quickly down her abdomen. Billy glanced at Cass for a reaction, but she was looking away.

"It's hard, isn't it?" Trista asked. "Riding all day when you're not used to it."

Billy nodded and turned as Rylynn jogged up on his other side, joining the small party. They turned to circle the lake toward a little collection of tiny vacation cabins.

"God, yeah, I bet it is rough," Rylynn said. She moved forward a bit, walking sideways to get a better view around Billy. She put a hand lightly on his arm to keep them from colliding. Billy suppressed a shudder, remembering Adam grabbing him—remembering so many times his arms had been held. "Is there any reason why Billy can't ride in the wagon? I'm sure he'd recover from his injuries better that way."

Rylynn was now looking at Cass, who had stiffened and slowed her pace, her eyes scanning the area.

"I suppose if he wanted—Cass?" Trista broke off as Cass took hold of her arm and steered her further back from the tree line. She slid her body between Trista's and the woods, gesturing harshly for Billy and Rylynn to move behind her, too.

Billy swore he could see the short, dark hairs on Cass's arm lift as she reached for her pistol and rolled her shoulder. No one breathed. Then, there came a grunt from the woods and the sound of scuffling.

"Cameron!" Cass's shout shattered the tense silence and forced a rushing, heart-pounding panic through the shards. She glanced across the pond, then charged into the trees, pistol lowered beside her. She lifted it just before she disappeared behind one of the decrepit-looking cabins. Billy flinched at the gunshot.

He hadn't realized he'd stepped in front of Rylynn and Trista until he turned at the sound of shouting and had to stand taller to see over their heads. Cam and several others were running around the lake.

There was a scream from the woods and Billy's gut flipped until his mind registered that it was a male voice. Another gunshot and Cass's voice screamed a name he'd heard once or twice in passing, "Trace."

"Stay with them," Cam shouted as he ran past. Drew was on Cam's heels and paused to look at the three of them.

"What happened?" he asked.

Billy shrugged his shoulders helplessly as Trista said, "We heard fighting. Cass went in. I think it's Trace."

Drew was already running, again.

There was another bloodcurdling scream and then shouting as Cam and Drew located the others. Derrick and Adam flew past and entered the trees, then Hank and a few others. Time seemed to slow as Billy listened. The shouting faded into tree-muffled conversation. Lena arrived just as people began to filter back out.

"What happened?" she asked.

"Drifters," Hank said. Billy heard Trista let out a shaky sigh. Her face had paled, and he reached a hand out as if to steady her, but never made contact. She caught him looking and swallowed.

"Rovers," she said.

"She get 'em?" Lena asked. Hank opened his mouth to answer, but Derrick's laughter interrupted.

"And then some," Derrick said. He and Adam continued walking past, but Billy caught Adam's raised eyebrow and knowing smile. He nodded at Billy, clearly thrilled with the timing of Cass's violence.

A tall, lanky man passed out from the trees, his shirt ripped and blood seeping from a shallow wound at his hairline. Drew clapped him lightly on the shoulder.

"We'll have Doc look at that. I'll go find him." As Drew jogged away, Cass stepped out of the trees. Billy's heart stopped, and he took a single step back.

"Jesus," Rylynn said. Trista clucked her teeth.

Cass was covered in blood from her collarbone down. She moved like an animal, smooth and sure, despite what must have happened behind the cabin. Her eyes were distant and her face hard. She stooped to wipe her knife on a clean patch of denim at her calf. She frowned at the handle and looked down at her clothing, searching for a way to clean the weapon.

"Here." Trace pulled his ruined shirt over his head and tossed it to her. He crouched near Cass. Billy could see a trembling in the man's legs as he watched her clean the knife and her hands. She sheathed the weapon and began to wipe blood from the skin on her arms and chest.

She tossed the stained shirt away from herself in a sudden show of emotion and looked up at Trace.

"Thank you," he said. He offered her his hand, and they clasped their arms together in a display of strength and affection that Billy would have envied if his blood wasn't still pounding in his ears. Trace pulled Cass to her feet and turned as Doc approached. Cass stepped away to talk to Cam, who had appeared from the trees. He was wiping Cass's gun with a piece of cloth. When he finished, he handed it to her and reached out to wipe a splatter of blood from her cheek. She shied away.

As she holstered the pistol, Rylynn stepped up between Trista and Billy and whispered, "Are you ever afraid of her?"

For a second, Billy thought she was asking him, and his throat tightened. He didn't want to answer that right now.

Trista let out a half-hearted laugh. "I used to be," she said. "When they first brought me into their group, and I started seeing

Cam, Cass hated me. I thought she was jealous of someone stealing her big brother. Then one day, in the dead of winter, we were raided by another group. They set fire to the house we were in—the house Cass and Cam grew up in—and we had to run in the middle of the night."

Trista glanced at Rylynn, then up at Billy. She kept her eyes on him as she continued. "Cam put me on a horse, but I couldn't ride. Cass had tried to teach me, but I didn't like spending time with her, so I hadn't learned. I fell off and got separated in the chaos. I panicked and started screaming for Cam and—" she sighed, "three Rover men found me." Trista's gaze turned to Rylynn, now. The younger woman rested a hand on Trista's shoulder.

"It was the first time I ever took a punch. But, I didn't get a chance to even try to fight back. Cass came." Trista let out a laugh and turned to look at Cass. Her eyes glazed as she went into memory again. "There was this swirl of snow, and she literally rode up on a white horse—on Smoke, actually—with a baseball bat. She took out *three* men with a *baseball bat*. And afterwards, I asked her why she saved me. She said that losing me would kill Cam." Billy turned to Cass, who met his gaze but made no move to come closer.

"It was the moment I realized that Cam was the one. And it was the moment I first understood Cass. She'll do *anything* to protect her family. And it's tough on her when her family grows. It makes it more likely she'll have to do what she just did to protect them—to go wherever she goes when she does that."

Trista greeted Cam as he came to check on her. At some point, Rylynn had left. But, Billy could only focus on the blood-covered figure before him, arms crossed over her chest, eyes searching his face almost as if waiting for judgement. Judgement from him, of all ridiculous things. Was she, like Rylynn, waiting to see if he feared her?

Fear was an emotion that pushed and when he looked at her all he felt was a pull. He began moving toward her. Her eyes widened. She dropped her arms and started to walk away, then stopped.

"Are you okay?" he asked at the same time she said, "I had to."

She cleared her throat and said, "He—uh—Trace. He went to set some traps. Seems he walked into one, instead. It was Rovers. We won't stay here tonight. I need to change, though, so can you help Lena get the horses ready to move on?"

He nodded, and she sped away, leaving him to walk back with a quiet Cam and Trista.

Six

CASS LEANED AGAINST A chain-link fence on the side of a hill. Behind her, the water tower the fence had once protected was leaking rhythmically. The first weeks of the trip had passed with little difficulty, and Cass was letting that fact sink in as the sun sank before her.

The Rovers that had attacked Trace were the only people they'd encountered. Though Cass's own hypervigilance had lasted days longer than anyone else's, she'd started to feel foolish. With mounted guards spaced throughout the caravan, it would be suicide for a small band of Rovers to take them on. And as they passed through what was once Colorado, Cass was beginning to doubt the existence of any group larger than their own. The population promised in Stronghold seemed a fairytale in the quiet of the world.

The only animals bigger than squirrels had been edible and more curious about humans than wary, so hunting had come easy, and the group had been well-fed. They were making better time than expected, even considering what others had dubbed the "weakling wagon" which carried Katie, David, and Rain. Conrad rode with this wagon; Darcy had been driving it, and Lena had taken to riding alongside as a "guard" although Cass suspected it was mostly because she enjoyed Katie's company. This stop was the first that would be longer than overnight. They would use the extra day to fish in a nearby creek and gather what fruit was ripe from the nearly idyllic orchard they were setting camp in.

Though Cass shuddered to remember the men she'd killed at the lake, her biggest complaint about the trip so far was that it had gone *so* smoothly people were letting their guard down. Everyone was relaxing into the dull, day-to-day travel and assuming because this much of the trip had gone so well, every day would. Cass tipped her chin downward and shook her head. She was as guilty as anyone.

She'd continued bringing up the rear of the group with Billy, and though he still refused to talk about himself, he had enough questions to ease Cass out of her self-consciousness, as hours and days had worn on peacefully. Cass had found herself opening up in that way people had always done on road trips Before. Something about the ground passing by and constantly changing scenery made people free.

Just when she had admonished herself and resolved not to answer a single question more until he answered some of hers, he'd begun asking about survival. Which plants were safe? How to find shelter if left without a tent? How to prevent himself being seen and heard by others? Cass had known she'd never be able to teach him by talking but needed to show him. So, she'd set Lena and Conrad the task of watching behind them while she and Billy broke off from the group to train.

Though Lena seemed to have a strong dislike of Billy, she'd welcomed the additional responsibility Cass was giving her. Conrad had been ultra-vigilant already and gave no argument.

So for the past several days, Cass and Billy had dipped in and out of their place in the caravan, into woods or down to creeks, frequently dismounting so she could instruct him. Cass was enjoying herself, and the guilt had been building. What if something happened to the group while she was away?

Cam and Drew had both dismissed her worry. Drew had pointed out that they were always within earshot. Cam had said she needed to train Billy sometime and asked her again if she felt unsafe with him. When she'd said "no," he'd considered the matter ended. He wasn't worried about an attack himself and was calm to the point of being blasé about her concerns.

A twig snapped behind her, and she froze, holding her breath and listening past the suddenly increased pace of her heartbeat. She heard a footstep, then another and just as she was about to reach for her pistol, she heard a familiar, soft rattle. She smiled, and her tension eased, though she kept her breathing soft so she could hear Billy as he crept closer to the fence behind her.

With a smooth movement like brushing a fly away, Cass pulled the knife from her arm sheath as she twisted and rose to her feet. She lifted the knife and pressed the blade against the fence, several inches from Billy's shocked face.

"That's a good way to get killed, you know," she said. "Sneaking up on people."

Billy let out a huff of air and crossed his arms over his chest. "You told me to."

"I said you wouldn't be able to."

"Yes, and that's just as good as challenging me to try."

"I could've killed you." Cass tapped her knife blade against the fence twice for emphasis.

Billy set his jaw and shook his head. "You knew it was me."

Cass nodded and moved to replace her knife only to find the

sheath hanging from her arm at an angle. Designed for divers, the sheath's straps were neoprene and Velcro. They'd been wearing thin, and one had finally broken through.

"Damn." She released the second strap and pulled the sheath from her sweaty skin, sticking the knife into it before assessing whether it could be repaired. "And I hate sewing."

She started to walk along the outside of the fence and lifted her hand to trail it along the chain link. Billy followed along inside the fence and likewise raised his hand, running it across the wires. Their hands began a kind of dance, swapping positions. First Billy's on top, then Cass's. They were careful not to brush their fingers together as they crossed the midpoint of their pattern. They were equally careful not to look into one another's eyes.

Too soon, they came to the gap in the fence where the gate had once been. Billy jogged through and caught up to Cass. They passed away from sunset and down the hill into the lantern and firelight of camp.

"So, how'd you know it was me?" Billy asked. "I know I stepped on a twig, but that could have been anyone—Lena, Derrick, someone else from your fan club."

Cass shook her head, half-smiling and looked pointedly at his hip as they walked. He'd attached his fire starter to his belt loop with a carabiner.

"That jingles when you walk."

Billy shook his head and looked at the ground in front of him.

"That's a bad place to keep it, anyway," Cass added. "Too easy to lose. Put it in your pocket or your pack."

She turned toward the tents and Billy halted.

"Aren't you going to dinner?" he asked.

"I need to put this in my tent." Cass held up the knife in its broken sheath.

"Oh." Billy held out his hand. "I can take it for you. I need to change my shirt, anyway."

Cass stared at his hand for a moment before meeting his eyes. He hadn't been given a weapon, yet. Cam hadn't wanted him to have one until they knew he could be trusted. But, that was miles ago. He'd had every opportunity to hurt her over the past week while they'd been alone in the woods.

She remembered all the times they'd sat together, and he'd been careful not to get too close. All the things she'd handed him when he'd gone out of his way to keep their hands from brushing. And the way he'd leaped away from Marie on his first night. He couldn't touch people; how would he manage to kill someone?

Billy watched her, his face sinking as he seemed to realize the reason for her hesitation. She handed him the knife.

"Just toss it in there," she said. "Thanks."

As she walked away, Billy called after her. "Save me a spot."

She nodded and picked up her pace.

"HOW'S IT GOING WITH Billy?" Cam asked as he came up beside her to fill a plate.

Cass raised an eyebrow. "How's what going? I mean, he's working hard—trying to learn. What do you want to know?"

"Well, mostly I'm wondering what *you've* learned about *him*. Who is he? What did he do Before? Has he told you why he was locked up?"

Cass swallowed. She'd gotten more information out of Billy, but didn't know everything her brother was asking. She was also hesitant to share it without permission. She glanced around to make sure no one was eavesdropping before answering. "He was a student. Living in L.A. Had part-time jobs." She shrugged.

"In L.A.?" Cam stopped filling his plate to stare at her. "How'd he survive? I don't know of anyone who was in or around a major city who lived."

Cass shook her head. "He was dirt biking with a neighbor or something. Outside the city. The guy was like a martial arts expert, and he kept Billy safe. At least for a while." She shrugged again when her brother's frown didn't disappear. "He doesn't talk much about himself, honestly. And I'm not going to pry. I know what it's like, you know. Not wanting to share everything."

Cam's posture loosened and he nodded. "But you trust him? You feel safe with him?"

"Yes." She met Cam's gaze and let him see the truth there, hoping he couldn't read any of the other emotions she was feeling for Billy.

"Okay, then. He seems comfortable enough with you. Not with anyone else but, with you... I'm sure he'll tell you more eventually."

"Sure."

Cam smiled and carried his heaping plate to where Trista sat with a larger group. Cass didn't feel like so much company and knew Billy wouldn't either. She plopped herself down inside a semi-circle of bushes with a fairly good view of the other diners.

It wasn't until she had to call out to Billy to let him know where she was sitting that she realized she'd chosen a fairly secluded spot.

"If I'd known about the cherries, I wouldn't have changed," he said, settling down and pointing to Cass's fingers, stained with red juice from the handful of cherries she was finishing.

"Just take it off," Cass said, after spitting out a pit. Then, she flushed with embarrassment. She cleared her throat and avoided looking at Billy as she added, "I mean no one cares, guys have been riding all day without shirts, so . . ."

In her peripheral vision, she saw Billy lift the bottom of his shirt on one side and run his hand along the bruises on his rib cage. Unable to help herself, she turned to look. The bruises were still visible and would be for a while, but they were fading and morphing from purple to brown.

She looked down at her plate again and added, "No one cares. We've all looked like that."

Billy pulled the shirt over his head just as Drew stepped into their area with Brick on his heels.

"Whoa," he said, glancing from Cass to Billy and back. "Should I leave?" There was a glimmer in his eyes and Cass shot him a warning look, setting her jaw.

"Sit your ass down," she said. Drew scooted next to her, and Brick stretched out in the grass nearby. Cass smiled at the dog. It already seemed so normal to see him with Drew, like he'd always been around.

They ate in silence for a while. Cass had been ignoring both men and was surprised when Drew spoke.

"She likes to people watch," Drew said. "Which is odd for someone who doesn't seem to like people, isn't it?"

Billy nodded. "I've noticed."

Cass felt her cheeks warm slightly as she realized they'd been watching her. Derrick walked into her field of vision just then, talking with Adam.

"I don't like snakes either," Cass said. "All the more reason to keep an eye on them when they're around."

Billy laughed. Drew said, "True," and nudged her foot with his.

She pulled her foot away, and Drew cleared his throat. "Has she told you about her interest in people's "reasons," yet?"

Cass's eyes widened.

"Reasons?" Billy asked, turning to her.

She felt trapped. Drew was the only person she'd ever talked to about that topic. It felt almost as if he had stripped her naked.

Drew bumped Cass with his elbow. She glared at him. But, Billy's gaze was intent, anticipating. Her hands felt unsteady as she placed another cherry in her mouth to buy time. How could she describe this small, ill-formed impulse she had.

"This world sucks, you know? At least, a lot of the time it does. And it's not enough for people to just wake up and fight for the sake of survival. I just thought—I mean, I think—everyone has some other—greater—"reason" to get up in the morning. I sort of collect them."

She finally glanced at Billy, feeling overly invested in his response. He gave a nod.

"That makes sense," he said.

"I don't usually have to talk to someone or even *like* them to know their reason," she said, wiping juice from her chin with the back of her hand. She looked away and pointed across the crowd.

Billy scooted closer and followed the line of her finger to Katie and Conrad. Hands clasped carefully around her arm, Conrad helped the pregnant woman lower herself to the ground.

"His reason is her, which is obvious to anyone who watches for five minutes although he still thinks it's his secret."

"And hers?"

Cass watched Katie for a moment longer as the woman recovered her protruding belly with the men's shirt she wore. She lovingly stroked her abdomen, oblivious to Conrad settling down beside her. Katie looked up only when Lena and Darcy joined them.

"The baby," Cass finally replied.

"It's not his, is it?" Billy asked.

She met his eyes again, startled by how close he was, and shook her head.

Doc passed by without noticing them in their semi-hidden enclave.

"And Doc's?" Billy asked, his voice a weighted whisper now, so close to her ear she felt his breath on her shoulder. Chills rolled down her arm and radiated all through her. She swallowed.

"Helping people," she said. "He wears it on his sleeve. Some people do. For others, it's more complex." She turned her gaze back to him.

"What's yours?"

She shook her head. "I can't tell you that." The truth was she wasn't sure she had one. Keeping her family alive? Maybe. Her uncertainty about why she pulled herself out of her tent every morning was what inspired her interest in the "reasons" of others.

Billy lowered his gaze to her arm, and she felt her gut clench as she realized he was looking at the jagged scar usually covered by the knife sheath. Her breathing wavered as he reached out a finger and moved it through the air, tracing the scar an inch away from her skin. She could have sworn she could feel his touch and was mesmerized by watching his hand.

"Can you tell me about *this*?" he asked.

She knew she couldn't tell him. But, as his eyes met hers again, she saw in them an intensity independent of her answer. Her glance swept over his shoulders and chest. Suddenly, she couldn't see the bruises—just bare skin radiating heat. The tip of his finger came to rest on her arm just above the scar. When she looked up, his gaze was on her lips. She felt herself leaning toward him.

Drew cleared his throat. The two of them jerked away from one another and looked at Drew to find he wasn't watching them. He was watching Derrick, approaching with his usual purposeful strides. Billy pulled away, nestling himself further into the bushes with his plate.

Cass's breathing returned to normal, and she managed a nod as Derrick crouched down opposite her.

"Nice night, isn't it?" He nodded to Drew. His look passed over Billy as if he weren't there before returning to Cass. "I'm taking some of my men hunting tomorrow," Derrick said. "I thought you might like to join us."

Cass hesitated. Tension was rushing from Billy, washing over her. It took all her effort to ignore it and think. She'd been wanting to hunt for a while. But, she'd imagined going alone, or with Billy to teach him. Her eyes cut to the side, and she saw he was putting his shirt back on.

"Is anyone invited?" Drew asked. Cass knew he was trying to buy more time for her and also offering to come with them for her sake. He'd have much preferred to fish.

Derrick nodded without looking at Drew. "Sure."

Drew was watching her, now. And Billy's gaze was on the side of her face like the heat of the sun, burning her skin. She couldn't think.

"I thought you'd want to go," Derrick said. "Everyone *says* you're the best hunter in your group."

He was challenging her. Cass wasn't sure she wanted to be around him and Adam for hours. But, he was goading her. Doubting her.

"I'm the best *shot*," she said, her tone certain. "That doesn't make me the best hunter."

"The best *killer*, then?"

Cass raised an eyebrow. He'd leaned in closer and unlike his other advances, this one felt genuine. She could feel his true interest this time, and it turned her stomach.

"I'll go," she said and feigned interest in the food remaining on her plate.

"Great," Derrick said. There was a pause in which Cass continued to push food around, knowing he was still looking at her. His voice deepened, weighted by sultry promises that groped at her like hands. "I'll come by your tent." He didn't say he'd come by in the morning. He left the time open for interpretation.

Drew shot Derrick a look that made Brick stand and skulk away. Only the fact he'd kept his distance from her kept Cass's anger in check.

"I wake up early," she said. "I won't be there."

His confident grin said he'd received her message, but wouldn't give up.

"Okay, then," he said. With a nod at Drew, he left.

Cass's mind was spinning. She *was* a killer. In many ways, that's exactly what she'd meant when she said she was the best shot. But, it was something she saw as a necessary evil, a cross to bear for those who couldn't. It had turned *him* on.

She shuddered. She didn't regret the choices she'd made; she'd killed in self-defense or in defense of others. She'd killed to survive. In those moments, her body and soul seemed numb to her decisions, precise and cold as a machine. But, in the quiet of night, she considered them black marks on her humanity.

She remembered the need she'd felt to explain herself to Billy after the incident at the lake. It was hardly the first time she'd felt guilt for killing, but it was unusual for her to apologize for protecting her family.

She realized her eyes had been closed only when they opened and darted to Billy. What must he think of her? This man who still took delight in a bird's nest or a herd of elk? Who had been brutally beaten and still managed to smile more than anyone she knew? A person she was certain bore no blood on his hands?

He stood and left. She watched his feet until they were swallowed up among others. Then, she looked at his half-full plate where he'd left it.

"I don't like Derrick," Drew said. "I don't trust "his men"."

Cass's layer of stone drew up around her again, and she turned, blank-faced. "You're not worrying about *me* are you?"

Drew met her gaze and held it, his face serious. "Not *just* you."

"*They* should be afraid of going into the woods with *me*. I'm not a woman so much as a monster, Drew."

"That's not true."

They sat in silence for a moment before Drew said, "I wanted to talk to you about our cover story." Cass felt a splash of ice water in her chest.

"With women from Derrick's band hitting on every man in sight, I suppose you want to be a couple," she said. Her voice dropped a few notches, and she said, "I screwed up. I told Billy we weren't together. I suppose that could always change, though."

"You did?" Drew sounded surprised but not angry. "No, it's fine. That's why I wanted to talk to you. It seems Derrick encourages women from his group to behave that way. Rylynn says he tells them that men don't take what's readily available."

Cass's anger flared, and she felt her upper lip curl. "What?"

"Some of them don't mind. Marie seems happy enough, but Rylynn? She's just holding out for Stronghold, I guess. Anyway, the point is I already told them we're not a couple but that I'm not interested in getting involved with them. So, I'm sure the whole camp knows by now."

Drew seemed amused by the look on Cass's face, so she closed her gaping mouth. "Are you sure?" She leaned in closer. "Don't you worry they'll start talk?"

"With the "monster" as my best friend, no one would dare to out me," he said, then laughed. "Maybe you're right, anyway. Maybe no one would care."

The group that left him to die in a winter storm had cared. People had reverted to the worst forms of themselves right after The End. Prejudice and general malice had run hot. They'd beaten him thoroughly and left him for dead in the snow. Cass remembered how he'd looked when she'd found him. In comparison, Billy had looked healthy the day she'd met him.

"I don't want to put you at risk on a hope and a prayer," she said.

"It's done. They might just think I'm prude or scared of diseases. I'm more interested in the fact that you told Billy we weren't together. I can't offer a buffer against advances like Derrick's if you've put yourself publicly on the market."

Cass didn't say anything. She'd spotted Billy, talking to Derrick, Adam, and a couple of others across the crowd. What was he saying to *them*?

"Or maybe you don't *want* to be protected from advances," Drew continued. "What are you looking at?"

As Drew leaned over to see around a bush, Adam's face turned sour, and he shoved Billy with enough force to knock him back several steps.

"What the hell?" Cass said, moving to stand up. Billy was raising a hand and talking quickly, but Adam advanced and shoved him again.

Drew grabbed Cass's arm and pulled her back to the grass. "You won't be helping him if you go over there."

Billy bumped into a woman who'd just gotten a plate, and her food flew to the ground. Billy was turning to apologize, and Adam was coming at him again. Just then, Cam stepped into Adam's path and spoke. Adam turned away and left. Cam said a few words to Derrick and turned to help Billy and the woman clean up. In a moment, Cam had steered the woman back to the food table, and Billy had headed back toward Cass and Drew.

Already, the crowd had gone back to the usual murmur of conversation. But, Cass's blood was surging with restless, unused aggression. She moved back into her old spot and steadied her breathing as Billy sat down. She waited for him to meet her gaze, but he didn't look up.

"Are you okay?" she asked when she couldn't stand his silence any longer.

His eyes met hers, confident and hard. A flush of embarrassment or anger colored his cheekbones. "Fine. Unpopular, but fine."

"What was that about?" Drew asked.

Billy addressed his answer to Cass. "I'm not welcome on your hunting trip."

"You asked to go?" Cass asked.

Billy nodded.

"They're bastards, Billy," Drew said. "Never mind it."

Billy picked at his food. Cass felt the need to keep away the silence, an impulse she seldom had. Her limbs were anxious. She needed to either talk or move, and she had nowhere to go.

"I'm surprised Derrick let him come at you," Cass said, as much to herself as either of the men. "He usually clamps down on violence in his group pretty fast."

"Notice his group is the only one that ever has violence to clamp," Drew added quietly.

Cass nodded and found Billy looking at her with such intensity it startled her. "Don't trust him, Cass." Billy lifted the side of his shirt, exposing his bruises once more. "He did this himself. Didn't seem too non-violent, right then."

As Billy dropped his shirt, Cass read his face like a book he'd left open for her. He wasn't just a man who found wonder in the little things. He used those things as his "reason" to keep waking up after years of captivity and torture. To keep waking up even when he had to grovel to the men who'd nearly killed him while they "rescued" him.

He may not have any himself, but he knew black marks on humanity as well as anyone. And he didn't seem to see them on her.

BILLY WOKE TO SCRATCHING on his tent and opened his eyes to see it was still dark. The scratching came again, and he sat up in his sleeping bag.

"Billy?"

It was Cass, whispering outside his tent door.

"Yeah?"

"Can I come in?" His insides gave such a leap at the prospect he thought he might lose last night's dinner.

"Yeah, sure," he said.

The tent flap unzipped, and Cass ducked through. She paused.

"I don't want to step on you," she said, keeping her voice low.

Without thinking, Billy reached out and took her hand, pulling her straight down, so she was sitting next to his exposed head and torso where they jutted out from the fluffy cocoon of his sleeping bag. He felt her hand tremble in his own and realized he had touched her without flinching. The thought made him anxious, and he pulled his hand away.

"What's up?" he asked, squirming upright.

"I want to teach you to fight," she said. "To defend yourself. We talked about it, remember?"

"I remember."

"I think it's time."

There was a long pause. Billy knew she was doing this because of last night's incident, an embarrassment he wasn't keen on reliving just now. He'd wanted to fight Adam. He remembered every hit Adam landed on him while he was tied to a tree outside the house he was imprisoned in. He'd wanted to fight Derrick; to break *his* ribs, tell him Cass was not a killer, and to sod off because Cass was not his for the taking.

But, he knew nothing about fighting. Not for real. He'd only mimed it on camera, and not often. Watching Derrick spar had looked so different from what he'd done. He might look good throwing a punch but how effective would it be? How could he think about protecting Cass when he needed her protection so badly?

She was offering to teach him as she'd taught many from her group. But, to learn to fight, he'd have to touch her, and she'd have to touch him. The thought excited and horrified him.

He'd love to be physical with her. He'd known this for a while now. Of course, in his imagination, they weren't exactly fighting. But in reality, every time they touched his skin crawled. He'd think of all the times he'd been touched against his will—forcefully—by someone who repulsed him. He hadn't figured out how to separate the two.

Though he'd done it just now, grabbing Cass's hand without flinching.

"What about your hunting trip?" he asked.

"I'm not a fucking circus act. I'm not going along to perform for Derrick and his men." Her voice grew softer. "Especially after what you told me last night."

Billy didn't answer for a while. He stroked the stubble on his jaw as he thought. When Cass spoke again, her voice seemed hesitant, almost hurt.

"I mean, you don't have to," she said. "I might be able to get someone else to teach you, if you'd like—"

He cut her off. "No. You. Let's go."

"I'll wait outside." He could hear her smiling even if he could barely see it in the pre-dawn grayness.

A few minutes later, he was jogging along behind her. The sky seemed to grow lighter with each step, just as his mind darkened. The more he tried to push memories away, the stronger they grew until they drug his head and shoulders down and he began to stumble through the trees, falling further and further behind.

At one point, he stopped and ran a hand across his face. He shook his head as if to clear away the rush of memories that made it hard to breathe. He heard Cass call to him and hurried to catch up, walking right into a low hanging limb. Colors burst behind his eye, and he let himself fall to the ground in an inhuman heap.

DREW ACCEPTED THE STEAMING cup that Derrick held out to

him and took a tentative sniff. It certainly smelled like coffee.

"Where'd this come from?" he asked, stifling a yawn.

"Instant coffee, sealed in individual packets. Lasts for years. Adam found some in that house we passed yesterday."

Drew blew on the surface of the liquid and took a small sip. It was bitter but warm and strong. "Wow."

"Not everyone is getting that, you know. Consider yourself lucky you're coming hunting with us." Derrick straightened and looked out over the small group of people crawling from their tents. Then, he turned back to peer at the people saddling up and gathering supplies for the hunt. Drew noticed he hadn't drunk from the second cup of coffee he was holding.

"So where's Cass?" Derrick asked.

Drew managed to contain his amusement to a half-smile, which he hid behind his cup. "She's not coming. Something came up."

When Derrick met his gaze a moment later, Drew was shocked to see the hardness in his eyes.

"Something came up?" He asked, his voice calm despite the tension now rolling off his body. "Something to do with that prisoner? I don't see him, either."

Derrick's voice was like a knife blade and Drew suddenly felt it was important not to say all he knew.

"I dunno," he gave what he hoped was a convincing shrug. "I don't track her every move. She does what she does and goes wherever she pleases." He used Brick, who was sniffing a spot on his pant leg, as an excuse to look away.

Derrick lifted his shoulder and let out a breath as if he'd made a decision. He was a study of opposites; his eyes blazed, but his body had become fluid and casual.

"It's not safe to run off alone with someone like him," Derrick said. "Trusting the wrong people will get her—or someone she loves—killed."

Drew's lips opened to let out a huff of warm air. Derrick's anger had morphed into genuine sadness and concern. Now, he transitioned just as smoothly back to anger.

He turned away from Drew and flung the cup of coffee to the ground. Brick shied away from the motion. The plastic cup landed in a patch of grass and settled as Derrick stormed away. Drew knelt to retrieve the cup, which was now split down the side, and watched the still-steaming brown liquid soak into a patch of earth.

Maybe it wasn't so funny.

Seven

THROUGH THE RINGING IN his ears, Billy was aware of Cass's feet pounding to his side. He felt her kneeling beside him and lifting his head onto her folded legs. But, when he forced his eyes open, she was holding her hands out away from his face with a trapped and tense expression. She didn't want to touch him.

He squinched his eyes shut again and said, "God, I'm a total wanker." His accent was crystal clear as he said it and he stopped breathing for a second.

"A what?"

He decided to gamble. "What? Not funny this time?"

There was a long pause, and he finally had to open his eyes again. Cass looked down at him, her choppy brown hair framing her face so that she looked like a dangling portrait. She held the bandana that had been in her hair near his face.

"What are you saying? How hard did you hit that branch? Did

you black out?"

The only reaction he could muster was a fake chuckle as he raised his hand to his face. There was a scrape up his cheekbone and into the corner of his right eye. His fingers came away bloody.

"I know, we need to keep it out of your eye, here—" she bit her lip. "Can I do it?"

He nodded, and she pressed the cloth to his face, blotting away blood and grit. The cloth was damp with icy water, and he sucked in a breath.

"Sorry, it's from my water bottle. It sat outside last night."

"It's fine," he said. She finished and looked down at him, frowning. He felt a rush of shame. He couldn't even follow her through some trees, and he wanted to follow her to Stronghold. And to the end of the earth if need be. "It didn't knock me out," he offered pathetically. "I was just—overwhelmed."

"Maybe we shouldn't do this," she said.

"I need to get over it."

"We don't have to rush."

He clenched his teeth and sat up so quickly he almost cracked her head with his. When he was sitting at eye level, he glared at her.

"Why aren't you tough on me, Cass? You're tough on everyone else."

She looked away and shook her head. He thought for a moment she was going to say something, but then her posture stiffened and she stood.

"Get up," she said, and she started off through the trees again. She'd forgotten her bandanna, and he snatched it up and stuffed the blue material into his pocket before following behind her, careful of the limbs this time.

She led him to a small clear area near a trickling creek. The camp was collecting their water a bit further down, but the trees were thick enough that they couldn't be seen by anyone there.

Cass had dropped her water bottle next to a rock, and she was now removing her gun holster and setting it in the grass. She turned back to him and began to roll up her sleeves.

"I'm not going to bother asking you what happened to you in that basement." Shocked by the force of her voice and the forward way she'd just brought it up unbidden, Billy took a step back.

"What you need is therapy. There was a time I needed it, too. But, it wasn't exactly the right option for me then and it sure as hell isn't an option for you, now. There are no psychiatrists, and there is—no—time." She accentuated each word with her jaw set, but Billy could see a gleaming in her eyes that made his chest ache.

Cass cleared her throat. "I never told my uncle that he saved my life." She began to pace a short track in front of him, talking with her hands. "Not just the day I took the pills, but every day after."

Billy took another step back. He'd known there was something dark in her past but hadn't expected it all to spill out like this.

"And he saved me by empowering me. Everything that kept me alive back then and since The End, he taught me. Or he found someone to teach me. Because *that* was what I needed. I didn't need drugs. I didn't need to talk about it. I needed to know that no one would ever be able to hurt me again. I needed to know I could defend myself."

She stopped pacing and rolled her shoulder in its socket before turning on him. She moved forward fast. Billy planted his feet and held both hands out; palms turned to her. He flinched, half expecting her to punch him. Instead, she placed her open hands against his. He met her gaze and let out a puff of air. Her palms were warm and steady. He was shaking.

At first, shock kept away all thought but then his heart rate increased, and he could swear he smelled the dampness of the basement lingering in the damp grass of the clearing.

"Stop," she said. "Look at me."

He hadn't realized he was looking away. He met her gaze.

"This is life or death, Billy," she said, her voice quieter and soft. The way she mouthed his name echoed in his memory even as she went on. "You don't want people to touch you. Why?"

He couldn't believe he was speaking as he said, "Because *they* did. *She* did. And her brothers—"

"That's enough. Do you want me to stop touching you right now?"

Billy blinked and swallowed. She'd linked her fingers with his so their hands were clasped together between them. "No," he said.

There was a hitch before she continued. Her eyebrows lifted in surprise. She pulled her fingers free and slid them down to loop around his wrists, loosely circling the fading pink scars where the rope had held him. "What if I were Derrick? Or anyone else trying to tie you up again. Anyone else trying to make you do something against your will?"

Billy's hands shook more noticeably than before, and he struggled to pull in a decent breath. Cass let go of his hands and took a step back, but he followed, taking two. Her hands were at her sides, and she held his gaze with the intensity of her own

"I want to teach you to prevent that. Do you want to learn?"

"Yes."

"Then, you'll have to risk touching me and letting me touch you," she said. "But, don't ever forget that this is *your* decision. And we can stop the second you say."

Billy nodded.

"Bring your hands up to defend your face like this," Cass said without preamble. She widened her stance, bouncing lightly, and raised her arms. Billy did the same.

His breath returned, steady and full.

*   *   *

CASS TAUGHT BILLY WITH fervor. She pushed him harder and expected more than she had with anyone else. It seemed more imperative since his conflict the night before. But when the time came that they would need to "attack" one another by grabbing and holding, she hesitated. The day had heated up, and the air was humid. They were both panting and drenched with sweat.

She didn't want to push him too far. He hadn't seemed to panic again since that moment in the trees, but she wanted to stop on a strong note.

Or maybe *she* wasn't ready to be close to him, yet.

"What's wrong? What's next?" Billy asked. Then, he went down to one knee and wiped sweat from his hairline.

"Water," Cass said, and she went to retrieve her bottle. She took a swig and tossed it to him. As he drank, she plopped into the grass. "And then nothing. Rest. Food. We're done."

Billy screwed the cap back onto the bottle and folded to the ground himself. "Okay. But just for now, right?"

"You're sure as hell not finished," she said.

Billy laughed and fell to his back and Cass glanced up at the sky. The sun had disappeared behind a cloud. She waited in vain for it to reappear as she listened to her own breathing and Billy's, both slowing and steadying. She recovered quicker, as expected. When Billy could finally speak without panting, he asked her a question she'd known she should expect.

"Do you want to talk about it? What you said about your past?"

"Do you want to talk about yours?"

There was no response except a cool breeze. It was strong and sudden, and Cass chilled instantly.

"The weather's turning," she said.

"I can smell it," Billy said. "A storm."

She nodded, though he was still looking at the sky. "Let's head back to camp. We'll see it better from the water tower hill. If it's a bad one, we have a lot to do."

Billy pushed himself off the ground in response, wincing. Cass felt bad for a moment, knowing that he'd be sore tomorrow. She studied his eye, bruised from its rough encounter with the tree branch. The wound had reopened, and there was a line of blood.

He caught her look and reached up to touch it.

"Everyone will think I kicked the crap out of you," she said.

"A lot of them probably won't mind."

"A lot of them probably won't be surprised."

They smiled at one another for a moment before Cass retrieved her gun and headed back to camp. She glanced down. Her shirt was torn, and there were grass stains on her pants. Billy looked equally disheveled. What a sight they'd be.

IN A TREE-LINED GULLY, the group of hunters was mounting their horses after a successful kill. Derrick cleared his throat and approached Cam on the side of his horse opposite the other men so that they could speak somewhat privately.

"I don't want to offend," he said, shoving his hands into his pockets, leaning in, and lowering his voice. "But, I'm worried about your sister."

Cam raised an eyebrow but seemed willing to hear. "Why?"

"I just don't trust the prisoner," Derrick said. He raised his hands in a surrendering gesture. "I know Cass can take care of herself under normal circumstances; it's just that a woman falling in love is not a normal circumstance."

Cam's hand came to rest on his saddle horn, and he frowned at the leather seat for a moment. When he turned back, his eyes were shielded.

"What makes you think she's in love with Billy?"

"Well, she doesn't strike me as the type to screw a man she

doesn't love." Cam's jaw hardened, and Derrick felt a bit of his confidence slipping. This had to go his way. "Or at least not a man she doesn't trust." Derrick read Cam's expression again. He seemed to be listening.

"Anyway, it's none of my business. I just like the two of you, and I'd hate to see her get hurt."

"Cass makes good decisions. She's smart. I'm sure she's fine." He picked up his reins. The first drops of rain had begun to spit from the sky, and though their group was sheltered from the brunt of the wind, they could hear it howling a promise of a rough return trip.

Derrick stepped back from Cam's horse. "I've seen a smart woman make a bad choice in a man. In fact, I've been the bad choice that got a smart woman killed." Cam turned in response to this honest sliver of information. "I just want better for Cass, is all."

Derrick turned and headed for his horse. They may have only had time to kill two deer, but the trip was a success anyhow.

AS BILLY HOOKED THE last horse to a high line, he looked for Cass. She was shouting back and forth with Lena, her face creased with the struggle of hearing over the wind and the worry over Cam and Drew. The hunting party was still out.

The storm put him on edge. He'd never been away from a building in a storm, much less been sleeping rough in one. His nerves weren't helped by the people staring at the two of them; eying their dirty clothing and his blackening eye without much effort at being covert.

The minute they'd reached camp, Cass had been in action, directing Lena, Darcy, and Waylon, reminding everyone to double check the stakes on their tents. She'd sent Hank to check out the large garage where the orchard owners had stored equipment. Finding it large and solid enough for the group to shelter in through the storm, Hank had reported back to her like she was in charge. In every meaningful way, she was.

She'd made Billy useful as well, sending him with extra tent stakes, then charging him with helping the cooks move the tables and lunch into the garage and tear down their tarp tent. Then he'd found her gathering the horses and helped with that. As they worked side by side, he felt closer to her than he'd felt to another person since long before The End. He worried she could read it right out of his mind with every glance.

She was smiling now. Derrick and Cam were coming through a gap in the trees. She rushed toward them, and he followed on her heels. People appeared out of the shelter, and the harsh crack of lightning overhead added urgency as everyone helped to untack and secure the horses. The field-dressed deer carcasses were protected and left to chill in the creek until the storm passed and they could be prepared.

The storm was in full swing, rain sheeting down on everyone, by the time they began to dart into the garage. Billy sprinted for his tent, slipping more than once on the wet grass. He retrieved his backpack and was zipping his tent flap when he heard the splash of footsteps behind him. He turned, expecting Cass, only to be knocked to the ground by Adam as he and another of Derrick's men ran past. Billy hit the ground with a grunt and heard their laughter receding as they disappeared into the grayness.

Adrenaline ran hot through his limbs as he picked himself up and ran for the shelter. He nearly collided with Drew just inside the doorway. The man's black hair was plastered to his forehead, accenting his brown skin and providing a stark contrast to the whites of his widened eyes.

"Is it raining?" Drew asked.

Billy heard Cass's laugh and turned to see that he'd burst in on their discussion.

"A sprinkle," he said. "Sorry to interrupt." He moved to pass between them into the garage, but Cass's hand closed gently over his arm.

He looked down at her hand and for an instant he felt sure that if his arm weren't dripping with rainwater, it would spark. He met her eyes and kept them as if to prove to them both that her touch was welcome.

"Did you fall?" she said, her tone grown serious.

"Yep. Slick out there," he said. She let him go, but he could see she knew he was lying.

After a hasty meal, Cass ran out to check the horses, and he wandered around looking for an unoccupied corner. Cam and Trista sat together in the cab of a tractor. Trista slept nestled in Cam's arms. Over her head, Cam gave Billy a chilly nod. He nodded back, heading for a nearby pickup. He climbed into the truck bed and settled himself in the dust with his back against the cab.

Producing Cass's knife and broken sheath from his pack, he pulled a thread from the hem of his shirt and threaded a needle he'd borrowed from Katie. He tucked the knife safely away and began to repair the sheath.

The storm had faded, but the rain was steady on the roof when Cass and Drew arrived a bit later, both shaking water from their clothes. Cass made a noise of surprise and hopped into the truck bed. Drew climbed into the cab.

"What?" Billy asked, seeing Cass's look of wonderment. "Can't believe I actually know how to do something?"

"You know how to do a lot of things," she said, settling in the opposite corner and leaning her head against the back window of the truck.

She watched him work in silence. Occasionally, he glanced up at her. When he'd finished, he used his teeth to break the thread away and looked up, expecting to show her the results. But, she was sleeping.

He'd never seen her so peaceful, and he let his hands fall to his lap and tipped his head to the side, watching her. Her hair was drying, and a piece of it flew away from her face and fell back with each breath. He glanced down at her hand lying palm up on the truck bed, and he longed to place his own palm against it.

Unprepared to do so, he replaced the knife in its sheath and laid that across her palm. When he looked up, Drew was staring at him through the window glass with a look not only incredulous but also angry. The expression faded to blankness as Drew gave a nod and settled down to sleep on the seat of the pickup.

Billy pondered the meaning behind that look for quite a while before falling asleep.

THE ARGUMENT BROKE OUT before Cass woke, and it momentarily prevented her from processing the fact she'd fallen asleep. She hadn't been able to sleep in the open among strangers—well, ever—and it had caused her many exhausted nights and panic attacks since The End.

There was no time to mull it over. Billy and Drew were gone. The garage door was open wide, letting in light and raised voices from outside. One of them sounded very much like Lena's.

Cass's hand brushed her knife in its sheath, and she grabbed it, noting the repaired strap. She hopped out of the truck bed and jogged between the parked vehicles and equipment. She was squinting against the light when she burst through the doors into the middle of a fight.

Waylon was physically restraining Lena who fought her way toward Adam. Cam stood between the fiery girl and the man, whose arms were relaxed over his chest, matching his smug expression. Adam was flanked by Derrick, who seemed amused, despite the tension coming in on them from all sides.

"Cass will tell you," Lena said, her bright red ponytail flipping over her forehead as she flung herself against her father's arm again. Waylon struggled to hold the girl.

"Tell them what?" Cass said, raising a hand in an attempt to steady Lena. It seemed to work. The girl began to calm.

"That I would never make a mistake with the horses," Lena said.

Cass turned to Cam for clarification. Her brother's eyes raked over her, and she wondered how disheveled she looked.

"One of the high lines broke loose last night, and we're missing the three horses that were on it," Cam said. "Also, a tree smashed one of the supply wagons and scattered a lot of things."

"It's not my fault," Lena yelled again. "*He* was supposed to be on watch. How did he miss the horses running away, huh?"

"I already admitted my fault," Adam said. "I fell asleep. I was tired from the hunt, and I didn't think there would be much risk of being attacked or robbed in the storm. I woke when the storm cleared, but I thought the wagon was the only damage."

"Which he reported to me immediately," Derrick said. "I'm less concerned with the horses than with my other man, Marshall. He's missing."

"Maybe *he* took the horses," Lena said.

Ignoring the girl, Adam turned to Cass, "She says she hung the picket lines herself because you weren't in camp. How can you be sure it was done right?"

"Lena knows what she's doing." But, Cass was thrown, and she heard it in her voice. Lena was smart and skilled, but Cass usually supervised everything. Instead, she'd been with Billy. She couldn't keep herself from searching for him. He was looking back at her, pale faced. She held his look for a moment before turning back to Adam.

"*There's* the truth," Adam said. "You were off rolling in the woods with him when you should've been doing your job. You don't know it was done right at all. You couldn't."

Cass dropped her knife and headed toward Adam, but Cam stepped into her path. "Cass," he warned.

"I think there's truth to Lena's theory." Drew's voice rang out over the crowd as he pushed his way into the melee. "The deer meat is missing, as well."

Cass took a steadying breath and backed away from Cam. He looked doubtful and disappointed, the way he'd looked when she'd written a nasty message about a bully of hers on the bathroom wall at their school. The way he'd looked when he'd stepped behind the barn to find her and Trace with their clothes half-off. Her heart sank as he turned away.

"Is it possible Marshall did this?" Cam asked, directing his question to Derrick with obvious skepticism.

"Marshall isn't a horseman. I doubt he could've managed one horse in that storm, let alone three."

"Why would he leave us, anyway?" Adam asked. "Marshall wants to go to Stronghold. Horses and an uncooked deer dinner would never lead him to betray Derrick."

"What happened to the deer, then?" Billy asked. He avoided looking in Cass's direction. "I mean the tree was clearly the storm, but what about the deer? Did hundreds of pound of meat just blow away?"

Adam looked ready to punch Billy, but Lena cried out again, drawing attention back to her pointing finger, aimed at Billy.

"It was him," she said. "*He* must have messed up the high line. *He* doesn't know what he's doing."

Cass's heart had stopped for a moment. It had sounded at first as if Lena was accusing Billy of taking the horses or the meat.

"Enough, Lena," Cass said. Her voice was sterner than she'd meant, but she was stiff with stress and couldn't help it. Regret washed through her when Lena shot her a tear-filled look of betrayal. The girl ran off, charging through the crowd and Cass was instantly exhausted.

"We're wasting time," she said, fighting away her guilt. "It doesn't matter how the horses got loose. If they weren't stolen, if the line failed, then we need to go find them before they get any further away."

"Agreed," said Derrick. Cass shot him a look he probably didn't deserve, but she had no desire for his backup. She picked up her knife and headed for the horses.

Behind her, she heard Cam naming people to help salvage supplies from the broken wagon and calling on Drew to see if it could be repaired. She found the broken high line, cursing her luck that Cowboy had been on it and was one of the missing horses. *Please don't let me lose my two best horses on this godforsaken trip.*

She picked up the end of the rope and examined it. It wasn't broken. It was still threaded through the rings where the horses had been attached, and there were no lead ropes, halters, or pieces of either anywhere she could see. To see this result, no fewer than four knots would have had to come undone.

It would have been impossible even if she hadn't checked them the night before. Granted it had been dark and windy. She stood and began to coil the rope, her leftover adrenaline making her hands shake. She scanned the trees around her wishing she'd fought the decision to stay there. Someone had been in their camp; she was sure of it.

She felt a presence at her shoulder and turned to see Billy.

"You shouldn't be around me today," she said.

"Cass."

"Seriously," she caught his eye. "I'm making you a bigger target. I'm not acting like myself."

Billy shook his head and looked at the ground. "They didn't just 'get loose' did they?"

"No," she said.

She headed for the wagon, skirting the people sorting through the wreckage. She scanned the spilled contents as she walked.

She caught Drew's eye when he stood up from peering under the wagon and gestured him over.

"You two should probably lay low," he said. "This has everyone on edge, looking for someone to blame. Cam's trying to calm it all down."

"Why should we lay low?" Cass said, finding herself much angrier than she'd thought. "I do my fucking job. Every day. And that line didn't break or fail; someone took it down."

"Shh," Drew said, stepping closer. "Relax. I know you didn't do anything wrong." His eyes darted in Billy's direction then came back to Cass. He raised his brows, but his usual smirk was absent. "Whatever you were doing."

Cass ignored his comment. "Look, was anything missing from the wagon?"

Drew shrugged. "One of the saddles was crushed. It's trash now, but most of it is salvageable."

"No, was anything *missing*? Not ruined, but gone."

Cass hadn't realized Cam had arrived until he spoke. "Yes, actually," he said. "Some people have reported some items missing from their tents, and one of Hank's people is missing a bike."

"Did you hear what I said about the line?" she asked.

"Cass, it happened. The line wasn't secure; it came down— whatever. We just need to find the horses, now."

"Cam," Cass said, trying to get him to meet her eyes. "I checked the line. You know me, I don't take sloppy chances."

Cam looked at her at last and then glanced at Billy. When his gaze returned to her, he frowned. "You haven't been sharing much with me, lately. I'm not sure what chances you're taking."

Cass's hurt at his doubt was replaced with anger at his censure.

How dare he assume things about her and Billy? And even if she was screwing him, what difference did it make? How could her brother claim not to know her?

Her voice shook as she said, "I'm not the only one who's been keeping things hidden."

She and her brother glared, locked in a painful contest, and just when Cass thought she might win, someone shouted.

It took a moment for her to realize the voice was calling for her and Cam. They exchanged a look and took off. There was a crowd gathered below the water tower, spilling out of the fence, but people made way for them. A dead body lay crumpled there, a pool of watered-down blood surrounding it. Cass couldn't see his face, but she understood that it was Marshall, the missing member of Clan Mason. Derrick was kneeling beside the body rubbing a hand on the back of his neck.

As they approached, Derrick looked up with pleading eyes.

"Do you think he fell? God, he couldn't have jumped, could he? He was one of my best."

Eight

THE MOOD AROUND CAMP was somber after the discovery of the body. Billy felt oddly numb to it, despite the fact he'd had no beef with Marshall. Marshall had been one of the few men in Derrick's inner circle who hadn't taken a turn "questioning" Billy when he'd been found.

He *was* shocked by Derrick's strong reaction. Marshall hadn't seemed a favorite.

Billy had stepped into the garage for a moment of peace and to retrieve his pack. He was just about to step back outside when he heard familiar voices outside the door and halted.

"There's a dead body to deal with, for God's sake." It was Cam, and he sounded worn and irritated. "I have more important things to do than babysit."

Cass's voice had taken on a pleading quality that Billy hadn't heard before. "He can help with the burial, then."

"Cass—"

"Cam, *what* is your problem? Where did this come from, anyway?"

"People said they saw him by the tents in the storm."

"His own tent. Cam, I was watching him. And where the hell would he hide a bicycle?" Cass threw her arms out to her sides. "Two days ago, you agreed to teach him to shoot. Now, you can't even keep an eye on him while I go look for the horses?"

"Two days ago he wasn't screwing my little sister."

Their voices came in a rush now as they talked over one another. Billy's heart pounded in his chest as he struggled to make out their words.

"We're not having sex, Cam!" The voices quieted for a moment before Cass continued. "I've been training him. That's all."

"You like him, though, Cass. I'm not blind. I just worry it's clouding your judgment. Mistakes are being made. One of those horses wasn't even ours."

"The horses were released, Cam. Why don't you believe me?"

"Who did it, then?"

Cass didn't answer, and there was the sound of feet scuffing the ground.

"I've got to go," Cass finally said. "People don't trust Billy all of a sudden and I think having him with me all the time is making it worse. Please, Cam. Just keep an eye on him while I'm gone."

Billy heard Cam sigh.

"Alright," he said. "I don't want you distracted, though. Be careful out there."

"What's the need?" Cass's voice had turned bitter. "If there's no possible way anyone could have snuck in while our guard slept that must mean there's no threat out there, right?"

There was a long pause before Cam said, "Where *is* Billy?"

"I'll send him before I leave," Cass said. "Oh look, here comes the mother of your child."

There was a pause and footsteps as Cass walked away. "You finally told her?" It was Trista.

"No," Cam said.

Billy waited until the couple left to exit the garage.

DREW WAS BARELY DOZING when he heard familiar footsteps approaching the tent. He leaned up on one arm and watched Cass's silhouette outside as she doused her lantern. When she crawled through the flap, she did a double take upon finding him awake.

"Hey," she whispered. "Sorry to wake you."

"Back late," Drew said. "How'd it go?"

Cass sighed as she settled into her sleeping bag. "No luck." She yawned. "How about you? Any luck with the wagon?"

"It's toast."

"Crap."

"Did you eat? There's meat."

Cass nodded. "Yeah. Who hunted?"

"Derrick. Went off by himself, which was the key to his success. He can hardly be around people without talking. When I went with them yesterday, it was ridiculous. More than half a dozen men laughing and crashing through the brush on horseback, then wondering where the game is."

Cass chuckled quietly. "I can't imagine why we don't eat like kings."

There was a stretch of silence in which Cass stared over to where Billy's tent was set up as if trying to spot his silhouette through the fabric and the darkness.

"Cass?" Drew said, his voice as soft as it could go.

"Yeah?"

"Do we tell each other everything?"

"You know we do."

"So there's nothing to tell? About Billy?"

After a pause, Cass's hand found Drew's between their sleeping bags and she gave it a squeeze. "You worried about me, too?"

"Shouldn't I be?" He squeezed her hand in return. "It's not the same as it was with Trace, is it?"

Cass pulled her hand away and moved it up to ruffle his hair. "I'm alright, Drew. Good night."

He heard it in her tone, though. Billy wasn't the same. Never had he wanted to protect her more and never had he been less able to do so. He told his best friend in the world "good night" and fell into a troubled sleep beside her.

THE SECOND DAY OF searching for the missing horses found Cass and Cam riding side by side in silence. Finally, they spotted a familiar, if mud-covered mare. The quiet tension was replaced by a familiar pattern of cooperation as they recaptured the horse. The mare was spooked from a day and a half on her own, and it was no easy task.

They were finally successful, and as Cass remounted and dallied the mare's lead around her saddle horn, she met Cam's eyes and grinned. He grinned back. As they looked at one another, their smiles faded, and finally Cam cleared his throat.

"Let's get back," he said. "We'll call this a victory. We can't spend any more time here."

They headed back toward the orchard in a strange state—feeling close due to their recent teamwork and also unwilling to forgive one another. Cass's seething anger finally got the better of her. She rolled her shoulder, straightened in the saddle and broke the silence.

"You know it's none of your business who I sleep with, right?" she said.

"Not now, Cass."

"Dammit, Cameron, don't put me off," she kept her voice controlled and pressed her heels downward to remind herself to keep her legs quiet so as not to upset her mount.

"I care about you, Cassidy, and that makes it my business. You're not Marie, or Rylynn, or any of them. You don't have to—"

"Jesus, Cameron, you know it's not the same thing. I've had three partners in twenty-eight years. And no one holds a gun to their heads, either, you know. Their bodies are their own. Who says they don't like their choices?"

"Yeah, well. Sex shouldn't be just for fun—"

Cass twisted in her saddle, her face hot with anger. "I don't need you to tell me what's what! Nothing's 'just for fun,' I know that. There are reasons for everything—"

"There was a reason for you and Trace, then? Besides making me crazy?"

Cass let out a growl and faced forward again. She took a deep breath. "Cam, Trace and I needed each other, then. No, I didn't love him, and he didn't love me, but shit. At least he didn't get me pregnant."

She heard a gush of breath from Cam and turned to see him shake his head and run his free hand across his face.

"I'm sorry I didn't tell you," he said. "I knew you'd be upset."

"I see Waylon," she said. "I see the way he looks at his daughters, and I know what a risk it is to love like that. I worry about Trista. I worry about all that could go wrong, and I worry what it would do to you."

"*I* worry about *you*, Cass. About being with men—with your history." Cass shuddered and glared at him. But, Cam pressed on. "I just don't want you to choose carelessly because there are consequences. More for you than most."

"Your concern is noted." Cass held up a hand, sticking out her fingers with each sentence, ticking off her points. "But, my issues are mine to deal with. My body is mine to worry about. I'm not having sex with Billy. I'm not *sorry* for having sex with Trace. And Cam," she dropped her hand, "this is a man's life we're talking about here. If you shut Billy out, everyone else will, too. It's his *life*, Cam. And maybe mine."

She turned away from a fresh intensity in Cam's expression. They rode in silence for a minute.

"So you're not sleeping with Billy?"

"What did I say, Cam?"

"Do you want him?"

She shot him a glare that made him lift his hands in surrender.

"Alright," he said. "Let's get back, little sister."

BILLY'S EYES SHUT REFLEXIVELY as the gun fired in his grip. He opened them to check his target. The can he'd aimed for was gone from the row that remained.

"Better," Drew said.

The two men were lying side by side on their stomachs facing a hill. The sun was high in the sky and sounds of talking could be heard from the direction their feet pointed. It had been two days since the storm and Marshall's death. Unable to repair the broken wagon, Drew had agreed to pass the time teaching Billy to shoot. Cass and Cam had gone to try to replace damaged supplies and look for the horses, again.

The search party from the first day had had no success. But, overnight, Cowboy had wandered back into camp. When Cass had found him grazing with the others, she'd said more to the horse than she'd said to Billy in two days.

Billy took a breath, cocked the rifle, and aimed for the next can in the line. *Squeeze*, he reminded himself, *don't pull.*

He heard the shot and then the plunk as the can fell. That was the first time he'd gotten two in a row.

"You *are* a quick learner."

Billy turned his head to the side and met Drew's gaze.

"Cass said that," Drew said, frowning. "We need to talk about her."

Billy's heart sank. He knew it. There was no way there was nothing between Drew and Cass. How could anyone share a tent and be so connected and not have a history?

"Let's talk, then," he said, laying the rifle down in the grass beside him and leaning up on one elbow.

Drew turned back to his target and fired off a shot. It was a miss.

"I love her, you know," he said. Billy's limbs were heavy, a slight ringing in his ears telling of the increased adrenaline in his system. He swallowed and kept his gaze steady on the side of Drew's face, trying to remind himself he'd done nothing wrong. Cass had said there was nothing between them. Besides, Drew wasn't speaking like an angry rival.

Drew took aim and fired again. Billy didn't have to look to know he'd taken down the final can.

"She trusts you. A lot," Drew said, rolling slightly to the side and making eye contact.

"I'm not so sure of that," Billy said. "Does she really trust anyone?"

"She slept beside you the other night," Drew said. "It's not my place to tell you why that's big, but it's big. Take my word for it."

"So what are you asking me?"

"I'm telling you," Drew said, and he leaned forward a bit to emphasize his words, "that I've decided to trust you, too."

Billy's shock must have been evident on his face because Drew leaned back and cracked a smile. "You're not public enemy number one. It just feels that way."

Billy was struggling to find a meaningful reply when a horse neighed loudly nearby. He and Drew looked up to see Cass and Cam riding into camp, leading another horse on a bright, new lead rope. The lead rope seemed especially clean considering the mud-caked condition of the horse.

Drew stood up and sorted through the cans, replacing a few that could still be set upright. Billy alternated between watching him and watching Cass as she dismounted and spoke with her brother. They were smiling, and Cam lightly punched her shoulder. They must have reconciled on their journey.

Drew cleared his throat, bringing Billy's attention back.

"Back to work," he said. "I want all these cans down by the time I get back." There was amusement in his expression that belied the gruff lecture in his tone. He left, and Billy picked up the rifle again. The weight of it in his hands was becoming more familiar. He glanced back at Cass. Drew had reached her and was listening to what she said with a frown.

He forced himself to turn away and focus. He'd fired off several more shots with some success when he heard footsteps approach. Assuming Drew was back, he continued to shoot, pleased when the bullet clanked off a can and sent it spinning away.

"Nice." The voice behind him was not Drew's, but Cam's.

Billy was still for a moment before he twisted his torso around. "I imagine it's harder to hit a moving target."

"And harder still to hit *any* target when you're riding," said Cam. "Still, you're learning quicker than I did."

"You were younger, though. You and Cass? You were kids when you learned, right?"

"That means it's harder for you. Kids are sponges," Cam said. He paused, sniffed, and added, "And I learned a long time before Cass did. I said you were learning quicker than me, not her. She learned fast."

Billy said nothing, but let his questions surface in his expression. The other man stared down at him for a moment before picking up the rifle Drew had left and aiming.

"Our dad," Cam said, firing his first shot, "didn't believe in women learning things like shooting." After a pause and another shot he added, "Probably because it'd be harder to beat and insult a woman who was armed."

Billy's throat seemed to swell, which was fine because he didn't know how to respond, anyway. Cam hit another can.

"Cass didn't learn to shoot until we moved in with my uncle," said Cam. "She was better than me right away. She's the best shot in our group." Cam lowered the rifle to his side. "Probably the best in all three." He smiled. For just a moment he looked chuffed to bits to be Cass's big brother. But, the pride deflated quickly.

Billy turned back to the cans to find they'd all been cleared away. He climbed to his feet and handed his gun to Cam, who seemed to be waiting for it.

"Enough wasted ammo for now. Go give her a hand with that horse," Cam said. As Billy turned away, Cam spoke again. "It's nobody's business. How much time you spend together or how you spend it."

Billy nodded over his shoulder, feeling stronger and fully welcome for the first time.

CASS WATCHED TRISTA SQUEEZE the rag out over the horse's body again. The slender woman stepped back to avoid the stream of brown water pouring down the horse's side, and Cass could see the bump forming low on her abdomen. Trista caught her looking and flushed, her eyes uncertain.

"I should have told you congratulations," Cass said.

Trista continued rinsing mud from the horse. "You don't have to say what you don't feel. Not to me."

Cass scrubbed at the horse's hip with her brush, trying to work away her guilt with elbow grease. "Congratulations."

Trista looked up again, eyes narrowed as she read Cass's expression. Cass hoped she looked sincere. She *was* happy for the woman; more worried than happy, maybe, but happy just the same.

"Thank you," Trista said, her smile genuine and seeming to turn inward as she glanced down at her stomach. Cass had moved to the other side of the horse, and she was surprised when Trista spoke again. "I know you don't think it's a smart idea. We didn't plan it—"

"Trista," Cass was shaking her head as she cut the woman off. "I worry. It's what I do. But, I'm glad if you're glad." After a pause, Cass thought to ask, "How are you feeling? Still sick?"

Trista shook her head. "That's over. Doc heard the heartbeat the other day, and Katie's been sharing her prenatal vitamins with me. They're expired but who knows? Maybe they still help."

"Good."

"I'm sorry we didn't tell you," Trista said.

"I get it. No worries." Cass's eyes widened as Trista's dirty hand covered her own over the horse's withers.

"You're going to be an aunt," Trista said, her eyes alight. For a moment, Cass felt a warmth in her chest, a thrill of affection for this woman and the unborn child she carried. Cass managed a nod, but Trista wasn't watching. Following Trista's gaze, she turned to look over her shoulder and saw Billy, approaching hesitantly.

"Oh, good," Trista said, laying the rag across the horse's back and shaking her hands off. "He can help with the dirty job."

"Fishing isn't much cleaner," Cass said, knowing where Trista would head for the afternoon.

The woman chuckled as she walked away.

Cass could feel Billy's approach more than she heard it. She'd missed him the last day and a half. She wasn't sure what to do with that emotion. She grabbed the dirty rag off the horse's back and flung it at him. It smacked him in the chest with a sloppy sound, and he caught it as it fell, half-smiling.

"She won't clean herself," she said. Billy stepped forward and dipped the rag in the water bucket before beginning to scrub at dirt clods on the same side Cass was working. Something about it felt very intimate. She watched the water drip down over Billy's bare forearms and the air around them electrified.

The spark fizzled as Cass noticed a rough, oval-shaped scar on Billy's right arm. She hadn't noticed that before.

"Only got two of the horses back?" he asked.

Cass blinked and nodded. "I'd worry more if I actually thought they were missing. But, I think they're being cared for."

Billy nodded, and she could tell he agreed with her. Maybe he felt he had to agree with her.

"Sorry I ditched you," she said. "It was for—"

"I missed you," Billy said, cutting her off and causing her chest to flood with emotion.

Cass moved to the horse's head and worked her way around to the opposite side, looking the animal over. She struggled to keep her eyes off Billy and her mind off what he'd said. It took her a few moments to feel she could manage a normal voice.

"Well, she looks uninjured, besides a few scratches. She ran her finger along a strip of reddened skin that was missing hair and then passed behind Billy, giving him a wide berth.

"Let's hobble her with the others and start packing," she said. "We leave tomorrow." Billy nodded and followed with the bucket as she led the horse.

There was no indication of awkwardness between them for the rest of the day. Billy never left her side but helped her repack things to fit into one less wagon. She never thought of sending him away, even when Adam passed by them with a dark stare. Billy didn't seem to notice, and so the awkwardness was kept at bay until after dinner when they walked back to their tents together.

Cass was conscious of glances from other people making their ways to bed. Some had moved their sleeping bags into the garage after the storm, but she and Drew, Billy, and several others remained outside. She got the feeling Billy wanted to say something, so she slowed her steps, waiting. At her tent, she stopped and looked up. Swallowing back the fluttery feeling in her gut, she chose to examine his eye. The bruise from two days ago was faded, and just a scratch remained on his cheekbone.

"That tree left its mark on you." She smiled and pointed to his face. Then she caught her breath and held it as Billy reached out and stroked his knuckles across her cheekbone.

"Yours is faded," he said. It took Cass a few heart-pounding seconds of his fingers against her skin to remember she'd scratched her face when Huck had died. There must still be a line there. She didn't often check her reflection.

Billy's long fingers swept back to tuck a few strands of her hair behind her ear, and then he stepped away. "Yours is faded, but we're alike, aren't we?"

He moved to his tent and crawled into it without looking back.

THEIR PROGRESS WAS SLOW for the next two days. Billy and Cass had offered up their mounts to others since the group was now down two horses, a bike, and a wagon. They could no longer train without falling too far behind.

Billy took the opportunity to look at her from the corner of his eye as they moved. She was frowning again and rubbing her shoulder. She seemed out of place without a horse.

Turning to look at him, she offered a tight smile.

"You still seem familiar to me sometimes," she said.

Billy's stomach lurched and he forced a laugh, "Well, aren't I familiar? We've known one another for a while, now."

Cass nodded. "True."

Guilt left a sour taste in his mouth as he plodded onward. Lena was mounted on Cowboy, and occasionally she tossed a glance at them over her shoulder. He caught her look, now. More like a glare, really. He'd seen Cass try to speak to the younger girl once or twice, but Lena's hostility hadn't yet faded.

Cass seemed more troubled than before, and for a moment he contemplated confessing if only to ease some of her strain. He could remove this one worry from her plate.

She sidled closer, her eyes distant. "I feel like I'm ignoring my instincts."

He paused mid-step. Did she mean about him? "How so?"

"About the stuff stolen from camp. About Marshall's death. About continuing on like nothing happened."

"You think whoever took it had something to do with Marshall's death?"

Cass shrugged. "Seems like quite a coincidence if not."

She seemed content to let the subject drop but Billy found himself asking, "What do your instincts tell you about me?"

She opened her mouth to speak once, twice. Then she stopped and reached out a hand to stop him, too. He looked up and realized he'd almost walked into the back of the wagon, which had halted.

Cass moved forward and helped Katie climb down to relieve herself. Their conversation was suspended, so Billy moved into the shade of some trees beside the road, leaning against a rusted sign advertising a motel. When Cass had helped Katie into the wagon again, he stepped back over and began to follow the lagging end of the caravan.

"Uh, wait," Cass said, reaching out for his arm without making contact. Her eyes flicked up to his as if asking permission as she plucked a small bug off his arm, touching him as little as possible. She dropped a small brown creature into her palm.

"A tick," she said. Billy leaned forward to examine it. "Ever seen one before?"

Billy shook his head. "Pictures." He shrugged and gave her a grin. "City boy."

She pinched the creature between her fingers and flicked it away. "Stronghold might be just your speed." Her voice teased, flirted even.

Billy remained close to her, conscious of the growing separation between the wagon and the two of them. Cass's gaze fell to his forearms, which were crossed over his chest. He sucked in a breath as she reached out her index finger and slowly traced the red scar of a burn on his right arm.

"What happened here?" she asked.

His face paled, and he rubbed the other hand across the mark as if to erase it. "Uh, it's a burn. Not a big deal." He took a step back and watched Cass's face fall. He pushed away the churn of guilt in his gut. After all, she wasn't too keen on sharing the details of her own scars.

Billy shook his head and ran his hands through his hair.

"Feel something crawling?" Cass asked. She wasn't looking at him, but staring after the caravan, her expression grown as distant as her gaze.

He stopped pawing through his hair. "Maybe."

Her gaze returned for a moment, brushing across the blonde curls on his head. Her expression changed to one that might have been longing, and she took half a step toward him, as if about to offer to check for ticks herself.

Then, the thought was gone, and she turned toward the caravan.

"You'd better check for more, then," she said, walking away from him with decisive strides.

Billy didn't expect to find any ticks, but he ran his fingers halfheartedly over his scalp, giving himself a minute. He hadn't thought of an excuse for the burn marks. In addition to the one on his arm, where the sensation of Cass's touch lingered, there were similar burns on his side and bum.

He could tell the truth. He could look Cass in the eye and tell her the woman who'd held him captive was jealous of the memories the tattoos represented, and she'd burned them off in two separate nights of agonizing torture. He knew Cass wouldn't push further.

But what if learning they'd been tattoos helped spark her memory? What if she realized who he was? She must be close to it. He kept catching her singing that song deep in her throat as her lips barely moved. That scar on her lip—it was so bloody distracting. Everything about her was distracting.

He took a deep breath and jogged after her.

He'd only just managed to catch up when the group stopped for lunch outside a little commuter town with dead cars blocking almost all the roads. Some of the faster eaters volunteered to check out a few cars and businesses on the near side of the town, looking for supplies.

Cass glanced his direction but didn't invite him to follow her. Instead, she fell into stride beside Doc. Billy watched the two of them enter a pharmacy. They exited within a few minutes, both looking disappointed. Doc gestured to the cars and Cass nodded. They spoke for another moment and then split up, Cass crossing to the store next door to the pharmacy as Doc began to search trunks and glove boxes.

Cass stopped in the parking lot of a pet shop, staring at the sign. Unable to bear watching her anymore, Billy stood and jogged through the ditch to join her. He knew she heard him crashing through the long grass and then, his boots slapping the pavement, but she didn't say anything.

Birds were nesting in the cracked neon sign, which he found

amusing, and the door hung at an angle still half-attached to its frame.

Cass put her hands on her hips and sighed. "I have to go in there."

"Okay?"

"I don't want to go in there."

"Why not?"

She glanced at him out of the corner of her eye. "Dead bodies."

"Oh." He'd seen what it could look like when no one had come to clear the dead away from a place. He glanced back at the pet shop window, and the posters advertising cat food and a sale on goldfinches seemed more ominous than before.

"On the one hand," Cass said. "There aren't any bodies in the cars. But it's not only humans that might be dead in there."

What happened to all the animals in a place like this when The End came and humans just—stopped coming?

"Maybe someone took them away," he said. Cass raised an eyebrow, but he met her skepticism head on. "They may have. Someone got rid of the human bodies. Why not the animals, too?"

He saw a light flicker in her eyes. She gave a nod and turned toward the door. Suddenly, he didn't want her to go in. He didn't want to watch that little light dim if he was wrong.

"I'll go in," he said, causing Cass to halt mid-step. He reached out and touched her arm. "What do you need?"

"I can be a big girl," she said. "I've seen plenty of gore, Billy."

"I know that," he said, now trailing his hand down her arm to her hand. He softly tugged it back toward him. He could almost swear he felt her shiver. His chest tightened, and he released her, balling his hand into a fist as it fell to his side. "I know you're tougher than me, but *I* didn't just lose a friend."

She must not have expected his words, though clearly, she'd been thinking about Huck. She looked away.

"Let me go," he said.

"Come with me." This time, she turned to face him, her eyes glistening with dampness.

He nodded and the two of them approached the store. He took shallow breaths as they came to the broken door, half expecting to be assaulted by the stench of rotted animals. Cass gave the door a solid kick and it broke free and clattered to the ground. They stepped across it and looked around.

Cass made a noise of surprise and Billy grinned. There were no animals here. Spots where tanks and cages had once lined shelves were bare and layered in dust. Tall metal shelving on the back wall stood empty under signage advertising brands of dog food. The place had the dusty, distant smell of an empty building.

Cass turned to him, mouth half open, head shaking. "I'll be damned. You were right."

"I was. Thank God."

Cass laughed. "The place is so empty; I don't know if I'll be able to find what I'm looking for. She walked down an aisle, chuckling and flicking a tiny bell hung from a mirror that would've decorated a birdcage. Many of the toys remained.

Billy followed as she walked up the next aisle with greater speed. She stopped in front of a display of dog collars and Billy instantly knew why she'd come. She picked out a leather collar and held it up.

"For Brick," she said, smiling.

For Drew, Billy thought with a rush of jealousy. Catching his shadowed expression, Cass shrugged.

"I know it's frivolous."

Billy shook his head and forced a smile. "No. It keeps up morale." He looked around and found a tugging rope and a squeaky tennis ball. He squeezed the ball, making a face as it sounded. Cass laughed, and he tossed the ball to her. Encouraged, he made a show of wrapping the rope around his neck and pretended to hang himself.

He was rewarded by another laugh as she snatched the rope away. They gathered a few more small toys and headed out. They helped pack up a few new supplies in the wagons and started off once more in their position at the back of the group.

He continued his clowning, beginning to feel like his old self again; his "Before" self.

Lena turned to stare at them, and Cass stifled her laughter behind her hand. He watched her little finger brush across the scar on her lower lip and knew he'd be a clown for her forever if she wanted. He'd be anything for her.

A COLICKING HORSE KEPT Cass up that night, and Billy found it impossible to leave her side. On foot again the following day, Billy was too knackered to do much more than walk. He wasn't very adept at that either as he once again almost ran into the back of the wagon when the whole caravan abruptly stopped. Conrad pushed his horse forward, heading for the front of the group probably to answer the question Cass now asked.

"Why are we stopping?" She stepped out around the wagon and horses for a better view. She stood on tiptoe for a moment, her hair band falling loose as she bounced back down to her normal height. She retrieved the band but left her hair down. Billy smiled. She'd cut it that morning by lobbing off part of her mocha brown ponytail. He slipped a hand into his pocket, fingering the blue bandanna there. He thought of returning it.

Conrad trotted back up to the wagon. "We're stopping for the day," he said. "I guess Derrick knows this place."

Cass groaned and muttered, "It's barely afternoon."

The next couple of hours were a blur. They were staying at what seemed to be a guest mansion; a historic place people used to rent out for weddings or retirement parties Before. Now, obscene graffiti covered the statues lining the front drive, and all the windows and doors of the once-gorgeous house were busted. The top floor seemed to be partially collapsed. Still, everyone worked quickly to set up for the night, eager to get into the old building to explore.

The three group leaders gave a speech at the top of the stairs to the house, thanking everyone for working together to recover from the losses after the storm. They said a few words in remembrance of Marshall, something no one seemed to have remembered to do yet. They encouraged everyone to explore and kick back for the rest of the evening.

It was clear Cass didn't want to kick back. Billy knew she would have preferred to cover more ground today. She looked ready to charge at Cam and give him a piece of her mind when Drew arrived.

"Let's go check out the house," Drew said. He slung an arm around Cass and steered her into the crowd filing up the stairs. Billy was separated from them by a man and woman with linked arms who darted across his path, eager to get inside.

When he reached the foyer, he stepped carefully, avoiding takeaway containers and broken limbs that had blown in onto the cracked tile floors. A chandelier dangled above his head, askew and destined to fall in the near future. He hoped it wouldn't be on anyone's head, though the way people were pounding up the stairs to the upper levels, howling as they went, he thought it might happen soon.

He heard the sound of music and his head whipped around. A once-beautiful grand piano stood off to the left, and a couple of older women were testing the keys. Some of them seemed to be missing as was the piano's lid. People gathered around to peer in at the strings. With a shudder, Billy looked away, searching for Cass.

He spotted her through a large doorway to the right in what must have been a banquet room. A few scattered tables and chairs remained on the outskirts of what appeared to be a wooden dance floor with a layer of dust over it. Some people had taken to dancing around the open area, weaving in and out of the beams of light streaming through broken windows. Drew was trying his best to entice Cass to dance with him, and Billy's jaw tensed in a moment of jealousy he quickly dismissed. He wondered once again whose decision it was that they weren't together.

The room was filling with rising dust as the dancers kicked it up and Cass coughed and laughed. She grabbed a coughing Drew by the shirt and dragged him through a door halfway down the room. She paused, spotting Billy, and called out to him.

A minute behind them, he almost collided with Derrick. Up close, he was reminded how much height the man had on him. He was leaving the room Cass and Drew had just entered with Adam in tow, ever the faithful dog.

"Nothing for you in there, basement boy," Adam said as the two of them surged past. Billy gritted his teeth but said nothing as he stepped inside. It was a kitchen, and much more light was streaming in through a broken skylight overhead. Drew was leaning against the counter, watching Billy as he entered. Cass was gazing out the window hugging herself, stiff as a board.

"They even took the cupboard doors and drawers," Drew said indicating the gaping cupboards lining the room. Billy's gaze came to rest on a wall with a peculiar-looking coat of arms on it. He stepped closer and found it was made of corks from wine bottles.

"Is anyone even on watch?" Cass said as much to the shattered window as to either of them. "Let's just forget to protect ourselves why don't we?"

"Derrick said he and Adam were going to secure the perimeter," Drew replied, his tone skeptical.

"They also said they were searching for knives. Like there's anything of value left in here," Cass said.

"Maybe they were after more instant coffee," Drew said. He

laughed. "Lighten up, Cass." He spun to face her and must have been making faces because her expression softened. Billy wandered closer, just as Drew pointed at a spot on the floor.

Someone had kicked aside a broken piece of countertop, exposing a tile different from the rest. It was the same color but featured a design of grapes.

"Oh, uh-uh. They couldn't have missed it." Drew descended on the tile as he spoke, brushing away dirt with his hands.

Cass said "who?" at the same time Billy said "missed what?" but Drew didn't care to answer either of them. Instead, he found a metal loop in the tile and pulled it upward. A door lifted up from the floor to reveal a wooden staircase spiraling down into darkness. Past the dust motes, Billy could see dozens of dark-colored circles as the light glinted off them.

"Is that a wine cellar?" he asked.

"Hell yeah," Drew said. "We need a light."

Cass darted outside for a lantern while Drew began to lower himself down the stairs, feeling his way through the dark. Billy looked up at Cass jogging in through a different door just as a thud sounded from below.

"Damn," Drew said.

"You couldn't have waited two minutes?" Cass asked as she lit the lantern. "You okay?"

"Bottom step broke," Drew called up. "Watch it when you come down..."

Cass held the lantern over the door. It was indeed a walk-in wine cellar, and it was still fully stocked.

"Jesus," Cass said.

Billy's mouth watered at the prospect of tasting wine again.

Cass descended the stairs, the room lighting more with each step. Billy moved to follow. He paused halfway down as the murky, damp smell assaulted his nostrils. It smelled just like the basement.

Then, the staircase was swirling beneath him, and his breathing was too shallow to afford him any oxygen. He spun and flew back up the stairs, heedless of Cass calling for him. He tripped over debris as he raced through the kitchen and out the door Cass had used when she went for the lamp. He stumbled down the stairs and went to his knees on the grass.

A breeze revived him and pulled him from his dark memories. He rested there on his hands and knees, breathing in the fresh, open air and blinking up into the sunlight. He was free. No bars. No ropes. He was free.

But, he wasn't really. "Basement Boy" Adam had called him. "Actor," "prisoner," "responsibility." So many names were haunting him. Lives were haunting him. What had he survived for if his life was to be about fear? And not even the healthy fear of danger, but a fear of the past.

He pushed himself to his feet and walked back up the stairs and into the kitchen at a steady pace. He paused by the cellar door and glanced down to see Cass halfway up the stairs. She stopped and tilted her head, her searching eyes appraising him, understanding him. When he put a foot on the first stair, she backed down herself and struck up a conversation with Drew, half-turning away from him.

He shut his eyes and focused on his breathing, listening as Cass and Drew talked. Their calm voices echoed around the space, making it entirely different from the barked orders and sickening whispers that had been the soundtrack of his captivity. He opened his eyes, focused on Cass's silhouette in the lantern light, and made his way downward. Step by step he descended until he reached the broken step and jumped past it.

He held on to the railing for a moment. Drew was working on a wine bottle with the corkscrew of a Swiss army knife.

Drew caught Billy's gaze and grinned, "I never thought I'd use this part of it." Then, turning to Cass, he said, "Do we have to share with everyone?"

"Selfish much?" Cass said just as the bottle opened with a pop. Drew lifted it to his lips and took a swig. He groaned.

"Oh, yeah," he said and took another drink. He passed the bottle to Cass, who handed it on to Billy without drinking. Billy lifted it to his lips. It was a shock. It was such a strong and wild taste after all these years of being lucky to get clean water. He drank again and could already feel the heat of it traveling down to his gut.

He passed the bottle back to Drew and watched Cass as she circled the small room, running her hands across the bottles. There was mold on the walls and the wine racks, and some of the labels were damaged. But there wasn't much dust. Still, she brushed her hands on her jeans as she came back to the stairs. She climbed a few and sat, now eye level with Billy.

Their eyes met, and he felt very much alone with her. He waited for the tightening in his chest, the panic. But, the taste of wine in his mouth, his muscles tired from travel—it was all so different. Cass's eyes didn't make him think of bars or ropes. They called up visions of shade trees and grass fields to run through. The panic didn't rise.

Drew shoved the bottle at Billy again, and he drank, never taking his eyes from Cass's. She flushed and turned to Drew.

"Maybe we shouldn't tell them," she said, glancing back up the stairs and then down at the lantern on the step beside her. "I'm not sure we all need to be drunk."

"Not all of us, but definitely you," Drew said swiping the bottle away from Billy and drinking again. Then, he held it out to Cass.

She shook her head. "I can't," she said. "I might need to take watch tonight. Plus, we're not staying, I can't be hung over tomorrow."

Drew advanced on her and tipped the bottle quickly up, pressing it to her mouth. She gasped and grabbed the bottle away, swallowing a mouthful of wine. She glared at Drew, but he had left, chuckling. He circled the room again, pulling out a bottle here and there to read the label.

Cass wiped the red liquid from her chin and brushed her hand along her neck where the excess had run down into her shirt. Billy's eyes traced the path to where it disappeared and then flicked back up to her face. She was reading the wine label, licking her lips.

"That's actually really good," she said as she drank again. She passed it to him and he drank deeply, already feeling his shoulders releasing their tension. He saw her look at him; at his lips, his hand as she took the bottle. Their fingers brushed, and their eyes met again.

She lifted the bottle, and he watched her neck move as she swallowed the last. A few drops ran down her bottom lip, and Billy found himself grabbing her free hand as she moved to wipe her mouth. He hadn't even known he was close enough. Then, before he really understood his plan he closed the distance between them, leaning against her knees where they jutted out from the steps and covering her mouth with his own.

The wine bottle dropped down the stairs and spun on the concrete as he let his tongue trace her bottom lip, capturing the wine and lingering over the raised flesh of her scar. Then he ran it over her top lip, increasing the pressure. He closed his mouth, caressing, and just as he was about to pull away, she responded, moving her lips against his. He felt her tongue flick against him as he pulled back, every nerve in his body crackling. He let out a shuddering breath and saw she was gripping the railing on the stairs with both hands.

Her eyes widened, and she glanced at Drew. Billy had all but forgotten the other man was there. Drew appeared intensely interested in the label of the wine bottle he held, but he wasn't managing to hide his grin.

Cass cleared her throat and said, "Bring up a couple of bottles. I'll go tell Cam what we found."

Her boots clattered as she tore up the stairs, her legs just flashes of denim in the light of the jolting lantern. Billy stood with his hands at his sides, staring after her.

"That was ballsy," Drew said as he passed by, arms laden with bottles. "Hot, though. Too bad you're straight." Drew disappeared up into the kitchen, and Billy shook his head. *Oh*, he thought. *That's why they're not a couple.*

All thought of Drew fled as he remembered something more important. She'd kissed him back.

Nine

LENA'S HAND CLAMPED FIRMLY around the neck of a wine bottle. She lowered it to her side and walked swiftly away from the table heavy-laden with others. She'd go to Katie's tent to drink it. The other woman may not approve, but she wouldn't rat Lena out.

A few feet ahead, Adam stumbled into her path, chatting with one of the women from the California band. He reached out a clumsy hand and rubbed it down the woman's arm.

"No, seriously," he said, his voice overloud. "I once saw a cat that rode along on the back of the saddle. Rode everywhere like that."

Lena dodged, the rest of their conversation lost in the noise of the crowd as she picked her way through the people. She came up to the row of tents, glancing over toward where her father was standing watch. There were *two* figures there in the lamplight. Marie had joined him. Lena's frown was deep across her forehead as she paused to call out to Katie before ducking into the tent.

"Baby kicking tonight?" Lena asked.

Katie let out a good-natured groan. "Yes. It's fine, though. Not like I'd get much sleep with all the fun going on out there. I only wish I could have some my—" Katie caught sight of the wine bottle as she looked up from the strands of horsehair strung across her lap. She raised an eyebrow.

Lena averted her eyes for a moment and then straightened her shoulders as she set about opening the bottle. "It's not like I'm going to get a MIP, you know. Or a DUI."

Katie pursed her lips and then nodded. She looked back down at her work, her fingers pinching the horsehair as she crossed it over itself in the complicated braid.

"Just don't drink too much," she said. "You'll regret it tomorrow. Believe me."

"I'll take it slow." Lena looked around. Her father had a Swiss army knife with a corkscrew, but she couldn't very well ask for it. Her focus landed on Katie's hands and she watched for a moment. "You didn't have to do a design that complicated, you know. A simple braid would've been fine."

Katie smiled. "I like doing this. Besides, Cass is a rough and tumble, 'gal. She's probably pretty hard on jewelry. It needs to be strong just like she is."

Lena raised an eyebrow and her desire for a drink increased. "I don't suppose you have a corkscrew lying around." When Katie looked up, Lena lifted the wine bottle with the cork now exposed.

Katie gave a half-smile, her eyes distant. "Come trade me," she said.

Lena crawled over and took the ends of the horsehair, pulling them taut but looking down at the jewelry as if it were a snake. Katie picked up the wine bottle and fished a knife from her backpack. She stuck the tip of the knife carefully between the cork and the bottle and began twisting with a practiced rotation of her wrist. Soon the cork popped free, and she laughed.

"Not your first time doing that," Lena stated.

"No, but probably the last." She smiled at the younger woman as they maneuvered around her large belly to trade the wine bottle for the strands of horsehair. "Unless there happens to be a vineyard up and running still somewhere."

Lena ran her fingers through the loose end of Huckleberry's tail-hair and sighed. It'd be the last time she was able to do that; Katie was almost finished. She tipped the bottle to her lips, took in a swig of the liquid and made a face. The loss of such a foul-tasting beverage was hardly a tragedy. All the same, she raised the bottle to her lips a second time.

DERRICK WATCHED AS MARIE straddled Waylon, kissing him and slipping her hands into his shirt. Waylon's knee bumped the wine bottles beside them, and they clanked together, falling to the ground along with the humans. He smiled and started quietly down the row of tents, knowing by the time he passed near the two of them, they would be too involved to notice him.

To his surprise, Cass had been flushed with drink already when she'd emerged from the wine cellar earlier. Drew and Billy had followed, carrying several bottles of wine in their arms. Derrick's joy had been lost amid the excitement of the group at large, though his was for a very different reason.

Discovering the cellar had seemed to overshadow any suspicions Cass may have had at finding him and Adam in the kitchen. He'd barely had time to pocket the note he'd been looking for; a map to a meeting point.

The wine had also presented an opportunity. As expected, the ever-wary Cass had insisted on setting a watchman, and when Waylon had volunteered, she'd been satisfied. So had Derrick.

He'd seen the middle-aged man, burdened most nights by chaperoning his teenage daughters, sneaking glances at Marie. It was easy enough to suggest she seek him out for a drink and more.

With the watchman occupied and everyone else busy getting drunk, no one paid him any mind. He'd had the foresight to wrap the wine bottles resting in his pack in a couple of T-shirts, to reduce noise. It was no challenge at all to sneak out of camp and into the woods.

When he'd been walking for about half a mile on an overgrown trail, he came to a clearing with a gazebo, or what was left of it, in the center. A tree had grown up through the washed-out boards, and the weather had all but destroyed the roof.

Gathered around the gazebo were four men, two of whom carried lanterns while the others were armed. He didn't raise his arms or slow his pace despite the guns aimed at him. As he approached, the weapons lowered and the nearest man, John, called out a greeting.

"Took you long enough."

"Would you rather I rushed and got caught?" Derrick asked, keeping his voice calm.

"How are they reacting? Does anyone suspect?" As Derrick listened, the gray cat he'd met around the same time he'd met John strolled up and began to rub itself against his leg.

"One. A woman. Cass." He looked down at the cat in displeasure.

"Only her?"

"Yes, but she's the second of the Montana band. And smart."

"I've seen her," said another man, one of Stronghold's recruiters. "With the prisoner."

When Stronghold recruiters traveled to find new members they went in groups of three. Unfortunately, two of the men they'd sent west were secretly loyal to a rebel cause. They had, of course, eliminated the third man. They had also had a secret travel companion. A leader of the rebel cause; John.

John had stayed behind the scenes, not visiting the bands of survivors, but waiting to reveal himself to the right partner for their plan—partner they had found in Derrick.

"Yes," Derrick said, nodding.

"They seem close. How'd you let that happen?" John asked. Derrick kicked the cat away from his legs, and it let out a yowl of complaint. He stepped forward.

"It's actually helping. It discredits her. Even in her brother's eyes." Derrick said, willing down the surge of anger he felt at being doubted. They'd have nothing if it weren't for him, after all. He imagined his fists pounding into the man, slamming his head against the broken boards of the gazebo. He pushed the image away.

"Well, if you want to keep them around, I suggest you get them out of the back of your caravan tomorrow."

Derrick stiffened. "Why?"

John paused and strode a few steps closer before answering. A bead of sweat lined the man's forehead. He wasn't as cool as he seemed. Still, his voice came out firm.

"Do you have any attachment to anyone in the back wagon? Your dead weight?"

Derrick set his jaw. "No."

"We need to speed you up."

"It's your fault we're behind schedule in the first place," Derrick said, his voice more a growl than he'd hoped. He cursed himself before moving on. "You're the reason we were delayed and the reason we're short horses."

"And we'll be the reason you pick up speed," John said. "You have to slow down and stop too often for that wagon."

An image of Katie, her swollen belly jutting out beneath her shirt, flashed into his mind. He saw her laughing in the wagon with the elderly couple. For a moment, her face was replaced by Abby's.

But, it was for Abby—for her memory—that he needed this alliance. So he could prevent it from happening again.

He could protect these people, now. Or protect many more later.

"You've seen their guards?" Derrick asked.

"One man and the redheaded girl. *If* you manage to get the prisoner and this Cass away."

"I'll manage," Derrick said, adrenaline charging through him now that he'd decided how to proceed. His head was starting to ache in time with his heartbeat as if he'd had too much wine, though he'd had none. "So long as this doesn't change our arrangement."

"Why would it?"

"You agreed to give me leadership of New Danville if I brought you women, supplies, horses, and loyal fli—" he cleared his throat, "fighters. And if I kept your secret. Now, you've taken horses and supplies, and you're about to take people. Not to mention I was forced to eliminate Marshall. The more you take, the less appealing my offering looks when we get there."

"Don't worry, Derrick," John said, reaching out a hand. Derrick shook it hard enough the lantern in John's other hand swung, setting shadows spinning across the grass. The man smiled from beneath his dark beard. "I won't forget a thing."

"In that case," Derrick said, removing the pack from his shoulders. He slipped out four bottles of wine and passed them to John and another man who stepped forward.

"Nice," John said. "We'll enjoy that."

Derrick nodded and waved them off. The men passed into the woods on the opposite side of the gazebo, their lantern lights disappearing like fireflies switching off behind the trees. He waited for his eyes to adjust to the pale moonlight again and picked his way back to camp.

He paused a minute to peek into the tall grass where Marie was fast asleep on Waylon's chest; her head tucked up tightly beneath his chin. Waylon was snoring. The noise of continued revelry further into camp rose up with the smoke from the dying fire.

No one saw him pass back along the row, but two lights illuminated two tents set up close together. They glowed like strange lampshades in the dark. Each bore the silhouette of a single human figure, the two leaning close together to whisper through the thin material. He stilled his breathing and recognized the voices.

"—trusts you," Cass said.

"It's not my secret to tell," came Billy's reply.

He knew he should linger and listen, but his head was pounding, now. He wished they'd just climb into the same tent for once and get it over with. What might have been a pinch of jealousy hit him, but it faded quickly. The more they isolated themselves, the better. He just might need to use them, still.

LENA ALMOST KEPT RIDING on when the wagon stopped beside her. It was her horse's hesitation that finally pulled her out of her own mind and caused her to stop. She blinked a few times and looked around. Darcy was helping Katie down out of the wagon. The pregnant woman must need to pee, again.

"Sorry," Katie said, mostly addressing Cass and Billy, who followed along on foot. "I suppose I ought to have Drew just cut a hole in the wagon I could pee into. Often as I have to stop."

Cass offered a forced smile. She seemed distracted today. Had she gotten as drunk as everyone else? Maybe Cass, like Lena's father, had gotten laid last night. Lena felt a scowl pinch her brow. *And I'm the child? I'm the reckless and irresponsible one?*

"That wouldn't be so pleasant for the two of them, walking behind," David joked. His hand rested on Rain's shoulder as she napped with her head in his lap.

"Sounds like a plan to me," Lena said. She knew she'd killed the humor, but she didn't care. Her scowl bored into Cass, waiting for a reaction.

"No worse than what the horses leave behind," Conrad said. Cass eagerly turned her gaze away to look at him. Lena followed suit. Conrad looked terrible. He'd had a lot to drink the night before, and his face was pallid. Occasionally, he frowned and clutched at his gut, slumping in the saddle. Lena hoped her father felt even worse.

She remembered how she'd found them early this morning, her father flat on his back snoring, the blanket mercifully pulled halfway up his naked belly. Curled under his arm, drooling on his chest hair was Marie. *California whore.* There was no generosity in Lena today. She was aware of it and didn't care.

Billy leaned in and whispered something in Cass's ear. Cass looked surprised for a moment. After a glance back at Katie, who was just rising out of the tall grass in the ditch, she followed him. She stayed a few strides behind as he climbed the nearby rise, but her steps didn't hesitate.

She'd better be screwing him. I mean if she's going to sell me out and practically ignore me through this whole trip, she'd better at least be getting sex out of it.

"Lena. Hello?" Lena snapped out of her thoughts again. It was Darcy, her feet scuffing over a crack in the road as she approached Cowboy's neck. "Did you hear me?"

"I dunno. Did you actually say something worthwhile for a change? If you did, I probably didn't realize it was you."

Lena felt a twinge of guilt as Darcy looked away, a flush creeping up her pale neck. *She should be wearing a hat*, Lena thought. Then, she dismissed it. *Why am I always looking out for people who won't look out for themselves?*

Darcy's voice was low when she spoke again, her words meant for only Lena. "Look, if this is about Cass and Billy again—get over it. You've always liked Cass. Why don't you want her to be happy?"

Lena glanced up to see first Billy, then Cass crest the rise and disappear.

"I want her to be happy, just not stupid," Lena said.

"Finding love isn't stupid, Lena."

Lena hesitated for a second wondering if that's what was really happening. She swallowed. "Is that what Dad was finding with Marie last night?"

Darcy's eyes widened, and she scanned Lena's face for an explanation. Then her expression settled back to resigned calm. "Comfort," she said. "I'm sure that Dad was finding comfort last night." Darcy cleared her throat and started to walk away, but paused. "Not everyone is like you, Lena. Some people need things that you don't seem to need."

Lena felt a burn of tears behind her eyes. She needed things. She glanced at Katie. Conrad had dismounted and was helping her back into the wagon. He always looked at Katie in the same way—like she was home for his eyes. Lena loved it. Her father had once looked at her mother like that.

Conrad jogged off into the bushes by the roadside to relieve himself and Lena settled down further into the saddle. Her leg muscles twitched with her desire to push her horse forward and get moving again. Unable to help herself, she glanced back up the hill where Billy and Cass had disappeared. A little rush of air puffed out of her, bearing guilt and realization. Billy was starting to look at Cass that way—like she was where his gaze belonged.

THEY STOOD SIDE BY side at the edge of the hill. The tension rippled between them, a transparent but nearly tangible wave of discomfort and desire. Cass imagined reaching out and touching Billy, clearing away the awkwardness with the brush of her fingertips on his arm.

Below them, the main group was already turning onto a 90-degree switchback along the old highway that was bringing them out of the mountainous area toward the flatter plain. It had been weeks since Cass had looked over the maps, but she knew they wouldn't hit mountains again. In a day or two, they'd be in Nebraska, and it would be flat land the rest of the way. The last of the visible caravan veered around a dusty abandoned car on the left side of the road and disappeared, snakelike, beyond the curve. She knew they should head back down to the wagon.

But she wanted to know why he'd brought her away from the others. She wanted to know what was behind the tantalizing "come with me" spoken in her ear. She didn't know how to start the conversation because she wasn't sure which conversation they were having.

They'd been up late last night, talking through their tents. She'd felt drunker on sharing and discussion than on wine. Yet, they'd avoided the obvious topic: the kiss. It had been impulsive and shocking. Billy had only recently realized he could touch her arm, much less press his lips to hers. Especially with the power *that* kiss had held.

She felt overly conscious of every inch of herself as she stood there. And she was becoming equally aware of him. Had he been so close a minute ago?

He'd stood for so long in silence she almost jumped when he finally spoke. "So, any idea when we might get another chance to train?"

Cass raised her eyebrows and rotated to face him. She pretended to think for a moment, not willing to reveal her eagerness. He didn't need to know she'd already planned out the next opportunity for them to be alone.

"Well, we'll be taking a turn on horseback tomorrow and the next day, so we may have a chance, then. Even if we don't, Katie is already past due according to Doc. When she gives birth, we'll have to stop for two or three days at least. That should give us plenty of time."

Billy moved closer as she spoke, his arms still crossed over his chest, providing a barrier despite his proximity. His eyes flicked back and forth across her face, to her lips and the scar there, then down to arms that fell to her sides under his gaze. When the heat of his expression increased until Cass couldn't handle it any longer, she let out a false laugh.

"Are you so eager to get your butt kicked?" she asked.

Billy just smiled and dropped his arms, taking another step closer. Cass could swear she felt heat coursing from him even against the summer warmth. She tore her gaze away from his body and met his eyes.

"Really, though," she said, "are you sure you're ready? It'll be more physical this time." She heard a huskiness in her voice she hadn't meant to come through.

"More eager all the time," Billy said, his voice also deeper than usual.

Cass swallowed. "We should..."

"Talk about last night?" Billy finished when she couldn't. "The wine cellar?"

Trotting hoofbeats broke into Cass's awareness. The surging of her blood in her ears faded. She looked to the hill behind them in time to see a dark horse crest the rise they'd walked up. Derrick trotted toward them, and she and Billy sprung back from one another. She heard a frustrated sigh pass between Billy's lips just as Derrick spoke.

"You two need to catch up," Derrick's voice was commanding, and Cass's jaw protested as she gritted her teeth. She forced her hands not to clench into fists.

"Your brother needs to talk to you, Cass." He nodded down the hill in front of them. The road cut back and through a wooded area, and she could just see her brother and a few others passing out of the trees. "If you cut diagonal there, you can catch up easy enough."

Without waiting for an answer, Derrick directed his horse between Cass and Billy, tromping over the very spot where they'd just stood together. She moved back to allow the horse space and saw as the black rump passed down the hill that Billy had stumbled back as well. They shared a look of mutual fury.

"We should hurry," she said. "It could be important." She glanced back to see where the wagon, Lena, and Conrad were. She couldn't see them. They must have rounded the sharp corner, maybe already caught up to the group. Cass had lost track of time. She gestured to Billy and headed down the hill at a jog.

Billy caught up, wearing a fresh, wild expression. He was grinning and staring at the expanse of open land ahead of them, dotted here and there with a bush or a tree. He turned to her, his look filled with a joy that almost stopped Cass in her tracks.

"Let's run," he said. Then he shook his head. "Let's race."

Cass's brow furrowed even as his smile infected her. "What?"

"Please, let's race," he said. He started to jog and turned to face her, running backward. "I'll bet I'm faster than you."

Cass felt her head shaking even as she adjusted the straps of her pack on her shoulders. She walked quicker. The distance between them was increasing, and she didn't want that.

"I guess *you're* not hungover." Cass felt her feet picking up speed. She was jogging now, her hands moving to pump at her sides.

"Oh, I *am*," he said, raising his voice and starting to turn. "I'm suffering the effects of being cooped up for three years. And here's a cure." He took off, his legs powering him forward and away from Cass much quicker than she'd expected.

Cass let out a little scoff of surprise and ran after him. She tore along behind him, her headache protesting the quickened heart rate.

Her legs already felt sluggish, and she was jealous of Billy's long stride. She caught him with effort, but as soon as he saw her in his peripheral, he smiled and pulled ahead again. Cass felt a surge of competition now and fought off her sluggishness. Soon, they were neck and neck as they rapidly approached the head of the caravan. Heads were turning to watch them.

Billy pulled ahead again, and Cass saw her hand reach out for him. *Am I really trying to pull him back?* The next thing she knew, he reached back and gripped her wrist, pulling her forward. Arm in arm, they approached a wooden fence, the top board of which was down. Cass realized Billy meant to jump it, and she panicked, not sure she could clear it with her pack on.

Just then, she stepped on something, and her foot rolled sideways. She saw the fence's missing board buried in the grass just as her arm pulled out of Billy's grasp and she fell. She tucked and rolled, managing to slow herself just as her shoulder hit the fence post. She laughed as she came to a stop and heard laughing close beside her. Billy slid to a stop and sat, one leg jutting underneath the fence.

"Are you okay?"

Cass was still laughing. Her ankle hurt a little. She had twisted it on the board.

"I miss riding," she said. She hadn't been this out of breath for the sake of fun since Before. Her laughter faded as she watched thin, white clouds passing quickly behind Billy's head. His eyes were the same striking blue as the sky, today.

"Cassidy?"

It was Cam. Her brother had stopped in the ditch on the other side of the fence. He wore such a peculiar look that she laughed again.

"What are you doing?" he asked. In answer, Cass laughed even harder. *What* were *they doing?*

She laughed until her gut hurt and finally Billy took hold of her shaking arms and pulled her to her feet. The caravan was passing on the road, and she distantly noted the strange looks she was getting. Some people shot stares of disapproval, probably thinking they'd been in the wine again this morning. Others were laughing.

She heard Billy snickering behind her as she took down her messy hair and told her brother that Derrick had summoned them.

"Oh," Cam said. "Well, it could've waited. Let's get back on the road, and we'll talk."

When Whiskey turned and surged up out of the ditch, Cass and Billy followed, stepping over the fence rail and sneaking joyful glances at one another like scolded children.

"I *WAS* KIDDING ABOUT the hole in the wagon," Katie said. "Now, it seems like a smart idea."

Hearing the undercurrent of distress in the usually light-hearted tone of the woman, Lena turned to her. Katie was stroking her belly and holding the back of the wagon seat to balance herself. Conrad was looking at Katie with such an openly terrified expression that Lena wanted to chastise him. No need to worry everyone.

A huge, fallen tree blocked the road ahead. It had grown at an angle from a steep rise. The roots now stuck in midair on that side. On the other, the ditch was too steep for the wagon to navigate.

"Lena, how'd the other wagons get around?" Darcy asked. Lena knew her sister's voice well, and it was too tight, now. Even ditsy Darcy knew something wasn't right. She could sense it in the air.

Lena only shook her head and looked to Conrad.

Conrad had ridden over to the base of the tree where the roots still dropped damp earth onto the ground below. He was shaking his head, his frown a much deeper ridge than the normal one he wore.

"This couldn't have been down when they passed," said David, rubbing a hand across Rain's back. Rain's eyes, usually twinkling with mischief, were now wide with worry.

Lena caught herself glancing behind the wagon, wishing Cass was still there. She even wanted Billy to be there. Her anger had turned into a sharp fear in her chest, and she couldn't seem to settle it.

"Conrad," she said, keeping her voice as steady as possible. "One of us needs to catch the others. We can't move this on our own." Her gaze skimmed over the people in the wagon; Katie's big belly, Rain, and David—both fragile and arthritic, his back hunched with age. Darcy still clutched the reins as she shifted in her seat, turning from Conrad to Lena and back.

Conrad looked at Katie. A silent communication passed between them, ending as Katie nodded toward Conrad's buckskin mount.

"Buck is young and fast," he said. "I'll go."

"Hurry," Lena said as she pulled her pistol from her holster and rested it across her lap.

Conrad nodded and fixed Katie was such a longing look that Lena had to turn away to scan the road behind them and the woods to one side. As Conrad directed his horse down into the ditch and galloped away, she turned to examine the downed tree, again. It was alive, healthy even. This wasn't right.

Cold panic threatened in her gut, and she forced it away. *Cass,* she thought, *we need you.*

Ten

CASS WOULD ALWAYS REMEMBER that she was still on foot in the ditch when she heard the pounding hoofbeats. She would always remember the twang in her twisted ankle as she scrambled up onto the road. She would remember Billy asking something she didn't hear over the panicked questioning of others and almost getting kicked for shoving behind a horse's rump to get a better view.

The riderless buckskin came to an uneasy standstill alongside the group. Its nostrils flared, and it trembled all the way down to its hooves which slid a bit on the pavement with the force of its shaking.

She should have been the one to go to it with a calm voice and take hold of it. Instead, she spent what seemed an eternity staring, as her brain roiled and tried to piece together sense. Finally, she managed to breathe.

"Is that Conrad's horse?" she asked. No one answered. Cass took off toward the back of the group but stopped. She already knew the wagon wouldn't be there. Where had she lost them? She'd been sure they'd caught up. She yanked at clumps of her hair.

"Cam!" she shouted, spinning in a circle, trying to decide which horse to commandeer. The next thing she knew, Hank had dismounted and led his horse to her. Someone handed her a rifle, but the cool feel of the metal did not have the usual numbing effect.

Her unused energy transmitted to the horse through her seat and her hands. The animal spun and shied beneath her. She wanted to scream. Finally, search party gathered, Cam gave the word, and she turned the horse and dug in her heels. The animal kicked out as he broke into a run.

Cass felt a tug on her memory as if she had forgotten something and she turned her head back, searching for Billy's face. She couldn't see him in the crowd of people milling anxiously, listening to Derrick's shouted directions.

She faced forward. He was safe. She had to focus on keeping the others safe, now.

LENA'S CONSCIOUSNESS PULSED BACK to her in rhythmic flashes of fuzzy gray. Her ears rang with a memory of the sound of the class bell at school which jolted her back to reality more than anything. She blinked and tried to move, watching as shapes grew up around her and gradually clarified.

She was lying on the ground nearly underneath the wagon. Everything ached, and she thought she must have fallen from her horse. Her arms groped sluggishly for something to help her stand, and her hand landed in a puddle of warm liquid. She groaned as she turned her head to look. Her hand was covered in blood. She opened her mouth to scream, but no sound came. The fluid was dripping down out of the wagon.

She heard a gunshot and the wagon jolted as the horses pulled against the brake. She needed to move, but her body felt weighted. She was squirming away from the wagon and the blood, trying to get her muscles to help her roll when rough hands seized her and yanked her upward. The movement seemed to rip through her skull and everything faded to dark red and black.

BILLY FOLLOWED BEHIND THE crowds of people, wagons, and horses filing away from the road and tucking against a nearby ridge. The distance between him and the rest increased, yet he couldn't stop pausing and turning to stare back the way they'd come as if he could see what was happening.

As he watched, he caught a flash of movement. He could hear hoofbeats. It was Cowboy. Lena had been riding him. Without knowing what he was doing, he raised both arms at his sides and called out to the animal.

"Whoa," he said, trying to mimic Cass's calming tone.

The horse changed course as if to run right by and then began to slow, front legs jarring into the earth. He came to a stop, snorting, his saddle crooked to the side on his back and his reins, which had been tied together, laying diagonally between his ears. Cowboy shook his head.

Billy began to smile at his success at stopping the horse when he heard a snort from behind him. He turned to see Derrick looming there, astride his horse. That was why Cowboy had stopped. Derrick looked down at him, eyes wide but unreadable. Billy turned back to the horse and everything inside him pulled the same direction. He grabbed hold of the reins and ran them back down Cowboy's neck.

Ignoring the shying of the horse, he righted the saddle and tightened the cinch. It took him two tries to mount the skittering animal, but once he had, he tucked his feet firmly into the stirrups and shot a look back at Derrick, expecting the man to try to stop him.

Derrick said nothing and his face was a nearly blank canvas, bearing only the typical hardness of distaste it always held for Billy. Billy jerked Cowboy's head around and kicked, hunkering down as the horse blasted back the direction he'd come.

NO ONE IN THE rescue party had bothered to attempt to catch Cowboy as he flew past. Cass had cast a glance at him as he went by. The horse seemed unharmed, but, knowing that both Lena and Conrad were on foot was a fresh terror in her gut. She urged her unfamiliar mount forward to take the lead.

When she spotted a patch of blood-darkened pavement, she held up a hand and shouted for the group to stop. She dismounted and followed another trail of blood into the deep grass of the ditch where flies, already drawn to Conrad's body, buzzed.

His face was barely recognizable, flesh torn and skull separated. His clothing was bloodied and grass-stained where someone had dragged him off the road. She wouldn't have known it was Conrad if not for the empty, but recognizable knife sheath at his belt. His boots were also missing, and something about his dirty socks being exposed torqued Cass's insides. Seeing him without his boots and knife was harder to bear than the gore of blood and brain matter scattered around him.

She stood and met Cam's eyes, shaking her head.

"We've gotta get to the others." The voice was Drew's and Cass blinked at him for a second before she returned to her horse. She hadn't noticed who had joined them on this likely doomed mission. As she mounted, she realized two of the Oregonians were there as well as Waylon, who had already kicked his horse onward.

As Cass's horse picked up speed and the wind lifted her loose hair, she felt herself praying to a God she wasn't sure existed. Her insides spun as she thought over and over with each hoofbeat, *please, let his daughters be okay. Please.*

Cass spotted the downed tree across the road and the horseless wagon standing behind it. Cam and Drew were the first to round the tree, so close Cass thought for a moment their horses would collide while descending the steep ditch.

She followed them, already casting her eyes side to side as her horse clattered up onto the pavement on the opposite side of the tree. A seed of hope sprouted inside her. There were no bodies on the ground. Then, she saw a boot lying along the edge of the road where the grass began. There were horseshoes drawn on it in faded purple marker. It was Lena's.

"Shit," came Cam's voice. He was directing his horse closer to the wagon. The animal was reluctant, and when its hooves splashed into a red puddle, Cass knew why. She drove her mount in next to Cam's and raised herself in the stirrups to see. Two bodies lay sprawled one over the other in the wagon.

"Oh, God," said Waylon. He dismounted and clambered into the wagon, and Cass was about to call out for him to stop when he stopped on his own and jumped back down.

"It's David and Rain," he said. Cam was nodding. "They're gone."

"We need to go," Cass said. "Katie and the girls aren't here. They can't have gotten far with them."

"If they'd meant to kill them, they'd have done it here," Cam said. "How many do you think there are?"

When no one answered, Cass realized he was looking at her. She shook her head. "Five or more? They must have taken Conrad out at the same time they were here taking the wagon. Lena wouldn't have gone without a fight."

"We need to go," Waylon said, his voice practically a growl.

"We need to track them," one of the men from Oregon said, shifting his weight to dismount. He stopped with his leg raised over the saddle as a scream tore through the air.

"Darcy," Waylon said. He directed his horse off the road in the direction of the scream.

"Dammit, Waylon wait!" Cam's call was no use. He turned to Cass. "If we ride up on them like that they'll kill the girls."

"Please, Waylon, stop!" she cried. First, she saw the man's shoulders slump and then he hauled on the reins and circled back, waiting on the other side of the ditch. Tears streamed down his face.

"We have to find them," he said, his eyes imploring Cass to fix this.

"We will," Cam said. "But we can't let them know we're coming."

COWBOY FOUGHT WHEN THEY rode up on a dead body Billy assumed was Conrad's. He didn't see for sure due to the horse's rearing and charging out around the road and the ditch. Cowboy nearly unseated Billy, dodging a road sign and a dilapidated fence. But with clumsy and rough steering and lots of kicking, he brought the horse back onto the road and headed in the correct direction.

He'd just managed to regain his composure and was congratulating himself on staying in the saddle when they approached the downed tree, and Cowboy reared, turned on a heel, and threw Billy to the road.

The fall came with a brief whirl of colors and shapes, the feeling of clutching for something no longer there, and his stomach rising into his throat. He landed on his arm and shoulder, skidding and then rolling downhill into the tall, scratching grass of the ditch. The impact knocked the wind from his lungs, and he flailed on the ground, struggling for air as he listened to Cowboy's receding hoofbeats.

When he could breathe again, he took stock of his injuries. His arm ached, already bruising in the spots where flesh hadn't been torn away. Those spots were oozing blood. But, he could move it. His head ached as well, though he couldn't remember hitting it. He climbed onto unsteady legs, scrambled out of the ditch, and made his way to the wagon.

He peered over the edge and backpedaled in horror, tripping over his feet and bruising his tailbone as he went down. He flipped onto his hands and knees, bracing himself on his good arm and tucking the injured one out of the way of the contents of his stomach, which came forth with violence.

When he finally stopped retching, he heaved himself up off the ground. He took a few deep breaths, hands braced on his knees. What would Cass have done? How would she have known where to go?

He stood up, a new energy about him, and starting searching both sides of the road, looking for tracks or disturbed grass and brush—any sort of trail he could follow. He saw what he was looking for, a pattern of turned-down grass heading into the trees. He plunged forward.

THE MAN'S DIRTY HAND was clamped so tightly over Lena's mouth that she could barely breathe. He smelled of horses and sweat. She wished she could bite him, but there wasn't room to open her jaw. He had her neck cranked to the side so sharply that pain shot up into her head and down her spine. Maybe he'd break it. Maybe this was how she'd die.

Darcy twitched on the ground beside her, and she let out a breath through her nose. She hadn't been sure her sister had survived that blow to the head. Tears of relief prickled Lena's eyes until they spilled out over the man's huge hand. In response, he gripped her tighter.

Darcy didn't get up, and Lena was glad. Her own and her sister's hands were bound, but Katie's were not. Katie's hands were up, surrendering to a man who aimed a gun at her. An obvious pulse of pain passed through Katie's body, and she grabbed her pregnant belly and fell back off her knees into the grass. She'd been having contractions for several minutes. Lena struggled and tried to scream.

"Shut up," the man said in her ear. His breath stunk like her father's had that morning—like alcohol. She thought of her father and the cruel words she'd said earlier, but she had little time to regret. More people burst through the bushes into the clearing with them.

Lena struggled to turn her head, and to her surprise, the man released her mouth. She wanted to scream, but instead, her jaw dropped open as she caught sight of the new arrivals. One of the kidnappers manhandled a wide-eyed Billy forward with a knife held to his throat.

CASS FINALLY FELT THE familiar chill of numbness overtaking her as she aimed her gun at the head of the man who held Lena. She couldn't take the shot. Lena was too close. She trained her gun on the man standing over Katie next. If she killed him, he might fire his weapon which was still pointed at the pregnant woman. It was pointless, anyway. Cam had told her to hold.

Beside her, Waylon was pale and sweating. He trembled even as she watched. Which was why his gun had been taken. Cooler heads were taking aim while Cam crept toward the clearing ahead, ready to announce himself and begin to negotiate. Cass scanned the trees again and saw her brother. He was still holding up his fist, telling them to hold. She felt an anxious rush in her limbs, a need for action.

She shoved it down and cast her gaze over the area again. What had they done with the horses?

As she turned her gun back, she saw that Katie had fallen and the man who watched her was looking terrified. Lena's struggling intensified and then, out from the trees, came a man with a hostage.

Cass recognized the blonde hair first, darker here in the shade. Her heart dropped, and her throat contracted. Heat seared through her body, hollowing her out and replacing the numbness with fear. She couldn't breathe. It was Billy.

He was taller than the man who held him, and they moved awkwardly as they came forward, Billy unable to walk well with his back bent. His upper body pulled away from the knife, shoving harder against his captor's chest and arm.

Through the trees behind them came another pair of men, arguing. Her gaze returned to Billy. The man said something in his ear that made Billy set his jaw and shake his head. The man shouted. Lena and Katie's guards hauled them to their feet, Katie crying out in protest.

Cass looked back for Cam. He wasn't where he had been.

"Do you see Cam?" she whispered.

"Yes," Waylon said. "He's giving the hold signal."

"What?" A fresh surge of adrenaline rolled through Cass. A man was lifting Darcy to her feet, now. There was blood running down from her hairline, and she wobbled as she stood. Lena tried to move toward her sister. Cass's eyes found Billy again. A line of red had appeared beneath the long knife at his throat, and his face tightened in pain, but the man continued to press forward. They were trying to leave.

The tension in the woods amped up. A man shoved Lena into Darcy, and the sisters fell to the ground, Waylon gasping at Cass's side as it happened. Katie let out a scream, and the man guarding her shouted something.

"Now?" Cass's voice wavered.

"Hold," Waylon said. "He says to hold." But this time, Cass could tell the man did not agree with her brother and neither did she. Every nerve ending inside her screamed to act now, or it would be too late. She had to save them. To save *him*. Still, she had no shot.

Then the man who held Billy shoved him forward. Billy's foot hooked under an exposed root, and he went down to his knees, the knife slicing the side of his face as he fell. For a moment, the captor stood in shock, and then his head was knocked backward by the force of Cass's bullet. He crumpled to the ground.

Billy looked back at the man and then turned toward her. For a fraction of a second, their gazes met. Then Cass turned and took aim at the man looming over Katie. A shot fired and he went down as a volley of shots rang out through the trees. Cass took aim at the man who'd been guarding Lena. He was darting for cover, but not fast enough. Her bullet exploded through his chest, and his body dropped heavily to the earth.

Waylon ran across the clearing to his daughters. Cass's feet carried her toward Billy, even as she took aim at one of the men behind him. The man was aiming a gun back at her. With a quick intake of breath, Cass squeezed the trigger, and her shot flew way off. She looked down somewhat in shock to discover her gun had fallen from her grasp. Her right arm burned, and she glanced down at it as if it belonged to someone else. Blood ran down to her fingertips and dripped from them.

Another shot. Cam had taken down the man she'd missed. She ran forward. Billy was trying to stand, reaching out a hand for her, blood running from the wound on his face and trickling down his neck. Cass paused, surprised by the fear in his eyes, and realized he wasn't reaching for her but pointing behind her. She spun just as a fist powered down on her. It caught her on the side of the face, and her body was flung toward the ground.

She rolled onto her back when she landed and kicked out hard at her attacker, managing to make contact only with his reaching arms. He shoved her legs away and bent toward her again. Another shot rang out. Blood spattered down over Cass's arms and chest and the man fell onto her. She shoved him away as the sound of his gasp crawled her spine like an insect. He continued to reach for her, but his eyes were now full of terror and desperation.

She reached for her knife just as Drew walked up, the beats of his footfalls uneven, though his limp was hardly noticeable. He stood over the man, aimed his pistol and before he pulled the trigger, his eyes met Cass's and held them as he fired.

CASS SLUMPED BACKWARD AND caught her weight with her hands. Her right arm exploded in heat at the impact and collapsed. She cried out as she landed on her injured arm and struggled to roll onto her back to relieve the agony. Through the haze of pain and the grass obscuring her vision, she saw something small and gray dart off into the trees with a lithe, leaping motion.

Then, Drew was lifting her up.

"What—" Her upper body continued to lift, and her arm twisted. She moaned in protest.

Propping her against him, Drew began wrapping her injury tightly in a strip of cloth the same color as his shirt. It felt as though he was sawing off her arm. He looked at her without apology when she growled her displeasure.

"Buck up, babe, you'll be fine," Drew said. She gritted her teeth and nodded, knowing it wasn't serious. Drew would tell her if it were.

Across the small clearing, Cass heard pleading voices and arguing, then a sob. She reached across with her good arm and clamped onto Drew's shoulder, using him to pull herself up. He helped her to sit on her own, then stood and jogged away. She watched him go for a second, but dizziness descended like a waterfall, and she had to look away from the movement of his feet.

Cass took in a few deep breaths, leaning forward. As her senses began to clear, she could feel Billy's presence like a fire on a cold night. She turned toward that heat, and when she opened her eyes, she was staring straight at him. He was on one knee a couple of yards away from her, looking through his sweat-dampened hair. His bloody arm rested across his knee and in it was the knife that had been at his throat. He hadn't wiped the blood from his face or his neck.

His gaze was steady on hers and expectant. He seemed to be waiting—no, bracing—for something.

Cass flinched as she heard an angry cry from behind her. It was Lena. Using her left arm to clutch at grass, she pulled herself onto her knees and twisted her body, still not trusting herself to stand. Her hand landed on a patch of damp grass, and she looked down to see she was sitting in a small pool of blood. From her arm, she guessed, or was it from the man whose body lay a few feet away?

Lena railed at Cam, her arms flailing. Behind her, Darcy huddled in Waylon's arms, shaking her head. Drew knelt in the grass nearby and beside him, protruding from behind a rock, was Katie's belly. Her shirt was half pulled up, and both its fabric and her skin were stained with blood. Worse was the unnatural stillness. The woman wasn't breathing.

Cass's eyes flicked back to her brother as she heard him shout, "Lena! Enough! There's nothing we can do."

Lena turned from him, disgust and anguish contorting her features. Her shoulders were hunched, and she began to fold in on herself, her knees bending. Then, her eyes met Cass's, and she straightened.

Cam moved to stop Lena, but she darted out of his reach and

bore down on Cass. Cass waited, her head tilting upward in slow motion as the girl's heavy footsteps grew closer. She was detached from what was about to happen as if it were a scene in a story she knew by heart. In fact, the only surprise she felt as Lena's arm swung toward her came when she was struck with an open hand. She had been expecting a fist, though the slap was effective in whipping Cass's head aside and almost unseating her.

Ignoring the sting of her cheek and the burn in her wounded arm, which she'd again used to catch herself, Cass turned back to look up at Lena. The fist she'd expected came down on her then. She flinched away, and it struck her ear. Her arm folded under her, and she went to the ground.

"What the hell is wrong with you? You bitch!" Lena shouted. Cass rolled onto her side in time to see a booted foot drawing back to kick her. She tensed in anticipation, but suddenly legs appeared between the two of them. Billy stood over her, his hands held out in surrender. This further infuriated Lena, but as the girl reached back to swing at Billy, arms clamped around her body from behind and lifted her away.

Billy knelt down beside Cass and put a hand on her shoulder. She glanced at his hand and arm which sported a nasty road rash. Her head felt heavy and slow, as though it moved through mud. She forced it to tilt so she could look up at him. Behind his head floated Cam's, his features hard. And fading.

Her stomach gave a flip as the world twirled to the right and she was consumed by dark.

Eleven

CASS WAKENED TO A steady thrumming in her ears mirrored by surges of pain from her arm. Slowly, other sounds clarified; the even pace of horse hooves on pavement and the rolling of wheels. Whispered voices occasionally broke the more monotonous sounds. Cass shifted her body and realized she was lying in the wagon, cool boards pressing into her shoulder and hip. She was covered with a blanket that scratched against her neck as the wagon turned. Her body rotated, and she would have been rocked onto her stomach had a large, warm mass not kept her propped on her side.

Someone sat beside her, keeping her lying steady between the side of the wagon and themselves. Her breath caught. Billy?

She opened her eyelids to find it wasn't much lighter on the other side of them. The wagon was a shaded brown against a deep blue sky. She looked upward and took in the stars and the glow of moonlight. Then the person beside her shifted, turning to peer into her face.

"Welcome back," Doc said.

Cass pushed away the sinking feeling of disappointment and tried to speak. Her voice came out as a dry croak.

"Billy. Water?" Doc said.

Cass began to turn her head, looking for Billy. But, a light shone on her face, and she squinted, flinching away.

"Ah-ah," Doc said, his hand on the side of her face, "open them."

Cass forced her eyes to open, her frowning brow fighting and her eyes watering against the incredible brightness in the dark. The light shone brighter in one eye, then the other, and it disappeared with a click.

"A flashlight?" she whispered, her hoarseness causing her to cough several times before a hand was placed on the back of her neck and the steel rim of a water bottle pressed to her lips.

She took a sip, another, and the bottle was pulled away.

"Yes," Doc said. "We found some that worked in a fallout shelter. The last of my batteries, though." He cleared his throat and tucked the flashlight into an inner pocket of his coat. "How's your head?"

Cass's eyes had begun to adjust, and she blinked into the darkness, first focusing on Doc's face and then seeking Billy's. He sat against the opposite side of the wagon, watching in silence, the whites of his eyes catching moonlight.

Cass cautiously lifted her head from the pillow someone had fashioned for her by balling up a coat. Her head ached, but she wasn't dizzy. Her arm pulsed with pain but nothing too strong.

"I'm okay," she said. She moved to sit upright and Doc did not stop her though she saw Billy tense. She pushed the blankets away, letting the chill of the night wake her further. She glanced up to see Darcy driving the wagon and, with a sick sweep of horror, she realized this was the wagon where Rain and David's bodies were found.

Almost as an answer to her thoughts, a cloud passed away from the moon. Earth was bathed in a brighter white illumination, revealing dark stains on the boards of the wagon between her feet and Billy's. She suppressed a shudder.

"Katie?" she whispered. Billy dropped his gaze away, and she turned to see Doc shaking his head. "The baby?" He held the water bottle out to her and looked away.

"Drink."

Cass took it, but before she drank, she glanced up at the horses pulling their wagon.

"You found the horses," she said.

"They were tied nearby in the woods," Doc said. "Cass—"

"What's the plan?" She now turned to Billy. "Do they think these guys were the ones who stole stuff in the storm? In the orchard?"

"Cass," Doc reached out and closed his hand over her wrist. "Drink."

Cass's nostrils flared, and she felt the clutch of anger grabbing her insides. She felt ready to fling the water bottle into the night. Faster-paced hoofbeats came up beside the wagon, distracting her. She turned to see a horseman, edging his mount closer, keeping pace with them.

"Drew." She practically sobbed his name and reached out for him. His hand clasped hers over the side of the wagon, and she felt a surge of strength as if he had gifted it to her.

"How is she, Doc?" Drew asked.

"She needs to learn to take on one thing at a time," Doc said, a sour note in his voice. "But, she's fine."

"Of course, I'm fine," Cass added. "Is everyone okay? Lena? Cam? Where is Cam? Did any of them get away?"

Drew responded by squeezing her hand until she quieted. "Stop," he said. "Cam sent me to check on you. We're not stopping until tomorrow night. He'll come to you when it's light. For now, rest."

"No," Cass said, gritting her teeth to keep her voice controlled. Darcy had turned to watch her. "I need to be helping keep watch."

"Cam doesn't want you right now," Drew said. His tone was guarded, gentle, but blunt. The kind honesty of the Drew she loved. Still, she pulled her hand free and turned away.

"First light," she said, her voice clipped.

"I love you, Cassidy," Drew said softly, as his horse moved further away.

Cass's eyes darted to Billy. He had shifted so he faced the front of the wagon, watching as they weaved between two long-abandoned cars stopped on the highway. His face was neutral but stiff as if he knew she was looking and didn't want to show any reaction.

Doc cleared his throat. "You'll be interested to know that the bullet just grazed your arm. It's not in there."

"Okay," she replied, not moving her gaze from Billy.

"But you have stitches. And you've lost quite a bit of blood."

Cass nodded.

"Now drink. And sleep," Doc said. He moved toward the back of the wagon, settling in among the various supplies.

Cass took a long swig of the water, feeling it cool the inside of her body to match the outside. Each time her glace landed on Billy, she envisioned driving her gaze into him, making him look at her, making him talk to her. But he didn't turn. Finally, she pulled the blanket up around her shoulders and turned to Darcy.

"How's Lena?" she whispered. Darcy's shoulders stiffened. It took a moment for her to relax again. Cass had almost given up on getting an answer, though she couldn't blame Darcy for being angry with her. She should have been there for them—should have been there to save Katie. And David. And Rain.

Cass's eyes had filled with burning tears when Darcy finally answered.

"Lena's alright."

Cass let out a loud, shaking sigh of relief, praying her tears stayed dancing on her eyes and wouldn't run down her cheeks. But, as Darcy turned and gave her a sympathetic look, they spilled over, hot on her face. Darcy's eyes widened in shock, and she looked away.

Cass slumped down further into the blanket and wiped the tears with the back of her hand. When she looked up, Billy had turned to face her. Her look brushed across him; his cheek swollen and angry but stitched up, his collarbone still caked with dried blood. Bandages covered the wounds on his neck and arm.

She met his eyes again, nodded, and sunk back to her side on her makeshift bed. Eventually, she heard him snoring. Doc, too. But she spent her night watching Billy and the stars, unable to sleep.

IT WAS DAWN, AND Derrick was yawning when the group pulled to a stop. Cam announced that everyone should rest for a moment and have a bite to eat, while the leaders had a quick meeting. Derrick felt a flicker of hot anger at hearing the announcement spoken from Cam's lips, but he was tired and distracted and shoved the feeling aside.

As he followed Cam, he heard Hank call out for a man to join them, so he also gave a nod to Adam, who followed. It wasn't until they came to the end of the caravan and he saw Cass sitting in the wagon that he realized Cam had brought someone else with him. The man, Trace, seemed wildly uncomfortable to be replacing Cass.

She leaned against the wagon, tracking the leaders as they passed and Trace shrugged at her. She shook her head and smiled briefly before letting her gaze become stone again. It spoke volumes about their relationship that she even bothered to reassure him.

Meanwhile, Cam never acknowledged his sister. Derrick

suppressed a smile. At least part of his plan was working out.

A last look at Cass pulled him into the past. Something about her posture and the set of her jaw made him imagine that she was Abby sitting there; disapproving, despairing.

How would Abby look at him, now? Knowing that he'd allowed—even encouraged—what had been done to a pregnant woman and two people too weak to defend themselves? How would she react knowing what would've happened to the teenage girls? They would've suffered the same fate she had, known the same terror that had crossed her face.

He'd never forget that detail, though he'd forgotten so many others—her eyes on him as they forced him to watch. Strong arms restraining him, beating him, proving to him that he couldn't protect her anymore. Voices telling him it wouldn't have happened if only he'd shared her in the first place.

He turned away, the familiar grinding ache in his head returning. It didn't matter. Abby would've written him off long ago if she'd been watching the things he'd done. But she wasn't watching. She was dead and dead was gone. All that mattered was this life. And ultimately, the power he gained from his actions—however terrible— would allow him to protect more people than he'd harmed. He could save someone else's lover.

He dismounted, clearing his head as the small group of men formed a circle, each of them stretching their tired, stiff muscles. Cam was beginning to speak when Derrick saw the prisoner approaching their group. He held up a hand, his temper flaring.

"What?" he said, warning Billy off with his stare.

"I—uh..." Billy said. He held his hands out in front of him, offering up a long knife with an antler handle. The blade gleamed in the rising sunlight as Billy turned and held the knife out to Hank. "I think this was Conrad's."

Hank reached out and took the knife, nodding. "It was," he said.

He ran his thumb across the butt of the knife, then narrowed his eyes at Billy. "I'm told you went after the kidnapped girls. Tried to help."

Billy's eyes dropped at first but flicked back up to Hank more confidently.

"I wanted to help, yes," Billy said. "I wasn't successful."

Derrick looked to Cam expectantly, waiting for him to agree—to condemn the rash actions of Billy and Cass that had gotten Katie killed. Instead, Cam stood with his arms across his chest, just watching.

Derrick cleared his throat. "No, you weren't successful," he said. His tone was of the type to close the conversation, and as Billy made eye contact with him, he raised his eyebrows, lifted his shoulders to their full height and leaned forward, trying to convey to Billy that it was time for him to leave.

Billy gave a nod and began to turn away. Hank stopped him with a hand on his arm. The man tipped the knife toward Billy, whose eyes widened.

"It's the knife that threatened you, you should have it," Hank said.

Billy did not reach for the weapon but said, "I couldn't accept this."

Hank shook his head and continued to offer the knife. "With Katie gone you have more claim to it than anyone. You tried to do the right thing. Trying counts."

The handle of the knife bumped Billy's chest, and he reached up to clasp his hand over it. "Thank you," he said.

Derrick turned to Cam again, but though the Montanan leader had raised an eyebrow, he seemed more thoughtful than inclined to disagree. Derrick groped about in his mind for a logical protest, but none came quick enough. The prisoner had already left, knife held firmly at his side.

Cam started to speak, and Derrick shook his head to clear his thoughts. It was all pointless planning, anyway. They wouldn't be attacked again. But he needed to appear concerned and proactive. He needed to show himself to be as strong a leader as Cam or Hank.

He shoved aside his irritation at the peace that had come between the other bands and Billy. Cass was still on the outs, after all. He turned his focus to the meeting, but what had happened with the knife gnawed at the back of his mind.

DREW TURNED TO CASS the minute the leaders finished their meeting. He was not surprised to see her rising to her feet and charging toward her brother. She spoke to Cam and stepped around him, heading for the closest patch of trees. Cam followed. Drew debated whether to leave the siblings to talk alone until he saw Cass roll her shoulder. He shook his head, sighed, and went after them.

He wasn't the only one tracking Cass, and when he saw Billy beginning to follow the Hoods into the trees, he jogged forward to intercept the other man.

"Nope," he said, putting a hand up in front of Billy's chest. "You stay."

"I should be there. This is more my fault than hers," Billy said, though he had stopped.

Drew shook his head. "If you get in the middle you'll complicate things. Again." Drew turned and followed the sounds of arguing into the woods, not bothering to check over his shoulder to see if Billy had listened.

"—disobeyed my signal to hold!" Cam was shouting, and Cass was in his face smiling as if proximity made his anger easier to bear.

"Ha," she said. "You've known me all my life Cam, how often do I *obey*?"

"Always when it's important. When it's life or death—Cass, Katie is dead!"

"I know it!" Cass screamed the words then let her breath out in a rush as if someone had punched her. She took a step back and turned away. Drew could tell she was fighting tears. "Cam, I couldn't hold, we had to *act*."

"No, Cass." Cam's voice was firm as he closed the distance between them once more. "You should have held. I need to be able to count on you. I need your head to be cool under pressure. What if that had been Trista?"

Cass looked up at him, wide eyes brimming with liquid. She absorbed what he had said and swallowed forcefully. "So, what now, Cam? I'm not your second anymore?"

"You'll always be my second." Cam's voice was softer now, and he reached out to place a hand on Cass's shoulder. She jerked out of reach like his hand would burn. Cam hardened again and said, "But I think you should take a break from some of those duties until you get your head on straight again. Trace will fill in."

Drew's jaw dropped open, and he felt Cass's anger welling up in his own chest. He watched his best friend nod and cut a path back through the trees toward the group, her face flushed and her upper body tense. She didn't look at Drew as she moved past him, but covered the bandage on her injured arm with her opposite hand and lifted her chin.

Drew turned to Cam, struggling to hold back the rage. He swallowed and took a deep breath, but Cam spoke before he could.

"She should have waited for my signal."

Drew let out a snort of laughter. "You're not getting this," he said. "Picture it like she did, *big brother*." Drew's tone was derisive, and he widened his shoulders as he spoke, increasing the space he took up in the woods. "You said Katie could have been Trista, but you're thinking like *you*. Cass didn't need a *stand-in* to represent her mate. He was there."

Drew turned to leave but stopped after a few steps to toss

another thought over his shoulder. "How cool would *your* head have been if that blade had been against *Trista's* throat? If that knife had scarred *her* face?"

DAYS RAN TOGETHER FOR Billy. All he was aware of was his exhaustion and the way it was mirrored in all the other drawn faces with circles beneath their eyes. They moved out before dawn every morning, traveled all day, and made camp each twilight. Concerned about another attack, they varied their route, making their path longer. Hunting was seldom a priority, and their supplies dwindled.

Billy had expected to be punished; yelled at or even kicked out of the band. But, after Hank's decision to give him Conrad's knife, Cam seemed to warm to him as well. He even assigned Billy a rifle at the start of each day, tasking him to defend the group, though he also arrived to take it back as soon as they halted each night.

Billy felt his fate was better than Cass's. *She* seemed to be taking the punishment that *he* deserved. Trace had been acting as Cam's second, not that there had been a need for one since all they were doing was running. And since the hidden but overheard fight in the woods, Cass and Cam had not spoken.

Cass spent sweat and blood caring for the horses in darkness each night when they stopped and each morning before they left. Billy helped her, but she spoke to him as little as possible. He didn't blame her. She'd been forced to protect him, forced to make good on her promise to keep him alive. The cost had been two other lives.

He wanted to apologize—to thank her. But, instead, he let Drew take that role. More than once he'd overheard the man telling Cass it wasn't her fault. Katie might have died anyway if she hadn't acted and who knows who else would have been killed, too?

Drew had stepped up where Lena had stepped out. The girl was impossible. She helped with the horses less and less, and completely ignored him and Cass when she did. Billy preferred the chilly silence to the way she'd used Cass as a punching bag in the clearing. He only wished she'd gotten in her shots at him, instead.

Drew had stepped in for Cam as well, acting as an emissary between brother and sister. Every time Cass passed her brother without speaking to him—every time he called on Trace to act as his second instead of her—Billy saw her shoulders sink a bit more toward the ground. Miserable with guilt though he was, he still couldn't keep from watching her.

The group had stopped at what must have been a factory and were eating near a receiving dock. Billy had settled against the concrete beneath one of the doors with his dinner plate. He let his gaze drift to her, again. She was sitting in a camping chair, letting Doc examine her arm. The bags beneath her eyes were deep and obvious even from this distance. She barely nodded her head in response to Doc's words.

He'd gone after her that day because she'd opened up his world and filled most of it with her strength. And in return, he'd closed her off from the few people she'd let in. The ache to thank her for saving his life was worse than the ache of hunger. Worse than the ache to touch her again, to kiss her. He hadn't known anything could top those longings.

"What the hell are you doing with that?" a voice asked, high and razor sharp.

Billy blinked and turned his face up to see Lena standing over him, scowling. The crowd near them had already been eating quietly, with little energy for conversation, but now they grew silent.

Billy glanced back down at his lap where he had been turning Conrad's knife over in his hands. He had been so deep in his thoughts he hadn't noticed he was holding it. He looked back up into her reddening face, surprised she hadn't already noticed that he wore it on his belt. Then again, Lena made a point not to look at him.

"Did you take that off his body?" Spit flew from Lena's mouth as she spoke. She advanced on him, hands in fists.

Billy glanced around hoping to spot Hank somewhere nearby. But Lena kept moving forward and quickly blocked his view.

"It was given to me," he began.

"Like hell," Lena said, reaching down and snatching the knife away. Reluctant to take it in the beginning, he had since grown fond of it, and he had to resist the urge to grab it back from her.

"By Hank," he said, holding his hands up in surrender but leaning forward, meeting her eyes.

Lena hesitated, uncertainty in her body language now.

"It's true." Derrick took a couple of steps toward them from where he'd been sitting on a short stack of decaying pallets. The man spoke louder than Lena had, calling attention from more of those sitting around in the lantern light. "Hank offered it to him as a kind of reward for attempting to rescue you and Darcy and Katie."

"That's bullshit!" Lena shouted. There was a murmur through the crowd, and it sounded more like agreement than disapproval. "He's the reason Katie's dead. He fucked everything up."

There was a scuff of gravel. Cass strode toward them, trailed by a harried Doc. He held one end of an off-white cloth that was unraveling from Cass's arm as she moved.

"For her," Lena continued. "For you." She turned to Cass, stopping the older woman in her tracks. "He didn't come after us; he came after you. Following you around like he has been this whole time, trying to get in your pants or whatever the fuck he wants. And you're worse. Mooning over him like some horny teenager and letting him distract you and put everyone in danger—"

"Lena Danielle!" Waylon's voice boomed across the crowd as he shoved his way past clumps of people, seated and standing. "That's enough."

The appearance of her father angered Lena further. She had

risen onto the balls of her feet, bouncing like a boxer waiting for the first hit.

"You don't get to reprimand me, Dad. You're just worried I'll tell everyone what you've been doing—who you've been fucking—on the nights when you were supposed to be on watch."

"Lena!" Cass silenced the girl but did nothing to calm her. Billy stood quietly, adrenaline numbing his body to his actions. He had never truly feared Lena until he'd seen her strike Cass and move to kick her. She seemed as angry now as she'd been then. And this time, she gripped his knife by the handle. The sheath was unfastened when she'd taken it, and now, the leather had begun to slip down, exposing the blade.

Billy's eyes moved from the blade to Cass, who showed no sign she'd noticed it but kept her glare fixed on Lena's face. Over her shoulder, Cam approached. The growing crowd closed up behind him, eager faces rushing to catch the drama.

Derrick moved forward. His arms hung loosely from his shoulders, and he was a picture of alert assurance. "Lena," he said. "Your father deserves a night or two of comfort. He hasn't put us in danger. And Billy is Cass's responsibility, like one of the horses. That's all."

Billy felt his shoulders stiffen, but Lena snorted, distracting him from taking offense.

"I know them better than you do," she said. She glared first at her father, and then at Cass. Seeing Cam standing tall behind his sister, she dropped her gaze to the knife in her hand. She turned to Billy and lowered her voice. "You showed up and got Katie killed. Conrad wouldn't *want* you to have this." She shook the knife at him and then chucked it to the ground at his feet. It struck his boot, bruising the top of his foot. "Whatever."

Lena turned to leave and then stopped and whipped the backpack off her shoulders. As she dug through it, Billy recognized it as the one Katie had worn. It had been sitting in the wagon and was stained with traces of copper-brown blood-splatter.

"Since we're all about giving away dead people's stuff today—here," Lena said. She flung something toward Cass. Cass tried to catch it, fumbled, and bent to retrieve it. It was a necklace made of braided horse hair. Cass stared down, running her thumb over it.

"Katie made it," Lena said, shouldering the backpack again. "For you." With tears on her face, Lena strode away, shoving through the crowd.

Derrick muttered something as he turned and made his way after the girl, rubbing his temples. Cass swiped a hand across her cheek and then closed the necklace in her fist and lowered her arm to her side.

Billy bent to retrieve the knife and his plate from where it had fallen when he'd stood, and felt her looking at him. She was standing alone, her arm properly bandaged and the crowd mostly dispersed, though people still watched them from all angles.

For a moment, the two of them just gazed at one another through the dim light, two pairs of tired eyes briefly awakened to take the measure of the other. It seemed Cass was trying to decide whether he was worth this trouble and he supposed he was also assessing the depth of his feelings for her. He wasn't surprised to find his breathing speeding up and his chest swelling as they braved really looking at one another for the first time since the kidnapping. Every part of him pulled toward her, begging him to go to her.

He was taken aback when she spoke. "Why *did* you follow us?" she asked.

Because I was scared for you. Because I'm in love with you. A thousand explanations flitted through his thoughts before he blurted out a question of his own.

"Why did you shoot when Cam told you not to?" he asked.

Cass's eyes widened and shimmered with moisture. It wasn't

really all that long before Cass dropped her gaze and spun on her heel, moving back the way she'd come, but it felt like a year's worth of emotion had passed between them. His heart sunk as she disappeared around the corner of a building. He wanted to follow her now as much as he'd wanted to that day. He'd been so sure she was in danger then, and now he knew she wasn't, but it didn't stop him from longing to keep her in his sight. This time, however, he turned and walked in a different direction, letting his heart go after her without him.

Twelve

THE WORST PART OF being at odds with her brother was not having answers people assumed she'd know. Cass was approached daily by members of the group wondering when they were going to slow, stop to rest, and most often wondering when they were going to hunt again.

Cass felt as worn as the rest of them and her belly rumbled just as often. Her relationship with Cam was frayed, her friendship with Lena destroyed, and whatever had been happening between her and Billy—well, that was probably over. If it hadn't been for Drew, she wouldn't have bothered to remain civil to anyone, especially after the embarrassing debacle of the night before last.

After Lena had outed everyone, Cass had attempted to ride separately from Billy. She'd expected him to try to follow her to a new traveling spot, further up in the caravan with Drew, but he hadn't. She guessed he hadn't appreciated being likened to a lovesick puppy dog by Lena or livestock by Derrick.

But she'd only made it for about an hour before a worry spasmed through her, causing her limbs to twitch with restlessness. She hadn't liked Derrick's declaration that he blamed the two of them for the deaths. And Billy hadn't even been quick enough to keep Lena from taking his knife. She worried he wouldn't be able to defend himself against Derrick's eager goons if a situation arose. Not to mention she still had a nagging sense they were being followed.

So she'd taken her leave from an amused Drew, and brought Cowboy into step with Smoke at the rear of the group. But, the next two days had been as awkward and silent as the ones before. One of them would catch the other glancing in his or her direction, and they'd quickly look away.

On the second day after the scene at dinner, they came to a stop earlier than expected in a river valley. The water was slow running in the drought, but it was water. Cam and Derrick had scouted a couple of miles downstream and found a sparsely wooded area with game trails. It seemed they would be staying more than one night here, and the chances of fresh meat for dinner tomorrow were good.

Cam rode up to the two of them before they'd even had a chance to dismount. Cass was surprised to see Cam sidling his horse up next to hers. He met her gaze, his eyes more gentle than angry.

"I'm planning to show Hank and Derrick what bow-hunting is all about tomorrow," Cam said. "Any recommendations?"

"Duct tape for Derrick's mouth?" Cass said. Cam laughed and then turned to locate Derrick, silencing himself. Cass didn't crack a smile.

"I'm not coming then, I take it," she said.

Cam let out a breath. "I don't think it's a good idea for you to come. Either of you." He lifted his chin toward Billy as if tossing the words over to him.

Cass tried to hold her tongue, but her thoughts burst out in a whisper despite her. "Why? I made a mistake, so suddenly I'm not useful at all? I get that you're punishing me, but Cam—"

"Cassidy, enough," Cam said. "I don't want any drama tomorrow, that's all. I said you're still my second or at least you will be when you remember how to be cautious and diplomatic again. Good-bye."

Cam slammed his heels into Whiskey's sides, and the horse shot forward and away. Cowboy shied and Cass was shaking with anger, further agitating him. She freed her feet from the stirrups and swung down from his back, glorying in the sharp concussion of her boots on the packed earth.

CASS HAD BEEN HAVING nightmares of Katie and Conrad, David and Rain. Almost every night she'd seen the ways they might have died. She knew they'd all died of gunshot wounds, but her subconscious often cooked up more gruesome ends. Sometimes, it was Lena or Darcy who died. Sometimes, it was Billy.

She stood on a ridge overlooking the camp. Her watch was uneventful and she couldn't keep the nightmares from haunting her even when wakefulness should have brought relief. So she paced and alternated her gaze between the goings-on down at the camp and the open space on higher ground. She hummed the song that had twirled and teased inside her memory for months and tried to remember the lyrics.

And when all else failed—when she couldn't stop herself thinking of the dead—she let her mind slip to the few good memories she had of each of them alive. She got stuck in a memory of Conrad.

The day had been like today, warm and exhausting, and it had been sunset then, too. She'd watched Conrad as he watched Katie with such love and longing. The love was like Cam's for Trista, but the longing was something Cass could neither define nor compare.

Did Conrad think of Katie when he died? Was his final thought her dark hair in its charming pixie cut? Her laugh or the soft touch of her fingers on his arm?

"God, I hope it," Cass said aloud. She hoped it fiercely. Partly because she wanted to think he hadn't had time to feel pain or fear. But mostly she hoped he hadn't died regretting the things he'd never said to Katie—the chance he'd never taken.

Cass moved back to the edge of the ridge and looked down at the people, again. This time, her eyes scanned the crowd with purpose.

THERE HAD BEEN TIME for some fishing before dark. Billy had been a model student as Drew and Trista taught him how to clean a fish. He ate with the two of them, as well. Trista seemed to be at odds with Cam. The tall man chatted with Hank and kept his distance.

Between bites, Trista asked the question Billy had been dying to have answered. "Where's Cass tonight?"

Drew nodded up toward the ridge above. "On watch. Why? Is she speaking to you, 'cause she doesn't seem to have much to say to me or Billy."

Trista nodded and took a sip of water. "I worry about what she's feeling and *not* saying. Her guilt is loud."

"She's not guilty," Drew said firmly, looking across the crowd at Cam. "She did the right thing."

"I know," Trista said, earning herself a look of surprise from Drew that mirrored Billy's own shock. "But she *feels* guilty. She's punishing herself—cutting herself off from everyone."

Drew shook his head. "It's not about punishment. It's about simplifying things. She doesn't think she can keep us safe and love us at the same time." Drew met Billy's gaze pointedly, his expression intense. "She doesn't think she can make choices based on what *she* wants without losing the warrior in her."

Billy found his focus drawn to the ridge above. To his surprise, he could see a lean figure, hair dark against the evening sky and lifting gently away from her neck as the breeze blew. She held a lantern in one hand while the other rested against the strap of the rifle on her shoulder. It was Cass, and the way his guts rolled, he was sure she'd been watching him.

The figure disappeared, and Billy stood.

"Good night," he said. He paused and turned back. "Thanks—for the disgusting fish lesson."

Trista chuckled and waved him away. Drew just fixed him with a lopsided grin that left Billy feeling exposed and uninformed. He went to the table the food was laid out on and piled a bit of the remaining fish and corn onto his plate. Then, he set out on the steep upward trail, squinting in the fading daylight.

When he neared the top of the trail, his feet stepped into a circle of lantern light, and he squinted up into Cass's face.

"What are you doing?" she asked as he crested the rise and paused, catching his breath.

He offered the plate of food without answering her question.

Her eyes traced their way up his arm to his face. They scanned over him, halting at the knife sheath on his belt. She rolled her shoulder with a frown and let out a sigh as if she had come to some necessary but unwanted decision.

"That's the same knife, isn't it?" she asked, meeting his gaze again before looking back at the knife. "Conrad's? That's the knife that—" her voice cracked.

"That gave me this?" he asked. He ran a thumb along the new, pink scar that split his cheek, then trailed it down to the shallower scar on his neck. Cass followed the motion of his hands as if they possessed hypnotizing power. "Yes, that's the knife."

He still held the plate, though his arm had begun to tire. Finally, she set her lantern down and took it, walking away to scan the darkened landscape before them.

She finished eating, and Billy grew restless, shifting where he stood. She tossed her plastic plate back toward the boulder and the sound of it striking the rock seemed like an explosion after the quiet. Billy's body tired of standing. He wondered absently what time it was and how long he'd been waiting, wanting to talk to her—wanting her to talk to him.

Finally, the tension began to bubble up in him, and he had to speak.

"I'm sorry, Cassidy," he said in a gush of air. Her shoulders stiffened. "For following you," he continued. "For complicating things. For Katie—" She held up a hand, halting his speech.

"It's not your fault," she said. "But, why *did* you follow?"

Billy knew he couldn't avoid answering again. He ran through a list of responses in his head. Had it been because he wanted to help? Not really. He wasn't naive enough to think he could do anything unarmed. Had he been worried about the wagon's occupants? Yes. But that wasn't why he'd followed.

Before he could lose his nerve, he dove in. "I was worried about you," he said. "I didn't want anything to happen to you, and I couldn't help myself."

Cass again looked at the knife on his belt.

"I'll never forget that knife," she said. "What I felt when I saw it at your throat..."

She swallowed hard, and Billy felt his own throat thickening. His heart pounded in his chest so loud that he thought it would startle the people moving off to sleep in the camp below.

"You don't have to feel responsible for me, Cass. I know it's what you do, but if anything should happen to me it's—"

She stepped toward him, stopping the flow of his words.

"Listen," she said. "I have a responsibility to keep my family and the members of my group alive. And you became part of that the minute I spoke for you." She caught her breath before charging on. "But—with you—it hasn't been about obligation for a long time. Maybe it never was."

Cass began to pace in front of him, and Billy let out a shaky breath, only then realizing he'd been holding it. He tracked her movement as always, refreshed to watch her without trying to hide what he was doing.

"I have gone over and over what happened in the woods, wondering why I made the choice I made. I've been telling myself it was instinct. The same instinct I ignored when the camp was sabotaged in that orchard. And I know I made the right choice—at least, I know I didn't make anything worse that day. But, the truth is—if the risks had been greater I would've chosen the same." Cass's eyes gleamed in the moonlight, her words breathy and damp as though they also bore unshed tears. "I was afraid of losing you. There's something in you that I need, and I am sorry I've been shutting you out..."

Billy closed the distance between them and took hold of both of her arms, careful to avoid clamping his hand over her injury. He could almost feel the wound as if it was his own. Cass let out a little gasp as he grabbed her but her ragged breathing soon synchronized with his own. He leaned toward her, aching to kiss her, and saw her lean in as well.

Boots scuffed on the dirt trail coming up the side of the ridge, and the two of them parted, whirling to face whoever approached. It was Trace. He shielded his eyes against the shine of the lantern.

"Cass," he said. "And Billy. Hello."

Billy nodded, suddenly remembering what Cass had said to her brother about "screwing" Trace. He looked at the tall, lanky man with a new interest and almost laughed when he realized Trace looked quite a bit like himself. He turned to watch Cass's reaction to the man.

"What's up?" Her tone was casual, though her body language was as stiff and startled as his own.

"Cam sent me to relieve you," Trace said, stepping forward with a slight hesitation as though sensing he had interrupted something. He gave Billy a nod.

"You're not hunting tomorrow?" Cass asked.

"Nope," Trace said. "Plenty of eager takers for that. I plan to eat and sleep and do nothing."

Cass chuckled and swung the rifle down from her shoulder. She offered it to Trace and elbowed him as she passed by.

He turned and said, "Hey, Cass? About this thing with Cam, I—"

Cass was shaking her head. "Don't worry about it. There's no bad blood between you and me. Ever." Trace nodded. "I'll leave my lantern here for you." Then, she glanced at Billy as she slowed her step. "Walk me back?" she asked.

Pleasure burst in Billy's chest, and he followed. Cass grabbed her discarded plate. As eager as he was to be alone with her again, it was awkward picking their way back down in the dark. Cass dropped the plate twice, he slipped and almost fell arse over tit once, and they didn't speak much.

The tents were nestled just under the ridge, making the journey far too short. They came to a hesitant halt watching a few people still milling about, whispering and settling in for the night.

"I think you could use some more self-defense training," she said, looking up through the darkness. Her voice wavered.

Billy nodded.

"I'll find you in the morning." As she started to walk away, Billy reached down and caught her hand. Sensation shot up his arm like electrical current when she closed her fingers around his. He could see she felt the connection, too.

Billy lowered his voice and whispered, "Good night."

Cass gave him a quick half-smile and pulled away. She climbed into her tent and zipped it behind her. Billy stood there numb for a few seconds and then climbed into his own, listening for her movements next door until her soft snoring soothed him to sleep.

DREW KNEW CASS WAS awake already when he rose and began to dress, but he still crept about their tent as quietly as he could. She'd woken an hour earlier with a start and lain as still as a corpse, barely breathing. He hadn't bothered asking what was wrong. He'd never yet managed to pry information out of her—if she needed to talk, she'd talk.

Brick trotted out of the tent behind him, and he scratched the dog's chin before patting his leg in an unnecessary invitation. He hurried to the supply wagon where his rod and reel were waiting and nearly ran headlong into Derrick and Cam. The three men exchanged nods and maneuvered around one another. The two of them were planning the hunt to come. Derrick, not a bow-hunter, was unarmed and joining just to watch.

Drew set to sorting through his tackle box looking for a specific lure. He was vaguely aware of a couple more men joining Cam and Derrick beside the wagon but was so involved in his search he didn't realize someone had spoken to him until Derrick reached over and knocked his knuckles against the wagon.

"Earth to fisherman," Derrick said.

"What was that?"

"Just wondering why you weren't joining us this morning," Derrick said.

"Oh—," Drew covered a yawn. "I think there are plenty of you. Besides, I like fish."

Derrick nodded.

"And where's your girl, Cass?" Adam's tone was not light or

quiet as befitted the morning. "Thought she was the great hunter in your group. *I* haven't seen it."

Drew raised an eyebrow at the sudden hostility, but before he could reply, Cam spoke up.

"Her arm is troubling her," he said. "I told her to take it easy."

Drew tried to keep his face passive, not sure why Cam was lying. He didn't know why Cass wasn't hunting, but he suspected it had more to do with her distaste for the company than any physical ailment. Especially since her wound was healing fine.

He felt Adam watching him as he turned back to his tackle box and snapped the closure. His eyes met Cam's, and he gave a nod. "Good luck," he said, walking away with his gear in hand and his dog trotting close behind.

CASS KNELT, PANTING AND glaring up at the sun, exhausted. Billy's butt was planted in the grass nearby, his feet on the ground in front of him making his knees jut into the air. It was comical—until he put his lips to the water bottle and swallowed, his Adam's apple moving with each gulp. He pulled the bottle away, leaving a bead of dampness decorating his lower lip. She thought of the wine.

He poured some of the liquid into his palm and trickled it onto his head, running his hands through his hair and bringing them to rest on the back of his neck. Wet, blonde tendrils fell forward against his cheeks and Cass looked away.

She'd awakened this morning terrified. Terrified of moments like this. Moments alone with him in the heat, adrenaline already coursing through her, the two of them panting as they tracked each other's bodies. Granted, they were supposed to be planning and defending against punches and holds, but Cass's mind was unfocused today. She shook her head. Her mind was always unfocused with Billy.

"What's wrong?" he asked. His voice was husky from exertion, a fact which didn't help her come up with an excuse about what she'd been thinking.

"Nothing."

"I know what you're thinking." Cass held her breath as her insides sunk deeper into her abdomen. "You're thinking I'm doomed. And you're doomed to continue watching over me. Because your grandmother could probably kick my ass."

Cass faked a chuckle, relieved.

"I never knew my grandma," she said. "And you're not doing so bad. I swear it's like you've done all this before. You're a quick learner."

Billy smiled. "I did get in a couple hits on you. I think you might even have felt one of them."

Cass's smile was real now. He *had* gotten her. She'd been thrilled, not only because he was learning to take care of himself, but also because the shock of the slight pain had helped her focus.

As her smile faded, she realized Billy's expression had also changed. His brow was creased in a frown, and he dug his hands into the dry grass on either side of him.

"Okay," she said drawing his gaze, "now what's wrong with *you?*" Though her tone had been playful, he didn't smile. In fact, he looked ill.

"I have to tell you something," he began.

Cass leaned back a bit, steadying herself for what promised to be a serious conversation. But Lena and Darcy jogged past just then, laughing together which was a strange enough sight to pull both Cass's and Billy's attention.

Waylon was following along behind the girls, and he slowed. With a quick glance between the two sweat-stained and flushed figures, he told Cass the hunters had returned and were looking for help bringing in the meat.

Cass nodded as Waylon left. "Their horses will need to be looked after, too. We'd better go."

Billy looked relieved. He was already getting to his feet, and she was a bit disappointed he wasn't more sore and tired from the workout. Maybe she'd been too easy on him. He offered her a hand up, but she pretended not to notice and stood on her own.

They picked up a jog side by side and Cass was struck by the now familiar and terrifying desire always to be as close to him as possible.

"You're not tired enough, yet," she said.

"Says you."

As they came to the edge of camp, Cass spotted at least three horses with deer carcasses on their backs. She frowned when she saw Cowboy among them. He'd never been one for packing meat, and he'd be a nervous wreck. She increased her pace.

IN THE CLAMOR OF people eager to thank the hunters for the food, Derrick hadn't noticed Cass and Billy run up. He hadn't been expecting them but as soon as he heard Adam's raised voice he knew who it was directed toward.

"—lying to your brother, now. Anything to get a little extra time with your boy."

"What?" Cass kept her tone cool, but her face was flushed. So was Billy's. It seemed they had run here together, though their clothes were too sweaty and rumpled for just a short run. "I didn't lie to Cam."

She looked around for Cam and spotted him, but her brother had not yet seen her.

"Arm wasn't buggin' ya too much for rolling around in the grass with our pretty parolee, was it?"

Derrick confirmed with a glance. Cass's arm seemed fine. It

wasn't bandaged anymore. Adam was advancing on Cass, stepping into her space, causing the horse she held—the skittish one she usually rode—to flail its head away. She didn't step back, not that Derrick expected her to.

He moved toward the commotion. Their argument was drawing a crowd. Cass handed the horse's lead to Billy and stepped forward and away from the animal, brushing against Adam's shoulder as she did. Adam followed her, pushing his chest against her shoulder as she moved, changing her course. Someone in the crowd gasped.

Derrick felt emotion battling in his brain. On one hand, this was just what he wanted. He wanted public opinion turned against Billy. He wanted Cass on her heels. But seeing Adam get physical with her was setting off alarms in his head.

Derrick couldn't hear the whispered conversation between the two of them. But Cass, finding her exit blocked by onlookers, stopped and spoke loud and clear. "We were sparring. I'm teaching Billy to defend himself."

"Bullshit," Adam said. "You're visiting the boneyard."

The term brought Derrick's time in prison to mind and his back stiffened. He could tell Cass understood Adam's meaning, if not where the phrase had come from.

He stepped a bit closer to the two of them. "That's enough, Adam."

"But—" Adam began to protest, fueling the fire that had begun to burn behind Derrick's eyes. He felt his fists clenching beside him.

"The woman can do what she wants," Derrick said.

"Who she wants," said a voice in the crowd. Derrick couldn't place it.

"David and Rain were decent people," Adam directed this comment at Cass, his face so close she flinched as spittle flew from his mouth. Adam turned back to Derrick, lifting a pointed finger at Cass. "They're dead because this *bitch* was spreading for some—"

Adam's words were cut off by Cass's fist slamming into his face. Since he'd been facing Derrick, she'd gotten him in the mouth, and he stumbled back, unbalanced by the surprise hit. Cass was quick, diving in and landing a second blow to Adam's gut with her left hand. The hit wasn't hard, but Adam stumbled a bit, causing the horse behind him to shy away. Billy maneuvered around, trying to direct the horse through the crowd, telling people to step back.

Cass had eased her attack, perhaps intending to stop, but Adam had let the hit rotate his upper body for a reason. As he swung back around, he lifted his arm and backhanded Cass hard across the face.

She grunted and caught herself, managing not to fall flat but to go down on one knee. Derrick was running forward, knowing she wouldn't recover in time. Adam had already raised his fist and was powering it down toward Cass's face.

Derrick let the swirl of hot red take his body, and he tackled Adam to the ground. He landed on the smaller man, shoving downward as if the tackle couldn't drive him deep enough into the ground. Adam had raised one hand up by his face in surrender, with no intention of striking his leader, but Derrick couldn't let it go.

Adam had hit a woman. Adam had single-handedly gone too far and pushed the public opinion out of Derrick's favor. People would care for Cass again if they saw her feminine face bruised at the hand of Derrick's second.

He cracked first his right, then his left fist into Adam's face. The skin on his right knuckles split with the third hit, but the spray of blood was coming from Adam's broken lip, not his own hand. As the fourth and fifth blows landed, Derrick could hear voices of protest through the ringing of his ears. His sixth punch ruptured a tooth from Adam's jaw. He knew the feeling and the sound of it from experience. Memories of his days in the ring came washing back, causing him to pause. He'd have been thrown out for behavior like this.

In his peripheral vision, he could see Cam and Hank coming at him from both sides, ready to pull him away. He raised a hand, palm flat, in Cam's direction. As his anger faded, he knew he needed to salvage his reputation. He shouldn't have done this.

Still, his muscles craved more of the familiar violence. Adam was conscious, though bruised and bloodied. One eye was already beginning to swell beneath the splatter of blood. Derrick took a deep breath, gritting his teeth.

"When I say enough," he growled. "I mean enough."

Derrick shoved himself up from his victim, kneeing Adam in the stomach as he did so. He ended the discussion with a relatively soft kick to Adam's ribs. He glanced up to see the somewhat pale face of another of his men in the crowd nearby. He couldn't remember the man's name through the swirl of hazy anger.

"Get 'im up," he said, straightening his jacket and moving away.

The crowd began to part for him, but he stopped and glanced at Cass. She was on both knees now, her hands limp beside her body. Her eyes were wide, and her brow creased. Already, her red cheekbone was darkening into purple.

"You okay?" he asked.

"I started it," she said, breathless.

"He needs discipline," Derrick said. He left, regretting those last words.

Thirteen

BILLY CAUGHT HIMSELF STARING at the large bruise on Cass's face for what must have been the thirtieth time that night. He wanted to run his fingers over it, to cool it, to ask her if it hurt. He felt eyes on him and turned to see Cam watching.

"How's your face?" Cam asked, bringing other conversation in their little dinner group to a crashing halt as all eyes turned to Cass. Billy had been near her all through the afternoon and evening and no one—except him—had asked her if she was okay before now. Her response to his own concern had been a terse "of course" and then an order to hold Cowboy steady while she checked on a crack in his hoof.

For the first time since the fight, she smiled. "Worried about me big brother?" she asked. "I'm tougher than *you,* you know."

Trista laughed and Drew put on one of his goofy grins. Cam nodded, smiling, his gaze turning briefly back to Billy. Cam had been the one to haul his sister to her feet after the fight, with no show of concern whatsoever. But he'd kept to her side, and they'd talked extensively, too quietly for Billy to hear.

"I remember you being a hothead, that's what I remember. Why is my baby sister always the one getting into fistfights?"

"I know," she said. She looked down at her feet for a moment. "I shouldn't have done it." The silence grew oppressive. Then, Cass sucked in a breath and cracked a half-smile. "I should've turned the other cheek."

Trista chuckled, and Drew let out a snort. Cam chucked his apple core at Cass. She deflected it, and it hit Billy's bare foot. As she retrieved it, her arm brushed across his shin. Their eyes met in a flash of questioning. Brick ran up and sat in front of Cass, mouth open in a comical pant, tail wagging in the dirt.

Cass tossed the apple core to the dog as the conversation turned to Trista's fishing prowess, which was apparently much greater than Drew's. The little group felt warm again. They'd reconciled without apology, and it was like no time or conflict had passed between those first stressful, exciting days of the journey and now. As he watched the four of them jibing one another, he missed the interactions of his own family.

"Why on Earth would I name my baby after your childhood cat, Drew?" Trista asked. Cam laughed beside her.

"He was a great cat," Drew said. "I only suggested it because naming him Drew would challenge Cam's masculinity."

"Ha," Cam said, smiling around the bite of fish he'd just put in his mouth.

"I like Caleb," Trista said.

"Caleb's nice," Cass said with a shrug. "If you want to stick with the "C" names."

"So that's a family choice," Billy said. "I wondered." They all nodded. "What about Christopher?" Billy trailed off, sensing the stiffening of everyone around him. Drew caught Billy's eye and gave his head a single shake. "Uh—or—what was your uncle's name?"

Cass and Cam exchanged a look. Cam swallowed and said, "His middle name was Dallas. We're leaning toward that for a girl."

"But, I'm not sure I want to break the "C" tradition," Trista said, her voice sweet and hesitant.

Cass's face was downturned as she said, "Maybe you should." Her tone was conversational but carried shades of meaning Billy ached to know.

"There's always Collin," Drew offered.

"Or Calvin," Billy said. And again, the group froze. Trista turned to Cam and Drew turned to Cass waiting for reactions. Brother and sister only shared another long, indecipherable look.

"There was already a Calvin in the family," Cass said. Billy's whole body felt flush with his embarrassment. Had he brought up the name of another dead relative? Two in a row? Feeling like a complete ass, he decided to keep his mouth closed for the rest of the meal.

But, it was too late. Cass stood and left without a word, leaving the rest of them to shift awkwardly in her wake.

"Sorry," Billy said, a bit of his accent trickling into the word.

"You couldn't know," Cam said.

"She hasn't talked to you about her father?" Drew asked, earning himself a slightly shocked look from Trista.

"No," Billy said.

Drew sniffed and took a swig from his canteen. "She will," he said.

CASS WAS GRATEFUL THEY'D decided to stay over another day. She slept into the afternoon the day after the fight, then found Doc to ask about Adam. When she learned he was fine, she set out to take stock of the condition of the horses and supplies, but as she rounded a large boulder that had fallen from the ridge above, she nearly ran into Hank.

Her blood pumped double-time. She'd hardly been able to speak to him since the kidnapping, so great was her guilt. He apologized for the near collision and moved to step around her.

She built up her courage as quickly as she could, like filling a pitcher from a fire hose until it overflowed. "I'm sorry, Hank," she said. She stared at the dark skin of his collarbone.

"For what?" Cass swallowed and fumbled, but Hank reached out and touched her good arm. In his eyes, she found the forgiveness she'd never hoped for. "You said you'd make an effort, and you did," he said. He gave her a melancholy smile and walked away.

For a while, Cass stood there by the boulder. But soon she felt the need to talk to someone. It was such a new sensation—wanting company. A good portion of the camp was at the creek, washing clothes. Cass gathered her own laundry and went to join them. She was surprised to find Lena and Billy working side by side in silence.

She sat down with them, which caused Lena to make a hasty exit. Shaking her head, Cass set to her work.

"I'm sorry I left so quick last night," she said after a few moments of silence.

"*I'm* sorry," Billy said. "For putting my foot in my mouth."

"I was just tired. And sore." She indicated her puffy cheek which she knew was at its ugliest today. She'd been getting stares everywhere she went.

"I hated seeing you fight him," Billy said.

Cass nodded, giving him a long look before changing the subject to Hank and then onto a hundred less serious topics. The stiffness and hesitation between them were forced out by the flow of conversation.

That evening, after another hefty meal at sunset, someone

started a fire and people began to gather around it. Some danced, but it wasn't the raucous affair that had taken place after the wine drinking. Even after the day's rest, the group was still drained from the events of the past weeks. The guitar wound down into a soft, subdued melody.

Cass felt alone; as the group around her was waning, she was buzzing. She and Cam were speaking again. Lena seemed to be easing up on her hatred of Billy. It seemed that Billy's interest in her matched her own in him. They'd spent the day together, only splitting up after dinner when Drew had pulled Cass off to dance for a bit.

Cass spotted Drew now, helping Cam to lift a sleeping Trista and carry her away from the fire. Several people had fallen asleep leaning against rocks, luggage, and one another. Talking had ceased, and some had begun to filter away to their tents. She let her gaze lift cautiously across the fire to Billy. He was leaning forward, chin resting on his hand as he watched the guitarist play. His expression was quietly hungry. *He* didn't look tired, she reflected and then banished the thought.

Cass stood, careful not to disturb the woman leaning against the tack trunk next to her legs. Marie offered up a sleepy smile, and Cass's eyes widened as she spotted Waylon asleep with his head cradled in her lap. Cass was a bit stunned to see a relationship progressing between them. She felt guilty for any passing judgments she'd made.

Once free of the circle of people, Cass crossed the stream at a narrow spot where a log had been placed as a bridge. The horses grazed in an open area on the other side. A few heads lifted as she approached and then dropped back to their grazing. Cass stretched as she walked and stared up at the full moon, so bright it dimmed the stars.

Suddenly, she felt weighed down. She shrugged out of her

jacket, letting it fall behind her. With practiced ease, she dug a toe into the opposite boot heel and pulled her foot free. She did the same with the other boot, reached down for her socks and jerked them off her feet. She wiggled her toes in the lush, cool grass and as she walked, her steps took on a familiar rhythm.

She was far enough from camp that the guitar was just a soft hum on the breeze when she began to dance. She let her memory conjure up the song that had been drifting in and out of her mind since Utah. And why not—alone here in the open with a freshness in her mind and no audience but animals? She closed her eyes and let her head fall back, but the song stalled.

With a small smile, she let herself picture Billy's face and the melody she'd been repressing burst forth, eager for her voice. She began to spin and hum, swaying her arms and her hips. She cut herself free of consciousness and simply moved to the sound of a guitar in her head—more real to her than the one she'd just heard at the campfire.

With each breath, she took in the musk of horses and the secret clarity of night air. Finally, the song came to a close in her memory, and she opened her eyes to stars and treetops whirling in her vision. With a dizzy smile, she gave in and folded to the ground, burying her fingers in the grass.

The snorting of a horse broke through her bliss, and she looked up to see Billy standing at ease a few yards away. Smoke had gone over to greet him, and he absently offered the horse his hand to sniff while he smiled at Cass. There was something sad in his expression.

She allowed herself a moment of embarrassment, then chose to let it go. She chuckled, falling backward once more. Billy approached and stretched out on the ground beside her. The intake of breath before he spoke was startlingly close, so she was prepared when his voice resonated directly beside her ear.

"I bet you haven't done that since Before."

"Done what?" Cass replied and swallowed away her hoarseness. "Made a fool of myself when no one was supposed to be watching?"

His laugh was all breath, and she could feel the warmth of it against her cheek. "Danced barefoot in a pasture after dark," he answered.

Cass risked a minuscule turn of her head to look at him. His face was close enough she could watch his pupils adjust as a cloud covered the moon, stealing away the brightness. Cass lost track of time as everything inside her body decided to defy gravity and float weightless within her. It seemed the only thing holding her down was her right hand, flat against the earth and millimeters from his left hand. She wasn't sure how she knew this, as she'd never torn her gaze away from his to check, but there was no doubt in her mind it was so.

It could have been seconds or hours, but neither of them moved. Billy remained silent, never prompting her to answer. When she finally did speak, it seemed a lifetime had passed between them, but she remembered the question without struggle.

"I never did that before you."

Billy missed a breath—or more. Her lungs were burning too when he finally let out a soft gasp of air and breathed in again. His pinky finger fell across her own. Her lips parted in wonder as she tried to sort out why that tiny touch was so much more intimate than anything she'd experienced in her life to date. More intimate even than the kiss in the wine cellar.

Eventually, her breathing steadied, and she relaxed under his gaze. She shut her eyes and twined her little finger tighter around his.

BILLY'S THOUGHTS GREW HEAVY as he watched Cass fall asleep beside him. He'd followed her out here to tell her so many things. To ask her things, too. He wanted to tell her he'd realized who had hurt her. Last night in his tent as he'd thought about everyone's reactions to his name suggestions at dinner, it had become painfully and disgustingly clear to him.

He wanted to tell her he was glad her father was dead. He'd have wanted to kill the man who'd harmed her before she could defend herself. Because he loved her. He loved her even if it seemed crazy. He had to tell her who he was—the stupid reason she had recognized him and the stupid life he'd lived Before. He needed to tell her and hope to heaven and hell she would understand why he'd hidden it.

But, when he'd seen her dancing out here in the moonlight—singing *his* song—he'd been so stunned. Even though it had been the perfect time to confess, he couldn't bring himself to do it—couldn't bring himself to do anything but be near her and touch her in whatever small and pathetic manner they could both tolerate.

Billy's eyes stayed locked on her face, memorizing—until the lids closed heavily over them. Even then, he dreamed of her.

CASS SHIVERED AS SHE drifted into consciousness. Her back and shoulders were chilled while her arms and the front of her body were warm. She was just wondering what had happened with her sleeping bag when she was wakened further by a horse's snort. With a jolt, she remembered the night before—dancing in the pasture, falling into the grass, and Billy. Her eyes flew open and struggled to adjust in the fuzzy pre-dawn light.

Her hands were the first things to come into focus. They were pressed against the gray cotton of a T-shirt and warmed by the rhythmically expanding chest beneath it. One hand was spread, her palm flat, the other was loosely fisted in the shirt. Billy's jacket enclosed much of the both of them; one of his arms rested under her neck, and the other was draped across her upper body. She took stock and realized their legs intertwined in an impossibly comfortable way.

She lay still, dealing with her surprise. She had somehow managed to sleep beside him in the truck bed at the orchard, but Drew had been there, just a few inches away on the other side of the window glass. She'd drifted in and out of consciousness in the back of the wagon with him and Doc, but it hardly counted when she'd been concussed.

And this was vastly different. They were holding one another; an intimacy she'd never known. She couldn't believe she was experiencing it while lying in the grass somewhere in Missouri with a man she'd only known a couple of months.

She wished she could see his face—wondered how he looked when he slept—but her head was tucked under his chin, the scar on his neck at the level of her eyes. She let out her breath in an unintended gush. Billy stirred and stiffened, and she knew she'd woken him. She waited for his reaction.

His hand flexed on her arm as he breathed out with exaggerated control. She felt the muscles of his forearm beneath her neck as he moved that hand in the grass. Slowly, he pulled away, his jacket slipping and exposing her bare arms to the cool air. She wasn't sure if the following shiver was caused by that chill or by meeting his eyes.

The blue of those eyes stood out like she'd never seen it before against his pale skin and hair in the washed-out gray light. They were wide, and his mouth was open like he had started to say something and lost the will. He blinked a few times as the two of them shifted and disentangled their legs. He rolled onto his stomach, but not before Cass had realized why he'd want to. The evidence of his arousal had been pressed against her. She flushed.

He propped himself up on his arms and Cass folded an arm beneath her head, trying to find the appropriate words. In the end, it was Billy's hoarse voice that broke their silence.

"Good morning," he said. "Are we okay?"

Cass searched his face for more information. He was staring at her like an animal tamer trying to calm a frightened creature. Wasn't *he* was the one who should be frightened of this?

"Okay that we fell asleep out here? Okay that we woke up like that? Or are you asking if we should sneak back to camp before anyone sees us like this?"

Billy raised his brows. "Yes? All of that?"

"Are *you* okay?" she asked, looking away and propping herself higher on her arm, scanning their surroundings.

It seemed a very long time before he replied.

"I've been wanting to hold you. I guess I needed to be asleep to do it. But, yes, I'm okay."

Cass felt a shy smile spread across her lips, unbidden, as she met his hopeful gaze. Her heart thudded in her chest, and she rolled onto her own stomach almost as an excuse to turn away from his affection for a moment.

Hoofbeats approached, and they turned as Smoke sauntered up. She snuffled Billy's back and the top of his head, bringing about welcome laughter, and then wandered off again to graze.

"She likes you," Cass said. "She always had good taste." Cass was pulled into memories of Smoke. The horse would put up with any number of balance issues or clumsy cues in exchange for kind hands and good judgment. She'd act like a lazy sow for the first couple rides with anyone, but if she liked a rider, she'd come to respond. If she didn't like someone, they might as well find a new mount.

The horse had loved the man who'd died on her back. The patient first boyfriend who had handled Cass with the same sort of care he'd shown the gray mare. Cass tried to recall his face but this scene was far away from anything she'd known with him. She'd never slept with him—even after sex. She'd never opened herself to that with anyone.

Billy was the first.

He tossed his head, flicking back a long strand of hair that had fallen into his eye. It was a gesture of long practice. He was used to his hair being this long. More important, the gesture forced guitar chords into Cass's mind, again. The familiarity was overwhelming right now when she was so open to her feelings.

"Who are you to me?" she asked, thinking the wonder in her voice sounded a tad dramatic, though not unwarranted.

Billy cast his eyes down at the grass and shook his head. "Whoever you want me to be," he said.

She searched his face for more recognizable features, frowning. "You just still seem so familiar, sometimes."

Billy reached out and ran his thumb over the scar on her arm as he had done once before. Her body reacted almost as intensely as it had then. Her skin tingled as all the tiny hairs lifted and her breathing grew shallow as if even her lungs were afraid of breaking the spell of his soft touch.

"It was your father, wasn't it?" Billy asked, still staring at Cass's scar. "He was the one who hurt you." Cass had the uneasy sense that the world was dropping out from under her. Her fingers dug into the grass before her, tensing her whole frame, but Billy went on.

"Did he give you this?"

When Billy saw her face, he jerked his head back and dropped his hand. Cass felt a tremor in her shoulders. Billy shook his head, mouth agape, and started to reach out to her.

Cass pushed herself to her feet and moved away.

"We should go," she said. She hurried over to her boots and coat where they'd been discarded the night before. She picked up a jog and leaped the creek without hesitation, refusing to look back.

Fourteen

B Y MIDDAY, BILLY WAS exhausted from the effort of starting to apologize—or say anything—and shutting himself up. He had put his foot in it already, and he didn't want to make things worse.

Granted, Cass had been acting as if nothing were wrong. She talked to him as usual and was riding beside him now, occasionally commenting. Things weren't right, though. There was a stiffness in the way she spoke, the way she moved. She was avoiding eye contact.

Through every phase of getting to know her, there had been a sense of opening. A sense that he was moving from room to room heading for the center of a building. A new door had been opened when they'd awakened in each other's arms this morning. And he'd gotten it slammed in his face.

He deserved it. He knew that he should tell her why she recognized him—come clean about his true identity from Before. He'd tried. But, every time he was close to fessing up he got scared of her reaction. He worried she would be hurt and angry that he lied, just as she'd been hurt when Cam had kept Trista's pregnancy from her. But *he* wasn't family, and she could choose to push him away for good.

But, he *felt* like Billy. This man Cass was learning to trust—this person she was teaching and working beside was the new him. This was what came out on the other side of an apocalypse, three years of imprisonment, and a handful of near-death experiences. He was Billy now, and he was hers. William Wyson had died when all hope of going home to find his family had been lost.

He'd panicked this morning because he didn't want her to see anyone but Billy when she looked at him. It had been a reflex to deflect her attention. But he hadn't intended to demand information about her past. It wasn't fair to ask her to tell her darkest secrets when he wasn't even willing to give her his true name.

He jerked back to attention as hoofbeats approached. Drew observed the two of them with poorly hidden curiosity as he rode up.

"Cassidy, my Cassidy," Drew said. "Thy brother beckons thee." Drew's faux British accent was horrendous, though Billy reminded himself he shouldn't say so.

Cass nudged Cowboy into a trot and headed out. Drew maneuvered his mount into the space she'd vacated and pulled the horse closer to Billy.

Billy glanced over at the man and for a moment tried to ignore his expectantly raised eyebrows and the knowing glint in his eye. Deciding it wasn't worth it, he sighed.

"What is it?"

"Cass didn't come back to the tent last night," Drew said, his voice quiet but eager.

Billy felt a flush creeping onto his cheekbones. "Huh," he said. "Are you sure? Maybe you were sleeping and didn't hear her."

Drew gave an exaggerated shrug. "I suppose it could happen. But it didn't."

Billy just frowned.

"Know how I know?" Drew asked.

Billy gave his head a shake. Might as well get this over with. He was apprehensive to know what might have been seen last night—considering the mercurial opinions about a relationship between him and Cass.

"I woke up worried about her, so I went looking for her," Drew continued. "You were adorable, you know. Snuggled up together in the pasture." Drew's lighthearted tone had taken on a sharper edge toward the end, and a hardness in Drew's features belied the playful way he'd broached the topic.

"Nothing happened," Billy said.

Drew scoffed. "Yes, it did. She spent the night with you. Again."

"We just *slept*," Billy said, worried he was about to get knocked off his horse by an impressively-muscled and perhaps justified friend.

"Exactly," Drew said, lowering his voice further. "I wouldn't be here if she was just having sex with you. She trusts you enough to *sleep* next to you, and I'm getting the impression you still don't understand what that means."

Billy signaled Smoke to stop, and Drew halted beside him. The wagon pulled ahead and soon they had created a kind of privacy through space.

"She sleeps with *you*," Billy said, hearing a note of unintended jealousy in his voice.

"She feels safe with me," Drew said. "Look, I'm sure you've figured out she didn't have the best childhood. For a long time after The End, she hardly slept at all because she had to sleep out in the open with strangers. Cam used to wrack his brain looking for ways to make her feel secure at night because she had two nervous breakdowns."

Billy felt like he'd been slapped. God, he was dumb. She'd been so vulnerable, and he'd asked her about her childhood abuser.

"When she saved me—that wasn't the first time we'd met. We knew each other Before. Since she rarely slept anyway, she sat up with me. In exchange, I told her everything about myself. We bonded. And she ended up falling asleep in a chair beside me every night. So when I was better, we shared a room or a tent or whatever we had. And I'm the only person she's slept with since. Until you."

"She didn't tell me," Billy said.

"She used to sneak off to be with Trace and sneak back in an hour later," Drew said. "But, I knew you weren't like Trace from day one. You mean *a lot* to her."

Billy rocked back into the saddle, slouching. Smoke shifted her weight beneath him. He ran a hand over his eyes. "I fucked up," he said, a bit of accent riding along with the desperation on his words. "I didn't know how important it was to her."

Drew's eyes flared for a moment and then calmed. He looked up and stiffened. Billy followed the other man's gaze to see Cass coming back. Drew sat up straight and asked, without looking, "Do you love her?"

Billy sucked in a breath. "Yes."

"Then, fix it," Drew said, kicking his horse forward.

CASS FROWNED UP AT the sun. The caravan had come to a stop, and it wasn't even noon. Her brother had told her that it might be a short travel day—that they might even reach their destination. There was a campsite just within the border of Stronghold's territory where they were to camp and wait for an envoy to come and escort them into the city. Surely they weren't there already. She ran a hand along Cowboy's rump and patted him, risking a glance at Billy.

Billy was scratching at a mosquito bite on the back of his hand. Cass had several like it from their night outdoors. Billy caught her watching him.

"I'll go find out what the hold-up is." She cleared her throat as she directed Cowboy away.

The three leaders were up ahead of the caravan, at the precipice of a hill, looking down. When she rode up, she found Derrick and Hank holding out a map between the necks of their horses, heads bent in study. Cam looked on with a smile that widened when she pulled up beside him.

"Why are we stopped?" she asked.

"Because we're there."

Cass felt an unexpected smile cross her face. A soft tingle of expectation and hope spread through her, and she turned to look down the hill. They were coming up to a wooded area and sure enough, not more than a mile further, a dirt drive led away from the road to an overgrown campground. A flag bearing Stronghold's symbol flew above the lean-tos and corrals. From this distance, the structures seemed in good repair.

Beyond the campsite, Cass could see the blue water of a lake. It was exactly as the recruiters had described. She looked up to see Hank folding the map and nodding to Derrick.

"This is it," Derrick said, his body language more relaxed than she'd ever seen it and his voice honestly pleased. At that moment, she felt a strong kinship with the man.

She giggled. Shocked that such a sound had left her lips, she laughed harder. The three men started laughing as well. Adam rode up with a quizzical expression and peered at each of them in turn.

"What's going on?" he asked. He rode forward and took the map from Hank's hand. He spread it, his horse sidestepping beneath him and looked down the hill. His bruised jaw dropped, and his still-puffy eyes widened. His expression made Cass laugh harder still.

She glanced back at the group to find several people watching them as though they'd lost their minds.

"Tell them," Cam said to the now suddenly-composed Derrick. "I know you want to."

Derrick nodded and rode back toward the head of the group, lifting his hand to gather everyone's attention. Cass wiped moisture from the corners of her eyes.

"We've made it!" Derrick called out. "This is the place!"

A slow whoop lifted up from the crowd, followed by others as the news traveled back through the group to the people who hadn't heard.

"Let's go, already," Hank shouted, and he kicked his horse forward and disappeared down the hill, causing something of a controlled stampede to follow. Cass pulled Cowboy out of the path of the frenzy. It seemed anyone on horseback or biking was rushing past.

Cam was on foot, stopping the wagon Trista rode in so she could climb down and leap into his arms. Cam kissed her and held her against him, then bent to kiss her growing belly.

Before the wagon could pull forward again, a shout caused Darcy to pull the reins once more. Waylon rode up, his stirrup and booted foot scraping the side of the wagon as he reached for Marie, who rode inside. She grabbed and kissed him, nearly pulling him from the horse's back. A few people passing by let out whistles at the display of affection.

Cass turned at the sound of hooves bearing down on her. It was Drew and Billy, riding up fast.

"What are you doing, dummy?" Drew called out. "Let's go!"

She grinned and turned Cowboy sharply, sending him forward and down the hill. She held him back a bit on the slope, but when she hit flat ground, she urged him forward as she lifted herself in the saddle. She heard hoofbeats behind her and glanced over her shoulder, surprised to see Billy had overtaken Drew. He was riding well, with an excited grin on his face which grew as he saw her looking.

She slowed as she turned up the drive. People were jumping up and down, someone was kissing the ground, riderless and confused horses were milling about. Normally, she would have hated the chaos, but today she could only laugh. She pulled Cowboy off to the side of the commotion and dismounted.

Billy dismounted and on impulse, she grabbed his hand and pulled him after her into the trees. The woods weren't dense here, but within a few yards she found a sizable old tree and ducked behind it.

She moved to wrap her arms around him, but his expression turned from thrill to apprehension. Forceful was more her style, but she swallowed back her eagerness. She tugged him forward by the hands until his body pressed against hers. Then, she waited.

His eyes were shadowed with hesitation. She leaned her head toward him, feeling his breath against her face.

"Billy," she said. "Just kiss me, already."

Her plea seemed to erase the doubt clouding his eyes, and he met her lips. They stood there, hands linked, bodies pressed close as the kiss slowly heated up. Cass let herself get lost in the movement of his lips, the thudding of his heart, and the warmth of his form.

The wagons rolled up on the road, breaking the spell. Billy pulled away, and she released his hands, taking a gasping breath and wiping her lips. She looked at him and cleared the passion from her throat before speaking.

"We made it."

Fifteen

CASS STOOD ON THE creaky roof of an old outhouse overlooking the lake. The splashing and shouting of swimmers took her back to a less dangerous time in her life. Before the world had ended. Before she'd killed anyone. Before she'd taken responsibility for anyone but herself and Huckleberry. Back when her biggest concern had been the exposure of her body in a bathing suit rather than the possibility the swimmers might be attacked as they backstroked. The press of the rifle between her shoulder blades was a welcome comfort.

Cass had insisted on taking her turn at guard, despite Cam's assurance that they were now within Stronghold's protected territory. He was sure the flag would deter any Rovers from attacking them and equally certain whoever had been following them had given up the chase long ago. Still, Cass had taken the first watch, determined not to let her guard down when they were so close. Lena and Billy had seen to the horses.

But, they were done. Billy was approaching the lake carrying a bundle of bright-colored cloth under one arm. His gaze had locked onto her on her perch just as she'd spotted him, and she was having just as much trouble pulling her gaze away as he seemed to be. She needed to either focus or dive into the lake. The cool water might do her good after their last kiss.

Billy almost ran into someone, and she laughed under her breath. The laughter stopped abruptly as she realized someone was calling her. She looked down and met Lena's hard gaze. From the irritation in her expression and her proximity to the outhouse, Cass knew the girl must have hailed her more than once.

"Honest to God, Cass, you're not even trying to hide it anymore," Lena said as Cass leaned down closer.

"I don't have anything to hide from you, Lena," Cass said.

"True." Lena put her hands on her hips. "I'm well aware of your lust and incompetence, so..."

Cass turned away for a moment and let out her breath in a huff. "What did you need, Lena?"

"My father is coming to relieve you," she said. As she spoke, Cass spotted Waylon approaching with Marie.

Cass stood and scanned the open spaces on the opposite side of the lake, then she turned and looked along the treeline behind her. People were lounging in the shade there, and beyond them the camping area was quiet. She slipped out of the rifle strap and handed the weapon down to Lena, butt first. Then, she turned and moved to swing down from the roof, but her hand scraped against something sharp, and she lost her grip. She fell straight down to her knees.

Lena snickered as Cass pushed back up to her feet. The girl handed the rifle to her father and strode away. Cass watched her go, rubbing at her bruised knees. She spotted Billy, now at the edge of the lake.

He had taken off his belt and was sliding his knife sheath off the end. He laid the weapon down on the bright towel he'd been carrying. Her mouth went dry as it hit her. He would soon be removing clothing.

"You'll have to forgive her."

Cass was startled. She'd almost forgotten Waylon and Marie were there. He gave her a sympathetic smile.

"She really looks up to you. She doesn't know how to behave now that you've taken such a strong interest in a man."

Cass's focus drifted back to Billy. He had stripped off his T-shirt and twisted around to look at his side, running his fingers over his ribcage. The bruises had faded to the point where Cass couldn't see them from this distance. Satisfied, he glanced up and found her looking. He turned away almost shyly, but not before she'd seen his small smile.

Cass turned her attention back to Waylon, who had gone on talking about his daughter. He was oblivious to the fact she'd tuned out.

"—was never like normal girls, you know. I mean not that she's abnormal—but she never went in for boys the way other girls did." Waylon paused and grunted as he helped Marie to unfold a stubborn camping chair. Cass turned back to the lakeside.

Billy was now standing with his jeans around his ankles, wearing boxers. He stepped out of the jeans and glanced back in her direction. Cass clenched her teeth to keep her jaw from dropping. He'd filled out a bit over the past several weeks, and though still thin, he was well put together. He had a model's body to match the gorgeous face. Even considering the scars. There were burn marks on his ribcage that matched the one she'd noticed on his arm. She'd never noticed them before, probably because the bruises had always drawn focus.

Still, Cass could tell no one would care about a few scars. A pair of girls had stopped swimming to gawk from the shallow water just off shore. Cass felt a rush of jealousy, and suddenly she wanted to be beside him.

Thoughts of swimming with him in the cool lake water took over—slippery skin against skin and inhibitions eased by the buoyancy of their bodies. Apparently, the feeling was mutual because he turned to face her, head cocked to the side and his eyes drifting over her. She turned impatiently back to Waylon.

"—sister got her a poster of some actor for her birthday one year, and she never hung it up. Finally, Darcy took it back and hung it in their bathroom. Prob'ly still there if the house is still standing."

"A poster of some actor." Those words brought down a revelation Cass had been seeking. In an instant, the sunny day grayed out, and the joyful sounds around her became hollow echoes.

Cass had once been kicked in the gut by a horse; her body flung back into the corner of a shed. She'd crumpled to the ground, all the wind gone out of her. She hadn't even been able to gasp in surprise. It was that moment she was drawn back to as realization sucker-punched her now.

She was vaguely conscious of staring at the boulder behind Waylon's legs, but she was seeing her old room, back at her uncle's house. There had been three posters on the wall behind her bed. Three posters she hadn't thought of in years; a photo of paint horses running through a field, a print of the cover of her favorite book, and next to them, a full-sized theater poster.

The poster had featured the cast of a recently-released movie. Three beautiful teen girls and two beautiful teen boys. And one of them had been Billy.

Her head whipped back to look at him. He'd changed, of course, but she could see it now, so clearly. The cheekbones, the jawline, the hair and the way he tossed his head to flick it back out of his eyes. She remembered he'd been a musician, too. She'd listened to his work on the Internet. That song—the song that had been haunting her all this time—was his. Her eyes flashed down to his side and the peculiar burn mark. It had been a tattoo.

Cass staggered back a step and heard Waylon asking if she was okay. Billy's shoulders sunk as she looked. His eyes were sad and dark with understanding. His lips moved in the shape of her name, but she had begun to shake her head.

The spiral of embarrassment and shock inside her increased to such a wild pace she thought she'd be ripped apart, and she took off at a run along the treeline.

"CASS, WAIT!"

She kept running, and Billy spent a second caught in conflict wondering if it was better to leave her be or to chase her and beg forgiveness. He couldn't shake the panicked feeling he'd never see her again if he didn't go, so he sprinted after her.

People who'd been staring at Cass as she flew past, turned to stare at him. He ignored them. He called out her name almost without meaning to, his tone desperate. He thought she was heading for the horses, and she did indeed make it to the corral, but she turned sharp right and headed for the trees.

"Cass!" he called again. She only moved faster. His lungs burned, and he found more speed somehow. He hadn't known he could run this fast unless he were running for his life; which he felt he was.

Cass leaped onto an overgrown trail, her arm slamming into what was left of the wooden sign identifying it. This slowed her. She clutched her arm and stumbled a step or two, giving him the opportunity to catch up, just as the shade of the woods closed around them.

He reached toward her, suddenly not sure how he intended to stop her. It was well established she could put him on the ground—or in it—if need be. But before he could touch her, she whirled around and shoved her index finger into his chest. It brought him to an abrupt halt, just a foot from her. He winced, more at her anger than the pain.

"Let me be clear," she said. "I do *not* want to talk. Don't follow me."

She spun back around and took off running, again. Though he wished it, his feet would not follow. Billy stared after her for a long moment before his gaze fell to his own arm, still extended out before him. It seemed not to be a part of him just then—he couldn't feel it. He couldn't feel much of anything.

AS HE WALKED, DREW bent to run a hand over Brick's head. The dog's rear end wiggled, and his front paws popped off the ground in his pleasure, eliciting a smile that swiped away Drew's troubles—if only for a moment.

Dogs were easy. They shared everything in the way they held their bodies and often expressed themselves so easily the power of speech would have been redundant. His human best friend shared a lot in her body language, as well, though she'd hate to have that pointed out. But without words, she was harder to *understand*. She was impossible right now.

Drew knew she and Billy had a fight at the lake. After watching her tearing through the crowd, holding back tears with Billy sprinting after her screaming her name, everyone knew. But she wouldn't tell what had happened.

As Drew came up to the supper table and began to fill a plate, he scanned the crowd looking for Billy. He hoped to get details from the other half of the conflict. He spotted his target sitting on a log, but he wasn't alone. Rylynn was sitting next to him, her arm pressed up against his as she laughed, open-mouthed.

Drew hesitated. Though it made his heart sink a bit for Cass's sake, he wasn't the type to get in the way of a person moving on. But Billy was perched on the very end of the log like a soft shove would send him toppling. More telling was the fact Rylynn's plate was sitting a few feet away from her on the opposite side as if she'd started scooting closer and Billy had moved away again and again until there was no more log.

Drew turned toward them with purposeful steps, and Brick trotted ahead, stopping occasionally to get a pet and a scrap of food from people in the crowd. As Drew watched, Rylynn leaned closer and stole a piece of pheasant meat from Billy's plate, grabbing hold of his hand to keep the plate steady. Billy's discomfort was clear.

Drew picked up his pace and Brick, infected by the speed, passed him. To his great amusement, Brick trotted straight up to Rylynn's plate where it waited on the log and began to help himself to her unfinished food. The woman let out a screech as she stood and chased the dog away. Her plate had fallen to the ground, and she was bending to pick up the mess just as Drew arrived and sat down in the spot she'd left.

Billy looked up, and relief flooded his face. Rylynn's face was painted in surprise and irritation.

"Yeah, you'll want to watch your plate around Brick," Drew said. "He's quick to go after other people's leftovers." Drew took a dramatic pause and raised his brows. "You know?"

Rylynn frowned, then made a breathy sound of annoyance and departed.

Drew scooted down the log, giving Billy space.

"Thanks," Billy said.

"Why don't you just tell her you're taken? Next time she comes 'round."

Billy turned to Drew with a frown and shook his head. "Because I'm not."

"Yes, you are."

Billy cleared his throat and whistled for Brick, setting his plate on the ground. The dog burst out of the bushes behind them and set to work on cleaning without hesitation. Billy ran a hand down the red-flecked fur on Brick's back.

"You don't know the whole story."

"She won't talk to me, no. I thought *you* might."

Billy crossed his arms over his chest with a sigh. "Did she ever tell you the reason she saved me that day on the trailer?"

Drew's forehead creased. He knew she'd saved Billy because she thought everyone deserved a fair shot at survival. Because she was afraid of being alone in the world, herself. But more than once in those first few days, she'd mentioned Billy had seemed familiar.

"She was right?" Drew asked. "She *did* recognize you?"

Billy set his jaw and nodded. Drew was filled with questions but didn't want to bombard the other man. He ate his dinner and waited.

Brick finished eating and wormed the top half of his body into Billy's lap. As the man held and scratched the dog, his stiff shoulders loosened and finally, in a rush, he confessed.

"I was an actor. She knew me from a film."

Drew's eyebrows flew up, and his chewing first stopped, then continued at a more thoughtful pace. He studied Billy's face as covertly as he could and tried to remember movies from Before. When he'd swallowed, he set his plate aside.

"Anything I might remember?"

Billy shot him an incredulous look. "What? That's not the point. The point is she asked, and I knew where she recognized me from, and I lied." Billy sighed and ran both hands harshly through his hair. "She has no reason to trust me."

"Eh," Drew said. "She does anyway. Whether you've given her reason or not. It's a feeling, an instinct. Cass trusts her gut." Billy was looking at him wide-eyed again, and Drew stifled a laugh.

"Everybody hides things. I don't know why you'd keep *that* quiet, though. I'd brag about it. Get special treatment."

Billy's expression grew heavy, and Drew regretted his flippant tone. He'd meant to cheer Billy up, make light of it. Apparently not the right move.

"That's not how it worked for me," Billy said. His words were weighted with dark implications and Drew remembered the few details Cass had shared about Billy's imprisonment. Billy didn't seem to have any plans to elaborate so Drew leaned forward, resting his elbows on his knees.

"You had reasons," Drew said. "And you don't need to share them with me, but you should tell her. She's in love with you." Billy turned to Drew, looking skeptical. "She is. I know her. But, I don't think she's ever been in love before. Not really. And for that to happen in this fucked up life—to someone who had a fucked up life Before…" Drew shook his head.

"She trusted me, and I lied to her. All along," Billy leaned forward, miming Drew. "If she cared about me before, she doesn't now that she knows."

Drew laughed aloud. "Right, I forgot. You can just turn love off. Just like sexuality. A flick of a switch and suddenly I'll be straight."

Billy raised his eyebrows and then cracked a half-smile.

"We all keep secrets to stay safe," Drew said. "She'll understand."

Billy nodded and his look of doubt gradually morphed into one of determination. He stood and offered his fist to Drew. They pounded their knuckles together.

"Thanks," Billy said. "Do you know where she is?"

Drew sat up straight and began to speak when a distant crack, like thunder, sounded. Both men flinched, and Brick gave a sharp bark. Around them, people had ducked or dropped plates and were now looking at the sky and at one another in confusion. Another crack sounded, this one softer. Then, another and another.

Someone shouted, and heads began to turn. People stood, leaving their spots and rushing to the lakeside. Drew and Billy exchanged a troubled glance and jogged after them.

Across the lake, a series of clouds were rising, a glow of orange reflected in them. After several explosions, the noise stopped, though the smoke lingered and the glow intensified. People were running toward them, converging on the lake, shouting and questioning.

Drew heard Billy speak and turned to see Cam standing beside them.

"Could that be Stronghold?" Billy was asking. "I mean. That's that direction, right?"

Cam nodded, his face grave in the bouncing light of lanterns held by various people. But Billy's gaze was now fixated on the trees, and Drew followed his look. Cass stood there, just at the tree line, hands on her knees as though she was panting. She slowly stood and pressed a hand into her side, staring into the glowing distance with a look of defeat.

Sixteen

CASS HAD ALREADY TACKED up Cowboy by lantern light and waited at the lake's edge, staring off toward Stronghold. Her body ached from standing here through the night, arguing with Cam and Derrick. She'd wanted to ride to Stronghold right after the explosions, but they had insisted it was foolish to leave before first light. She rubbed a hand across her tired eyes. Maybe they had been right.

But now, the sky was turning blue in increments and the morning chill was making her restless. The distant fires were dying away after burning all night, and Cass was increasingly worried there would be nothing left of Stronghold by the time they arrived. When she heard footsteps approaching, she sighed in relief.

"Finally," she said, turning. "I'm ready to—"

But, it wasn't Cam. It was Billy. He paused, waiting for her to finish her sentence. She turned back to look out over the lake, and he came to stand beside her.

She had shut down her emotions, closed off thoughts of him as best she could, choosing instead to focus on the explosions and the potential danger and conflict they now faced. But his proximity was tangible, a battering ram against those young walls she'd built. Even standing there quietly he was pressing, begging his way back in.

"I thought you were Cam," she said, unable to bear heavy silence. She was too anxious to be near him without distracting herself somehow.

"I'm coming with you," he said. It was a simple, direct statement and yet Cass was baffled.

"Like hell," she said. The bite in her tone somehow surprised her. She hadn't had adequate time to process her discovery of his identity, and hearing her own hurt and anger so clearly intoned in those two little words brought everything crashing back.

"You can't stop me." Billy's tone was mild. "I already spoke to Cam."

Cass let out a dry "ha" of a laugh. "We'll see about that. Where the hell *is* my brother, anyway?" She turned and began to maneuver Cowboy around Billy, who remained unmoving, arms across his chest.

"He's eating," Billy said. "It'll be a while."

Cass felt tension beginning in her chest and expanding out through her limbs. She felt a tremor of anger rolling inside. She couldn't think of anything to say and knew she'd never manage to avoid screaming at him if she tried to speak. So she shoved her way past, her shoulder connecting with his arm and sending an unwanted but familiar thrill through her. Cowboy sidestepped out away from Billy, who stayed grounded like a statue.

Cass tied Cowboy and wandered toward the soft murmur of voices and the clatter of plates. Not many people were up yet, but her brother sat in a circle with a few others, making a meal of last night's leftovers. A hitch came into her stride. She couldn't yell at Cam about Billy in front of the others, especially with Derrick there. She didn't want to let everyone in on the conflict—didn't want to let up on her implied protection of Billy.

She came to a complete stop. *Why should I care? He's a liar. He used me to keep himself alive, putting his acting skills to practical use. He let me wonder all this time, let me think I was crazy, and all along he knew why I recognized him and just kept quiet. Why should I keep protecting him?*

Derrick turned and spotted her, then pointed her out to the others and waved her over. Cass sighed. She knew it didn't matter. She would keep protecting him. Because the curious, searching look Derrick gave her as she approached caused a mild alarm to ring in the back of her head. She tasted the panic she'd felt last night when the explosions rocked the ground. She'd run back to camp, not for a better view, but to ensure everyone—especially Billy—was alright.

The others were looking up at her expectantly, so she knelt on the ground beside them and cleared her throat.

"When do we leave?" she asked.

THE PATH IN FRONT of Drew's feet was growing visible as he followed the small party to the horse paddock. Cass had gone on ahead, more restless than she was letting on, he knew. She had tied the required horses and was running a brush across Whiskey's side. She turned to watch them walking up, and there was such strain on her face Drew regretted not urging the others to hurry.

Though, he suspected at least some of that strain came from Billy's presence. He was tightening the cinch on Smoke in another corner of the paddock with a resolute expression that almost made Drew chuckle.

Drew lifted a booted foot and moved to heft himself over the paddock fence, but he paused. He'd heard something in the distance. He twisted around to look out toward the lake and strained to hear better, cocking his head to the side.

"What is that?" Cass asked. She had come to stand just on the other side of the fence.

Hank and Cam had been chatting as they approached the corral, but they grew silent when she spoke and soon Cam was walking back toward the lake, tension in his shoulders.

The muffled noise was growing louder and separating out into a series of sounds, a rhythm of beats. Hoofbeats. He opened his mouth, but Cass beat him to it.

"Riders," she said.

Drew felt a tightening in his chest as everyone moved at once. He leaped down from the fence and reached to his hip for his gun. Cam was shouting at the camp at large, calling everyone to arms. Cass flew over the railing like a deer and shouted something to Billy about rifles at the gate. She pulled out her pistol and jogged forward to join Drew, flanking Cam. She rolled her shoulder and turned on the hard and startlingly cold look he had come to expect from her in a fight.

By the time the riders became visible in the dim light, much of the camp was spread out near the lake with rifles aimed. Cam and Derrick stood out in front, Hank just a step behind. Drew, Cass, and Trace—who shivered in nothing but unbuttoned jeans—stood a pace behind them.

It wasn't a large party; Drew counted four approaching, and two of them held flags. One flag bore the symbol of Stronghold, a match to the flag waving above the campground. The other bore a similar symbol with different colors. The lead man held up a hand to halt his group as they rode into shouting distance. He dropped his reins.

"I'm going to dismount," he called. "To come talk to you."

"Are you from Stronghold?" Cam called back. The man was

dismounting and didn't answer right off. Instead, he raised his hands and then pointed to his side.

"I'm going to remove my weapon," he called. He did so slowly and stepped to the nearest rider to hand up the gun. Then he turned and walked toward Cam and Derrick, arms held in the air. "I'm unarmed," he called unnecessarily. Cam was the first to lower his weapon, followed by a reluctant Derrick. Seeing Cass had no intention of lowering hers, Drew held fast.

"Are you from Stronghold?" Cam repeated. The man stopped and shook his head.

"No. We're from New Danville, a sort of—well, sister city to Stronghold," the man glanced at Cass and Drew and then over to Trace. "Can we speak without the weapons, maybe?"

Drew looked to Cam, who turned and said simply, "Cass." Cass lowered her gun, and Drew and Trace followed suit.

"Thank you," the man said, lowering his arms. He pulled off his gloves and stepped forward with his hand extended to Derrick, who shook it. In turn, the three group leaders introduced themselves, and it became known that the man was John. When the introductions concluded, John cleared his throat and spoke.

"I'm sure you saw last night's explosion from here. There's been an accident."

"We saw," Derrick said. "We were getting ready to ride out there, see what had happened."

The man shook his head, his expression glum. "There's not much left of Stronghold, I'm afraid." He nodded when gasps rose up from the assembled people and raised his voice to be heard over the buzz. John gestured behind himself, at the mounted men. "Most of our people are there now, helping survivors. We knew you all had arrived and thought we should come and tell you the news."

"What kind of accident was it?" Cam asked, arms across his chest.

The man sighed and shook his head again. "Stronghold had a problem with Rovers coming in through a woodland area to the north of the city. Stealing, murdering, raping. They were looking into setting up a minefield. Tapped one of New Danville's most talented minds to come up with formulas for the explosives and detonators. Not an easy thing to accomplish, I'm sure you understand." The man put his hands on his lower back now, with more sorrowful head-shaking that seemed a bit affected. "There must have been an accident. Sadly, our man is nowhere to be found."

"It wasn't an attack, then?" Cam asked, arms still crossed.

"No, sir," John replied. Doc approached Hank and spoke into his ear.

Nodding, Hank said, "Do you have a doctor to help the survivors?"

John frowned. "Unfortunately, no."

Doc stepped forward, "I'm not exactly a doctor. I was an EMT, and my wife was a surgeon. She taught me what she could. I'd love to come and help treat any survivors."

John paused for a moment, cleared his throat, and said, "Well. Sounds like you're the closest thing."

"Didn't Stronghold have a doctor?" Cass asked. Drew glanced her way. Billy had—unsurprisingly—appeared at her side.

John turned to Cass, and a half-grin appeared on his face for a moment before he wiped it away and answered. "Yes, they did. Unfortunately, we heard he passed away a couple of weeks ago."

"Ah," Cass said. "That's too bad."

"It is," John said, turning back to Doc. "We'd be very appreciative of any help you could offer us."

"I'll get a horse ready, and we'll head to Stronghold," Doc said, already turning back toward the paddocks.

"Sure, but we'll be taking you to an encampment of ours instead. We've moved the injured there," John said.

"You've been moving them?" Doc asked, now stopped in his tracks.

John shrugged. "There are still fires burning in Stronghold. We needed to get them to safety. The camp was a sort of meeting place, halfway between Stronghold and New Danville."

Doc nodded and jogged away. Cass stepped forward and addressed John again. "Since doctors are so scarce, you'll understand if we don't send ours to an encampment we've never seen without sending a guard with him."

John raised an eyebrow, and his smirk returned as he regarded Cass. Drew held back a smile. People were always surprised by her—she wasn't the kind of beautiful that stopped traffic, but once someone noticed her looks and the quietly forceful way she held herself, it was difficult to turn away.

"Of course. Send a guard. Come yourself if you'd like," John said.

"I'll do that," Cass said.

"No," Cam interjected. "We'll send someone else."

Drew wasn't surprised. Cam valued Cass much more than Doc, even with the upcoming birth of his child taken into account. But, he definitely wouldn't want to risk losing both of them.

Drew almost felt a chill as Cass turned to her brother. "Why not me?"

"I want you here," he said. A message passed between the two of them, carried on the look they shared. Cass gritted her teeth and nodded. Drew could hardly believe she'd conceded.

But, he knew a perfect alternative.

"I'll go," he said, taking a step forward. Cass looked at him, and he could see the conflict in her expression. She always hated for him to be away, hated for him to take risks without her by his side. But, at the same time, she considered his eyes and his skills to be the next best thing to her own. "You can trust me to keep him safe."

Cam glanced at Cass, who nodded her approval, and then he

turned to Trace. Seeing the man barely dressed he looked to Derrick. "Anyone you'd like to send? That way Doc will have two guards, and we'll have sent someone from each group."

Derrick shrugged. "I don't see the need."

Cam nodded, but Cass stiffened.

"I think we should send another guard. No sense taking chances when we're not sure we're in safe territory."

"What makes you think we're not safe?" John spoke up, having watched all the goings-on with interest.

Cass shrugged. "I'm sure we're not the only ones who saw that explosion," she said.

Cam was nodding. "If Stronghold had enemies sly enough to sneak through the wall, they're sure to be watching."

"It would be a perfect time for an attack," Drew said, realizing this "sister city's" encampment might be at risk. He was willing to protect Doc but wasn't sure he wanted to be apart from his group in a war.

John was shaking his head. "I swear to you, any friends of New Danville will be safe here. We are more than ready to step up and take over for Stronghold in protecting these lands. It wouldn't be the first time."

"Why weren't you there, then?" Cam asked, crossing his arms again. "Why two cities, instead of one?"

John cleared his throat and hitched up his belt. "There were some differences of opinion about rules and regulations. Differences between Stronghold's council and our old leaders. We have new leaders, now. We'd been working to settle those differences. Sadly, we'll never know what the two cities could've been together."

"Is there any chance of rebuilding?" Derrick asked. "We've traveled a long way to have to turn around and travel back. We'd never make it before winter."

John smiled. "You are all welcome to join *us*. Perhaps, when this tragedy is sorted we can discuss it."

Drew felt a rush of uncertainty in his gut, and he turned to watch Cam's reaction.

"A generous offer," Derrick said.

"Very," Hank agreed.

"We'll discuss it," Cam said. And he turned away, looking over the crowd and making his way toward Trista.

John and Derrick met eyes for a moment before John turned back to his waiting party. "We'll lead you there when you're ready," he called back over his shoulder.

"Cowboy's ready?" Drew asked.

"Billy will bring him," Cass said. Drew's eyebrow went up. "Drew." She stepped close to him and lowered her voice, "Be careful."

"Something wrong?" Drew asked, matching her volume.

"Who knows," she said. "Everything? Maybe nothing. This isn't what we signed up for. Find out what you can about these guys. Check their story. Just—be careful."

"Always." He leaned forward and kissed her forehead. "I'm a good detective, you know."

"I know," Cass conceded. There was no end to the surprises with this girl today. "But, I wish I was going with you," Cass added.

"Uh-uh," Drew said, shaking his head. "You need to stay. Keep everyone else safe. And talk to Billy."

Cass shot him a sharp look.

"No, seriously. Cass, you're happier around him. And you two are a good team. See?" Drew nodded at Billy, who was leading Cowboy toward them. Doc rode alongside, and the two of them were discussing something to do with Smoke. Every few sentences, Billy would gesture toward the gray mare. "You have a connection. And these days, you can't afford to waste that. Got it?"

Cass was still frowning when she turned to him, but she nodded. "I'll talk to him." It sounded more like she intended to rip Billy a new one than have an intelligent and fair discussion, but Drew didn't have time to argue. There were bigger concerns today.

He took Cowboy's reins from Billy and mounted. As he settled his frostbite scarred foot in the stirrups, wiggling his toes in the extra boot space created by the two missing ones, he spotted Brick. The dog had made himself scarce during the earlier standoff and now paced, staring up at Drew expectantly. He would've liked to bring the dog, but wouldn't want him in harm's way.

"Tie Brick up for me?" he asked, looking down at Cass. She nodded and reached down to grip the leather collar she'd given him. It felt so comforting to have a companion like Brick. As he looked down at Cass, whose gaze had honed in on Billy once more, he thought it might be nice to have romantic companionship someday soon, as well. After all, how could he give advice about taking chances when he didn't take any himself?

Cam and the other leaders came by to see them off.

"Take care of my doctor," Trista said. She smiled up at him, clinging to Cam's hand. "I need him."

Drew assured her he would.

Cam stepped away from Trista and added quietly, "Find out what you can about their city and their ways. See if John's story checks out."

Drew nodded, not bothering to say that he and Cass had already discussed this.

"Be careful," Cam added.

With another nod, Drew clucked to his mount.

BILLY WATCHED DREW RIDE away and then watched Cass stare at the spot where they had disappeared. She knelt beside Brick. The dog had whined for a few seconds as Drew left without him and now leaned quietly against Cass's legs. The gathering of people slowly dispersed and Cass stood, patting her leg for Brick.

Billy followed as she led the dog to the corrals and secured him to a signpost with a lead rope. She stood with her hands on her hips, staring into space until Cam approached and stood before her with his hands jammed in his pockets and a frown creasing his forehead. He nodded at Billy and turned back to his sister.

"What do you think?" he asked.

"We don't know anything," she said. "We're probably in as much trouble right now as we ever have been and just don't know it yet."

Cam nodded. "Probably. Maybe not."

Cass let out her breath and shook her head. "Well, it *is* your job to be the optimistic sibling. Always has been."

Cam nodded again and reached forward to put a hand on her shoulder. "Yes. Optimism is inspiring, but it isn't what's kept us alive. That was you."

Billy watched as Cass stared at her brother with a kind of nervous wonder. He wanted desperately to move forward, to see her face a bit better as she took in what her brother was crediting her with.

"I have a lot to apologize for, Cass," Cam went on. "And one day, I'll say what needs said. But, today? I want you to talk to Drew and Doc the second they get back and then tell me your instinct. I have a feeling your gut is what's going to keep us safe, again."

Cam left, nodding at Billy as he passed. For a few moments, Billy stood frozen, afraid to breathe too loudly or shift his weight and break the spell. He didn't want to remind her of his presence and all the doubts she must have. He saw her swipe the back of her hand across first one cheek, then the other. She sniffed and turned to him.

First, she looked to the left and right over his shoulders. When she met his gaze, it was as if he looked at a steel door. Her face was passive and her eyes hard.

"So, William Wyson, you ready for an interview?"

Billy felt like his soul was coming apart inside his chest, hearing the bite of his given name spoken in her voice. He could hardly contain the grasping desperation to make things right and the blind panic that promised he never would.

"I GUESS I KNOW why you took to it so easily. You've had to learn how to fake a lot of things in your life. Though, this is the first time you were acting to actually *save* your life so I suppose I should be honored that the performance was just for me."

Cass struggled to contain her emotion, but she was failing. She wanted to scream at him, to rip him to shreds. She wanted to rip out her own hair and cry. Mostly, she wanted to grab him and kiss him. She wanted to believe the sorrow and regret in his eyes were real and pretend she'd never figured it out at all. She hated herself for that thought and gritted her teeth against it, feeling tears threaten behind her eyes.

"Cass," Billy said. She cut him off with a slash of her hand.

"Not here." A couple passed behind him, headed for the lake with breakfast plates. She spun on her heel, thankful for an excuse to put her body in motion. "Follow." There. That had come out like an order, not the shaky plea of a person in love. Relocating was already helping.

She pushed her way into the trees, slowing as her eyes adjusted. Though the sun was rising, it was still a dark blue in the woods. She felt his eyes on her back and listened to his obedient footsteps close behind. Her face contorted, and she ground her teeth again. Her heart thrilled like it always did when he was near and her body, so completely attuned to him, recognized that they were alone here, even despite her anger.

She stopped and rolled her shoulder in two complete circuits before whirling, ready to confront him. He stood closer than she'd expected, looking ill and braced as if he expected to be beaten. There was such longing in his face, akin to the way he'd always looked at her but so intense here in the half-light it made her question everything she knew in the world.

Suddenly she wanted to run. He must have known what she was thinking.

"Please stay," he said weakly. Cass swallowed and tried to remember all the accusations she'd planned—all the questions she'd had for him. She settled on one with relatively little importance.

"What was the song called?"

""Divine"." His voice had turned robotic, and his expression settled as if he intended to answer questions all day.

She approached him purposefully and considered slapping his face, too pretty in the filtered dawn light. To his credit, he didn't move. She took in a deep breath.

"And how did you *really* survive The End?"

"The friend I told you about was a fight choreographer. We were on location working on a scene when it happened. And he did keep me safe. For a while."

"What did you do to get locked up?"

He turned his face up to the trees, frowning as if trying to find the words. "I existed. When the man who saved me—I called him Nash—when he got tired of taking care of me, he—sold me." He stopped when Cass's eyebrows lifted and took a breath before charging on. "This group of people thought they could use me. They thought I had connections or people looking for me—people who wanted me back. They assumed that because I had money, I had resources. But nothing I had was worth a *damn*. You know that. And eventually, they realized I was no use, so they traded me to the woman who put me in the basement."

Cass turned and continued to push her way through the trees until she burst out into a field on the other side. She stopped and put her hands on her hips.

"So, you really didn't do anything?" she asked when Billy emerged from the trees after her.

He shook his head.

"Why didn't you tell Derrick all that?"

He sighed and pinched the bridge of his nose with his fingers. "Nobody recognized me anymore, so I didn't *have* to tell, and I realized I didn't want to. The things that happened in that basement..." He shook his head. "She was sick. Obsessed. And I didn't want to be the object of her obsession anymore. I didn't want to be someone who got other people killed."

A frown crossed Cass's face. The thought had occurred to her that there was some greater reason he'd changed his identity. But, why from her? Why wouldn't he trust her after all this time she'd spent protecting him—getting close with him?

She shoved her doubts aside and let anger take her tongue, again. "Why did you hide it from me? I mean, I get why you didn't want to tell me at first but then—" she threw her hands out to her sides. "I thought you trusted me. You kissed me. You—we spent every waking moment together. We *slept* together, and now I find out that was all because of a poster?"

His jaw dropped. "A poster?"

"Yeah!" Despite her efforts to appear calm, she practically shrieked her reply. "That's how I remembered. I had a poster." Cass's tone changed from anger to disbelief as she continued. "A fucking poster! That's why I could sleep next to you? Because your face was on a poster in my room?"

"No!" Billy shouted back, horrified. "That's not why. You *know* that's not why. It's more than that."

Cass was surprised he'd raised his voice, and she noticed how pieces of his accent were slipping into his words as he got worked up. The night before when she'd figured out who he was, she'd thought back and remembered he was British. She'd noticed the twinges of the accent before and always thought it was just a fluke of speaking too quickly.

"Your fucking accent!" Cass exclaimed. "What? Are you just going to pick it back up now that I know?"

"It doesn't work that way," Billy answered. His anger quieted for a moment, but there was still tension in his voice. "I've been hiding it for so long—long before I met you—I don't know if I'll ever get it back. It slips back when I'm upset."

"*You're* upset," Cass said indignantly.

"Of course, I'm upset," he said. "I meant to tell you—"

"Clearly, I wasn't that big a fan," she went on, ignoring him. "I forgot about you, after all." She began to pace back and forth and saw his eyes tracking her. "But you knew." She turned and bore down on him, putting her face close to his. "You knew I recognized you. I gave you plenty of chances to tell me." She covered her face with her hands and hung her head. Her voice came out muffled as she continued. "That song. I sang your song, and I butchered it, but I *know* you knew it was yours."

She felt his fingers, gentle on her wrists, pulling her hands away from her face.

"I'm so sorry. Yes. Yes, I knew. And you didn't butcher it. If I could go back and write it again, I'd change it. I'd write it the way you sang it that night in the field."

Cass's heart soared and then plummeted to the bottom of her feet. She stepped back, jerking her arms away.

"Nice line." Spittle flew from her lips. "You should've been a screenwriter instead of an actor. Not that you're not a good one. I actually believed you had feelings for me."

His face contorted and became fiercer than she'd ever seen it.

"I do," he said. "I do have feelings for you. That's why I couldn't tell you."

Cass raised an eyebrow and opened her mouth to tell him what an idiot he was, but he went on.

"I wasn't worth a bloody thing after the world ended. I couldn't take care of myself the way you guys can. That's why I didn't tell you who I was."

Cass shook her head. "That doesn't make sense. You know that doesn't make sense, right?"

"It does," Billy was firm. "It was one thing for you to help the college student from California who worked part time in retail, it was another thing for you to help some guy who'd once been famous and wealthy. I mean, other people thought I was getting what I deserved—payback for the blessings I'd had Before."

Cass shook her head. "No. No, that's not how it works. It doesn't matter who you were Before. You could have told *me*."

"Cass, you were so amazing to me. Do you understand that? You were amazing! You were so tough and so resourceful. So independent and kind. I couldn't stand that you might think less of me."

"Jesus, Billy, think *less* of you?" Cass felt the tears she'd been holding back slip from her eyes. "I tried to kill myself!" Time and nature seemed to freeze after she spoke the words. Her lungs stiffened, and she had to gasp in a breath to jumpstart them. The breeze even seemed to pause.

"Things happened to me that seem—well, they were awful. But when you compare awful to the apocalypse it's just—they're just things. It wasn't just my dad. It was my brother, Calvin." She pulled up her left sleeve and pushed the knife sheath aside, fully exposing her scar. "He gave me this and worse when I didn't give him what he wanted. Cam had to save me, and we had to run away. And I couldn't get past it, even after I was safe. I tried to kill myself."

Cass paused to catch her breath and force back the tears.

"But you—what you went through." She stepped forward and

looked up into his face. "You were locked up in someone's basement for three years. And I can't even imagine what happened. And you never thought about giving up, did you?" His eyes glazed as he stared at the ground near her foot.

"And when you got out, you took another beating. And you still had the will to try. You appealed to a sense of justice in those around you. And you still find beauty in a herd of elk or a plant. In starting new relationships."

Without realizing it, Cass had stepped even closer to him. Her hands were held in front of her, and they were nearly against his chest. He eyed them, and she stopped moving, though she kept talking.

"Who you were Before—it wouldn't have mattered. It wouldn't have changed the person I was getting to know..." Cass trailed off, unsure if what she was saying was true. Would it have affected her decisions about him?

"If that's true," Billy said, taking a halting breath, "why does it matter now?" He took a slow step forward, pressing his chest against her palms. His gaze was steady on her, but Cass could feel from the lack of movement under her hands that he was holding his breath.

"I trusted you," she said.

"You still can. You know that. You know *me*. I'm Billy, Cass. Just Billy. Your Billy."

Seventeen

DREW AND DOC WERE ushered toward a tent the moment they dismounted. They'd stopped at the edge of the encampment which provided Drew no opportunity to get a good look at the scale of the place. It seemed larger than expected, given their claim it was used only for meetings and emergencies. He'd gotten the impression no one lived here, but the noise of voices and the people milling about seemed to indicate a settlement.

Unease followed him as he passed through a tent-flap, noting the ground beneath his feet was well-worn with deep tracks from a time when people had walked in the mud, and the sun had dried the imprints. Grass was growing up around the wooden tent supports.

As Drew's eyes adjusted to the lower light inside the tent, he saw large tables laid out cafeteria style. It looked like a mess hall in a war movie from Before. Several tables had been pushed aside to allow for the cots which lined one side of the tent. There were grooves worn into the ground where the tables had been.

Drew schooled his face into a less-conspicuous expression and nodded at the guard who was staring him down. The burly man held a rifle easy in his arms, and he turned and continued his slow circuit of the large tent without nodding back.

Doc had already run to the cots. Most were empty. Doc spoke in soft, urgent tones to a man who had been appointed to help familiarize him with the injuries of those people they'd pulled from Stronghold. Those five people. Just five.

On one cot, two women sat on either side of a young boy, huddled together as if they meant to cocoon him with their bodies. A couple of bags and a stuffed bear waited on the cot next to them. Across the way, a head with blood-caked brunette hair jutted out above a ratty blanket. The head shook. The whole cot shook.

Doc knelt beside a third cot, holding a man's hand lightly in his own, checking a pulse. No, he was checking *for* a pulse. He lowered the hand and moved to the neck. After several seconds of breathless watching, Doc shook his head. Four survivors.

Doc's voice grew louder, and the man he was speaking to frowned, his face reddening. Drew crossed over to them, the foot of the woman nearest him jerking away as he passed. Both women watched him warily. He put a hand on Doc's shoulder and felt it shudder.

"What?" Doc said.

Drew leaned down and spoke into Doc's ear. "A moment?"

"I need to see the other patients," Doc said, teeth gritted behind his lips.

"Thirty seconds, Doc."

The gray head nodded, and the man stood. Drew led him a few feet away as the red-faced man pulled the blanket up over the head of the dead body. The guard's stare followed their movements as Drew whispered, "Tread carefully. This isn't on the up and up."

"Five people, Drew," Doc said. "You're telling me there were only five survivors?"

"Help as much as you can, as quick as you can and don't let on that anything bothers you about any of this. Let's just get out of here, okay?"

Doc nodded and brushed past Drew on his way to the cot where the shaking woman lay. Drew stretched and turned. The guard was still watching him, so he faked a yawn and pretended to check his shirt buttons and his belt. His hand brushed across his gun, and he could see the bulges of the knives in his jeans pocket and his boot. He was only minorly reassured.

He knew the guard was still watching him, having lost all interest in the gray-haired and apparently unarmed Doc. Drew crossed over to one of the tables, making more of his limp than necessary. He let out a groan as he sat and finally the guard looked away. He rapped his fingers against the table, yawned, and alternated between watching Doc work and scuffing his boot in the dirt. After a few minutes, the guard grew bored and stepped out through the tent flap. Drew could see his legs there still, just outside the doorway.

The man with Doc seemed to have grown helpful. He ran back and forth to a collection of first aid kits, bringing gauze and alcohol. One of the women had stretched out on the cot with the boy beside her. The other moved to sit on the cot next to the injured woman's and watch Doc's ministrations.

Drew stood and crossed the tent to a place where a decent-sized hole had worn in the canvas. He bent and peered through. The rest of the camp was down a slight grade from here, and it was quite large.

There were a few permanent buildings including what seemed to be a stable. Beside it was a paddock where there grazed maybe twice as many horses as their group had brought. One building was a large steel garage or workshop set on a concrete foundation. An armed guard stood outside. What used to be a barn seemed to be some type of supply building with people passing in and out. And there were tents. A lot of tents.

Drew paced, regretting his decision to come here more every minute they stayed. When they'd been there for about an hour, the child began to cry. Doc spoke to one of the women, and she whispered back.

"Drew," Doc called over to him. "Could you find some drinking water?"

Drew nodded and started toward the tent flap. The guard's bulk appeared in the doorway.

"We need water for the survivors," Doc's helper said.

"I could get it if you just point me the right way," Drew said, trying to keep his tone light. "I need to take a leak, anyhow."

The guard stayed planted where he stood, forcing Drew to come to a stop. Drew met the guard's eyes and remembered what Cass had told him when she'd been teaching him to defend himself years ago. *The ones that are bigger than you will always underestimate you. When you see them doing that, you've got them.'* The guard's eyes panned briefly up and down Drew's frame.

"Come with me," he said.

"I know how to find a bush on my own," Drew said.

The guard laughed. "We have outhouses."

The guard indicated a row of man-sized wooden boxes before leaving to get water. Drew jogged down the hill, observing as much as he could about the camp. The first outhouse was occupied, so he stepped into the second, realizing it was not a pleasant place to stay if one didn't actually need to be there.

He stood awkwardly for a minute, listening for the person in the first outhouse to leave. The only noises coming from the box indicated that the occupant wasn't finished, so Drew opened the door on his own box and glanced around, looking for the guard. He was hopeful that he might get a few more minutes to snoop, and he slipped between the two outhouses for a better view.

That's when a glint of metal caught his eye. His heart juddered and restarted when he saw the bicycle leaning against the back of the outhouse. He'd almost knocked the thing over. He was supposed to be paying attention and keeping himself and Doc alive, and he'd let an inanimate object sneak up on him. He was cursing himself and turning away when something lying in the grass next to the bike caught his eye.

He glanced around for witnesses. Seeing none, he knelt in the tall grass and retrieved a plastic miniature vanity plate. He turned it over and over in his hand, wishing it didn't say what it did— wondering if maybe he'd misremembered the one he'd seen on the first day of their journey. No matter how he stared, it still featured the graphic silhouette of a nude bicycler with the words 'Keep Portland Weird' underneath.

He quickly tucked the plate into his boot and pulled his pant leg back down. As he stood up, he saw the guard returning, carrying a plastic gallon jug.

He walked up and raised a hand in greeting. A lump caught in his throat as he realized the large man was frowning at him.

"Where were you?" the guard asked.

"Uh—in the toilet?"

"You came from *behind* the outhouse."

"I just wanted to have a look at the camp," Drew said, slowly starting to walk back up toward the tent. "Your set-up is impressive." Drew grinned. "I mean, I gotta say, maybe we should've been coming to join you guys in the first place. Not to be disrespectful to those lost, of course."

The guard's face softened, and he shrugged, an awkward gesture for a bulky person with a rifle strap over his shoulder and a gallon jug in one hand.

"I didn't know anyone there," he said.

Drew held the tent flap for the guard, but before he could follow him through, he heard hoofbeats trotting up. He turned to look at the horse and rider and did a double take as he saw a gray cat perched half on the back of the man's saddle. Its claws dug into the saddle pad where the material extended beyond the leather. It would have been funny if he'd seen it anywhere else.

Something tickled in his memory, chilling him as he watched the pair move down the hill. But the guard was waiting, so he ducked into the tent. Doc made eye contact as they approached and Drew widened his eyes and mouthed the word "hurry." He sat at the table he'd occupied earlier for an uncomfortable wait.

THEY'D BEEN AT THE camp for only a few hours and were returning mid-afternoon, the sun hot in the sky. Drew's stress level had been ratcheting up bit by bit the entire time. John and two other men were accompanying him and Doc home. As they left the encampment, a man rode up to John and whispered with him for a moment.

The news he delivered seemed to please John, whose shoulders visibly lifted after the encounter. But Drew's were drawn down by his horrible realization. As if the bike and the vanity license plate hadn't been enough, he now remembered hearing Adam, drunk on wine, telling some story about a cat that rode horseback with its owner. It seemed too strange a coincidence.

Drew's tension and the resultant exhausting effort of hiding it didn't start to ease until he caught sight of the campground and people moving about by the lake. One of the distant figures froze in place for a moment and then let out a shout and ran deeper into the camp, toward the tents. He let out a grateful breath.

"Glad to be back, huh?" John's voice startled Drew. He hadn't realized the other man had ridden up so close. The ordeal was far from over, and he was caught distracted again.

Drew glanced at the other man and shrugged.

"It's okay if you are," John continued, resting his rein hand lazily on the saddle horn before him. "We're intimidating. We mean to be. There was no bad blood between us and Stronghold in the end, but those that left were mostly men and all armed, so..."

"Hey, that's the kind of protection we need, right?"

John nodded and looked Drew over. Drew faced forward, pretending not to notice the scrutinizing stare of the man beside him. The group by the lake expanded. They were close enough now he could pick out individuals.

"There's always room in the upper ranks of our group," John said. The man's tone suggested he was offering the donkey the carrot he'd be led by. "For you or maybe your friend, Cass. An—election— might be just the thing we'd need. After you got settled with us."

Drew forced a smile and hoped it looked genuine. "A very generous idea. I'll be sure to remember it when we're deciding."

As they closed in on the group, Drew scanned the crowd, looking for Cass. She wasn't there. When John halted his horse, Drew stopped beside him, and the two escorts came to a stop a horse-length behind. Doc, however, who'd been silent the whole return journey, weaved through the stopped horses and continued forward.

"Thank you for your services, Doc," John called out as the gray horse passed his own.

Doc waved a hand.

John looked down at Cam and Derrick, who had stepped forward. Cam held Cowboy's reins and eyed Drew's face briefly before turning to acknowledge John.

"Of course, we have no plans to send all you fine people back into the cold," John said. "We'd love to have you join us."

"A kind offer, John," Derrick said. "But, we aren't exactly one group here. We'll have to discuss it amongst ourselves."

John nodded, turning a smile and a nod to Cam and Hank in turn. "We'll stop back tomorrow afternoon," he said. "For your decision."

Drew watched Cam open his mouth and then close it. John turned his horse and headed off at a trot, the other men falling into ranks behind him as he left. For a long moment, no one said anything as they watched the riders leave. There was a current of tension running through the group. That current seemed to spike when Adam turned to Drew with a blank smile.

"They were welcoming?" he asked.

Drew let out a sigh and dismounted. He glanced back at the riders who had disappeared behind a bend in the road leaving a low-hanging puff of dust behind them.

"Drew?" Cam asked.

"If you call having an armed guard follow me around and yell at me when I dared to look at their campsite welcoming then yes, they were welcoming."

"What?" Derrick asked. Cam just lowered his gaze. He looked older, jaded even.

Drew bent to pull the license plate from his boot. The group of people waiting for his statement shifted and Cass rushed through. Her hair dripped with water as if she had splashed it over her head, but it didn't hide the puffiness of her eyes. She stopped between Hank and Derrick, running her gaze over Drew as if to ensure he was intact.

Now that Cass had appeared, Drew felt the need to purge himself of the story. He described New Danville's camp in as much detail as he could remember. He answered questions from both Cass and Derrick but kept a steady pace. When the moment was right, he produced the license plate.

"As if all that weren't enough," he said. "There was a bike there, and this was on the ground beside it."

He held it out to Hank. Frowning, Hank stepped forward. A second before he grabbed it, Drew saw him recognize the plate. He stopped, hesitant to take it. Instead, Cam pulled it from Drew's hand and held it up for Hank and Derrick to see. He raised it higher so the group at large could look. The crowd began to rumble with conversation and Drew took the opportunity to glance at Adam with fresh eyes. Could he be working with John?

"They might have—" Hank began, but he trailed off. He had accepted the plate from Cam and was studying it.

In the following pause, Doc's voice sounded from somewhere buried in the crowd. "The women with the boy," he said. "One was his mother, and one was his aunt. They were terrified of the men from New Danville. The mother begged me to get them out of there and when I said I couldn't; she asked me to take her son. They also told me that Stronghold hadn't been expecting any new recruits. The last recruiters they sent never returned."

Drew met Cass's eyes and willed her to feel his urgency.

He saw a restless energy take hold of her. She glanced over her shoulder for a moment and said, "Cam. We need to leave. Today."

Eighteen

WITH TREMENDOUS EFFORT, DERRICK had managed not to reach over and strangle Cassidy Hood in front of everyone. From the moment Drew had pulled that stupid license plate from his boot, Derrick had watched his plan spiral down the toilet and disappear. It was all over.

Maybe, if there hadn't been hard evidence, he'd have been able to work it through. He might've swayed popular opinion. But he'd been relying on these cocksuckers to be smart and discrete. And what had they done? They'd screwed him.

As chaos broke out over Cass's declaration, Derrick backed out of the crowd. He needed to think. He needed to decide on a plan. Cam would follow his sister. And his group would follow him. Hank was driven by fear, and Hank and Cam had bonded. So the Oregonians would follow Cam.

Derrick only saw two options for himself. One was leaving.

John and the others would have a place for him in their band. But, it would be a place *in* their band—*not* the head of it. If he didn't deliver all these people with the women, horses, and supplies he'd promised, they would never agree to let him lead.

It was likely they would attack this group the second they learned no one intended to join. Cass's idea to leave right away was the only way to get clear before New Danville realized and came down on them. John's group would come in and take what they wanted and eliminate the rest. They had the men and guns to do it.

So he could switch sides and become a cog in someone else's machine. Or he could choose option two—to stay and possibly end up dead with the rest of these people. He looked around. There was arguing and crying; some had already begun to run back to their tents, talking about packing. Cam had snuck through the crowd and was talking quietly with Doc and Trista.

Cass was in the midst of a heated argument with Adam. Derrick worked his way toward the two of them, listening.

"You can't make this decision for everyone, bitch," Adam said. He pushed Cass back a few steps with his hands and moved to advance on her, but Drew stepped between them.

"I'm not making this decision for everyone," Cass said. "Just for *my* group. We're getting the hell out of here."

People stopped talking to watch her, drawn to the spirit that had proved such a challenge to him.

"Who says you have the right to speak for *your* group?" Adam's aggression was wavering. For all his inadequacies, even he could feel the tide turning.

"She was right, though," Lena said, moving to stand beside Cass and Drew. Her clear voice carried out through the crowd. "She *said* someone stole from the orchard. Said that someone killed Marshall, and she was right."

His efforts to drag Cass through the mud had been useless.

When it came down to it, Cass's people still had faith in her. Cam took her decisions as his own. Hell, he saw some members of *his* group watching the argument, nodding at her every word.

A clinging frustration reached into his brain, worsening his now near-constant headache. If he couldn't destroy her image, he needed to destroy her.

A new hope bloomed in his chest. He could still end this in a favorable way. He could still end with all three groups united under his command. He just needed to get rid of Cassidy Hood. He took in the image before him as if it were an opponent's stance in one of his matches.

Adam was behaving like the villain and Derrick ignored the surge of anger that ran beneath his skull. Cass was confident, ready to take Adam on; this time not with fists but with words and an utter lack of need for anyone's approval.

He could do it—he could get her alone, take her by surprise.

He pushed between Drew and Adam and rotated to stand beside Cass.

"We're all getting the hell out of here," he said, his voice carrying over the crowd and silencing a good portion of them. "Cass is right; we need to leave."

"But—" Adam began to protest.

Derrick raised a hand. "We need to leave tonight before they realize what we've decided. If they come for us, we're in trouble. Listen to Cass. Get packing." People scattered. Adam cursed and stormed away, as well.

He turned to face her and found shock all over her features. He let his honest fear of what John and the others could do shine through as he spoke to her in soft tones. He felt tears welling up in his eyes.

"We need to hurry," he said, touching her wrist. "We need to protect them. I don't want to see anyone get hurt."

She nodded. "We will protect them," she said. "I'll get us out of here. Fast." She gently pulled her arm away and turned toward the horse corrals. Derrick moved to follow, but Drew stepped into his path.

"We need to talk," he said.

Derrick's hand formed a shaking fist at his side as he bit back a protest. Every second Cass was getting farther away. He needed to catch her now before she started working with the horses.

"I think you may have a mole," Drew said. "Someone working with New Danville."

Derrick's attention was fully Drew's now. The other man was glancing around them. He nodded his head toward the nearest patch of woods.

"Come on," Drew said.

Derrick followed, watching Drew's slight limp. He thought of Drew and Cass, so often walking together, his limp more pronounced beside her strong strides. It was different when she walked with Billy. Her strides were hesitant, body half-turning to face him. With Drew, she was all comfort and confidence.

As they passed into the seclusion of the trees, Derrick remembered Drew stepping between Cass and Adam just minutes ago. Her hand had curled around Drew's arm, half-gripping him, half-directing him out of the way. Hiding behind and protecting him in one motion.

Maybe Derrick didn't need to kill Cass. Maybe he just needed to break some supports, make her pliable.

Drew began to talk while walking, ducking branches and pushing deeper into the woods. Derrick needed it to be now, while Drew was lost in thought and paying attention to swerving through the trees.

Decision made, he reached under his shirt and slid his hand along his sweat-damp back until he found the object jammed into his waistband. He pulled it out and freed the antler-handled knife from the sheath.

He moved up, the mutterings of his victim clearer as he came close. His hand was sure and swift as he plunged the knife into Drew's back at an upward angle. The weapon resisted for a split second, and then his strength popped it through fabric, skin, and diaphragm until it slid through soft, human innards and sank to the hilt. Drew let out a gasp and half-turned, eyes wide and confused. Derrick ripped the knife from Drew's back and plunged it into his side. A moment of realization and understanding lit Drew's face, and then pain contorted it as the man sunk into the grass. He landed on a jutting root, his body at an awkward angle. He convulsed, gasping. Derrick went to one knee and plunged the knife into the thigh. Blood spurted from the last wound.

Derrick's shoulders heaved, and his breathing was harsh as he stood. The knife was wet in his hand, and there was some blood running down his arm. Drew's head had tilted back, eyes forever focused on some spot in the sky.

Derrick stepped back from the body to look at himself. His boots and jeans were bloody; he felt it seeping through the fabric to his skin. He arched his back and stretched his muscles.

His ears had been pulsing with adrenaline, and now the ringing was beginning to fade. He could hear a bird flapping not too far away. Beyond that, there was a steady beat of sound. Barking. It was Brick, yapping rhythmically.

Derrick looked back down at his hands. He tossed Billy's knife off into the trees, taking a moment to give thanks that the idiot had left it beside the lake. He rubbed his hands on a clean patch of tall grass. His tent wasn't far from the tree line, but he needed to hurry. With all the commotion, no one would notice him, but that dog was bound to find the body soon. He hurried through the trees, removing his clothing as he went.

Nineteen

"BILLY! LENA!" CASS CALLED as she ran up to the paddock. "Billy!" Where the hell were they? She had seen Lena down in the crowd, speaking up for her of all things, but where was Billy? How could he not have heard all the commotion?

Bark Bark Bark

Maybe he couldn't hear it over Brick's incessant barking.

Light, running footsteps approached behind her. Cass turned as Lena ran up. "Oh, thank God," she said.

"What's first?" Lena asked, climbing over the fence and heading for the nearest horse. Cass was glad to know she could count on Lena, despite her anger.

"We need to get the driving horses hitched up right away and get the wagons loaded. Then, just every saddle and pack on as quick as you can, but it's gotta be right. We might be riding all night."

Bark Bark Bark

Lena nodded as she led a horse by the halter. Cass reached for a horse herself, but her hands were shaking. She needed to know where Billy was. And Brick wasn't helping her nerves.

"Shut up, Brick," she said, looking around for the dog. A thrill of panic went through her gut. What if he was barking because there was trouble? Could John and the others have circled back and seen them packing up?

She spotted Brick still tied to the old signpost where she'd left him this morning. It was strange that Drew hadn't yet released the dog.

She glanced from Brick down in the direction he was looking. No Drew. As she tied the horse to the nearest paddock post, she looked toward the tents for him. She couldn't see much with all the people running about. She shielded her eyes and scanned the area by the lake. There was no one left down there. Cam was leading Cowboy toward her.

"Where's Drew?"

Bark Bark Bark

Cam paused and flipped Cowboy's reins around the paddock rail. "I thought he'd be here. Is he at the tents?"

"I can't tell," Cass said.

"Shut that dog up," Cam said. "Everyone's nervous enough as it is. We don't need a panic and sloppy mistakes."

"I'll let him go to Drew," she said. Unsteady from her emotional morning, she opted to crawl between the paddock rails instead of jumping them. In her rush, her shoulder cracked against the rail, and she cursed.

Brick was straining against the lead rope he'd been tied with, and he began to whine and paw as she approached.

"Okay, okay," she said. She couldn't undo the latch because the dog was pulling the lead taut. Impatient, she grabbed his scruff and pulled him back. Just as the clasp came free, Brick whirled and snapped at her hand before taking off down to the lake. "Ow, what the hell?"

"Did he bite you?" Lena called.

"Yeah," Cass glanced at her hand. The skin wasn't broken. She shook it, looking back up at Brick. The dog was nearly to the lake and veering left, into a stand of trees, barking the whole way. Hot panic spread in Cass's chest. "Something's wrong."

She charged down the road after the dog, arms pumping against her sides, willing her body to move faster.

Her shoulder and her hand burned from the concussion of every step, and the hot wind in her face was blinding. She heard footsteps running after her and Cam's voice calling out, asking what was wrong. But, she didn't slow.

As she jetted past the lake and headed toward the woods, she screamed. She meant to call for Brick but instead, Drew's name left her lips. She charged into the trees without slowing, branches slicing her skin as she swerved around obstacles.

"Brick," she called. "Come 'ere boy!" Lena and Cam were both shouting for her now as they crashed through the trees behind her.

She spotted a splash of red color to her left and adjusted her course toward it. *Brick!* she thought. But, it wasn't Brick. It was a streak of red on a tree trunk. Her eyes followed the trail of it down to a man's body, lying face up in the grass, jammed between a root and another tree trunk.

Brick stood at the head, licking and nudging the face with his nose. Cass had been moving so fast she almost tripped over the familiar boots. She flung her body to the side and landed hard. The man's knee bent under her weight, and the grass made an unnatural sloshing sound.

She rose up onto her hands and knees and crawled toward the body. That's what it was. It was a body. It was Drew's lifeless body.

No, he can't be dead!

Cass clambered almost on top of him, her hands gripping the bloody shirt as she worked her way up to his face. She grabbed his head. Brick shied away from her motion and laid down a few feet away.

"Drew!" she shouted. "Drew, wake up!" She slipped one hand to his neck and felt for a pulse. The other hand pressed into his chest and pushed, rocking him slightly back and forth. "Drew, come on," she said. "It's not funny, Drew." Her voice cracked.

She heard a sticky splash as Cam's foot slid through a puddle of Drew's blood. She could feel it soaking her clothes. "Oh, God," her brother said. He ducked around the tree whose root so offensively pressed into Drew's body and knelt, replacing Cass's now limp hand with his own at the neck.

Cass tucked her face against Drew's chest and listened as her brother said what she so longed to deny.

"He's dead."

The words echoed in her ears and became a steady ringing. She closed her eyes and let the world disappear. She focused on Drew's scent, trying to separate it from the sharp smell of his blood so she could remember him untainted.

CASS REMEMBERED NOTHING ABOUT her mother's death. When everyone else died in an apocalyptic blink, she'd been too busy trying to survive to think about all those losses. But, Cam remembered her mother's death, and he'd told her about it many times. He always said it was fuzzy. He'd been so young. He couldn't remember the funeral or the things people had said to him—couldn't put together a timeline. What he did remember were meaningless details; the color of the fabric on a chair he fell asleep in at the funeral home, the musty smell of the borrowed suit their father had worn, and hiding behind floral arrangements.

Those things were weird, perhaps. But they were all nice things. As she laid against Drew's cooling body, Cass wondered what she would remember later. What gruesome, unwanted detail would haunt her?

There was chaos all around her. People were crashing through the woods, Brick started barking again, someone stepped on her ankle, and twice people tried to pull her away from the body. There was constant talking. At first, the voices had been soft and sympathetic, sharing facts in mournful tones. Now, the voices were arguing.

It all seemed to her to be happening at a distance. Oh, she knew the voices were close, but it was almost as if she had pulled a thick blanket over herself and Drew, shutting everyone out and keeping them muffled. She liked this fake distance, this soft ringing in her ears.

But the illusion shattered when she heard Lena speak up over the steady murmur, silencing all other speakers. "We need to find Billy."

Cass's eyes opened, and she tuned in to reality again.

Cam was nodding, hands on his hips, "We should. Yeah. He can get Cass away from the body, away from here—"

"That's not what I mean," Lena said. Her voice was halting, hoarse. She was disturbed.

"What's *that?*"

Cass didn't dare turn her head to look at what her brother saw. She didn't want them to know she was listening. She didn't want to break her bubble completely. And maybe, she already knew somehow and didn't want to see.

Her fear was confirmed. "Is that Conrad's knife?" Cam asked.

"Billy's knife," Lena corrected, though for once there was no emotion in her voice. "Darcy found it. In the trees over there."

Cam sighed loudly. "Oh, God. Has anyone seen him?"

"He was washing something in the lake a bit ago." This voice was Derrick's. "I think he headed toward the tents."

"Find him," Cam growled. "Lena, stay with her."

The sound of retreating footsteps turned into the heavy, rapid thudding of Cass's heart. It couldn't be. Billy would never hurt Drew.

Cass thought of getting up, chasing after them. She knew it wasn't Billy. She tried to think of how she would convince them.

Billy hadn't had the knife—not last night, not this morning while they'd argued. Hadn't had it *on* him. It could've been in his tent.

They'd been talking—he'd been with her. Until Drew came back. She hadn't seen him since.

Still, everything in her screamed that it wasn't Billy. It couldn't have been. Billy could barely hit her when they sparred, forget about taking a life. He was too kind.

"Cass," Lena's voice was close beside her. She felt the soft touch of a hand on her back. "Can I help you at all? Can I do anything?"

Cass took in a deep breath, struggling to think. She needed to work this through, needed an answer.

"Okay," Lena said after a moment. The weight of the hand disappeared, and she heard Lena walk away. Cass glanced up as the girl lowered herself into the grass beside Brick, running a hand over the dog's back.

Billy was kind. Billy was naive. Or was he just acting?

Drew had trusted him. He could've gotten close to him. But could he have gotten the drop on him? Really?

Cass sat up so quickly it startled a bark out of Brick and a gasp out of Lena. She squirmed backward and began to examine Drew's body. There was one wound on the side she'd been lying on. But, following the blood, judging where the pool of it had come from there had to be another. His leg, at the point of the groin—femoral artery. But, if that were all, Drew would've seen his attacker. Might've fought him off.

It was hard to fake being an inexperienced fighter; hard to hide that from a sparring partner and harder still to hide when someone had a knife to your throat.

"Cass? What are you doing?"

Unless you're sure no one will hurt you. If you're working with the guy who's holding the knife.

"Cass? What are you looking at?"

"Help me turn him over," Cass said. She began to rotate Drew's body, trying to see his back.

"What? Cass!" Lena got up and came over but stood away from the body, as if she didn't want to touch it.

"Dammit, Lena." Cass gave up and grunted, forcing Drew's body up alone. She held its weight with one arm locked out and ran her free hand over his back, touching the bloody fabric and the wound there. She probed into the wound with her fingers.

"Cassidy!" Lena yelled.

The wound was deep, sure, angled upwards to slip beneath the ribcage and damage the organs there. This was an experienced kill. Someone had done this before. She slowly lowered the body, suddenly aware she'd been crying as she'd examined him. She ran the back of her hand over each cheek in turn and then under her chin.

Lena was staring at her. "Another stab wound?"

Cass nodded.

"I'm so sorry, Cass," Lena said. Cass looked at the girl; her blue eyes, sunburned red skin, and the red hair. Beyond Lena's hair, she saw Brick snap to attention and turn to stare into the trees. The dog stood and trotted over to Billy, his wagging rear end more subdued than usual. Billy didn't bend to greet the dog but stood staring at Drew's body. His face paled, and his mouth dropped open. He caught Cass's gaze and shook his head.

She may not have known him for long, but she could tell. She could tell by the way he looked nauseated, that he wasn't familiar enough with dead bodies to have made one. She could tell by the way his lips went white that he was experiencing a true horror. Actor or not, Cass realized she'd always somehow recognized when he was lying to her, and he wasn't lying, now.

Actors had the benefit of time and rehearsal and could school their performance to perfection. A little direction and the appropriate music and they could portray human emotion with sincerity—boil it down to its most basic form and offer it like a tonic to the viewer. Billy was just wrecked, experiencing every thought at once.

And if all that weren't enough, he still wore the exact clothing he'd been wearing earlier. It was stuck to his body with sweat and totally free of blood.

Cass glanced at Lena. The girl was kneeling, now. Someone else had closed Drew's eyelids, but Lena moved to brush the hair away from his forehead, oblivious to Billy's presence. Cass looked back up at him. He was taking in a breath to speak. She shook her head sharply, pressing her index finger to her lips to silence him, but she was too late.

"It's true," he said.

Lena whirled around to face Billy and reached to her side for her gun. She wasn't wearing it, and she groped at her hip in confusion for a moment.

"You bastard," Lena said. "You did this!" She took in a deep breath, ready to scream, to call for help.

Cass leaped forward and clapped a hand over Lena's mouth, wrapping her arms around the girl none too gently. "Lena, stop."

The girl twisted in Cass's arms, her eyes accusing as she fought to break the hold. She stomped on Cass's foot and elbowed her in the breast. Cass held on until Lena bit into her hand, harder than Brick had done earlier.

"Dammit, Lena!"

"Help!" Lena got out a single shout before Cass pulled her gun from its holster and aimed it at the ground halfway between Lena's feet and her own. Lena's blue eyes widened and then narrowed, and she took a step back. "What are you thinking, Cass?"

"He didn't do it, Lena."

"Oh, Jesus! What's wrong with you? He's a spy, a mole. He killed our people and now Drew. He'll kill you, too."

"I didn't kill anyone, I swear," Billy said. At some point, he had sunk onto his knees.

"Get up," Cass said. She turned to Billy for a moment. "Run," she said. "Run north. I'll catch up." Billy hesitated. "Go!"

He stood and jogged through the trees.

Cass turned to find Lena's cold eyes on her. The girl shook her head. "Look at you, holding a gun on me. I'm not the enemy Cass, he is." She pointed in the direction Billy had disappeared—which wasn't north. Cass had to hurry.

"I have to hold the gun on you. If I don't, you'll fight me, and you're good. You're quicker than me, and you're smart. All you'd have to do is keep me busy and call out. They won't listen to logic right now, and without my help, they'll catch him."

"Don't compliment me—"

"Right? Without my help they'll catch him, won't they?"

"Yes," Lena snapped.

"Think about that Lena. You are smart. Think about it. He didn't do this; he didn't get the drop on Drew." Cass prayed Lena would believe her. Lena didn't know Billy had been an actor. She wouldn't have *that* doubt.

Lena's conviction seemed to waver, and her gaze turned down to Drew's body.

"He's not a killer. He'd never have known where to aim a knife. I know you hate Billy but can you see him stabbing Drew three times?"

The doubt in Lena's eyes turned to clarity. She believed.

"We don't really know him," Lena said.

"And if he was clever enough to kill him so efficiently, why would he leave the knife right here? Someone wanted us to find it."

Cass heard shouting in the distance. The people looking for Billy were coming back. She locked eyes with Lena and took a risk. She replaced her pistol in her holster without looking away. Lena's eyes first tracked Cass's hand as she put away the weapon and then met her gaze again.

Tears welled up in Cass's eyes, and she swallowed back the cotton in her throat. "If you ever believed in me or trusted me at all, trust me now. *Believe* me now. Billy didn't do this. Lena, please. Tell my brother the killer is still here." Cass glanced down at Drew once more and bit her lip to hold back the tears. "I'll be back."

She sped away through the trees. She only hoped there'd been too much travel through the area for anyone to pick out her trail. Lena didn't yell for help. Cass heard a stick crack behind her and turned. It was Brick, following. She thought about sending the dog back and decided it was better if he stayed with her. The others might be able to use him to track them somehow.

When Cass burst out of the trees, she had to stop to let her eyes adjust for a moment. Billy came into focus. He stood by a little four-seater plane, overgrown with weeds but still mostly sound despite its emergency landing in the field.

For a moment, Cass just stared at him. The sun was lowering behind her, and the trees were casting shadows on his body and troubled face. But his golden hair was glowing in the sunlight, like a halo.

"That's West," she said. "I said North. Let's move."

Twenty

LENA TOOK A DEEP breath. She wasn't a good liar. Everything she felt tended to surface on her face and in her voice. She'd never been able to help it. And now, she had to lie for someone she didn't even like.

The panic bubbled up from her gut as she heard the voices growing closer. What was she going to say? How could she tell them she had let Cass and Billy leave? Her breathing was coming faster and shallower. She heard the crack of branches and swish of grass from people entering the trees and she darted away.

She traveled in a half-circle out around the scene of Drew's murder, picking up speed as voices called for her and Cass. She popped out of the trees and took a fumbling step into the lake, filling her boot with water. She cursed and bent to dump it out. As she did, she spotted a metal water bottle floating on the surface, jammed half under a bunch of driftwood at the lake's edge. Empty, it must have drifted over here from the shallower, sandy areas where people had been swimming yesterday.

Her mind whirled as she came up with a plan. She snatched the bottle from the water and unscrewed the top. As she pushed it down beneath the surface, she realized she'd filled this bottle before. For Katie. Her hands froze as lake water slowly ran into the mouth of the bottle.

With her breath still coming in short, ineffective gushes, she thought of Katie; recalled the woman's sweet face and large belly, her hands braiding the horsehair necklace, her infectious, eager laugh. Then the memory of her death came—the blank face with wide-open eyes and blood smeared across her abdomen. They hadn't let Lena get too close—hadn't wanted her to see the reason they were so sure the baby couldn't be saved.

Lena clenched her teeth and waited for the anger. She tried to picture Cass following Billy up the hill away from them that day. She'd conjured that image many times. But, now all she could see was Cass's clothing soaked in Drew's blood and the paleness of her face as she clutched his body, refusing to be pulled away.

She hadn't saved Drew, either. But, she hadn't been with Billy. She'd been with Lena, getting horses ready. The easiest image of Cass to summon was her covered in dirt, caring for the horses or hauling in meat. Cass sweating as she yelled at Lena not to fight fancy. *"Hit where it counts and end it. Show off and you'll wind up dead."* Cass cursing her, *"Jesus Christ, Lena! Never hold a gun like that."*

As she started to screw the lid onto the now-full water bottle, she noticed the streaks of Drew's blood still on her hands, though partially rinsed away in the water. She remembered holding Billy's knife. She'd held it twice. Most recently she had held it out away from herself, gawking at the drying blood. But, the first time, she swiped it from Billy's grasp with ease. She remembered something she'd heard him say to Cass. *"I'm just glad I'm strong enough to set the saddle on her gently, now. She hated me at first for lobbing it up there."* She pictured Billy, on his knees and clutching his gut as if he was about to be sick as he looked at Drew's body.

She tightened the cap with purpose and skirted the lake, jogging back toward the woods. Derrick burst from the trees and Lena almost crashed into him, stopping so suddenly the wet water bottle slipped from her grip and clanked to the ground.

"What's going on?" she asked. "I heard yelling."

"You were supposed to stay with her," Derrick said, his voice booming. Others began to filter out of the trees. "Where'd you go?"

Lena let her usual anger surface, hoping it would help her to be believable. "What are you talking about? Cass? She wanted water. I went to get some." Lena bent to retrieve the water bottle and held it up.

Trista stepped out from behind Derrick and came to place a hand on Lena's arm. "She's gone, Lena. We couldn't find Billy, and we came back here, and Cass was gone."

Lena was spared having to answer by Cam growling and spinning on his heel. He ran a hand through his hair and kicked a rock out into the lake.

"So help me, if anything's happened to her..." Cam said.

"Surely he wouldn't hurt *her,*" Trista said, pulling Lena toward her and wrapping an arm around her shoulders. Lena stiffened. Trista was probably the nicest person left on Earth, but Lena didn't like to be babied. Still, better this than questioning. She let the embrace continue.

"Why? Because he's hot on her?" Derrick asked.

"Like killing her best friend didn't hurt her," Cam said at the same time. The men exchanged a look. "I can't leave without my sister."

"No, of course not," Derrick said.

"Like hell we can't," Adam said, forcing himself into the space between Cam and Derrick. "Half an hour ago it was run or die; nothing's changed."

"We can't leave Cass," Trista said.

Adam glanced at Trista with distaste and then, seeing Lena tucked beneath her arm, he advanced on the two women. "How can we be sure he took her anyway? Maybe she went willingly. Maybe she's a part of it all, huh?" He was pointing his finger at the women and Lena felt Trista tense.

She shrugged away from the pregnant woman and met Adam. "I don't know, do I? I wasn't there." She flung the water bottle to the side and met Adam's gaze. The man shook his head and backed away. *It was easy lying to* him, she thought.

"Shouldn't we send out a search party?" Hank asked. "While there's still light?"

"We should," Derrick said. "If Billy's the mole he'll be heading for New Danville. He'll tell them we're leaving, and they'll be here in force."

"Which is why we should leave, now," Adam said. "It's our only chance of getting away before they get here.'

"I'm not leaving my sister." Cam's voice was quiet, but it held a note of danger and assurance.

"I can't believe Cass would ever hurt Drew or do anything to help his killer," Trista said. "She didn't leave of her own free will."

"I agree." This voice was Lena's father's.

Lena felt her cheeks and neck burning at their words. They were both right and wrong. Lena glanced at Cam. He had separated himself from the discussion and looked out across the lake as if he could see through the trees and spot his sister. This might be the only chance Lena would have to talk to him alone—to tell him the truth without revealing it to everyone.

The argument continued as Hank agreed with Trista and Waylon. Adam protested loudly, calling Cass's character into question. When Derrick's voice raised over everyone's, suggesting every able-bodied fighter should get a gun and a horse to go rescue Cass, Lena saw her chance. She darted over to Cam and clutched his arm.

"What's wron—" he began. But, Lena cut him off, her words quiet and frantic. She couldn't get it out fast enough.

"I was there when Billy came to Drew's body." Cam's eyes widened, and Lena charged ahead. "Cass left with him, to protect him."

"What?" Cam said, his voice a whisper.

"Cam, she said Billy didn't do it, and I believe her." Tears welled up in Lena's eyes, an unfamiliar feeling. "She said the killer is here with us still. And she said she'd find out who it was and come back."

Cam let out a deep breath, and Lena watched his expression. He was relieved, he was angry, but he was not all that surprised.

"Cam, I—" This time Lena was cut off as Adam and Derrick barged up.

"Cam, we need to go after them. We need to catch them before they get to New Danville," Derrick said. "They're on foot. We could overtake them and get your sister back."

Adam's eyes were hard on Lena's face. She looked away.

"What? Does she know something?" he asked. "Do you know something else?"

Adam moved toward Lena, but Cam rotated his body, blocking Adam's path.

"She was apologizing," Cam said. "For leaving Cass." Cam cleared his throat and turned to Derrick. "I appreciate you wanting to go after my sister. I wish we could. But, this is their territory. We can't split up. For all we know, Billy could've had a horse or others from New Danville waiting nearby. He might have a way to signal them."

The ridges of the frown on Derrick's forehead were deep. Lena had to drag her eyes away from his harsh face.

"We have to either run now or stay and fight. If we run, they will probably catch us anyway. Who knows how far we'd get and it will be dark soon. Besides, I won't leave my sister," Cam said. Voices raised in agreement and support. "We're stronger here. This spot is defensible."

Cam continued to plead his case, but Lena couldn't focus. She glanced from Adam, all fire and anger, holding his strength above his head on display—to Derrick, whose scarred face and massive upper body contrasted with his mild and relaxed demeanor. And yet, she'd seen his eyes change, seen him become a tornado. A chill ran down her spine as Cam concluded.

"I believe we could win if we fought them together," Cam said. "But, I won't blame anyone—even members of my own band," here he paused and looked around, "if they choose to leave."

For a moment, no one spoke. Derrick's eyes flicked back and forth almost as if clockwork moved behind them, rather than a brain. He nodded.

"Cam is right." Adam turned on Derrick in a fury, and one or two voices protested. Derrick turned to face the crowd and raised a hand over his head. "Once Billy warns New Danville, they'll be after us in force. If we split up, they'll run over the people here and come after the rest of us anyway. If we all leave, they'll run us down, just like Cam said. Our only option is to fight together."

Derrick let his words sink in for a moment. Murmurs of discussion passed around the crowd. Finally, Derrick turned to Hank.

Hank nodded. "We'll stay and fight," he said.

"Thank you," Cam said. He started giving orders, assigning people to set up watchpoints and putting others to work at protecting supplies and building defenses. Lena stood by his side, staring straight ahead, not seeing anything and not hearing much. They were talking about war, and the realization chilled her.

She jumped when Cam's arm came down over her shoulder. He steered her away, toward the lake.

"I just need to speak to her for a minute, Waylon," she heard him say.

Lena felt her boots sink into the softer, rocky sand near the lake and then Cam shook her arm, roughly. She blinked and focused her eyes on his face.

"Tell me everything," he said.

BILLY HAD BEEN OUTRUNNING Cass for quite a distance. He was so focused on getting away, keeping them out of trouble long enough to convince her he hadn't killed Drew. All he cared about was making her believe.

His lungs were burning, and he felt detached from his own legs. He was utterly spent by the time he realized they should stop. They could talk here and then turn back. Get Cass back to the safety of her group and let them deal with him however they pleased. He came to an old gas station and pushed his body through one more surge of speed to collapse against the building.

He turned around and let his back slide down the wall, the cinder blocks scratching his skin. A panting Brick trotted into the shade beside Billy and flopped onto his belly. Cass was further behind than he'd thought. When she saw he'd stopped, she stopped as well, though she was still a couple hundred feet away in a field. He wanted to tell her to come closer, to get some cover instead of standing there exposed, but before he could catch his breath to call out, she crumpled to the ground.

He jumped to his feet. His heart-rate, which hadn't had time to slow anyway, skyrocketed again. He ran for her, skidding to a stop near her feet. She wasn't unconscious, just sitting with her head between her hands, sobbing. She gasped for breath between agonized cries, and Billy wanted to hold her. But what right did he have?

He braced his own arm on his knees and rested his head on it, listening as her crying slowly slackened and stopped. She sat there sniffing, her breath steadying. When he lifted his head, she was looking at him through swollen eyes. She seemed to be waiting for something, so he said it.

"I didn't kill him."

"I know."

"I swear I didn't Cass." Billy charged on desperately, only wishing he could talk faster. "I would never hurt Drew. I needed to be alone for a bit, just to think—about us. And we can go back. I didn't intend to run; I just needed you to know I didn't do this. We have to get back where it's safe and let them do what they want to me. I'm fine with it so long as *you* know I didn't do it."

"Billy, I said I know," Cass said. "And—," she clapped her hands over her face, pressing the tips of her fingers over her eyes as if to soothe them, "—so you're gonna give up?"

Billy grappled for a response. He stuttered for a moment before he could speak. "I want you safe."

Cass gave a dry huff of a laugh. "I'm not safe there. No one is until we figure out who—" she trailed off and looked away. "We have to find out who did it."

She stood up, and Billy followed suit. She wavered on her feet for a moment and reached a hand out to him, her eyes shut tight. He grabbed the hand and gripped her arm as well.

"You okay?" he asked.

Cass took a deep breath before answering. "I haven't eaten today; that's all." She clutched his hand for a moment longer until the dizziness seemed to pass and then she pulled away and looked around. The grass swished as Brick rejoined them.

"Come on," she said. "We need to find someplace to hole up for the night."

Billy watched her get her bearings and adjust their direction, then followed her forward, his eyes taking in the unpleasant amount of Drew's blood still staining her clothing.

"Where are we going?" he asked.

"Stronghold."

Billy looked up at the horizon. He saw now what he'd missed while running blindly. Just a mile or two away, there was a wall. A couple of taller buildings were visible over the top and a thin trail of smoke still moved lazily heavenward on one end of the city.

Though he wished he knew her plan, he took comfort in the steady swishing of her feet in the grass beside him. He took comfort in her trust and decided the time to pick it apart would come all too soon. For now, he was just happy to be free and not alone.

STRONGHOLD'S ONCE-INTIMIDATING WALL NOW featured at least two new entrances. They couched in the shadows of a play structure at a park just outside the city for nearly half an hour. Then, Cass led Billy and Brick through the rubble of stones, shards of metal, and splintered wood that had once been a solid barrier. No one was guarding the city. In fact, the only movement was that of scavengers; carrion birds and wild dogs who were feasting on and fighting over the bodies.

Cass paused just inside the wall to take it all in. Buildings—a courthouse maybe, an apartment, a library judging by the books littering the ground—had been reduced to piles of debris not much taller than Cass. Houses had become foundations covered in rubble. But, the bodies were the most disturbing thing.

"I'm guessing the whole "sister-city" claim was a bit of a stretch," Billy said, crouching to hold Brick. "Since they didn't have the decency to take care of the bodies."

Billy's voice, usually silk in her ears, was more like gravel. Every movement he made, every irritating shift of his weight echoed around in her. His words nagged at her brain. *"I would never hurt Drew"* just a reminder Drew was dead, a fact she was trying to ignore to avoid falling apart. *"Let them do whatever they want with me"* stabbing her heart. He was a survivor and after everything he'd lived through, everything they'd been through together, and even after she'd given him forgiveness—how could he just roll over? How could he just give up?

She glanced down at Brick. Billy's hand held the dog in place with a firm but gentle grip on his leather collar. She remembered Drew's hands, fastening the collar there and she gritted her teeth.

She turned to the bodies. So many. She spun in a slow half-circle, earning a growl from a matted dog once golden-haired, now covered in soot. It was guarding a human corpse from her, its muzzle covered in gore. She frowned at the body. "Not all of these people died in the explosions."

Cass cleared her throat and bent to pick up a chunk of concrete. She held it firmly in one hand while she pulled her pistol from her belt with the other. She advanced on the dog confidently. "Get," she said. "Go on."

The dog shied back at first and then barked and moved to the body again. Cass chucked the concrete toward the dog. The animal ducked away as Cass's crude weapon struck the ground beside the body and bounced. She kept her pistol aimed at the dog as she moved to within a few feet of the body. Her eyes flicked back and forth between the still-growling animal and what was left of the corpse.

She backed away, allowing the dog to return to its meal, and would have stumbled over Billy and Brick, had Billy not reached out and touched her calf, stopping her.

"Gunshot," she said. "They were here when it happened. To finish off the survivors."

Billy let out a grunt of disgust.

"It'll be dark soon," Cass said. "We need to find a map and someplace intact enough to stay for the night."

"A map?"

She ignored Billy and moved on down the street.

Cass's tension grew as building after building was either demolished or too damaged to hide out in. She was beginning to doubt her decision to come here. She'd wanted to see for herself what had happened, but she hadn't imagined dead bodies would be littering the ground or half-hanging out of shattered windows. She'd thought this would be the last place anyone would look for them, but she hadn't understood how right that judgment was. She felt fragile, worn by Drew's death and weakened by hunger. The carnage wasn't helping.

"Look at that," Billy said after they'd walked for a bit, picking their way through rubble and the discarded belongings of those who'd tried to escape.

Cass followed Billy's gaze and squinted into the setting sun. Just a block ahead of them was an area that seemed untouched. There was a larger building with no sign, but it appeared to have been a natural grocery once, a high-end place. Around it, a cluster of three or four houses was miraculously unharmed. Cass picked up her pace.

"Why aren't they blown up?" she wondered aloud as she jogged forward.

If it weren't for Brick cautiously sniffing a blackened shoe that lay in the middle of one of the yards, this could look like a picture of a street corner from Before.

The glass front doors of the grocery store were boarded up, but a series of yellow, reflective arrows—once road markers—indicated a path around the side of the building.

"You don't suppose there's food left in there?" Billy asked.

Cass glanced at him and shrugged, not feeling quite as hopeful as he looked. "Let's find out."

She followed the arrows around the building to a side door. It was glass and Cass peered inside. There were a number of skylights, but with dark coming on, she couldn't make out much. There did appear to be rows of shelving in the center of the store.

She pulled her pistol from its holster and turned to Billy. She had opened her mouth to ask if he had a weapon on him when she remembered the antler-handled knife, white and tan striations covered in Drew's blood. Her mouth snapped closed, and she took a deep breath before pulling her own knife from her arm sheath and passing it wordlessly to Billy.

She pulled the door's handle. It was unlocked and swung open with barely a sound. Once inside, Cass scanned the area. The place was empty. She stood for a moment, listening and watching Brick as he trotted in without concern and took to sniffing the merchandise. Cass considered motioning to Billy to check the place, but it was a fairly small store, and she finally decided she had no energy for the tension of waiting.

"Hello!" she called out. "Anyone in here? We've come to help." Billy stared at her wide-eyed and tensed, bracing for a violent response. His expression eased as a minute passed with no sound but their own breathing and the clicking of Brick's toenails on the tile.

Cass wandered over to the check stands, holstering her gun as she walked. The computers were missing, of course, and the long unmoving belts were in disrepair. She found a lantern underneath a counter and felt around its base until her hands clasped a box of matches. When it was lit, she saw small, metal lockboxes where the computers would have been.

Cass lifted the lid on one of them and found a mixture of paper types inside. There was some money. She'd hadn't seen a lot of it since The End. She picked up a five and raised her brows. There were words and numbers scrawled across the bill. She glanced down at the other slips of paper and cardboard. They were similarly marked.

"Some kind of rationing or trading system," she said. She traded Billy the bill and the lantern for her knife and sheathed it.

"There's food," he said, indicating the shelves with a nod of his head. "You should eat."

Cass nodded and followed his direction. She picked an apple from a full crate and bit into it as she walked down the aisle. There were some fresh fruits and vegetables, loaves of bread and clear containers filled with jerky. There were shelves and shelves of preserved foods of all types in glass canning jars, each neatly labeled and dated.

Cass's mouth watered as she looked. *Can't stay here*, she thought. This was a valuable place, should Rovers or men from New Danville come looting.

"Find a bag and fill it with whatever you can," she called to Billy. "We need to find someplace else to sleep." Cass felt juice from her apple drip down her forearm, and she moved to wipe it. Glancing down before her fingers made contact, she froze. She'd almost forgotten she was covered in blood. The apple juice ran clear down to her wrist and then turned a rusty brown.

Cass glanced down at her front, suddenly acutely aware that Drew's dried blood stiffened her shirt and pants. It scratched her skin as her breathing picked up. She ran a shaking hand through her hair and felt patches caked with blood.

The apple dropped to the floor as she leaned forward and gripped the nearest shelf in both hands. She shut her eyes and focused on her breathing. Footsteps approached and stopped a few feet away. She opened her eyes to see Billy's boots, illuminated by the gently swinging light of the lantern

She looked up to find him holding out a pile of clothes balanced on his hand.

"They should fit you," he said. "And here," he produced a jug of water that had been tucked under his arm, "to clean up."

Cass bit down on her lip as tears stung the back of her eyes. She nodded and took the items. The restroom sign had been taken off the door, but it swung open, allowing Cass a view of a shadowed room full of boxes, chairs, and other furniture. She slipped in and fished in the bottom of her jeans pocket, removing the horsehair necklace and carefully hanging it on the door handle. She stripped out of her clothing, finding her skin sticky in places with more than sweat.

There was a hand towel among the clothes, and she soaked it with water and began to wipe her skin clean, struggling not to remember whose blood darkened the cloth.

When she'd squirmed into the clean clothes, she replaced her boots, belt, pistol, and knife sheath, and left without retrieving the bloodied jeans and t-shirt. They could rot there. Outside the door, she stared at the necklace for a moment, took a deep breath, and slipped it over her head.

She found Billy filling a backpack and a canvas tote with food and supplies. He looked up as she approached and spotted the horsehair necklace. His eyes dropped back to the floor.

"You said we needed a map," he said. "I couldn't find one."

Cass rolled her shoulder and let herself enjoy the feel of clean cotton on her skin for a fraction of a second.

"I don't know how to get to New Danville," she said. "I have a general idea but—I'm gonna need a map."

"We're going to New Danville?"

Cass knelt to zip up the backpack and slung it over her shoulders. "We'll have to split up."

She headed for the door, Brick skittering along beside her. She stepped back out into the warm evening and paused for Billy. Facing the undamaged street, she set him the task of searching houses on one side while she searched those on the other.

Cass's frustration boiled near the surface when the first small house she checked proved nearly impossible to search. More than one family had lived here, and though there were thankfully no bodies in the house, it was littered with stuff. Board games and extra blankets, reams and reams of paper, and hundreds of books. She tore through the place but found no map.

The last light was fading as she moved to the next house. She passed through the yard toward the back door only to freeze in place when Brick whined and refused to go further.

"What, Brick?" Cass asked. She watched the dog pace for a moment and then looked in the direction Brick was trying *not* to look. She squinted in the low light. There was another body in this yard.

She started to head into the house, but paused with her hand on the railing. They would need weapons. They hadn't been checking the bodies, but some of them might be armed. She headed over to the body. It was laying atop a rifle, and she let out a sigh of relief. There was also a pistol in a shoulder holster. It looked as if the man had just stepped out of the large toolshed behind him when he was shot. The door stood ajar.

What was he doing in the shed?

Cass had let Billy take the lantern. She called out for him, now.

She waited, shouting once more to let him know which direction to go. He arrived in the yard breathless and clutched her shoulder in his large hand. Cass shrugged away.

"I'm fine," she said. She nodded into the darker part of the yard. "I wanna see in that shed." Cass reached for the lantern. "Get his guns."

She walked up and pulled the door open. The shed was apparently just for storage. Small shelves held boxes of tools, books, vases, and knickknacks. There were also document boxes filled with paperwork. But Cass's attention was drawn to a small table under a window.

The window itself was odd as it faced another window. Cass could see into the house, though what room it might be was obscured by the descending darkness. The shed was close enough an occupant in the house could've reached into it and taken an item off the table.

It was the items on the table that were the most interesting. There were stacks of notebooks and on top of the tallest group was a tiny pyramid made from balls of off-white clay.

"What the hell?" she mumbled.

"What is it?" Billy's footsteps approached the shed door as she bent toward the balls, swinging the lantern lower. On closer inspection, they weren't so small. And there was something metallic sticking out of each one. The metallic pieces had strings attached, and for a moment Cass thought she'd simply stumbled upon some child's artwork.

"Holy shit," she said, as the truth came to her.

Suddenly, Billy was beside her, guiding her lantern arm away from the table.

"Let's not get the flame quite so close," he said.

"That's a bomb," Cass said.

Billy nodded. "C4."

"Really?" She frowned as he bent over the table, sniffing the explosive. "Can people still make that? I mean, they'd have what they needed?"

Billy nodded, again. "Yeah. If someone knew what they were doing, they could find it. Looks like John wasn't lying about their explosives expert." He crossed his arms and looked out the shed window, his frown deepening. "Doesn't make sense, though. They'd need a lot of C4 to do the damage that's been done to this town. This bit here is barely enough for the house—it's maybe—six pounds?" He rubbed the stubble on his chin.

"How do you know this?"

Billy raised his eyebrows and cleared his throat. "You know the film I was in—*Blackwatch*?"

"No."

He cracked a half smile. "Guess you *weren't* that big a fan," he said. "I played the son of a demolitions expert. It wasn't a big role, but I still did my homework."

Nodding, Cass felt a perverse sort of pride in him.

"I think maybe they intended to take out this house, specifically." He was looking through the window again.

Cass approached the table and again brought the lantern closer— this time more carefully. The notebooks appeared to be journals. The covers bore sets of dates all *after* The End.

"The house and the shed," she said. "Maybe this was the house of someone important to Stronghold." She rolled her shoulder. "We can't stay here."

"It won't explode until someone lights the fuse," Billy said. "But I could try to disarm it."

"No," Cass said. "They might come back for it. They have to know it didn't go off." She turned and stepped out onto the grass. Brick waited as far from the dead body as he could get without leaving the yard, whining.

Billy gathered up the rifle and Cass set a brisk pace away from the bomb and the body.

"We need to find a map and—"

"I've got one," Billy said. Cass stopped and turned to stare at him. "It's in my bag."

Cass let out a sigh and suppressed the urge to hug him. "Thank you." She lifted the lantern as if to light up the nearby houses. It was useless. "Now we just have to find a place to sleep."

Billy cleared his throat. "Follow me."

*　　*　　*

LENA SAT ON A rock, listening to the continued arguing as she watched the horses move about nervously in their corrals. The animals were tacked up, and Lena's excuse was keeping an eye out to make sure they didn't chew on their saddles. Really, she just didn't want to hear any more.

People were confused. If Billy had gone straight to New Danville, he'd have been there for a while. Everyone had been expecting the attack to come before now. Everyone except herself and Cam, anyway. As far as she knew, Cam hadn't told anyone—not even Trista—what Cass and Billy were really doing.

She wanted to tell her father. Waylon was upset by Cass's disappearance and insistent that the reason no attack had come was because Cass had discovered Billy's plan and killed him. While the others waited for an army, Waylon expected a distraught but victorious Cass to return alone. She wanted to tell him he was half right. But, Cam had given her strict instructions to keep quiet to avoid tipping off the real mole and giving him or her time to escape. So Lena waited.

Weapons were propped up in lines along the back walls of the lean-tos. The tents were folded and packed with almost all their other supplies in one of the wagons which stood down the road a bit, ready to be hitched up and moved out. The others formed a makeshift blockade near the lake.

There was little else to do until the fighting started. The group slept and ate in shifts, their anxiety growing as they prepared for an attack that would not come for quite some time if at all. Lena willed Cass luck.

Lena's expression softened as a gray cat leaped onto the top rail of the nearest corral fence, and started to make its way across. The cat had been around camp all evening, making friends here and there, earning the occasional scrap of food for a purr or a well-timed butt lift. The concensus was that he had once lived in Stronghold, but he didn't seem traumatized by the recent events. Everyone seemed to appreciate the lightened mood the animal inspired, especially since Brick had disappeared with Cass and Billy. At least, she hoped the dog was with them.

She stood and crossed over to the cat, lifting it into her arms as its claws gently gripped her jacket.

"This isn't a good place to hang out, cat," she said. She rubbed the animal's neck for a moment and turned, intending to walk it back over toward the crowd.

But the cat stiffened in her arms, and cranked its head around, staring. Lena turned to see Derrick and Cam approaching. Derrick's voice was raised to match his gesticulating hands. The cat hissed and dove out of Lena's arms, scratching her as it went.

"Ow," she said, sucking in a breath and putting a hand over the place where the scratch would be. It had sliced her through the fabric. She watched the cat dart into the darkness of the nearest trees.

Cat has good sense, I guess. To avoid him. Rubbing her arm, she wandered back to the gathering of people, beginning to feel exhaustion pulling at her senses.

Twenty-One

IT WAS FULL DARK as Cass followed Billy to the second of the houses he'd found. His first option would've been more comfortable but too far from the shed with the explosives. Cass wanted to know if any New Danville men came back for the bomb or returned to raid the grocery store. She intended to follow them back to their encampment.

The second house was almost uncomfortably close to the explosives. Also, half of it had been in range of another explosion. The large house was half-demolished. The right side was absent, but the left was intact enough they could pass through and gain access to the basement. They could see what was going on down the street through an egress window that would also provide a secondary means of escape if need be.

The trip down the stairs was a challenge for Billy. He stopped twice to retreat back to the top and breathe. Cass felt for him, though not as deeply as she normally would, not as intensely as she had in the wine cellar. She was tired, hungry, and numb.

She gave a half-hearted offer to stay in what was left of the first floor, but Billy refused. He finally sent her away, choosing to navigate the stairs on his own.

After shedding her weapons and backpack, Cass hung a heavy blanket over the blinds to block the light of their lantern from one window. She set to maneuvering a bookshelf to block the second window and was surprised when Billy arrived and lifted the other end.

"This is probably not necessary," she said, catching a book as it slid off the top of the shelf. "They probably wouldn't come until it was light, anyway."

"Maybe they won't come at all." Billy moved to crouch on the floor and began digging through the canvas bag, pulling out various food items and water bottles. "Maybe they don't know it didn't go off."

"Maybe," Cass said. "But their man never came back, either."

"Do you think they care?" Billy asked. "I mean—the sort of people who would do this..."

Cass shrugged. She removed her weapons and sat cross-legged on the opposite side of the lantern from Billy. She dug into the food with more vigor than she'd known she could muster and strove to think of anything other than death. And Drew.

When they'd each had their fill, they sat in silence. Billy stared at the steady flame in the lantern, stroking Brick, while Cass looked around the room. There was a bunk bed, and there was a king-sized mattress on the floor in the next room. There must have been multiple families in every home. Even though this city encompassed only the size of a small town, there must have been quite a lot of people here. People who were now dead.

Desperate to derail her train of thought, Cass watched Billy. His shoulders rose and fell steadily; he licked his lips, the moisture shimmering in the orange lantern light. It reminded her of the campfire they'd sat around the night after they'd met. She'd been trying to avoid thinking of a lost friend that night, too.

Sensing her gaze, Billy looked up. His frame seemed to crumple.

"Why did you trust me?" he asked. She stared down at her bare feet on the floor in front of her.

"I don't want to talk about Drew," she said.

"So don't. Talk about you and me. Cass, I need to know. Why do you believe me?"

Cass put her face in her hands. "Jesus Christ. Do we have to do this?" She paused and then added, "William," for spite.

"Don't call me that," he said, this time with anger in his tone. "But since you bring the name up. I lied to you, and yet you trusted me. I need to know why."

"You're not a killer," Cass said. Her anger was boiling now, causing her breath to come short and uneven. She felt she was gasping between every sentence. "You couldn't have stabbed someone three times. For God's sake, you can barely hit me when we spar. You can barely touch me at all." Cass stopped herself. Her tone had been hurt, almost jilted. She hadn't meant it that way.

There was a pause, and she saw him chewing the inside of his cheek.

"I don't know how to make this up to you," he said. "I don't know how to thank you for saving me again. I wish you *hadn't* run with me."

"Oh, please. You know going somewhere is as good as asking me to come. You know I'll follow you." Cass let out a little gasp when she realized what she'd said. Too agitated to stay still, she jumped to her feet and went into the other room.

"Cass—" Billy stood up and followed her.

She turned on him as he entered. "Everything I've worked for since The End is back there." She gestured vaguely in the direction of the campground. "I left everything I care about. Dead or alive. How did *you* get so important?" She shook her head and turned away, sinking to the cold, concrete floor.

In a moment, she heard the scuffing of feet as Billy moved to sit behind her, propping his back against hers. She leaned into him and they balanced, bracing one another. For a moment she just sat there, feeling the rhythm of his breathing against her back. A thought occurred to her, and she gave a dry laugh.

"At least Before, I knew you'd never give me the time of day. I wouldn't have left my best friend to be buried by someone else for—"

Billy pulled away so abruptly that Cass almost fell backward and had to catch herself. The heels of her hands slammed into the cold floor, and she rotated her body to find him kneeling, facing her.

"It's not Before!" he said, voice harsh. A hint of his accent was trickling back into his speech, again. "I'm not who I was then any more than you are. We've changed. Everyone's changed. We make our choices differently, now."

His irritation amped up the adrenaline in Cass once more, and her voice cracked as she shot back, "Well, why don't you just explain me to myself? How do I make my choices, now?"

"We choose like we're about to die," he said, the tendons in his neck taut with the strength of his emotion. "Like every choice could be the last."

Cass sank back onto her rear, grabbing a clump of hair in her fist and holding it against her head as if to ward off the truth of this speech. *I would*, she admitted silently. *I would choose to die with him.*

Billy had sunk onto his legs. His hands rested on his thighs, and he stared at them like they were foreign. "I might not have given you the time of day Before—even if somehow we'd met—but now—" he paused, frowning. His eyes found hers and locked on. "Now you keep me alive," his voice was almost a growl of emotion.

Cass shied away from the intensity and looked up at the ceiling, throwing her hands out to the sides as if pleading for answers. "Doesn't someone always? Didn't Nash or whatever his name was?"

Billy threw his head back, lips parting in exasperation. "Not just like today! Not just when my life is in danger. Every. Fucking. Day." He turned his eyes on her again, as if boring a hole past her defenses. "You're my Reason, Cass. You're my Reason, now." As he finished, his eyes shimmered, and his expression turned pleading. He reached out his hand and placed it against the side of Cass's face, running his thumb along her cheekbone.

Cass felt as if she lost control of herself, then. Her brow furrowed and then her eyes lit up, her face a confusion of doubt and furious hope. Her mouth opened, and a small gasp escaped, but she couldn't find words. She rocked forward onto her knees and captured his head between her hands, unsure if she was trembling or if it was him. His hands were on her shoulders, long fingers communicative; light, yet poised to draw her toward him.

She closed the gap between them, steady but so slow both of them were breathing raggedly by the time their lips touched. The kiss ached and tormented—everything she'd wanted, but not enough. Billy groaned, and Cass's eyes flew open. Then, as if she'd accepted a sip of cool water without realizing her own thirst, she threw herself against him, desperate for more.

For a moment, their kissing was frantic. Then, his tone changed. His hands dropped away from her body. Frustrated, Cass wrapped an arm around his neck and felt him tense. His lips stopped moving against hers, and suddenly she remembered. She released him and pulled away.

"I'm sorry," she said, gasping. Her eyes were wide behind her shaking hand as she touched her lips.

Billy shook his head and drew close again.

"*I'm* sorry," he said. "I—it's not that I don't want—"

"Shh," Cass said. "I know. You told me. I know what happened, I—I wasn't thinking." She swallowed, reached out for him and then dropped her hands to her sides. She placed them flat against her legs. "I just want to show you—how I feel."

Billy's eyes dropped away "You're probably used to guys being eager. Leaping at the chance."

Cass waited for him to look at her and when he didn't, she cleared her throat. "I'm used to being the one in control," she said. "Because of what happened to me, I've been strict. I've always been the one to initiate intimacy. I've been the one to pace it—to stop it." She took an unsteady breath and blew it out. "It'll be new territory for me, not taking that role. But, I want *you*," she said, watching his reaction carefully. He looked like it pained him to hear it and she saw him shift his weight toward her.

He offered his hands, and she reached forward and linked her fingers with his, hardly any pressure holding them together. Her gaze traced the outline of his face, raked through his messy hair, passed down over his shoulders, his chest, his abdomen, and hips. Her eyes flew back to his face as she flushed.

But, his eyes were on her body, too. His gaze rested on her hips as heavily as if his hands were there. She realized he was breathing hard, as was she. His eyes met hers again, burning.

"New territory that you're willing to wait for?"

"If we survive all this," she said. "I'll wait as long as you need."

His answering smile was so infectious she felt a grin spread across her own face. Her facial muscles were stiff from being downturned and practically frozen for days.

Reality dropped back onto her, and she sighed. Billy squeezed her hands.

They moved to the mattress and for a while they lay face to face, chatting about Drew; the person he had been, the best friend.

A pause in the conversation left Billy staring at the walls around them and the bare floor beams over their heads—things found in most basements. His face paled, and his breathing grew shallow. She laid her index finger across the back of his hand where it rested on the mattress between them.

"What were you like Before?" she asked.

"What?" Billy asked, his eyes flying back to her face.

"I mean what were you really like? I know what actors were supposed to be like." She laughed, glad to see his shoulders relaxing into the bed beside her. "According to the trashy magazines." Now he chuckled, a stiff sound but better than panicked silence. "But, Before—were you serious? Proud? Reckless?"

"Shallow."

Cass shook her head. "No, you weren't."

Billy's laugh was freer this time. "I *was* a little."

There was an unsteady silence between them as the conversation hung on a tipping point. Cass waited for him to say more, hoped he would.

"I was brave," he said at last. "I was the man who came down into the cellar and kissed the wine from your lips. If I was afraid of the water, I dove in faster. I was spontaneous and irreverent like the day I made you laugh in the pet store." He cleared his throat and moved his hand to her shoulder, running it along her arm. "I wouldn't have been afraid to touch you. I would've told you who I was. I never hid from anything."

With gentle pressure on her arm, Billy pulled her closer and kissed her again. Eventually, she turned her back to him and draped his arm over her shoulder. She worried she'd never fall asleep that way, but she needed the warmth, the nearness. She didn't worry long. Soon, the steady sounds of Billy's breathing lulled her to sleep.

DERRICK PACED BESIDE THE lake, knowing he shouldn't be

around people when he was in this sort of rage. His frustration rolled just beneath the surface like an undertow, ready to rip him out into deep water. Nothing was going as planned. He glanced up toward the fire.

People were gathered around, talking about Drew—talking about Cass. Maybe arguing still over whether she'd been kidnapped or gone with Billy willingly. Derrick paused his frantic steps for a moment. At least one thing had gone right. Everyone suspected Billy of Drew's murder.

Derrick continued pacing. He needed to get himself under control. These next hours were crucial. If he stayed, he needed to appear to be a calm and confident leader. The type of leader who could unite all three groups. No small feat considering how natural such things were to Cam. Not to mention how beloved he was.

But Cam was soft. Sympathetic. Weak. And to prevent what had happened to Abby from happening over and over again, a strong leader was needed. Derrick *had* to be in control.

He would find some way to override Cam. And Hank. It shouldn't be too hard, with Cass gone and her allegiance in question.

And there was always the easiest option—the one he was best at—a clean, efficient kill.

FOR A SECOND TIME, Billy woke with Cass in his arms. But, whereas the first time he'd woken startled and been eager to see her response; this time, he remembered exactly how they'd ended up this way, and he was desperate *not* to wake her so he could keep her there. Hardly daring to breathe, he shifted, bracing himself up on his arm as well as he could without moving it and waking her. He craned his head around so he could see her face.

She was so carefree in sleep; face calm, body relaxed. First, it made him smile and then it made him shudder. In this world, carefree meant only vulnerable. He never wanted her to be vulnerable.

She took in a sudden breath and frowned. Her eyelids fluttered and opened.

"Good morning," Billy said, and he dove down quickly to place a kiss on her cheek. She tensed and squirmed away from him. He pulled back. "I'm sorry."

Cass shook her head. "It's okay; it's fine. I'm just—still not used to waking up with someone. Like this." She studied him. Billy was still as she raised her hand and brushed her fingers across his forehead, arranging his hair. She smiled for a moment before the look slowly faded, and a frown creased her brow.

"I haven't heard anything," Billy offered, knowing where her thoughts had gone. "I've been awake for a bit, and I've been listening. I don't think they've come. Not yet, anyway."

Cass nodded. "Maybe you were right. Maybe they're not coming." She shifted around, extricating herself from the thin bedcovers which had tangled around the two of them in the night. When she managed to stand, she adjusted her clothing.

Brick shook and danced around her as she went into the next room.

Billy sniffed and stretched. He followed to find her crouched beside the open map, running her finger along it with eyes narrowed.

"You never told me what our plan is," he said. "I mean, I know you want to find out who—" he broke off, seeing how Cass's shoulders stiffened, "—who the mole is." She relaxed and began folding the map. "But, how do we do that?"

Cass stood and continued to get ready. As she tightened her belt and adjusted her pistol at her hip, he couldn't help but remember that first day he'd stood before her, intimidated not so much by the presence of the gun but the sureness in her eyes that promised she knew how to use it.

"Cass?"

She let out a sigh and picked up her knife, sliding the sheath up her arm and tightening the straps. Billy didn't move to gather his own things, but watched and waited. When she turned, she took a step toward him and then stopped suddenly. She backed up to the nearest wall and pressed herself against it.

"Come here," she said, letting her arms fall to her sides and arching her back. He tried not to show his eagerness as he came to stand before her.

"What is it, Cass?"

Instead of answering she reached out and wrapped her hands around his forearms, pulling him closer before releasing him. He placed a hand against the wall on either side of her, his body aligned with hers, pressing her into the cool, painted concrete. Her breath grew ragged, but she kept her hands down and her gaze steady on his.

"Maybe we should just leave," she said. "Go off on our own? Just you and me?"

Billy pushed against her harder. He heard the hitch in her breath at his movement, and he leaned in to take her mouth with his own. He felt her tremble as she responded. Her lips were so soft and her mouth so warm that, for a moment, he could think of nothing but her taste and the beat of her heart against his chest. He considered saying yes.

Pulling away, he looked at her face just as her eyes squinted shut. She tipped her head back against the wall twice—two dull thuds confirming what he already knew.

"We can't do that," he said. He leaned forward so his lips were at her ear and whispered, "You told me I couldn't give up, that I had to prove my innocence. I believe you said that because you want me to be with you... *and* your family." He pulled back to look in her eyes.

"You won't leave them."

She moved her hands forward to grasp his t-shirt on either side of his ribcage. "I won't leave *you,* either." A dark determination filled Cass's eyes as she let go of his shirt and Billy backed away.

"Get ready," she said. "We have to stop back at that shed before we go."

Billy had begun to gather the items for his pack but paused to ask, "What for?"

"The C4 is coming with us."

Twenty-Two

CASS'S MANIC ATTITUDE AND pace hadn't left much time for talking once they'd left the shed. The blasting caps and fuses had been carefully removed and separated from the balls of C4 Billy carried in an open, plastic container they'd found.

Periodically, Cass would turn back to check on him and her eyes would flick down to his deadly burden as if wary it would explode at any moment. He was amused by her lack of trust in his knowledge but not surprised or hurt. He didn't trust himself, truth be told. It was one thing to identify the explosive as homemade C4 and speculate on its placement. It was another thought entirely to try to handle the stuff. But he hadn't blown them up, yet.

Cass assured him they would need it—that they would need a good distraction. But the thought of her planning to blow something up and her darkly efficient attitude were more frightening than the C4 in his arms.

Still, Billy followed, the pistol at his side occasionally brushing against his elbow as he walked. It wasn't all that useful as they only had a few rounds for it. He missed his knife. He had come to find comfort in having the antler-handled weapon. The feel of it had been all familiar whereas the gun jutting out from his lean frame was foreign.

Brick romped along beside Cass, rarely stopping to sniff. The animal seemed to sense her determination as much as he did. How could he not? Everything about her posture and her movement was fiery. But, though he was used to Cass leaving him out of her head—used to following her without knowing for sure the why's and how's—there was something different about this silence.

"Cass, stop," he said. He planted his feet, but Cass continued forward.

"Can't. Walk and talk."

"Cass."

This time she swung around, walking backward a few steps. The distance between them increased less and less rapidly and finally she stopped.

"What?" she asked.

Billy approached, keeping his pace leisurely. "What aren't you telling me? What's bothering you?"

When he came within a few feet, she looked away.

"What, Cass?"

She turned her gaze on Brick, who was digging for a field mouse or some other small animal hidden in the grass.

"There's only one way we're going to find out who their inside man is, Billy. Have you thought about that?"

He hadn't. He did now. The tone of her voice brought him swiftly to the conclusion that hiding in the bushes outside their compound and listening wouldn't do the trick. They wouldn't just overhear one of the leaders identifying the mole. The realization of her plan hit him, and he tilted his head back to gaze at the sky. It was lovely today, like blue glass with thin strips of white cotton scattered sparsely over it. It made what Cass said next seem all the more heinous.

"We'll have to capture one of them. Someone high up in the leadership. Not John, but someone he trusts. And we'll have to get it out of them."

Billy stared at her. Her hair was pulled back taut in a band, and she crossed her arms over her chest. She'd rolled up the sleeves of the clean navy blue t-shirt, exposing her arms and leaving free access to the knife. The strap of the rifle cut across her chest, pulling the tucked-in end of the t-shirt tight across her abdomen. The pistol rested in its familiar spot on her hip. The jeans were tighter than the ones she'd discarded and new, clean; a stark contrast to the blood staining the tips of the worn boots that peeked out underneath. Those boots were what made her look capable of her plan.

Impatient, she crossed her arms over her chest. "Torture, Billy," she said. "That's what I'm talking about here. I'm talking about blowing up their weaponry, grabbing someone in the chaos, and taking him someplace to beat information out of him." Her voice didn't waver. "Maybe kill him."

Billy's eyebrows lifted before he could school them into stillness.

She shook her head and looked at Brick again. "We may not get to the weapons building and if we can't, we won't be able to risk him getting away and warning the others."

"Cass..."

"There will be blood on my hands by the time this day is through, Billy. Will you still want to go off alone with me, then?"

"Cass, not for me. Don't do this for me."

"Not *just* for you. For Waylon and his daughters. For Doc. For Cam and Trista. For my niece or nephew." Cass paused to swallow, the first sign of emotion she'd shown throughout this speech. "For

Drew. Especially for Drew."

Billy scrubbed a hand across his face. "There must be some other way."

"Not any way that's fast enough." She sighed and dropped her hands. She pulled them into fists and released them twice at her sides. "Listen, if you don't want to be a part of this, I get it. Go back to the house, and I'll come for you there when it's done. But, take Brick with you."

Cass turned and strode forward again. Billy watched her, indecision swirling in his chest. But as he stepped forward to follow, his doubts faded.

He focused on Cass's bouncing ponytail and took deep breaths. He saw it flick sideways as she turned to look at Brick, and then she stopped. Taking in the sudden tension in her posture, he also looked at the dog. Brick was stiff, staring ahead with his hackles lifted. Cass turned back, wide-eyed.

"Someone's coming," she said. She grabbed Billy by the arm and turned his body left 90 degrees before taking off running. "Brick, come!" she shouted. She brushed the dog's back with her hand as she ran past him and the animal let out a low bark and followed.

Billy caught up to Cass, despite the fact that he ran awkwardly with his arms loaded. He saw her intended destination. There was a ditch ahead, cutting through the middle of the field, with a trickle of muddy water running along it. A large metal pipe jutted out of a land bridge that crossed the creek, allowing the water to flow beneath.

She barreled down the hill, and he followed, nearly losing his footing as he splashed into the water. He slowed and let her take the lead as she shouted "get in," and disappeared into the tunnel. Billy set the box just out of the stream, then reached out and grabbed Brick by the scruff as he entered behind her. He crashed into Cass's shoulder.

*　　*　　*

CASS CLOSED HER HAND gently over Brick's muzzle and said "enough" for the second time. The dog quieted, and she traced her hand back over his head and along his body. Her vision was beginning to adjust to the low light in the culvert. The cold, fetid water was soaking into her clothing. Beside her, Billy held Brick's collar firmly in one hand and scratched the dog's chest with the other.

He met her gaze, and she knew he heard the pounding of hooves, too. There were a lot of horses moving across that field, and Cass knew with Stronghold gone there was only one guess as to who was riding them. But, this was too big a force to be retrieving a bomb from Stronghold. She was sure of that despite the fact she couldn't be sure of their direction.

"Wait here," she whispered.

Billy shook his head and reached for her, but she shoved the rifle into his hand and continued to move toward the end of the culvert.

"I have to see," she said as she continued her awkward maneuvering down the narrow tunnel.

She squinted as she came to where light shone in, illuminating the first couple feet of the tunnel. She took a deep breath and fell to her hands and knees, the cold water a fresh shock. She could feel the lazy current of it as she crawled out into the sun. Behind her, Brick let out a quiet whine.

She crept up the side of the irrigation ditch, dropping lower to the ground with each advancement. By the time she was ready to crest the rise, she was flat on her stomach, and she shimmied forward, hands digging into the earth. Grass obscured her vision, and she parted it.

Drew had said New Danville had maybe seventy-five horses, and she guessed they had every last one out in that field. A few pulled wagons and trailed near the back, but most bore only riders. Every rider held a gun—at least one gun, she corrected herself—and the wagons sported only a couple of humans apiece, so it was possible they were laden with weapons as well.

The force had turned to the south, and they were running along the highway she and Billy traveled beside the night before. They were not heading to Stronghold, but to the campground. They were headed toward her people.

She slid her legs around and let her body roll down the side of the ditch, keeping her arms tucked against her head on either side. When she splashed into the water, she unfurled herself and turned to see Billy peering out from the culvert, a hand shielding his eyes.

"Are you okay?" he asked.

"We have to go. Right now." Cass stood up and held out her hand for the rifle. Billy handed it to her and crawled out of the culvert.

"What'd you see?" he asked.

"They're going to the campground," she said, already running.

"Cass, the bomb."

She stopped, balanced on the incline, and looked at where New Danville's force was already disappearing behind a tree-covered hill. She clenched her teeth. The bomb would slow them down, but it could mean being able to *end* the fight when they did arrive.

"Go get it," she called.

She leaned into her running and said a silent prayer her brother had left. Failing that, she hoped they were prepared to hold off the onslaught until she could get there.

LENA HAD WATCHED THE sun come up, again listening as people argued. The decision before them now was whether to hold to the plan and fight or run for it, hoping Billy had somehow failed to deliver his message. Lena wondered if she cared anymore what they did. Stay or go, abandon Cass or look for her, leave now or wait.

Lena was numb with it all. But when the final decision was made to leave, she found her will wasn't with the choice.

She shared a glance with Cam over her horse's neck before she mounted. He didn't want to go, either. But what choice did they have? They couldn't tell Cass's secret without admitting she had left of her own will. And they couldn't explain *that* without revealing they knew Drew's killer was among them still.

At least they weren't going far. The leaders had pored over the maps looking for a defensible stop no more than a day's ride away. They would set up there and send a search party out for Cass and Billy. Lena was determined to be in that party. So she clucked to her horse, feeling fairly certain she'd be back soon and taking pleasure in the idea she'd find the answers to the mystery.

But, her pleasure and her certainty disappeared with the echoing of fast-approaching hooves. She tugged the reins around, turning her horse so she could see in the direction of the noise. People around her were beginning to shout and scream.

Around the corner, down the same road Drew and Doc had taken to New Danville's camp, a cloud of dust hovered over the rapidly approaching forms of a number of horses. She took in a harsh breath and then someone was tugging on her leg, yelling that she should get down and take cover.

She dismounted, and the reins were ripped from her hands as a horse's chest crashed into her from behind, knocking her to the ground. She scrambled to her feet and hurried away from the chaos of horses and people panicking.

"We need to leave," someone shouted.

Lena turned to locate Cam, whose eyes hardened. He raised his voice, straining to be heard over the din. "We'll never outrun them, now," he said. "Ready your weapons and take cover."

Lena pulled the pistol from her hip and checked it was loaded, watching out of her peripheral as Cam gathered Hank and Derrick and headed forward to meet the coming onslaught, arms raised. Her father's familiar voice was at her shoulder, and his arm spun her and pulled her away.

A barrage of gunshots sounded and there were several screams as the remaining crowd separated. Over her shoulder, Lena saw the three leaders dive to the ground, Cam turning in mid-air so that he could return fire when he landed.

Waylon's hand on her neck urged her forward faster, and she felt smaller hands on her arm, squeezing. Darcy. The three of them ducked behind a lean-to. Lena stumbled and felt Darcy's boot bite into her calf. The gunfire continued, and Lena pressed herself against the wall so she could see around the corner. Cam and a few others were cutting the frantic horses loose from the closest wagons, then pushing them back into the road where the blockade had been the night before. They used them for cover and returned fire.

Several others with rifles ran forward to help establish a defense. She watched as blood flew from someone's leg. He'd been hit under the wagon. As the man fell back and tried to crawl away, she saw it was Adam. She felt her father touching her shoulder, telling her to stay put and for once, Lena found herself lacking in courage. She had no intention of going anywhere. Her limbs were stiffened by her fear.

A scream and a gunshot close by made Lena duck fully behind their cover. Darcy held her gun with both hands, at arm's length like a pro. Lena looked where her sister had aimed to see a man on foot, just outside the tree line. He stared down at his chest and fell, his rifle falling to the ground beside him.

"Put the gun down, Darcy. You did good," Waylon said, as he ran forward to grab the fallen man's weapon.

Darcy lowered her arms and looked at her sister, eyes wide. Lena managed a nod and then turned back to the action on the road. Someone else had been shot, a woman this time, and she lay sprawled and quivering near the opposite tree line. Doc was picking his way toward her.

Lena longed to scream at him to get back, but she only watched. Behind him, a gray blur whipped through the trees. When it came out into open ground, Lena recognized its fast loping movement. It was the cat. It lunged straight into the line of horses, showing no fear of the bullets or the animals, and disappeared into the crowd.

What the hell? Lena thought. *Was the cat with them?* The vision of the cat hissing at Derrick and clawing her to get away flashed in Lena's head. All at once, she realized who the mole was. The only person who'd ever seen the cat before last night—Derrick.

Her thoughts were cut off as a bullet struck the ground near the fallen woman. Dirt fell to earth as Doc shouted. He dropped to the ground, hands covering his head, and Lena scanned the woods behind him, looking for the shooter. A man approached, aiming at Doc and shouting something.

Lena didn't bother trying to comprehend his words, but took aim and fired her gun. The bullet struck the man in the shoulder, and he stumbled back, hitting a tree. He looked from his shoulder to her. He stared right into her eyes as he lifted his gun.

Twenty-Three

CASS TWISTED HER ANKLE in a gopher hole and cursed, limping away.

"Okay?" Billy asked. She nodded, gnashing her teeth as sweat dripped from her forehead over her eyelid. She looked at the C4, glad they'd had the foresight to pack old towels around it. Even if Billy did assure her it was stable, it bounced a lot as he ran. Besides, he'd said it *should* be stable. He couldn't truly know if they'd made it right.

Well, this isn't nice enough to be heaven, she thought as her ankle twinged and her lungs burned. But, it isn't bad enough to be hell. So we're alive. We haven't blown up, yet. She hoped her family was as lucky.

"This is taking too long," she said, her voice almost a roar.

"I know," Billy called back, breathless. They couldn't keep up this pace. She cursed and slowed to a quick walk, readjusting the various straps across her body

"God knows what's happening at camp. They could all be dying as we're stumbling through this field."

"Shh," Billy said.

Cass opened her mouth to yell at him for shushing her, but he repeated the sound more urgently. Cass scanned the field, and a movement caught her eye. There were two horses charging toward them, one dragging a harness and the other saddled.

"Shit," Cass said, excitement pulsing through her. She began to shrug off her pack and the rifle. "Don't move, don't breathe."

The horses spotted them and slowed, lifting their heads even higher into the air and blowing their nostrils as they moved. They watched the pair of humans warily. Cass knew she had to be careful if she was to catch them.

She steadied her breathing and began to take slow steps forward. Gunshots echoed in the distance. With a low groan, she picked up her pace and held her hands out in front of her, palms up. She recognized the horses, but she couldn't remember their names on her life at that moment.

"Hey," she said, deep and low. Two sets of ears flicked as she spoke. She kept her pace steady in spite of the crackle of urgency that sped through her veins like sparking wire. She was nearly close enough to reach them when a bird flew overhead, its shadow crossing between her and the horses. At the same time, a gust of wind came up, rattling a patch of dried grass, and the saddled horse's eyes widened. His head lifted as his nostrils flared. He spun and bolted.

Cass's attention sprang to the other animal, and she saw the whites of her eyes as well. With a grunt, Cass leaped forward and grabbed the lone, long rein, attached at the bit and entangled in the harness on the horse's back. The horse spooked away from her motion and tried to run, but Cass braced her legs and held as the horse pulled against the leather.

"Easy," she said, letting up on her pressure. She stayed with the pulling animal, sometimes jogging along and sometimes being dragged, her feet catching on the tufts of grass as she struggled to stay upright. "Easy, hey." She managed to keep her voice calm as they stayed locked in a tug-of-war motion of give and take, the animal backing and bracing and Cass holding firm despite the rein slicing into her palm and filling her hand with blood.

When she thought she wouldn't be able to hold for one more jerk, the horse stopped, its front legs shaking as it tossed its head. Cass let out a breath.

"Good. Nice," she said. She spoke mostly nonsense, taking cautious steps forward, hand extended. She approached the mare at the side of her head, reeling in the rein as she went. When she finally placed a hand on the horse's shoulder, it left a streak of blood against the animal's rich, bay hair. She untangled the rein and turned to lead the mare back across the field to where Billy stood next to the bomb.

"So," she said. "We're about to find out just how good a rider you are."

DERRICK'S HEART WAS PUMPING too fast, and every beat drove spikes of pain through his brain. He'd ducked into the trees as the first shots were fired and returned their aggression. He hoped for a clean shot at John and anyone else who knew about his deal so he could make sure all his planning didn't fall apart. But, John was not in the front lines.

He'd watched as Adam bled out on the road—watched Lena kill two men before she and her father and sister had to retreat into the woods as New Danville's forces passed through the pathetic barricade of wagons Cam had made.

It was Cam he tracked through the woods. The man searched and called out for Trista.

Hank found Derrick first.

"Christ, Derrick!" Hank said. "Glad you're okay. Let's get out of here." The man turned away, gesturing to Derrick to follow him. "We'll have to cut our losses and regroup with the survivors. There's no winning thi—"

His words were cut off as Derrick's bullet shattered his skull. His body fell forward, and Derrick stepped over it. He'd lost Cam, and he squinted through the trees until he caught a flash of long, blonde hair.

CASS GRIPPED A FISTFUL of the mare's mane to steady herself as Billy used her arm to slide down from his spot behind her. His legs gave out as he landed and he fell. The tote full of explosives bumped against his chest and bounced onto the ground beside him. Cass saw him flinch at the same time she did. She shook her head.

"Oh yeah," she said. "You're *so* sure it's stable."

The horse was fidgeting, her flesh jumping at the sound of every gunshot. It had been a rough ride. The makeshift reins Cass had fashioned from the broken driving rein had been too short, pulling Cass's arms and body position forward until she crouched like a jockey on the mare's neck. Billy had clung to Cass, cursing in her ear, his accent heavy the whole way. The box of C4 had dug into her back, a constant reminder they might blow up. And the mare had been squirrely, requiring the best of Cass's skills to keep her moving toward the sound of the fighting.

The shots were fewer now and more worrisome as there were long pauses between them.

"We need to see what's happening in there," she said, nodding to indicate the woods. Her shaking fingers undid the bridle and freed it from behind the horse's ears. She rubbed the mare's muzzle and whispered a thank you as she turned away, leaving the horse free.

She had opened her mouth to suggest they hide the bomb when Rylynn came running through the trees, screaming. Her frantic steps were halted as a gunshot sounded and a bullet burst through her calf. Her leg cranked around unnaturally as she went down, her screams slicing along Cass's spine.

A man stepped out into the sunlight after the wounded woman, rifle aimed. Cass pulled her gun from its holster.

"Hey," she shouted. The man looked up but didn't have time to react before Cass put a bullet through his heart. As he fell, his gun fired again, and Cass heard the mare's retreating hoofbeats behind her.

She retrieved the rifle and returned to find Billy helping Rylynn tie his long-sleeved shirt over her wound. The woman eyed him warily, but he pretended not to notice. Cass had a moment of doubt about bringing him into the wooded campground with her. Chances were high her own people would be as quick to fire on him as the enemy.

"What about the bomb?" he asked.

Cass's answer was lost as another scream drew their attention. It was Darcy this time, ducking behind a tree far too skinny to provide any real cover. Clutching her bleeding arm, she slid down to the ground.

Cass turned, already aiming her pistol toward the rough area Darcy had come from. She spotted him and prepared to squeeze the trigger. Just before she did, a spot of darkness burst over the man's gut. He sunk forward onto his knees, clutching at his stomach as blood poured between his fingers.

"It's Waylon," Billy said. Cass looked down, only now realizing he had looped an arm around her waist as if to pull her out of harm's way. He released her and ran forward, reaching Darcy just as her father did.

"Is she okay?" Cass called out.

Waylon nodded as he slung his daughter's good arm around his neck.

"Hardly bleeding," Billy called, applying pressure to the wound. Waylon eyed Billy as they helped the girl out from the trees.

"Where's Lena?" Cass asked.

"I don't know," Waylon called back.

The numbness had taken Cass sometime earlier, as she and Billy had hurried toward these woods, hearing gunshots and imagining what might have happened to their friends. But, as the possibility of losing Lena swarmed her, a surge of hot anger brought feeling back to her limbs. And with it, urgency.

Cass helped the men lower Darcy to the ground near Rylynn.

"My brother?" she asked.

"Lena was looking for him," Darcy answered. "She ran off to find him."

"She said she needed to tell him something," Waylon added as he frowned at the plastic tote packed with towels. "What is that?"

"C4." Ignoring his open-mouthed disbelief, she said, "Waylon, are they all spread out like this through the trees?" Cass's voice was growing desperate. After all the trouble they had gone through to bring the bomb here, it would be useless if their enemies weren't together in roughly one spot.

Waylon shook his head. "No. They've captured some of us, so a lot of them are standing guard by the lean-tos. That's where our people are."

Billy returned, carrying a pistol and a knife he must have taken off the body of Darcy's shooter. The knife, his arm, and much of his white t-shirt were stained with blood and Cass let out a gasp when she saw him. He quickly shook his head.

"I'm fine," he said. "He wasn't dead." He met Cass's eyes and offered the gun to her, his hands shaking. "He is now."

Waylon stepped between Cass and Billy and leaned in close to her. "You trust him?" he asked, jutting his thumb back over his shoulder to indicate Billy.

"He didn't kill Drew," Cass said. "I swear it on my life."

"On all our lives," Darcy said, an edge to her tone Cass had only ever heard from Lena.

Cass swung the hand that held the pistol down toward Darcy's head, stopping mere inches from her face. Darcy flinched, then glared up at Cass. Cass held the look, her own eyes fierce.

"On everyone I've ever cared about." She watched her words register with the girl. "Take it," Cass said, loosening her grip on the pistol. Darcy took the weapon, and Cass turned back to Waylon, whose face was surprisingly passive. He stepped out from between Cass and Billy without comment.

"We need to get that bomb up to the lean-to," Cass said, taking a moment to remove the detonators from her pack and tuck them in beside the C4. "And we need to get our people out."

"The guards," Waylon said, checking his ammunition.

"I know. We need a distraction." Cass rolled her shoulder and stood up straighter.

"Find Lena," Darcy said. "She's distracting."

"I do need to find my daughter," Waylon said.

"And Cam," Cass agreed. She glanced back at the bomb. "Okay, listen. Darcy and Rylynn, crawl over there by those bushes for cover. Keep Brick with you. Waylon and Billy, move the bomb. Find a place near the lean-to but out of sight."

With one last check of the dead man's rifle, Cass turned to Waylon and fixed him with a commanding stare. "Waylon, I need you to stay there. Wait for the distraction and get our people out."

Waylon shook his head. "I'm going for my daughter."

"No, you have to trust me," Cass said. "The captives might not follow Billy. They won't trust him. But, they'll follow you. For all we know, Lena's in there."

"No, she's not," Darcy said.

Cass nodded. "Still. You have to trust me to find her for you." Cass turned to Billy and glanced at his hip where the firestarter she'd given him still hung from his belt loop by its carabiner. "You stay with the bomb until I come for it."

"I want to help you," Billy said, shaking his head.

"You have both sides gunning for you," she said. "You can't help if you're dead. But, you can guard the bomb and light it when the time comes."

"I want to stay with you," he said, though the fight had left his voice.

Cass glanced at Waylon and then closed the distance between herself and Billy. She lowered her gun to her side and wrapped one arm around him, laying her head against his chest. She felt the blood from his shirt soaking into the hair by her temple, but he put an arm around her back, and she didn't care.

"Stay alive," she said.

"I love you," he said, loud enough to be heard by the others. Cass froze for an instant and then her duties came rushing back to her.

Pulling away, she said, "Get moving." Then, she darted into the trees without looking back.

Twenty-Four

LENA HADN'T REALIZED HOW hard it actually was to slash someone's throat. *Of course*, she thought, *the knife is dull.* She felt separate from herself, a spectator in her own fight, until the man's blood splattered out over her hand and he fell back onto her, pinning her to the ground. She began to hyperventilate, flailing to extract herself from underneath him.

Arms dragged the still-gurgling man off of her and hands gripped her under her shoulders and hauled her to her feet. She shuddered, flashing back to rough arms around her and a sweaty hand covering her mouth.

But, this was Cam. He released her and began wiping her bloody hands off on his shirt.

"It's okay, you're okay, Lena," he was saying. "You saved me."

Through her shivering, she realized that she had. She'd tried to shoot the man who was fighting Cam, but her gun had misfired. No, it had been empty. So she'd come up behind him and tried to strangle him. But he'd fought.

That's when she'd seen the glimmer of the knife in the grass, and she'd grabbed it and brought it to his throat. It had pulled against the skin and stuck when she hadn't expected it to.

"Lena!" Cam shook her shoulders.

"It's Derrick," she sputtered. Yes, that had been what she'd been saying to herself, over and over as she sped through the woods looking for Cam.

"What about Derrick?" Cam asked.

"He's the mole."

"How do you—" Cam was cut off by a familiar and shockingly welcome voice.

"Cameron!" Cass called.

Lena glanced over and saw Cass weaving through the trees toward them. Then, her vision went white and she sunk between Cam's hands.

DERRICK'S HEAD WAS POUNDING fiercely with each step. And the squirming woman wasn't helping. He called out for John. He hardly knew how to think through the pain by the time he stumbled out onto the gravel road.

Guns were trained on them from all directions and Trista's muffled screams intensified, but Derrick hardly cared.

"I said I want to talk to John." Derrick was pleased with the calm in his voice, despite the storm in his brain.

"I'm here," said John. "We can talk." The man gave a signal and guns lowered all around. "I'm not sure what we have to talk about though, Derrick. You've chosen your side."

"I can give you her," Derrick said, jostling Trista so she stumbled to her knees. "And her baby. Population. Women, children.

Legistimancy." Derrick frowned. That hadn't sounded right. God, his head hurt. "And she'll call out for the daddy, and then we'll have Cameron Hood."

John frowned. "What do I want with him?"

"His band will fall without him," Derrick said. "You can still have what we agreed to. If I can still have what I was promiss—. Promised."

Laughter made Derrick's anger burn.

THERE IT IS, CASS thought. It was the distraction she'd been needing. It just wasn't a distraction she liked very well. She put a strong hand on Cam's arm, holding him in place.

They'd found Billy and Waylon, handed an unconscious Lena to her father, and heard Derrick shouting. All the guards had left the lean-to, running to the fence line with weapons aimed. Cam had begun ushering the captives out and leading them away when Derrick had said something that left them all frozen. Derrick had Trista.

The captives were out. The bomb was ready to be placed. But Derrick had Trista. And she was too close for them to blow the lean-to.

Cass clicked her tongue until Billy looked at her, then nodded at Cam. Billy's hand replaced hers on her brother's arm and she crept through the trees to get a better view. John was shaking his head, pressing his fingers to his temple. Most of the men looked at Derrick like he was crazy. There was little stopping them from murdering both Derrick and Trista on the spot.

"Well, that is something I want," John said. "Cameron Hood. And Cassidy. I would very much like to talk to the people who killed twice their own number in a clearing and sent the rest of my men running back empty-handed."

Cass's eyes widened. She'd known New Danville was responsible for the kidnapping and murders, but hearing John refer to it openly was a fresh shock. She heard the sounds of a scuffle. Billy was having trouble restraining Cam, and as she watched, Cam threw a punch that landed Billy on his ass. Freed, her brother ran into the fray, heedless of her whispered pleas for him to stop.

"I'm right here," Cam yelled. "Let her go."

"That way," John's voice commanded. "Find the sister. Bring her back alive."

And then Billy had her arm, and he was dragging her deeper into the trees, shadows closing in on them as he led her the same way Waylon and the captives had gone.

She dug in her heels.

"No." She tugged her arm away. "I won't leave them," she said. "I'm going back."

"Cass, there are too many," Billy said.

"Good thing we have a bomb."

"They're everywhere looking for you."

"But not for you." Cass grabbed his upper arms. "If I go back, they'll take me to John. They'll stop looking. You can get the bomb and light it."

"So you can be blown up, too?" he asked.

"I'll get us out," she said. "Whistle at me when it's set, and I'll get us out."

Cass pulled away from him before he could protest and threw herself back the way they'd come. Over her shoulder, she saw him dart off the trail, disappearing into the trees. Then, she slammed into someone. Hands grabbed her, yanking the rifle over her shoulder. She heard a pop and cried out as it dislocated. She clutched her arm, holding it up so the pain lessened.

Her pistol holster was checked, and she shuddered as rough hands brushed the bare skin near her hip. Her knife was pulled from the sheath on her arm and a hard, cold gun barrel pressed into her back.

"Move," a voice ordered.

She nodded and walked down the trail, wincing as the gun barrel was prodded into her at intervals. There were at least three men with her, but adrenaline was blacking out the edges of her vision, and she couldn't count. She could only focus on putting one foot in front of the next as she moved toward her fate. As they rounded the lean-to, she wanted so badly to glance down the tree line toward the spot where Billy should be moving up to retrieve the bomb. But her neck seemed cast in cement, head directed at John, who waited in the middle a group of armed men.

Cam was on his knees in front of John, his hands raised. John turned to watch her approach, a smile curving his mouth. Derrick still held Trista with a gun to her head. Various men pointed their guns in various directions; at Derrick, at Cam, at her. The affair looked comically dangerous, and she let out a dry laugh.

"What's funny?" John asked.

"Your men," she said, glancing around at the guns pointed every which way so if anyone missed, John would surely be shot.

"Weapons down," he ordered, the amusement gone from his expression. Weapons lowered—even the one at her back.

With the pressure of the gun gone, Cass had to fight the urge to charge at John. A sparkle came into his eyes as if he knew what she'd been thinking.

"No wonder we killed so many in that clearing," she said, then bit her tongue. Now was not the time to let her mouth run. John's jaw clenched and then released as his shoulders lifted and fell in a sigh.

"We want a surrender," John said. "Help us find your survivors and join us. We'll rebuild Stronghold and start fresh."

"Why would you rebuild the city that you bombed?" Cass asked.

John's head jolted back as if she'd hit him. Cass heard a thump from inside the lean-to and her eyes flicked over to it. No one had returned to guard it.

"Yeah, I know about that," she said. "I also know about the bomb that didn't get lit. I suppose I should have expected your men to be as sloppy with their guns as they are with their explosives."

A murmur circled her, passing through the ranks of the men. John frowned.

"The explosion was an accident," he said.

Cass glanced at Cam and fixed her eyes on his for a second, widening them. "No," she said, "I've been there."

She turned to look at Trista. Derrick still stood over her kneeling form, though his gun was lowered. Cass wiggled her fingers at her side, drawing Trista's gaze. She made a fist. "They had a hospital." She fixed Trista with a hard stare and flicked her eyes up at Derrick, praying the woman would do what a woman should know how.

"We could set up a hospital. We have your doctor." John indicated the lean-to behind him and Cass waited, praying to hear the whistle. She couldn't keep this up much longer.

"Join us, and you can build the place yourself," John said.

"You have our doctor," Cass said, glancing at Cam once more. "We have your bomb."

John shook his head. "No."

Cass shrugged, saying nothing as she let John read the calm honesty in her expression.

"Where is it?" John asked, stalking toward her. He was angry now, convinced. His face grew redder with each step. He grabbed her arms and shook her, his fingernails digging into her skin. "I burned half your state to the ground to get you here." Flecks of spit hit Cass's face as he spoke, but she couldn't convince her gaping mouth to close. Her eyes were wide with shock. *They* had started the fire?

John shook her again as he continued. "That was my mistake. I've lost men and horses and guns to you and so help me God, I'll lose nothing else. Where is the bomb?"

Cass shook her head, and he stepped back. He raised a hand, preparing to slap her and she flinched away, bumping into the guard who'd had the gun on her.

"Don't," she said. "It's in the wagon." She pointed with her good arm. Two wagons, horses hitched and waiting, were parked up the gravel drive, just around a bend.

John slapped her anyway, and Cass let her head whip back. Holding her cheek, she sunk to her knees.

"Check it!" he yelled.

Cass heard the sound of several feet rushing away.

"John, she's—" Derrick started.

"Shut-up, Derrick."

Cass waited a heartbeat, then two, before shouting, "Now, Trista!"

She drove her fist upward, delivering an uppercut to John's jaw. The force of the surprise hit knocked him over backward. He sat up, and she kicked her boot heel into his face, hearing a crunch as blood spattered out from the impact. He fell back again with a grunt. Cass stepped on his chest, his sternum giving beneath her weight as she bent and pulled his gun, a revolver, from its holster.

She aimed first in Derrick's direction, only to find that he was staggering away from Trista, holding his balls. Cam was rocketing toward him. Trista stood and ran into the trees, wobbling as she went and Cass turned to find a new target. Before she could, she was struck in the back of the head.

She went down face first and rocked her head back and forth, struggling to stay conscious. Gravel scraped her hands and face, and she blinked away dirt as she tried to reorient herself. Her dislocated shoulder hampered her attempts to stand. Someone kicked her in the ribs, and the air gushed out of her lungs. She curled in on herself and tried to roll away. Then a shot fired, followed by a second in quick succession. The man above her cried out. A gun fell to the ground beside her face and then a heavy weight pinned her legs down as the man fell on top of her, clutching his side.

She dragged her lower body out from under him and kicked his gun out of his reach. She looked up to see Billy, still holding the rifle, eyes wide. A man to his right aimed a gun at him, and Cass screamed wordlessly.

The man went down as Billy whipped around. Waylon had come back, and he stood, pistol in hand, nodding at Billy.

Someone tackled Waylon from behind, and Cass struggled to her feet, spots spinning in her vision. She sprinted toward the lean-to, passing Billy, who was bashing the butt of his gun into the shoulders of the man who tussled with Waylon.

Cass crawled through the fence and swung around the wall of the lean-to. The bomb sat in the center of the dirt floor. Billy had reconfigured it, molding it into one large lump. The fuse stretched along the ground to the door she'd come through. She'd probably stepped on the damn thing. She reached for it and remembered she had no way to light it.

Her growl became a string of curses, and she ran back out. The group of men who had been checking the wagons had almost torn them apart looking. The horses were prancing in place and rearing against the men who held them. She had to hurry.

The man Waylon and Billy fought fell, and Billy stepped back. He held the same bloody knife at his side, dripping. Cass charged past Waylon to lunge at Billy's hip. She grabbed his firestarter and yanked. He stumbled to the side, crashing into her and dropping the knife just as the fabric gave way and the firestarter tore free of his jeans.

"Get our people out of here," she said, flinging her useless arm toward where Cam had been.

As she passed Waylon again she screamed, "Get gone! Now!" The pain tearing through her injured arm gave volume to her order and her own voice sent waves of pain through her head.

She skidded into the lean-to, good hand scuffling in the dirt, searching for the fuse. She could hear approaching footsteps and knew she didn't have time for so much fuse.

She reached to her arm for her knife to cut it and touched the fabric of the sheath. Her roar of frustration was cut off as someone slammed into her from behind. Arms clamped over her own, and she and her attacker plowed forward, taking the bomb with them. Flesh and explosive skidded across the dirt coming to a stop as the C4 smacked into the back wall of the lean-to, its shape changing again.

Fresh pain sliced through Cass's wounded shoulder and arm. She squirmed to be free of her captor and heard fabric tear. The arms jerked her away from the bomb and tossed her onto her back. Strong, thick hands wrapped her throat and squeezed.

She sucked in tiny, rasping breaths. Derrick's face hovered above her, surrounded by a cloud of the dust that rose from the ground with their every movement. She gripped at his wrists and stared up into his bloodshot eyes, feeling as if her own would pop out of her skull from the incredible pressure. The world narrowed as dark circles closed in on the outer edges of her vision.

She felt herself weakening. A fingernail broke against Derrick's hand, and she lost her grip, unable to claw him further. With no other recourse, she pulled in the tiny amount of air she could manage through her nose and let her body go limp. Her hands fell away, and her head tipped to the side as she forced her eyes to focus on a cobweb hanging from the upper corner of the little shed. The ruse was easy, and for a moment, she thought she was truly dead.

Derrick's hands loosened and then released as he raised up onto his knees, letting out a yell of victory. As he celebrated, Cass sucked in a gulp of air, tucked her legs up, and slammed them into his thigh. His legs went out from under him, and he fell. Cass rolled as the concussion of his landing reverberated through the dirt.

Surprised, he didn't move for a moment. Cass propelled her foot toward his head with all the strength she could muster. He caught it and twisted. She screamed at the wrenching pain in her knee and hip and rolled her body with his motion, trying to keep the damage minimal.

With her free foot, she jabbed him in the ribs, but she was coughing from the dirt and the strangulation and didn't have much power. He laughed. His grip on her leg wouldn't loosen.

A beam of light came through the wood panels of the lean-to causing the dust around them to glow. Something glimmered at Derrick's calf. Billy's antler-handled knife was shoved into Derrick's boot, and it was working its way free as they struggled. She squirmed until she could reach and snatched it. It sliced into Derrick's leg as she jerked and he finally released her with a surprised grunt.

Derrick sat up, reaching for her wrist, but she was quick. She brought the handle of the knife slamming into his temple and knocked him flat. She set the tip of the blade against his left breast. There was no numbness here; heat pulsed through her body and her brain as she met his eyes.

She shoved the knife downward, leaning all her weight against it. It bent against a bone, then slid into his chest up to the hilt. He grunted and began gasping as she jerked the knife back out. Blood seeped up after the blade, and she met his panicked eyes once more before turning away.

Bile burned her throat as she scrabbled about in the dirt-clouded area, looking for the firestarter. It was under Derrick's still-convulsing leg, and she shoved at his boot to grab it. His body went still as she clambered over him and found the coil of fuse.

She sliced through it with the knife, shortening it and leaving a bloody line in the dirt. Her left hand was now completely numb due to her dislocated shoulder, and the firestarter slipped from her grasp. She retrieved it and fumbled with the cap. She had to position her near-useless fingers with the opposite hand to hold the small object. She struck it once, twice, again, and again; her heart pounding harder and harder as she heard shouts and scrambling feet growing closer. They were looking for her.

Finally, the fuse caught and began to spark and burn with the scent of phosphorous. Cass glanced at the bomb one last time. Her eyes passed over the blood-stained and bent knife that had threatened Billy, murdered Drew, and taken revenge on Derrick. She left it in the dirt. Knowing she had only seconds to get out, she leaped over Derrick's body, swung madly around the side of the building and threw herself to the ground to roll under the fence.

She risked a backward glance as her legs powered her away. Men were leaping the fence and entering the lean-to, John among them. She faced forward in time to narrowly miss a tree. As she swerved, she stumbled over a fallen limb and landed in a pile of bracken, sharp edges splitting her skin all over.

The blast came. Her body was powered along the ground, entangled with the tree limb she'd tripped over. All sound became an unbearable buzz. Debris struck her; she slammed into something solid, and her world closed off in darkness.

Twenty-Five

EXISTENCE CAME BACK IN flashes, even after she'd regained consciousness. Shouting and intense pain were interspersed with darkness and voices repeating mindless phrases of comfort.

White clouds and stars alternately rolled by above her head. Hands lifted her, poured water into her mouth, offered food, pulled back her hair as she was raised to vomit over the side of a wagon.

Voices spoke to her. By day, Billy, Doc, Cam, Lena, Trista, even Darcy. By night, the voices were sometimes Drew's or Derrick's. Or her father's. Even her mother's, once. So she thought.

She had moments of lucidity. She remembered what she'd learned during those moments. She knew who'd survived and who hadn't. She knew they thought she was brilliant and brave. Knew they'd been successful.

The daytime voices grew harsher; demanding that she eat, demanding that she move. The nighttime voices beckoned. She only wanted the gray peace of sleep.

And one day when the sun was fierce on her face, the voices argued.

"She won't talk to me."

"She won't talk to anyone."

"That's not her problem, right now. Her wounds—both physical and mental—will eventually heal. But only if she survives. If she doesn't start to eat or drink on her own, she'll die. It's that simple." Footsteps stomped away.

"Doc," this voice was Cam's. The tone was one she'd thought reserved for her own moments of greatest insensitivity.

"He has to hear it, Cam. I know it hurts him, but it's true. We have to find a way to reach her."

CAM FIXED BILLY WITH another long stare. His eyes were growing less sympathetic, more impatient. Billy got the message. They needed to get going. It was already late morning. He'd been at this for hours.

Cass was propped up against the side of the wagon, staring off into space like always. She was in there somewhere. She had to be.

"Come on, Cass," he said. "So, what?" He reached out and turned her head toward him with fingers marked up by healing wounds— wounds he'd gotten digging her broken body from the debris. "You're just gonna give up?"

Cass blinked at him, and as soon as his fingers fell away, she turned her head back to stare out at the trees.

"Okay." He shook his head. "Doc, help me."

Doc walked across the wagon bed and lifted under her left shoulder as Billy lifted the right. Doc was careful of the bandages covering the stump of her left arm, which had been severed above the elbow after sustaining traumatic damage in the blast. Together, they maneuvered the girl to the edge of the wagon. Billy jumped down and caught his breath.

She wasn't heavy. Lighter than ever, now, he guessed. But she tended to go limp when moved. She would roll over, crawl, and sometimes sit up on her own in the wagon. They'd even had her out walking once. But, if it wasn't her idea she didn't help.

He pulled her into his arms and carried her away from the wagon. After several yards, he set her on the ground and knelt beside her, clearing his throat.

"We are all—so sorry," he sucked in a shaking breath. "For what you went through. For what you lost and for what you sacrificed. He ran a thumb along what was left of her childhood scar; from the top edge where a tan line spoke of years of wearing the knife sheath there, down to where the scar disappeared beneath the white bandage. He knew the scarring underneath was extensive.

He saw the hairs on her arm stand on end and looked at her face. She shivered and tears glistened in her eyes. Billy held back his excitement at her response, keeping his voice level.

"But none of us can watch you do this to yourself, Cass."

She swallowed and opened her mouth. Billy's heart-rate rushed through the roof, and he put a hand on the ground to steady himself.

Her voice was hoarse. "I can't stop it from happening again." She let out a cough. "I can't save anybody like *this*." Her head jerked toward her missing arm.

"Fuck us, then," Billy said. Her eyes flicked up to find his, surprised at his tone. "Can you save yourself? That's all we want you to do."

She looked away again, and after a moment, her eyes turned to the legs of the horse standing nearby. Lena stood beside the mare, watching. Cass ignored the girl and eyed the horse. Billy knew she recognized her as the horse she had caught in the field. The mare that had somehow carried them and a bomb safely to the campground, despite her own terror.

He met Lena's eyes and nodded. Lena nodded back and walked away. He glanced over to see that the group had left. The wagon was disappearing around a bend. Cam sat astride his horse, his look a sharp warning. Finally, he shook his head and left as well.

"Here it is," he said. "These days, in our group, horses are the cars, cabs, and ambulances. So you've got to be able to ride even when you're dying." He leaned forward and adjusted the horsehair necklace around her throat, moving the clasp to the back. He pressed a kiss to her forehead.

With a sharp sniff, he stood and walked away. He didn't look back, but picked up a jog, then a run, and dashed around the corner. Smoke flung her head up as he arrived but went back to grazing right away. He patted the gray mare's shoulder and settled himself against a tree trunk nearby, watching the last of the group disappear down a hill, following the overgrown train tracks.

He waited and doubted himself. He counted his bullets, readjusted the knife sheath on his belt, and doubted himself. He pictured Cam slugging him in the face for a second time and doubted himself. The sun was high—nearly noon—when he realized how far his shoulders had sunk.

He was going to have to go back for her. His plan was going to fail. Which meant, unless someone else could think of some better way to reach her, he was going to lose the woman he loved.

He tugged the blue bandana from his pocket and worked it between his fingers for a moment before pushing himself to his feet. He wondered how much longer he should wait. That's when he heard the hoofbeats. The horse was walking his direction, slowly from the sound of it. It was possible the mare had just wandered off on her own.

Unable to wait any longer, he stepped out from behind the trees and instantly regretted it. The mare shied to the side and Cass—who miraculously sat astride her—had to clutch the saddle horn, her grip awkward with the reins bunched up in the same hand. Her only hand.

"Easy," Cass said, her voice scratchy. The mare calmed and stood as Cass readjusted her seat and her grip on the reins. She looked at Smoke grazing nearby, but she didn't look at Billy. For long minutes, she sat looking at everything but him.

Finally, she met his questioning gaze. Her eyes flicked down to the blue bandana in his hand.

"Her name is Claire?"

Billy's eyebrows lifted, and he took a tentative step forward. "Eclair," he said. "Like the pastry. She's from California, but no one claims her."

"That's an awful name," Cass said.

He wanted to remind her that her first horse was named after food as well, but he kept quiet, instead basking in the sound of her voice after so many worrisome weeks.

"We'll call her Dynamite," she said.

Billy laughed. "I like it."

Epilogue

LENA ADJUSTED THE LEAD rope of the mule she was ponying and gazed at the mountains. An early rainstorm had turned into sleet, forcing her and Cass to stay overnight on their supply run—the first of the season. Snow was falling in the higher elevations, but their path home was clear. It helped that they could ride on the Interstate the entire way from the city to the guest ranch they now called home.

She glanced over at Cass, met her eyes, and smiled. She received a nod in return. Cass could smile again, but she didn't do it often. Most of her smiles were reserved for Billy and Dynamite. Lena admired the bay mare her friend rode. As she watched, Cass pulled back the reins and said "whoa." Lena pulled up her own mount.

"What's up?" she asked. Cass didn't answer, but secured the lead rope of the pack horse she led and dismounted. Lena huffed in disbelief, her breath visible in the air before her. How was it possible

Cass had already adapted so well? She rode and worked like she'd never been injured, much less had an arm amputated.

Cass walked up to a vehicle and rubbed her hand across the driver's side rear window. Lena clucked at her horse and moved in closer, trying to see what had caught the woman's eye.

"Goodies?" she asked. Her eyebrows lifted as Cass turned to her, smiling.

Two hours later, she watched an even bigger smile cross Cass's face as they rode into camp and Billy spotted the guitar hanging across Cass's back. He stood back as she dismounted, shaking his head in disbelief.

Two of the group's newer members, a brown-haired boy and his aunt who Doc had rescued from New Danville, took Lena's horse and mule. Lena thanked the pair and turned to greet Darcy with a hug.

"We were worried about you," she said. "Was it just the weather?"

Lena nodded. "We didn't know how bad it would get so we found an old middle school to stay in. The horses slept in the gym."

Darcy laughed and made room for Trista, who joined them with a crying infant in her arms. She bounced the baby girl and shushed her until she quieted.

"How's Katie today?" Lena asked, wiggling her fingers at the baby.

"Not as bad as she'd have you believe," Trista said. "She has a flair for the dramatic already. Maybe Billy will teach her to act one day."

Lena and Darcy laughed, and all three women turned to watch as Billy inspected his new guitar and thanked Cass. He zipped up the soft case and leaned in to press his lips to Cass's forehead. He took her hand, and both of them paused to stare down at their intertwined fingers.

"They're getting better at that," Trista said. Darcy nodded and let out a little squeal. Lena rolled her eyes.

Katie began to cry again, and the lovebirds approached. "How's your girl?" Cass asked.

"She wants her auntie," Trista said, passing the baby over.

Lena watched in fascination as Cass took the baby and tucked her into the crook of her only arm. Someone had made Trista a sling to carry the baby as she worked and Cass often used it, but didn't need it. Katie was always content with Cass. She twined her little fingers around the horsehair necklace made by her namesake and tugged. Lena laughed to herself. *That's right*, she thought, *there was one other person who always ended up with Cass's smiles.*

CASS RAN HER CHEEK against the infant's. Katie was hungry and complained in half-hearted mews against Cass's face, trying to suck her aunt's soft flesh.

Trista appeared, already unzipping her jacket.

"Thank you," she said. Cass leaned back to let Trista scoop the child from her arm. She stayed reclined in her camping chair, watching the patches of fog dissipate over the nearby hills like wraiths disappearing into the clouds. The day was beginning to brighten and warm.

Cam arrived, carrying a wooden box. "We're having eggs with lunch," he said.

Trista let out a soft cheer as she headed for the house. On the porch, Rylynn clapped in excitement before gathering an armload of firewood and heading back indoors.

"First eggs, Cass," Cam repeated as he passed her, patting her leg. "Come have lunch." She half-smiled and looked back at the hills.

Once alone, Cass tilted back her head and closed her eyes. Before she'd achieved any kind of peace, something struck her boot. She looked down at the pebble spinning near her foot and traced its likely trajectory. Billy stood in the thin space between the porch and the hill it nestled against.

His eyes flashed as she watched him and he tipped his head back and to the right, toward their spot behind the hill. Cass was hungry now, but not for food.

She stood and followed where he'd already disappeared. She ran along the base of the hill until she collided with him, his arms keeping her upright. They kissed, deep and hot, each motion dragging at her, making her crave more.

She slid her hand under his jacket and shirt, running it up the skin of his back. She felt his hands slip down along her hip and into the waistband of her jeans. She leaned into him. He pulled his head away.

"We could wait," he said, eyes sparking mischief. "There's eggs for lunch."

"I don't want eggs," she said, pressing her lips against his again.

Later, with her back nestled comfortably into a nook at the foot of the hill, Cass moaned. Her eyes flicked open, and she found her vision blurred by Billy's hair. Through the blonde strands, she could see steam rising off his bare back, a miniature of the mist on the hills around them.

A surge of sensation pulsed through her, and she had to fight to keep her eyes open, clenching her teeth with the effort of keeping her hand to herself. Her arm stretched above her head in the sparse, cool grass. Every inch of her skin was burning, every muscle taut as she pressed her body into him, matching his movement.

Billy moaned and brushed his lips over her shoulder, and she shivered and tore at the grass, a clump of dirt popping free and crumbling in her grasp. She let out an agonized groan and tightened her legs around Billy's waist, pressing as much of her skin against his as she could manage.

Unable to stand it any longer she raised her arms, sharp pains radiating through the stump of the left. Bits of dirt and a few blades of grass rained down on her face and into Billy's hair as she placed her palm lightly on his shoulder.

This time, Billy didn't flinch or slow, but rather ran his hand down her side, gripping her hip and pushing deeper into her. Cass increased the pressure on his shoulder, her fingers indenting his flesh, then whitening. She bit her lip to stop herself as Billy lifted his head and met her eyes. They were steady and dark with lust. His expression showed no hesitation.

She slid her arm further around him, pulling her body up from the ground and tight against his, burying her face in his neck.

She hadn't told him that this was when the phantom sensations of her missing limb were the worst. Not being able to do things as easily as she once had was, at best, an annoyance and often worse. But not being able to hold him the way she longed to—that was her agony. Maybe she would tell him one day. Maybe he would understand that her body was crying out the depth of her feeling for him.

"I love you," she gasped, as the two of them climaxed together.

As Billy's breathing began to slow, Cass loosened her grip, but he pulled her harder against him.

"Don't let go yet," he whispered, trembling. Cass softened in his grasp but continued to cling to him. They waited like that until the spring breeze began to chill Cass's bare skin. She shivered and Billy released her, lowering her back into the little notch in the earth.

He stood and Cass watched his naked body, strong and lithe as he gathered their clothes and returned. She smiled and sat up, taking her shirt from the pile and pulling it over her head. This process was surprisingly easier than pulling on her underwear and pants. She shimmied them up her body, tugging on each side in turn. Billy, already dressed, was watching her.

"What?" she asked.

He wore a smile, but his eyes were uncertain. "You know what you said, don't you?"

Instead of answering, she finished maneuvering into her pants and leaned back on her elbow. For a long moment, she just watched him, still as a statue except for the movement of his hair in the wind. She felt her own blown back, her neck exposed and sending tingles down her spine.

"You're so beautiful," Billy said. The bottom dropped out of her gut.

"You're not bad yourself," she said, smiling. "William."

He shook his head with a crooked grin. "Billy."

Cass gave a single nod. "I love you, Billy."

He shut his eyes and tilted his head back as if lifting his face to the sun, though the sun still hung behind the clouds. "I love you, Cassidy."

She stood, crossed over to him, and pressed her lips to his. The kiss was gentle, sweet, and long.

A bark cut through the silence, startling them both. They jerked away from one another, chuckling as Brick shoved his way between their legs. They petted him and followed him back along the hill. Cass thought of the bag she'd loaded with toys and grooming supplies while she was in town. It was probably excessive.

But, Brick was all she had left of Drew. And Drew had loved her so well, the least she could do was spoil his dog.

Brick tired of their slow pace and bounded around the corner, out of sight. Cass caught Billy looking at her sidelong.

"That arm is getting strong," he said, a huskiness in his voice.

Cass nodded.

"And there's certainly nothing wrong with your legs," he added, slowing his pace so he could turn and look her up and down.

Remembering those legs, tight around him as he flexed and

arced between them, she stopped walking.

"Nothing at all," she said. Her own desires were mirrored in his eyes.

Cass reached out and took his hand, pulling it to her lips. She rubbed them across his knuckles, then drew his index finger into her mouth. She watched his shoulders rise and fall faster and released his hand, smiling.

"We could always stay back here for a little longer," she said.

Acknowledgements

Many thanks:
To Jane Curry for having faith in my story.
To Renee Barratt for designing the cover of my dreams.
To Mandy, Elease, Laura, and Sara for your input. You all made it so
much better than it was.
To the "poetry night" crew for starting the ball rolling in the first
place.

About the Author

Tara is living a dream one day at a time. She is happily married with two beautiful human children, three dogs, and a cat. She was born and raised in Montana, lived in the Pittsburgh area of Pennsylvania, and currently resides in North Dakota.

In addition to blogging and reviewing books, Tara enjoys participating in the Collaborative Writing Challenge's projects. Some of her work is included in their novel, The Map. Tara is also the Story Coordinator for their sixth novel, Esyld's Awakening.

Find Tara's short story "Initiations," in Twisted: A Horror Anthology. Find additional short stories and poetry on her website: www.tsdickerson.com.

Tara thanks you for reading her debut novel and would love to know what you thought. Please consider leaving a review online.